The voice in her head was quiet at first. Barely a whisper.

He's in the house.

Getting closer.

You should wake up.

That was before the piercing screams.

He doesn't need you anymore.

He's here for the children.

Before the children were taken.

Professor, you need to wake up.

Wake up now!

PROFESSOR!

Professor Rebecca Tempus's eyes snapped open at once.

"Jhonas!" she yelled frantically, jolting upright and jumping out of bed.

He had snatched the new-borns from their nursery and rushed them through the corridors of the dusty old mansion, then downstairs and into the laboratory; their innocent cries quickly fading into the distance. Dressed only in a nightgown, she propelled herself from the bed, her bare feet landing with a thud on the wooden floor below and ran as fast as she could.

The ceiling in the laboratory shook. Jhonas Spletka looked up, fragments of dust fell from the wooden beams and onto his face. The Professor is awake, he thought. No time to waste. He ran to the centre of the room and yanked off the green dust sheet that covered the Professor's time machine, whilst clutching both infants in the crook of his free arm. A huge upright silver disk stood to the rear of the machine, in front of which was an empty storage area then two red satin seats as you might expect to find in an old-fashioned carriage. He climbed carefully inside, and fastened the crying children into the passenger seat. Once they were strapped in, the front instrument panel suddenly burst into life. Jhonas smiled (He knew the children were the key) and fished in his pocket before producing two tiny luminous orange strips each with the word 'sleep' printed on them. He placed one on each child's forehead. They stopped crying and fell instantly into a deep sleep.

After adjusting the controls on the dash, he fixed an expectant glare on the green button, waiting not so patiently for it to flash.

"Don't!"

Rebecca was finally in the room, standing by the open doorway and pleadingly shaking her head. Her eyes, which were tired and red - worn out from the countless hours of tears that had passed through them over the past couple of days - were fixed firmly on the children.

The button on the dash began to glow green and she took a tentative step closer. As though on cue, Jhonas moved his hand, threatening to press it. She stopped her advance and he eased his hand.

"Just let them go. Please, Jhonas. You used to be our friend; it's not too late."

She started to cry again.

Jhonas Spletka sighed. "I'm sorry, Professor. It wasn't supposed to happen like this."

He shook his head, wiping the sweat from his brow.

"You have your sanctimonious father to thank for this." He said.

The Professor's next plea for him to release the children faded quickly into the background as Jhonas pushed the green button. The mechanism started to vibrate, the silver disc began to spin and the Professor dived forward, grasping the metal bar at the back of the machine. She knew that if she couldn't climb inside and quick, she would surely die and her children would be lost forever.

A blinding white light flashed around them, making the room disappear from sight. The Professor began to feel incredibly weak and dizzy, as she tightly held on to the back of the machine. The air around her felt both damp and suffocating, as if she was freezing and drowning at the same time.

The extreme cold came close to rendering her unconscious. Her skin was already drained of colour. Blue frostlike icicles had begun to form on the edges of her hair. One single thought, an image of the children kept the Professor awake and allowed her to delve into whatever energy stores she had left to climb in and behind Jhonas.

Jhonas' full attention had been focussed on the panel in front, he slowly and continually turned the silver dial whenever the green button flashed. He didn't notice the Professor sneak up on him. He did become more aware, however, that he was not alone when she wrapped her arm around his neck from behind.

Jhonas had to keep one hand on the silver dial to prevent the machine from spiralling out of control. He tried unsuccessfully, with his free arm to pull her from his windpipe. He thrashed violently from side to side. If it were a mere battle of brawn then her efforts would have been for nothing but her strength, all be it failing, was a mental one and she was doing what she could to control his movements from within. He felt her psychically probing inside his head, trying to will him to stop struggling, but on its own, her power was no match for his. It was just a matter of time.

Jhonas concentrated hard his eyes turn jet black. If he could catch a glimpse of the unwelcome passenger; if he could lock eyes with her, she would be unable to do anything but follow commands. That was his power. She knew this, of course and tightened the grasp around his neck whenever he attempted to turn and face her, but her strength was fading fast…

Jhonas continued to thrash left and right while the Professor, tired and exhausted, prayed for a miracle. She didn't have long to wait. The same internal voice that had warned of the intruder's presence rang out once again in the Professor's head.

"Look down my child."

As she lowered her head, a single bead of sweat fell, and she followed its progression right down to a series of luminous strips that had fallen from Jhonas' pocket to the floor. She used her remaining free hand to pick up a green 'obedience' strip and slap it on his forehead. Jhonas stopped struggling almost immediately and the lids of his eyes came down, submissive and restful. His hands came to rest by his side also. With no one to control the silver dial on the dash, however, it spun uncontrollably and the machine began to violently rock from side to side. The Professor used her remaining energy and psychic ability to stare at and control the movement of the dial. Within a moment the machine was as submissive and restful as Jhonas.

"Now" said the Professor, stepping back and gasping for breath, "Stand up and walk toward me." Jhonas compliantly climbed over the front seat and into the storage area.

"Now, step outside." He inched to the edge and stopped; his hands trembling furiously.

Deep down he knew that to step outside the time machine in flight was suicide, and he was fighting it for all he was worth. The veins in his forehead began to pop as he tried to battle the overwhelming will of the Professor and the obedience strip. The commands came in thick and fast:

"Jhonas, step outside!"

"It's safe. Do not worry."

"Jhonas you cannot resist. Step outside."

"Step outside now!"

An obedience strip had never been used to force someone to end their own life. The human's survival instinct is just too strong, and Jhonas Spletka's will was stronger than most.

He was using all his strength to defy Professor Tempus. She watched in bewildered amazement as his arm tensed, as though thousands of volts of electricity were running freely through his veins. He forced his hand up so that he was within grasping distance of the obedience strip. Acting as quickly as she could, she charged into

Jhonas Spletka's midriff just as he pulled the strip free of his head.

He was sent flying backward and out into the void. There was a moment's quiet. The Professor leaned over to see out of the machine. A kind of white mist surrounded it and looked almost heavenly. She breathed a huge sigh of relief. Was it finally over?

Suddenly and without warning a hand appeared from beneath the cloud, locking itself onto her wrist, pulling her half out of the machine. She tried to free herself but the grasp was too strong. Jhonas' head emerged from the thick cloud, his eyes were jet black. He stared directly into the Professor's eyes. She tried to look away, to avoid his hypnotic trance, but could not.

A sinister sound echoed in her brain.

Pull me up.

Pull me up now, Professor.

The Professor was perhaps one of the most intelligent and equally strong-willed women of her time, and bewitching her was not going to be as simple as Jhonas had hoped.

She fought for all she was worth before exhaustion took its toll and the Professor lost consciousness. With no fight to keep her inside, Jhonas pulled her clear of the machine. The instrument panel hissed, trying to initiate an emergency landing. Tiny sparks on the dashboard facilitated larger explosions till the whole panel burst into flames. A huge flash of light preceded total darkness and, finally, quiet.

21st Century

The room gradually came into focus as the Professor slowly opened her eyes. The housekeeper stood smiling over her exhausted and limp body.

"Sleep in your laboratory again last night, Professor?"

The Professor thought for a moment before answering.

"Who am I?"

Chapter Two

Arran and Molly

21st Century.

Mrs Anderson was not the sort of lady to put up with any nonsense, a wannabe school principle, whose recent appointment to become head of science served only to give her an overly inflated view of her own superiority.

She had dishevelled red hair and wore red horn-rimmed glasses, which balanced quite remarkably, on top of her thin, pointy nose. She looked so old that she may well have invented the well-known cliché "The bell is a signal for me, not for you."

Molly thought Mrs Anderson to be, by far the worst-tempered teacher in the school. She had a stare so intimidating and intense that children often referred to it as the death stare. For those unfortunates unlucky enough to be caught in her death stare, it was as though their very soul was being captured and melted from the inside, and was usually enough to drive even the most disruptive student to tears.

The classroom fell silent; all eyes yet again were on Molly and the teacher. Molly was sometimes known as the class clown. And at thirteen and three quarters years old, she was small for her age, something she more than made up for in attitude, never afraid to voice her opinion and very good at persuading others that her point of view was always right too.

"Step forward, girl," the teacher quietly commanded.

Molly's twin brother, Arran, was sitting third row from the left. He shook his head and sighed.

"This isn't the first time, is it?" Mrs Anderson asked.

Though it was a question, the teacher clearly was not expecting an answer. Molly took a step forward.

"No!" she retorted.

Her reply seemed all the more defiant when she stopped looking submissively at her own feet and began to stare directly into Mrs Anderson's eyes.

"Your beloved Professor is gone," said Mrs Anderson, "and you can't just pick fights with anyone who dares to question her sanity."

Professor Rebecca Tempus, to whom Mrs Anderson referred, was brilliant, some might say a genius, but as far as Arran and Molly were concerned, she was the cleverest person in the whole wide world, even cleverer than the lady who Daddy liked to watch on *Countdown*.

Mrs Anderson had never liked Professor Tempus; she found her to be a little too eccentric for her own conservative sensibilities.

The Professor was also thirteen years old, well, in a manner of speaking: Although she was nearing the ripe old age of thirty-four, an accident thirteen years ago left her with almost complete memory loss. Her earliest remembrance now was that of waking up dazed on the floor of her laboratory with no recollection of what had gone before. Only fragments of her recall remained. Though her intelligence and memories of all things scientific were intact, doctors held out little hope that her more intimate past would one day return. How wrong they were.

Her memory wasn't the only loss that fateful day. Her father, with whom she shared the house, had also disappeared; unexplained. Never to be seen again.

The Professor had been working on a rather unique invention practically every night following the accident. Recently her experiments had taken an unexpected turn for the better. This prompted her to leave her post as head of science at the school; she simply couldn't be distracted by meaningless pursuits, such as employment.

"Please, miss…" Arran raised his hand.

"Never one without the other, is there?" muttered Mrs Anderson without altering the direction of her gaze, which was firmly focused on Molly. "I really don't think you can help your sister out of this one, Arran."

"Molly didn't start it" said Arran earnestly. "It was…"

"She knows," interrupted Molly. "She was there. She was there and did nothing!"

"I'm not sure I like your tone, Molly!" bellowed the teacher.

"Oh, like I care!" shouted Molly.

The rest of the class, including Mrs Anderson, was stunned by Molly's temper. No one had ever dared to speak to the teacher like that, let alone not be frightened by her death stare.

It took only a moment for the gnome-like expression of shock to leave Mrs Anderson's face. This was unchartered territory; none of the children knew what she was going to do next. The metamorphosis which took place was quite remarkable though:

Her nostrils began to flare; her breathing slowed and was much more deliberate. Her face, like an eager volcano, grew a deep shade of red. Rage was slowly building from within. She clenched her fists and raised one arm.

The class was dumbfounded. Arran quickly arose from his seat and stood in-between his sister and the teacher.

"Leave her alone!" He paused, remembering that confrontation was not his strongest quality. "Please, miss."

He turned his face away. He wasn't about to let his sister be hit, but certainly did not want to see it coming if the purple-faced rage monster decided to attack.

The shocking red lipstick that was caked to the teacher's wafer-thin lips formed into a seditious smile. This was indeed a day for firsts. Arran and Molly had never seen Mrs Anderson smile before, and both wondered if the sudden shock to her face would cause it to crack. A few children in the class covered their eyes, too afraid to witness what was to follow.

"Well," Mrs Anderson finally said with all the calmness of a child psychologist, "you want to share in your sister's punishment, do you, Arran?"

"No, miss?"

"Very well."

She handed them each a pink slip of paper from her desk. The papers already had Arran and Molly's names scribbled on them.

"One week's suspension, to begin immediately. Now leave. You are no longer welcome in this classroom."

Relieved, Molly shrugged and turned to walk out of the classroom followed by her brother.

"Oh, and children?"

They both stopped without looking around.

"I'll be calling your father to see what he makes of all this!"

Molly quickly turned, this time a little more concerned. "Please, miss, don't. I'm sorry I…"

"Good-bye, children."

Mrs Anderson waited till they left before she continued with the day's lesson as though nothing had happened.

Chapter Three

Professor Tempus

The phone rang again. Professor Tempus hardly flinched, scribbling away in her notebook; a continuation of the journal her father had efficiently maintained till his sudden disappearance. The persistent and unrelenting sound forced the Professor to look up from her book and stare at the telephone.

"Batsy!" the Professor shouted.

The ringing noise continued. Much more impatient now, the Professor glared at the stairs that led out of the basement and slammed her pen down on the desk.

"Batsy!" she yelled again. "Will you please, for the love of my sanity and your own self-preservation, move down these stairs and answer this confounded telephone?"

Barely a moment later the telephone ringing was accompanied by an equally distasteful sound to the Professor's ears: A rather out-of-tune rendition of the *Annie* show song "The sun will come out tomorrow" was being hummed by Batsy, the Professor's ever-joyful housekeeper, which grew noisier and more irritating as she moved her plump and bouncy frame toward the telephone.

Of course, by the time she got there, the phone had stopped ringing. The Professor was not amused.

"Do you know who that was?" she quizzed Batsy rather sarcastically.

The housekeeper thought for a moment before answering. "Was it…" she paused, "the school offering you your job back?"

The Professor buried her head in her hands.

"No, no, obviously not," Batsy continued. "Was it, Arran? Molly? The Queen? No, not the Queen, how silly."

The Professor looked up and glared at her. "I don't know, do I?

It was rhetorical."

Batsy looked up and concentrated hard, as though she were trying to recall a distant memory, buried deep in the cobwebbed and vacant lot of her mind.

"Don't think we know anyone called terrorical, Professor."

"No, *rhetorical*. It means… Never mind. It was probably Uncle John, calling to see if I had changed my mind regarding the sale of my father's house. Call him back and say thanks for the offer but the answer is still no, I can't leave. This was my father's house, for Pete's sake!"

Thoughts of her father prompted the Professor to stand and walk toward the old dust sheet in the centre of the room. The unassuming stretch of army green material in front of her covered possibly the greatest invention of all time, quite literally. She ran her fingers across the rough edge of the cloth.

"Won't be long now, Dad; I'll finish what you started and we'll be together again. I promise," she quietly said to herself.

"Aren't you selling this house then, Professor?" asked Batsy.

Professor Tempus turned to face her. "Not that it's any of your concern, but," she smiled, "no, for a few reasons, the least of them being that if I do, you will become an unemployed homeless lady selling lucky clovers on street corners faster than you can click your fingers."

The housecleaner then bemused Tempus, as for the next two minutes she proceeded to try unsuccessfully to click her fingers. Her unrelenting focus was disturbed only when the Professor gently put her hand over hers and said calmly:

"Can you call Uncle John, today, and if possible before one of us dies of old age?"

The housecleaner did as she was told.

John was not actually the Professor's birth uncle but a close friend of the family, and more importantly a friend to her father since she was a child. This meant that he was now the closest family and link to her father she had. He also had two children, whom Tempus absolutely adored.

"You always do this," said Arran as he and Molly ambled slowly out of the school gate and down the country lane that led to Tempus's house.

"What?" said Molly. "Miss Anderson's not all that."

She laughed as she recalled her earlier defiance in front of possibly the meanest teacher in the school.

"Well, she certainly won this one," Arran pointed out. "We're suspended from school. Dad will kill us."

"Who cares?" replied Molly. "Besides, we're not going to Dad's, are we?"

They both smiled as they approached the Professor's front door. After three knocks the door slowly opened and out popped Batsy's smiling face.

"Children, come in." The housekeeper stepped aside to allow them passage into the house.

One after the other the children jumped in through the front doorway.

"Hi Batsy," said Arran.

"Is the Professor downstairs?" Molly added.

"Shouldn't you both be at school?" came a familiar inquisitive and friendly voice from the basement.

The housekeeper closed the front door as the two children rushed downstairs to see Tempus.

Chapter Four

John Pentka

The solicitor, Jeffrey Peabody pushed the papers back across the desk, toward John Pentka.

"It's her house." Jeffrey spoke calmly. "If she doesn't want to sell it, then she doesn't have to. Her father's instructions were quite specific, and basically giving her power of attorney over the whole estate and everything contained within it."

"Why now?" bellowed John. "And after all this time."

He took the papers, pressed them into the open briefcase on the desk, and slammed it shut, then picked it up and walked out of the office without saying good-bye.

The solicitor, rather used to his behaviour, thought nothing of it and proceeded to scribble into his notebook.

"Is it finished yet, Professor?" Molly asked Tempus.

"Yeah, can we see?" added Arran as they made their way toward the hidden object in the centre of the room.

"Stop right there," Tempus quietly directed. "You can see it soon." She paused and smiled. *Very soon*, she thought.

Batsy popped her head around the corner.

"Professor, that was John on the phone; he's coming over to see you, something about the house."

The Professor sighed and her eyes rolled up toward the heavens. "I know he means well," she suggested to the children, "but that father of yours can become a bit too embroiled in the affairs of other people."

"What does em-boiled mean?" asked Molly.

"It means she should tell Dad to mind his own business." Arran laughed.

"We'll have none of that sort of talk about your father." The Professor sent them upstairs with Batsy to sample some of the new double-chocolate cookie ice cream she had picked up for them when she went out to do her weekly shop—well, her *weekly* shop, which was as usual five weeks too late.

Once the children were out of sight, Tempus moved toward the centre of the room and in one swift movement yanked the sheet from the mysterious machine. A cloud of dust filled the air and settled onto the object that lay underneath. She marvelled momentarily at it in the time it took for the dust to settle.

The huge object was housed in a reinforced aluminium cage. Four red satin-covered seats, as you would expect to find in an old-fashioned carriage, both front and rear, an empty storage space and a huge silver disc which faced the front panel, which comprised two silver dials, a series of buttons, a screen, a lever, and a hollowed-out square panel.

She sat in what would be the driver's seat if it were a car and ran her fingers proudly across the front panel, glancing momentarily toward the lever. She smiled and her heart rate increased as she slowly moved her hand so she was touching it. Just one slight push and the

Professor would be sent hurtling through the fourth dimension; travelling through time.

The temptation was so great; there had been many occasions over the past two weeks, since she completed her father's machine, that she had dared herself to push that lever.

She was only completely sure the machine finally worked when Muffy, the housekeeper's pet hamster, reappeared after the Professor had sent him on an experimental trip a few days into the future, equipped with a mini electronic time piece and calendar all inside a miniaturized version of the time machine.

Tempus took a sentimental glance round her laboratory: her desk, her father's journal, her father's old camera; it was originally her father's laboratory. The time machine was his project, and in truth the main reason Rebecca finished it was in the hope that one day her father and she would once again somehow be reunited.

Okay, it's time, she thought. The hollowed-out panel was blank; she placed her fingers firmly in the middle of it and pushed. The panel began to glow a very bright white, and she removed her hands from the platform. As she did so the light in the panel gradually dimmed, and simultaneously the whole room began to glow that same bright light, so bright in fact that Tempus had to cover her eyes. A few seconds later the room looked exactly as it had before.

Tempus's eyes were now firmly fixed on the panel, which was still a dull glow, and she clenched one of her fists in eager anticipation. "Come on, please work."

All of a sudden, the dull, white, expressionless glow began to change and an image appeared in its place, gradually coming into focus like a developing photograph in a dark room.

The Professor afforded herself a huge grin and a triumphant punch into the air with her still clenched fist. The image of the room that surrounded her was now in firm focus on the panel.

"Okay, we'll store that image." She pushed a button to the right of the panel. "And now for…"

Her train of thought was interrupted by the sound of somebody walking down the stairs to the basement.

"Rebecca, Rebecca, are you down there?" John was close to the door but not yet in sight.

The Professor had just enough time to get out and cover the machine with the dust sheet, then quickly sit behind her desk, pick up a book, and pretend to be studiously reading.

The door opened.

"Working again, I see."

He paused, recalling the usual and unnecessary pleasantries that needed to be said before getting down to the order of business.

"How are you?" he enquired in his usual uncaring, business-like manner as he made his way to the Professor's desk. He carried a briefcase under his arm, which he pulled out with his free hand and slammed on her desk, prompting Rebecca Tempus to slowly put her book down and look up toward him.

"I'm fine, thank you, Uncle," she answered, sounding slightly irritated. She looked at the briefcase, then back at John. "To what do I owe this unexpected visit?"

Before John could answer, the temperature in the room suddenly fell quite dramatically; the Professor shivered and rubbed the sides of her arms in a futile effort to keep warm.

"I see you brought the weather with you, John."

John seemed inexplicably distracted by this temperature change as he started to sniff the air and walk slowly, with outstretched arms, toward the centre of the room. Each step resulted in a slight temperature drop.

"For pity's sake, what are you doing?" the Professor asked, perplexed.

John turned his head to look at the Professor and the room temperature returned to normal. He lowered his hands and reluctantly walked back toward the Professor and his briefcase.

"What was that all about?"

He looked accusingly at Tempus, studying her gaze before relaxing.

"Nothing," he said, "to business."

John released the catch to unlock his case, took out a small selection of papers, and handed them to the Professor. Before she could start reading, he pushed a pen toward her and raised one eyebrow.

"Come on, Rebecca, sign the papers; what do you want with this old house anyway?"

"Oh, Uncle, not again," she snapped and pushed the papers back across the desk toward him. "I've told you, many, many times. This was my father's house. I'm not selling it, not now, not ever. What do *you* want with it anyway?"

John's face started to glow that familiar red which meant he was about to lose his temper and begin shouting.

Their conversation was abruptly interrupted by the sound of Molly and Arran running down the stairs.

"Professor, Professor," Molly shouted, "Batsy said Father's on his…" Her sentence came to a sudden halt when she came face-to-face with John. "… way." She finished without the same bravado she had displayed earlier in front of Mrs Anderson.

"Hello, Father," she said very politely.

"Molly, Arran," John acknowledged without paying them much

attention.

"Hello, Father," said Arran. "We've been suspended from school; you see, Molly and the teacher…"

John, only half listening, interrupted. "You two are going to have to stay with the Professor tonight. I'm going away on business for a couple of days."

Trying hard to control their inner smiles, the children nodded their heads in agreement.

"I assume that's fine with you, Rebecca," he said. "We'll continue this discussion when I return."

Once John had left, the Professor ushered the children out of the basement and up the stairs, followed closely by the Professor herself, turning to take one last look at the object covered by the dust sheet and affording herself a cheeky smile as she did so.

Chapter Five

Just One Look

"What do you think the Professor is working on?" Molly quietly asked, whilst sitting up in her bed, staring at the motionless figure in the bunk across the room.

There was no response; of course, there wouldn't be. It was two in the morning and both kids were supposed to be fast asleep. Molly whispered again, hoping to wake her brother. There was still no answer apart from an outward sleepy snort sounding remarkably like a frog had just escaped from his mouth. He followed it by a rubbing of his eyes as he turned to continue his slumber.

Looking rather like she had given up on waking him, she resorted to speaking with Lancelot, her favourite teddy bear, instead. "What do you think the Professor is working on?" she asked the teddy, looking intently into his plastic eyes.

She raised the teddy bear's arms into a shrugging pose and in a deeper voice than her own natural tone mimicked Lancelot answering her back:

"I don't know, but she's being very secretive about it."

"Do you think Arran would know?" she continued in her natural tone.

She then made another shrugging movement with Lancelot's shoulders before smiling and throwing him with all her might at Arran's head, causing him to roll over, off the bed, and onto the floor.

"Oh, I'm sorry," said Molly very innocently. "Did I wake you?"

Arran got up from the floor, rubbing his head with one hand and carrying Lancelot in the other. "Either that or your stupid teddy learned how to fly and fancied a chat!"

"Oh, there he is; I've been looking for him." Molly held out her hands, indicating a desire to have her teddy bear safely returned to its owner.

Arran handed Lancelot to Molly. "So, what did you, erm, I mean Lancelot want to talk about?" He sat back on the bottom corner of his bed, rubbing his sore head to check for bruises.

"The Professor," Molly replied. "She spends every day in that basement, every night till way after we have gone to bed, and the only thing we're not allowed to see, the only thing that's kept secret is under that green sheet."

Arran nodded in agreement, and then shrugged his shoulders. He was not quite as inquisitive as his sister. "Remember the time the Professor threw her shoe at Batsy's head for trying to clean it?"

"Yeah." Molly chuckled. "Was quite impressive; she didn't even look up from her notebook. Kept writing with one hand whilst slipping off her shoe and bopping Batsy on the head with the other.

"Fancy a look?" Molly asked her brother with a raised eyebrow and a cheeky grin.

"The Professor would kill us!"

"She can't tell us off for what she doesn't know. Besides, I just want to see."

She walked out of the room and crept down the hallway toward the stairs, reluctantly followed by her brother.

The big old house looked rather different at night. Looming shadows from aging pieces of furniture appeared much more menacing than in daylight. Anonymous echoes amplified every movement the children made. The sound of creaking floorboards and wind rattling through the pipes was masked only by the ticking of the old grandfather clock outside the Professor's study.

"Why is it when you're trying to keep quiet, every footstep makes the house creak more?" Arran whispered as he carefully made his way down the stairs that led to the basement.

"Shhh." Molly looked round, with a finger pressed against her lip. She turned the handle and opened the basement door. Once inside she signalled for Arran to follow. He cautiously did so, reaching for the light switch on the wall, and with one flick illuminated the whole room.

"I'm not sure about this," said Arran with one foot out the door.

"I might go to bed."

"Go to bed then!" Molly snapped. "You'll never find out what's under that sheet, cos I won't tell you." She folded her arms and faced away from Arran.

Arran thought for a moment; he was, after all, now a little curious as to what was under the sheet. Not only that, walking on his own through the dark stairs and corridors back to bed was not his idea of fun.

"Okay, one look and we go back to bed," he said.

Molly was already advancing toward the hidden object. "Yes, just one look." She yanked off the cover and threw it over to the corner of the room.

Chapter Six

The First Flight

The time machine, now visible to both children, lay before them. "Cool," they said in amazement.

"What is it?" Arran asked.

Molly shrugged her shoulders. "I dunno." She circled it, studying the front panel and red satin seats.

"It's like an old-fashioned car without wheels."

"Of course!" Molly finally concluded. "It's a hovercraft."

Arran was unconvinced. "I don't think so."

"It is! Look, I'll drive. Get in."

With that she hopped into the driver's seat. Arran stayed put.

"Are you getting in or not?"

Arran shook his head.

Molly was a little deflated by her brother's lack of enthusiasm. "I promise I won't touch anything."

He cautiously walked around the machine and sat in the passenger seat.

"Good day, sir," Molly playfully said in her poshest voice. "I am your chauffer for the day. Would you care to go to the palace?"

Arran smiled. "Why yes, Jeeves. Go through the park first; you know how I love the park." He looked at the dashboard, then at the front panel. "Hey, Molly, look," he said, pointing at the image in front of him. "It's a picture of this room."

"Oh yeah, it's probably a safety thing." Molly said, as if she was very knowledgeable as to how hi-tech hovercrafts work. "It makes sure we don't bump into anything or hit the ceiling."

"How do you know?" he asked. "This is your first hovercraft too." *If that's even what this is*, he thought.

Molly shook her head, and using her usual *jump first, think later* philosophy by which she had lived her life so far, stretched out her hand and pressed the image in front of her.

The image began to glow, and she snatched her hand back as fast as she could; both children's heart rates increased.

"What did you do that for?" shouted her brother.

"I didn't do anything," she replied defensively. "But look at that." She pointed to a green button which had started flashing to the right of the image.

She glanced at Arran, who, like a rabbit caught in the headlights of a car, was too afraid to move anywhere, but was clearly not fond of the situation.

"I think I should press it," she said with a slight chuckle, and before Arran could voice any objection, she quickly pushed the button and held it there till the green stopped flashing.

For a moment nothing happened. Arran breathed a huge sigh of relief whilst Molly, rather disappointed, grunted.

"Fat lot of good that is. It doesn't even…"

She didn't get to finish her sentence as the time machine started vibrating; this was soon accompanied by a low-pitched hum, and the room around them began to fade and drift out of focus. It gave Molly a slight headache looking out; it was as though she were putting on a pair of glasses that were far too strong for her.

Arran didn't have the same feeling at all; he was too busy closing his eyes as tight as he could whilst pressing his hands against his ears. Normally Molly would have laughed at her brother behaving in this manner, but for the moment she was just as scared.

Suddenly there was a huge explosive flash of bright light outside the machine. As quick as it had arrived, the light faded and the children found themselves looking outside into the laboratory again, everything as it had been before.

But wait, something was different. The Professor was sitting at her desk, reading a book.

"We're in trouble now," said Arran. "Sorry, Professor," he mumbled. "It was Molly's fault. I told her I wanted to go to bed, but then she hit me with a teddy and so I switched on the light and now we're in your hovercraft."

The Professor didn't even look up from her book.

"See what you've done?" said Arran. "The Professor can't even look at us. I've never seen her *this* angry."

The basement door opened and in walked John, their father.

"Dad's here," said Molly.

"Shhh," said Arran. "Wait a minute, he's ignoring us too."

John Pentka was wearing the same boring suit he had on earlier that day and was carrying the same briefcase. He also had the same unsympathetic look on his face, though the children were used to that. Arran wondered what he was doing there in the middle of the night.

John walked across the room without so much as a glance toward the children and slammed his briefcase down on the Professor's desk; she put her book down and began speaking with their father.

"He can't have not noticed us," said Arran.

"He'll notice if we stand right between them," snapped Molly, who didn't like spending too long in any situation she didn't understand.

With that she turned round and attempted to get out of the time machine and banged her head.

"Ouch!"

There was an invisible wall surrounding the machine. It was both soundproof and inescapable. "I can't get out!" Molly shouted.

Arran wasn't paying any attention; he was much more concerned now with what was in the machine itself.

"Molly, look." He pointed at the dashboard. Directly under the picture of the room was a digital display that read:

Destination eight hours: thirty-two minutes into the past. Hover mode engaged.

"Oh, my goodness," said Arran. "It's a time machine. Professor Tempus has invented a time machine!"

Molly turned to look at the display in disbelief; she then turned to face her brother. "I mean, I'd have preferred a blue police box that was bigger on the inside, but still, a time machine. This must be earlier today when Father was here."

Materialization in twenty seconds.

"Twenty seconds?" shouted Arran. "It's counting down."

Nineteen, eighteen…

"What do we do?"

Molly's attention was firmly fixed on her father, who was now looking right at her from the other side of the room. "Dad's stretching out his arms. He's walking this way. Arran, he knows we're here!"

Arran was still looking at the display.

Thirteen, twelve…

"Molly, do something."

"Oh yeah. I'm quite the time traveller; I know exactly how this thing works!" Her father drew closer.

Six, five…

"Molly, now! Press anything!"

Molly began randomly pressing a series of buttons.

Four, three…

"If we end up landing in Jurassic Park, you're getting eaten before me!" Molly finally came to press the same green button that had transported them there in the first place. The display changed:

Flight mode.

The time machine began to vibrate and the laboratory disappeared from view. Almost immediately they found themselves back in the same place they started from.

Both children sat back in their seats and breathed a huge sigh of relief.

"That was close," Molly observed.

"Do you think?" shouted Arran in the most aggressive tone he could find. "I suggest we get out of here, put the sheet over this thing, and hope the Professor doesn't…"

"Oh no," Molly interrupted, "look over there. We're right back in time again."

Both children looked across the laboratory to see the Professor sitting behind her desk, reading her book as she had been doing a minute or so before.

"What are we going to do?" asked Arran.

There was a pause. Molly shrugged.

"Well, you can start by getting out of my machine before you hurt yourself," echoed the Professor's voice from behind the book.

"Professor? You can hear us?" Molly and Arran asked simultaneously.

Tempus peered over the top of her book and stared at the children. "Now would be good." She was beginning to sound more like Mrs Anderson.

Now afraid, having never heard the Professor speak in such a serious tone, both children alighted from the machine and walked slowly toward her. She put down her book and stared at the children.

"Do you know how dangerous that could have been?"

"Yes, Professor," both children answered whilst bowing their heads, in the same way a puppy does when he's being reprimanded for leaving a smelly parcel on the rug, instead of outside the house where he's supposed to.

"I would have warned you," scolded the Professor, "but it

should be impossible for anyone but me or one of my bloodline to even operate it. I've obviously miscalculated somewhere."

Tempus got up from her seat, walked round to the front of the desk, and propped herself up on it whilst facing the kids. She drew a huge breath before allowing a slight smile to appear on her face.

"So, what do you think—you like it?"

Relieved and unbelievably excited, both children embraced the Professor. "Like it?" Molly laughed. "It's amazing."

"It's a time machine." Arran was aware his input was screamingly obvious, but it seemed to be all he was able to add to the conversation.

"Yes, it is," answered Tempus. "And it is vitally important that this remains entirely between us. In the wrong hands this could be very dangerous."

Both children agreed.

"We have a project on Cleopatra at school," said Molly. "Can we go see her?"

The Professor allowed herself a slight chuckle.

"No, we can't interfere with history; what has gone has gone. Besides, the machine does not work like that, not yet. The furthest back in time this machine can go, well, you have already been. That image you must have pressed on the front panel was no ordinary image. The machine took an exact photograph of the room eight hours ago, and by 'exact' I mean every single atom and molecule was captured in that image, enough for it to act as a gateway for us to travel back to that point in time as we please. Forward time travel is much easier," Tempus continued. "We can travel forward to any point in time simply by the turn of a dial and the push of a lever."

She opened her old-fashioned pocket watch: 3.20 a.m. "Which reminds me, it's quite late; go get some rest. We'll go on a journey tomorrow."

The children's faces beamed with excitement.

"Remember, not a word to anyone," Tempus reminded them.

"Not even Dad?" asked Molly.

"Not even your father."

"Can we tell Batsy?" continued Arran.

The Professor allowed herself a cheeky smile. "No, though I'm not sure Batsy's only working brain cell would understand anyway. Now off you go to bed."

Chapter Seven

The Ghost

The night seemed to last forever in wait for the next morning; rather fitting as time seemed now to have lost all of its meaning. The children sat up for as long as they were able, talking in wonder of all the things they could now do, until Mother Nature asserted her own authority on the situation and eased them into a restful and somewhat reluctant slumber.

The Professor's sleep was less than restful.

Desperate sobs of a young girl woke Rebecca Tempus barely moments after her eyes had closed. She sat up in bed and listened carefully.

Not Molly, definitely not Molly, she thought.

The Professor knew all too well Molly's expressions of grief, after spending many hours through the years comforting her, usually as a result of John's terrible temper; which meant she was either imagining this or there was an intruder in the house.

The crying stopped; then the bedroom door creaked so that it was partially open. The Professor froze; her heart rate suddenly increased and made a thumping sound which seemed to drown out the grandfather clock's solemn chime in the background.

"Please help me," wheezed a weak and feeble female voice from the other side of the door.

The Professor wanted to answer, she wanted to help, but couldn't bring herself to move or even offer verbal reassurance that everything would be okay.

How could everything be okay? She was imagining this, she had to be. The young girl spoke again.

"Please, you're the only…"

A sudden door slam from across the corridor cut her sentence short and made the girl cry once more. Heavy footsteps with a menacing, dark, and meaningful purpose moved rapidly closer and closer to the bedroom. The young girl screamed; the Professor jumped out of bed and swung the door open. All was quiet; there was nobody there, and no sound but that of the ticking grandfather clock.

The screams and footsteps surely had to have woken more than just her, but there was no sign of Batsy, Arran, or Molly. Putting on her dressing gown, she decided to walk toward the children's room, just to be sure the sound had not come from Molly herself. Although she loved Molly dearly, there was a small part of her which hoped the tears and cries for help had indeed come from her. At least then she would have something to rationalize and make sense of what had just happened.

The moonlight shining in through the children's room was bright enough to show Rebecca Tempus that there was no way Molly could have made that sound earlier. She lay on her back, peaceful, one arm extended off the bed, with Lancelot lying on the floor beneath her hand. The Professor smiled, crouched down, picked up the teddy bear, placed it on the pillow, and kissed Molly's forehead.

Footsteps again, only now not heavy and menacing but those of a small child, could be heard running past the children's room. The Professor rushed out and looked down the corridor just in time to see a young girl turn and stare at her. For a moment both were transfixed in each other's gaze.

"Hello," said the Professor calmly, not wanting to alarm her.

The girl turned and ran down the stairs, quickly pursued by the Professor.

"Wait," she called after her, "I only want to talk!"

The young girl descended the stairs that led to the basement, ran inside, and slammed the door.

The Professor was barely three seconds behind. Once at the bottom of the stairs, she reached for the handle and turned it but the door wouldn't open. It was locked. Locked? That door hadn't been locked for as long as she could remember; there wasn't even a key for it.

"Please open the door," she called through the keyhole.

She tugged at the handle a few more times before stepping back to sit on the stairs. She buried her head in her hands and rubbed her eyes, trying to make sense of the evening's events. There was a click.

Sudden warmth from the room's light was now shining upon her face. She quickly looked up.

The door was open. She cautiously stepped inside the room, clueless in what to expect. The little girl she had chased earlier was on the ground, almost collapsed, looking like a lone survivor of a terrible disaster. Her clothes were now torn and dirty. There was little hope in her tired eyes, and she stretched out an exhausted hand with fading energy toward an empty space and part clenched it as if holding onto an invisible object. No sooner had her hand rested in its final position than she froze; the slow movement of her chest breathing in and out had stopped too. Her eyes fixed, staring endlessly into the empty space ahead of her. A single tear emerged from her right eye and began to roll slowly down her cheek till that single tear, only halfway through its journey, stopped. The little girl was as still as a statue.

The Professor cautiously moved toward her and reached out to wipe away the glistening tear from the girl's face. No sooner had her hand touched the tear than a sudden cold sensation passed through her own hand. She quickly snatched it back; or at least she tried to.

The Professor's hand was frozen solid. She was suddenly unable to move, it felt like invisible ice had spread through her veins like a ravenous virus, till she too, was frozen solid, unable to move or speak but somehow still conscious and very aware of her environment.

"My little angel."

A male voice spoke from behind her; it was accompanied by footsteps. The voice was very familiar, but who?

"Please don't cry."

The little girl started to sniffle and tears started to free flow down her cheeks. Mobility had at least returned to her. The Professor was still unable to move a muscle or make a sound. The little girl, who was now quite transparent, stood up and faced the Professor; she appeared ghostly—rather ironic, as the Professor felt like the girl was looking right through her.

The Professor had no choice but to stay put and let this play out.

"Oh, Daddy," cried the little girl, her gaze fixated on the unseen man behind the Professor. "I don't want to do it. I can't, and it's not fair!"

"We have no choice," the man replied solemnly.

"But, Daddy," the little girl said once again before burying her head in her hands, unable to face the finality of what was to happen.

The man walked past the Professor to comfort the girl, who obviously was his daughter. She didn't get to look at his face and could only see him from behind as he crouched down on one knee to hug the little girl.

He was partly transparent also, a man in his mid- to late thirties, she guessed, good head of white hair, albeit unstyled and rather erratic, and a rather strange taste in clothing. He wore an old tweed jacket, unfashionable corduroy trousers, and scuffed brown shoes. Was the girl Albert Einstein's daughter?

"One day you will understand, my daughter." The man spoke softly, and with that turned his head so he was no longer facing the little girl but looking directly into the Professor's eyes. She wanted to run, as fast as she could, but was still frozen to the spot.

The man feigned a slight smile. "Find me, Rebecca."

The Professor felt a tingling sensation return to her fingers, and the same feeling made its way round her entire body as her mobility began to return. Now able to move, but somehow transfixed on the man, she stared dreamily into his eyes. She felt fragmented memories returning, dormant lost images, like missing jigsaw pieces from her past falling slowly into place, and then there was the sudden realisation.

Tears formed in her eyes. "Daddy?" she said and started to cry. "You're my…"

A million unanswered questions, fleeting, without form, rushed through her mind, so many things she wanted to say, to ask, to express. She just needed to get a handle on the situation.

The moment was suddenly halted by an aggressive, deafening sound; footsteps, the same ones she had heard earlier, approached the door. They both rushed a look in that direction before her father shook his head.

"John must never get this." He reached inside his jacket pocket and pulled out a white envelope, which he then proceeded to place beneath a loose floorboard near the Professor's desk.

As the footsteps got closer, the little girl, who the Professor now understood was a younger version of herself, began to shiver, petrified.

Watching the young girl now felt like reliving an earlier past experience. To comfort her now would seem oddly self-serving, but the Professor walked toward her anyway. A sudden door slam made her turn and then, nothing.

The Professor was in bed. Her room, exactly as it should be, nothing out of place. Her dressing gown was still attached to the hook on the back of her bedroom door. She shook her head.

"Now *that* was a dream," she said to herself, whilst attempting a rather unconvincing snigger.

Just as she was about to take her attention from the door, it suddenly started to open, very slowly. Her heart race increased again and she instinctively buried her head under the duvet, not that it would offer much in the way of protection or camouflage. Tiny footsteps approached her bed. She clamped her eyes shut as the duvet was slowly pulled from her head.

Silence.

Gradually and reluctantly she resigned herself to open her eyes, only to see Arran and Molly's smiling faces beaming down on her.

"Mooning, Professor." Molly rubbed the remaining sleep from her eyes.

"What?" the Professor replied, this time laughing and very relieved.

"Molly keeps saying mooning instead of morning," Arran complained. "It's getting irritating."

The Professor pulled both children close in a heartfelt embrace. "Well, I think it sounds wonderful."

Chapter Eight

The Envelope

"Morning, Batsy," Arran said as the ever-joyful housekeeper made her way into the dining room, pushing a breakfast trolley containing scrambled eggs, toast, Rice Krispies, tea, coffee, and juice.

"Mooning, Arran." Batsy placed a bowl of breakfast cereal in front of him. Molly laughed.

"Did you say mooning?" Arran asked.

Batsy nodded eagerly, so much in fact that her little chef's hat nearly fell off her head.

"Just for you. Molly said it's your favourite word, and you like to pretend you simply hate it, so I have to say mooning to you every morning."

"Thanks," said Arran sarcastically, smiling as he propelled a Rice Krispy off his sister's nose. "So, Professor, where are we going in the you-know-what?"

The Professor was staring blankly into her empty coffee cup, lost in concentration.

"Earth to Professor Tempus?" Arran continued.

The Professor looked up and stared at him. "Sorry, yes, erm, I mean coffee would be great, thanks."

With that she stood up and walked out of the room, leaving her empty coffee cup and the two children at the table. Molly and Arran exchanged a confused glance before shrugging it off and tucking into their breakfast cereal.

Once at the door to her laboratory, the Professor paused, took a deep sigh, and pushed it open—everything as she left it, the machine still covered. She gazed at the wooden floorboards upon which the desk rested.

"Well," she said, "if it was a dream, there will be nothing under that floorboard but dust and dirt."

Kneeling down in front of it, she flexed her fingers in front of her face before tugging at what appeared to be a loose corner.

"What are you doing, Rebecca?"

Startled, the Professor spun around to see John standing in the doorway. She still wasn't sure if last night was a dream or not, but it had left her with an uneasy, untrusting feeling regarding him. Her father's last words were that John must never see the envelope that may or may not be lodged beneath the floorboard. She didn't know why, but she wanted John out of her house.

"John, you shouldn't creep up on people!" She stood up and pushed the loosened piece of floorboard down with her heel. "I thought you were going away for a few days."

John's eyebrows came close to meeting in the middle in that familiar way they always had done when he suspected someone was lying to him, or all was not quite right.

"No, my trip was cut short." He paused for thought. "I came to collect the children, but they tell me you're taking them on a trip?"

The Professor's eyes widened. "Oh yes, that's right," she replied. "Did they mention where?"

"No," said John. "Are you all right? You seem shaken up."

The Professor did a rather unconvincing impression of a smile. "No, no, I'm fine and breezy."

She placed her hand back to lean on her desk, which unfortunately missed and she was, without support, propelled backward onto the floor.

"Yes, still fine," she lied, stumbling again to her feet.

John rushed forward and took her hand in an effort to steady her upright.

"All right now?" he enquired, looking into her eyes.

"Strange dream, that's all," she concluded finally. "And I don't think I got any sleep last night."

"You had a strange dream, but didn't sleep?" John sat on the corner of her desk and regarded her accusingly. "What's going on, Rebecca?"

He turned his attention to the floorboard the Professor had been trying to loosen, bending over to examine it. "What were you doing on the floor when I walked in?"

Rebecca glanced at the floorboard, then back at John. "Nothing important. Thought I dropped an earring."

"You know, I don't think I've ever known you to wear earrings—didn't think you had your ears pierced."

She raised her hand to the bottom of her earlobe, hiding the fact that there was no hole.

"Clip-ons," she finally offered. "You know I'm not really into this girly stuff, but saw them as I was out shopping yesterday and thought," she gulped, "they looked rather nice."

Unconvinced, John knelt down over the loose floorboard.

"I'll help you look."

The Professor's eyes opened wide, her heart rate increasing as his hand neared the loose floorboard.

"No need, John, really. They were just cheap, nasty things."

"It's no trouble," he said as he pulled the floorboard up.

There it was, exactly where her father had placed it: a white envelope covered in dirt and dust. John turned his head and looked at the Professor before pushing his hand in the small crack. "Well, I've got it," he said, placing something in his hand and turning to face her. When his hand opened there was no envelope, instead a tiny clip-on earring.

"There you go." He handed it to her. "Have a good trip with the kids; bring me back something." John left the laboratory and walked back upstairs.

Walking to the doorway she listened to make sure John had left the house before approaching the loose floorboard. Had she just imagined the envelope? Where did the earring come from? She looked again where she'd seen the envelope, and there it was, plain as day. John couldn't have missed that, surely?

To the Professor's eyes there was nothing special about it, just a normal white envelope, slight yellow colouring around the edges. Nothing unusual in that. It had been there for over thirty years after all. On the reverse side, the words: To My Little Rebecca.

"Professor?" Batsy's voice echoed through the stairwell. "Would you like me to get the children ready? They say you're going on a trip."

She glanced at the empty doorway. "Yes, do please; I'll be up in a moment."

"Okey dokey," the housecleaner replied.

There was a letter inside the envelope and a few photographs. Pulling out the letter, her hand began to tremble. Though her logical mind couldn't explain it, last night was no dream. She began to read:

Rebecca my darling,

If my calculations are correct, you will have reached your 34th year by now. To confirm what you are no doubt aware, your vision last night was very real. Your memories have been hidden to protect you from John. As yet they are not complete and exist as mere fragments. I promise they will be restored when the time is right and not all at once, again for your protection.

John is not to be trusted. I can't divulge too much without awakening the resting images in your mind, so for now I will say, keep the two children safe and away from him without arousing suspicion.

Under no circumstances must he be aware you have completed the machine. The fact that he thinks you have not finished is the only reason you are still alive.

I wish I could be there with you.

All my love

Richard Tempus 3021

The Professor sat behind her desk. She put the letter down, then took out the photographs; they made very little sense. They were simply pictures of empty rooms. One looked very much like the laboratory she was sitting in but much more high-tech. Most of the equipment in the picture was alien to her. She placed the pictures on the desk and stood, looking again toward the basement door.

Chapter Nine

The First Planned Journey

Arran and Molly's faces, almost as if on cue, appeared round the corner.

"Mooning," said Molly with a cheery grin on her face.

Arran looked hard at her and rolled his eyes toward the heavens. "Can we leave her behind?"

Molly said nothing, feeling that the sharp kick in the leg he was about to receive would be answer enough.

"So where are we going?" Arran asked.

Molly kicked him in the leg. "Oh, I'm sorry," she said. "I slipped."

"*When* are we going?" they both asked, taking the dust sheet off the machine and climbing inside.

"Can I sit closer to the edge?" asked Molly.

The Professor afforded herself a smile as she walked round the desk to join them.

"You on the way there and Arran on the way back," the Professor said, placing her hand on Molly's head. Both children agreed.

"Well, if we can't go back in time," said Arran, "how far forward?"

The Professor thought back to the date on her father's letter. "The year 3021," she said. "One thousand years into the future."

The children cheered as the Professor made the necessary adjustments on the panel.

"Okay, here we go," she announced, pushing the lever forward.

Within moments the outside laboratory disappeared and the machine was surrounded by white light. The digital display rapidly increased from 2021 and they moved through the years as though they were seconds. Finally, the display read 3021 and the machine vibrated.

Hover mode engaged, was written on the display. *Dematerialisation in twenty seconds.*

"Yeah, we've seen that before." Arran laughed. This time they were in no hurry to return to 2021.

Once the display reached zero, both children eagerly looked at the Professor.

"Why can't we see anything outside the machine?" Arran asked.

"The machine is doing an environmental check. Give it a moment."

Gradually the room around them came into full focus.

The children were not impressed; their faces were rather reminiscent of youngsters eagerly opening a Christmas gift only to find it was filled with all their old toys.

"Are you sure we're one thousand years into the future?" Molly queried.

"Of course I am," the Professor answered with utmost certainty.

"But we're still in the laboratory, and it's exactly the same as it was before we left."

"Yes, interesting, isn't it?" The Professor stepped out of the machine. "Well, the air seems quite breathable," she said with a huge grin.

"Imagine that," said Molly, disappointed. "Come on, Arran; let's go see if Batsy has any of that ice cream left."

With that, the children clambered out of the machine and ran toward the doorway. Arran turned before following Molly upstairs.

"Sorry it didn't work, Professor. Would you like me to stay and help fix it?"

The Professor chuckled. "No, that'll be fine, go save me some ice cream. I'll be up in a moment."

She stood up, pulled the green button from the machine, pressed it between her fingers, and watched as the time machine disappeared from view. With that she placed the green button in her pocket and made her way upstairs to join the children, who, unable to find Batsy and convinced the machine was not working, had made their way outside to play in the garden.

Chapter Ten

Grombit

"It's a pity about the Professor's machine," said Arran.

"Yeah," said Molly as they ambled across the grass to the swings at the foot of the garden. "Do you think we were rude just running out like that? She may be upset."

Arran shrugged. "I got the impression she wanted to be alone. You know how she gets. You know what I think?"

"Good morning" came the reply.

Arran looked confused. "What?"

"I said good morning."

"Well, at least you're not saying *mooning* anymore; that was really annoying."

"Erm, Arran, that wasn't me." Molly pointed to a hedgehog perched on Arran's shoe.

"Ah, isn't he cute?" Arran smiled and crouched down to pick it up. Just before touching it, he had second thoughts. "Wait a minute, they may be cute, but these things are supposed to be riddled with fleas and stuff."

The hedgehog took a step backward before retorting, "Fleas indeed! Do I come into your bedroom, then turn up my nose for fear you will be riddled with lice? No, thank you very much. I've never heard such rudeness!"

Both children were astounded.

"I'm sorry, Mr. Hedgehog," Molly said.

"Quite all right, Miss Human," he replied. "I do have a name, you know."

"I'm dreaming," said Arran. "It's the only explanation."

"There's no explanation for rudeness," the hedgehog clarified. "My name is Grombit."

He twitched his nose in a very proud manner.

"Fourth generation if you please."

"Fourth generation?" the children said in unison, still trying to digest the fact that they had found a talking hedgehog.

"Yes, fourth generation. Do you two have mental problems?"

"But you're a talking hedgehog," they once again said together.

"So, you *do* have mental problems."

"But how is it you can talk, Grombit?" Molly asked.

Grombit looked confused before laughing deep and heartily. "Is this a joke? Am I being recorded? Did my fiancée put you up to this? Yes, yes, very funny, you can come out now, dear."

"No, really," said Molly. "We've never met a talking hedgehog, or any talking animal before."

"Except for parrots," added Arran.

"Talking parrots." Grombit chuckled. "I don't think so." He shuffled his spikes before continuing, "And how come you have never seen a talking animal? Where are you from, the early twenty-second century? Ha."

"Not exactly," said Arran, "the twenty-first. Is this the future?"

Both children now knew the Professor's machine worked all too well, and they were indeed one thousand years into the future.

Grombit opened his eyes wide so he could see them both more clearly, then said in a slower, more cautious tone: "Only if you're from the past children. Are you familiar with Professor Tempus?"

"Why yes," Molly said. "She's in the house."

"She? A woman?" Grombit laughed, rather confused. "Professor Tempus is a man, not a she—a *he*. He, he, he!"

"What's so funny?" Arran joked.

The hedgehog was not amused, though Molly found it quite

funny.

"Well, Professor Richard Tempus, *a man*, developed a kind of translation in the air if you like," lectured Grombit. "Humans, animals and even the environment exist in perfect harmony and understanding."

Standing in the doorway that opened out to the garden, the Professor watched as the children spoke to Grombit. Finally, she decided to approach.

"How do you do? I am…"

"Oh my worms," Grombit interrupted. "It can't be. Are you, excuse me for asking, Rebecca Tempus?"

The Professor nodded. "How do you know me?"

"It's my job to know you," he replied, "well, my family's job at any rate." Grombit bowed his head. "It is my honour, Rebecca Tempus. Your father was a great man."

"What do you mean *was*?"

"I do beg your pardon. Greatness never dies, of course."

Tempus shook her head. "That's not what I… Is my father," she paused, "dead?"

Grombit gasped. "Good heavens no. Definitely not." The Professor sighed with relief. "I don't think," he continued.

"What?" She gasped.

"Well, I'm not sure; some say he's dead. Others say he's being held captive and some even say he's missing."

"Missing?"

"Yes, missing, like the brain cells of these two children."

"Hey!" Molly marched toward Grombit, who on a reflex curled himself into a little ball.

"Sorry," he said from inside the ball. "Just my idea of a joke."

"That's okay." Arran laughed. "She can dish it out but she can't take it."

"Can too." Molly took a step back.

Grombit poked his nose from the little ball and regarded his three visitors.

"Okay, Miss Professor Tempus, come with me to the other side of the hedge. We have much work to do."

They followed him to the hedge and watched as he disappeared underneath.

"Are you coming?" he shouted from the other side.

"We can't fit under there," said Molly.

"Oh yes, you two are blessed with brain cells, aren't you? Perhaps you might try the gate. I don't know, this is supposed to be *your* house."

Tempus took the children by the hand and walked out of the same gate, like she had a thousand times before whilst making her way to the school. Once on the other side, she found that the similarity from her own time period ended there.

What was once a large expanse of fields enclosing a quiet suburban village, comprising a few hamlets and a quiet country lane which led to the local school, was now a bustling metropolis. The sky turned a beautiful scarlet colour, then back to bright blue. The sound of thunder could be heard in the distance, and the rain fell, but not everywhere; raindrops very specifically dropped on the trees, grass, and vegetation, leaving the people bone dry. One couple who were resting in the field, relaxing and taking in the sun, upon seeing the rain did…nothing at all. The rain seemed to completely bypass them. It was as though the weather planned itself around the convenience of the animals and humans.

All manner of people and animals seemed to be living quite harmoniously together too. Businessmen and women were walking together, smiling and laughing, in and out of busy office blocks. One middle-aged man crossed a road with a tiny white mouse on his shoulder; for all intents and purposes, it looked like he was having a conversation with the rodent. Having reached the other side of the road, he knelt down so the mouse could jump to the ground. After a short affectionate wave, the mouse continued with his day's business and the man walked in the opposite direction.

A young girl walked past the Professor, suddenly stopped, and began uncontrollably laughing, then did a strange dance, waving her hands up and down rather like a cartoon chicken. Molly laughed.

"Reminds me of your last girlfriend."

Arran looked scornfully at her. "She had a wasp in her hair, and you made fun of her for weeks after."

"I know," said Molly. "I put it there. Still was funny though."

"Are you all right?" the Professor called out.

The little blonde girl turned to face them. "Yes, we're fine thanks." She looked to her left, gave an affectionate wink to the empty space, then looked back at the Professor. "And you are?"

"Oh, I'm Professor Tempus."

The girl laughed again, this time at her, looking her up and down. "Like the network? Sure you are," and with that she turned and began to chat to her imaginary friend and walked off.

"What an odd girl." The Professor looked around the bottom of the hedge for some sign of the hedgehog. "Grombit, are you there?"

"Out in a moment," Grombit called from behind the tree. "Takes a while to get changed."

Arran laughed, imagining the hedgehog jumping out wearing mini trainers, tracksuit bottoms, and a baseball cap.

A young man stepped out from behind the tree, wearing jeans, a

T-shirt, and a pleasant smile.

"There, ready. Shall we be off?"

Both children exchanged a confused glance.

"And you are?" asked Molly.

"I'm Grombit, brain cell."

"Grombit brain cell?"

Grombit sighed. "No, just Grombit. *You* are the brain cell...or

not."

"That's amazing," exclaimed Tempus, walking around

Grombit. "Some sort of perception projector."

Grombit laughed. "You sound just like your father."

Now irritated, Molly shouted, "Professor, where is the

hedgehog?"

"I think he *is* the hedgehog." interjected Arran. "He just looks

human."

"Very clever," answered Grombit. "Are you sure you two are

related?"

Molly folded her arms and snorted in disgust. "So can all

animals here do that, walk around as humans?"

"No, no, no," Grombit replied. "Just me." He produced a small

black box from his pocket. "This was a gift from your father. He said I

was to use it if ever you should turn up. I'm still the same handsome hedgehog you met a few minutes ago. This box works as a kind of advanced hypnotism, and everyone connected to the Tempus network sees what I want them to see. I can even become a tree or a table."

"Fascinating." The Professor prodded him in the nose. "I can even touch you."

Grombit sneezed. "Yes, your father was a very clever man."

Tempus raised her eyebrow, unamused by his persistent use of the word "was" when describing her father.

"But we have just got here," said Arran, "and we're not connected to the Tempus network, whatever that is. How is it that we can see you as a young boy?"

"All will be explained in good time. For now, do you have any worms on you? I'm famished," Grombit asked, expectantly rubbing his belly.

"Yuck, revolting!" said Molly, twisting her face. "I was hungry before you said that."

"Oh, very well." Grombit sighed. "Let's go to a cake shop. I've been experimenting with human food recently."

The four of them crossed the road and headed toward the town centre.

Chapter Eleven

Bridget Fondue's Fanciful Fancies

"Oh, look!" Arran pointed toward a large 3D holographic spire emanating from one of the buildings. "They still have Mighty Burgers in the twenty-second century."

The moment they took an active interest in it, the 3D spire seemed to glide toward them from the top of the building and rest on the pavement in front of them. The "MB" brand that symbolized the Mighty Burger's chain multiplied itself to provide a path of "MB's" leading directly to the entrance.

"Cool," said Arran.

"No, no not cool, young sir," said Grombit. "That is the popular eating place of the Spletka Clan, and besides, I've heard they serve all manner of animals."

"What's wrong with that?" Molly had always thought of herself as an animal rights activist. "If animals are walking around, they should be served the same as everyone else."

"Quite so," said Grombit. "I meant to say that they are served as food. I heard of one family of hamsters that went in for a burger. They never came out; no one knows why, but Hamster McStuffin was on the menu the next day."

No sooner were the children repulsed by the idea of eating there than the glowing MB's disappeared.

"There is where we are going." Grombit pointed to a modest little shop, three doors down.

"How come that one hasn't all the bright lights McDonald's does outside of it?" Arran asked.

"Some things haven't changed since your century. No need for cheap advertising here; the food in this place speaks for itself!"

The children looked suspiciously at Grombit, who sighed and shook his head.

"Not literally. I mean it's very nice."

The sign above the shop door read: Bridget Fondue's Fanciful Fancies. Underneath that there was another sign:

Please wipe feet, fins, and paws before entering.

Looking through the window, they all licked their lips. "Is that a cake made from ice cream?" asked Molly

"No, it isn't," said Arran. "It's a sticky chocolate pudding with a river of Turkish delight flowing from the centre."

"It's whatever you want it to be," said Grombit. "If they have it in stock, the shop knows exactly what you are hungry for and shows you that. Everyone sees something different."

"Ah, that must be why I can see a cup of coffee," said Tempus.

"Well, quite." Grombit shrugged. "Just like your father. Shall we go in?"

"Oh, I haven't any money," said Tempus. "I imagine these are rather expensive."

"Money? Oh yes, I've read about that. Wealth is dependent upon your contribution to society and family; a little to do with your family too. Don't worry; I think we can assume as Professor Tempus's daughter, you will have endless credit. Just place your order and put your finger on the sensor pad over there." Grombit scratched his head, embarrassed. "Would you mind ordering for me? I look like a young boy but would register as a hedgehog."

Tempus shrugged. "Okay." She placed the order and then put her finger on the sensor.

"Thank you, Mrs Tempus, luv," the waitress said.

"That's *Miss* Tempus," the Professor corrected.

At the sound of her name, everyone eating or engaged in conversation stopped and looked at Rebecca Tempus. She gave a shy wave. After a moment the silence ended and everyone continued with their meals.

"I'll take you to yer table, luv," the waitress said, walking them across the room to the only free table in the room. "Sorry about them lot. You see, your dad is…well, he's quite well liked around these parts. We all miss him terribly."

"Thank you," the Professor said softly.

"I'll just get your refreshments. You have a good day, Mrs…" The waitress stopped talking mid-sentence and gave a cheeky wink with a playful nudge of her elbow. "I mean Miss Tempus."

The Professor shrugged this off, sipped her coffee. She took a notepad from her inside pocket and started writing.

"What are you doing, Professor?" asked Molly.

"Just making sure I don't leave anything out," Tempus answered, matter-of-fact.

Grombit, suspecting he was about to be asked multiple questions, finished the white chocolate and worm mousse in its entirety, then sat with his arms folded in wait, licking the leftover dessert from his lips.

"Okay, first," asked the Professor, "what is the Tempus network and why are we already connected to it?"

Grombit twitched his nose before speaking. "Everything and everyone on this planet, born in or after the twenty-second century, is automatically connected to the Tempus network. As you may be able to tell, it was invented by your father, brilliant man."

"Yeah, yeah," said Molly. "Our Professor is brilliant too, aren't you, Professor?"

The Professor didn't respond, except to gesture for Grombit to go on. When learning, she preferred to remain quiet and let others speak.

"Like the air around us," Grombit continued, "the Tempus network is everywhere. Well, almost. There is an area outside the city centre where it isn't as strong. In that place it rains all the time and is always night."

"Spooky." Molly nudged Arran and grinned. "Dare you to go there!" Arran shook his head.

"Quite right, young Arran. That isn't a place for children like you. Or anyone who has put a value on their own lives."

"Jus' joking," Molly mumbled and poked a finger in her ice cream cake, then licked it clean.

"So that's *where* it is," said Arran, "but what is it?"

"The good lady Professor's father described it as a low-level telepathic field that works in harmony with its environment," Grombit answered. "It's the reason you can understand animals, and we you. It's also the reason the elements work with us instead of in spite of us."

Grombit looked at the leftover Turkish delight on Arran's plate. "It's also the reason this fine establishment showed you exactly what you were hungry for when you came in."

"It can read minds too?" asked Arran, a little disturbed.

"It's a bit like computers in your time. You know when you order something online and the program has an insight into what you like and recommends similar items in the hope your shopping spree will continue with them? Well, the Tempus network does not need you to fill out any forms or manually log onto a machine; it knows everything about you and makes appropriate choices based around what you want and need."

The Professor looked rather concerned by this.

"That seems very invasive; people like their secrets. Sounds like big brother gone mad."

"Professor Tempus was far too decent a man for anything underhanded like that! People's and animal's secrets are their own and can't be removed or viewed without a specific operation. To my knowledge the operation is only carried out on the undesirable criminal elements in society to ensure they don't reoffend once they are back in the community."

"Okay," she said, unsatisfied. "And why are the children and I connected to it automatically?"

"Well, you are Professor Tempus's daughter. I assume his biological imprint is on you."

"What about us?" asked Arran.

"Oh, young man, and I thought you to be the clever one."

Molly considered covering Grombit's face in ice cream.

Grombit continued, "I assume as Professor Tempus's children you, too, share the biological imprint."

"You assume too much," the Professor interrupted. "They are not *my* children."

Molly and Arran nodded sadly in agreement.

Grombit was a little taken aback by this revelation. "Are your parents from this time?"

"Nope," said Molly. "We never knew our mother, and Dad is a businessman from the twenty-first century called John Pentka."

The name sent a visible shiver down the spine of Grombit. "Say his name again, young madam."

"John Pentka."

Grombit let out a huge sigh of relief. "Oh my worms, I thought you said something else. Thank goodness."

There was a pause in which Tempus and the two children stared at him expectantly.

Grombit clearly didn't want to speak his name but was now left with little choice. "I thought you said Jhonas Spletka."

"Jhonas Spletka?" Molly laughed.

At the mention of his name, everyone in the room stopped and stared at her, and this time the look on their faces was not one of admiration but more disdain and fear.

"What?" she protested.

The waitress who had served earlier them walked over to the table.

"Out of respect for you and your father, I'm not throwing you out of here, but can you control your little friend's language?" With that she returned to the counter.

Grombit smiled politely at the waitress and turned to face the children. "Jhonas, erm, you know, has not been seen for thirteen years, but he swore he'd return one day to finish what he started. He is evil through and through."

"What did he start?" asked Arran.

"Death, young man, death to everything good and decent on this planet. Many of his disciples are still around patiently awaiting his return."

"Is that the Spletka Clan you spoke of outside Mighty Burger?" quizzed the Professor.

"Yes, he'd enlisted the services of people and animal alike; an ever-growing army. And there they lie, on the outskirts of town, just waiting."

There was an uneasy atmosphere in Fondues Fanciful Fancies from that moment. Sensing this, Grombit suggested they get on with the order of business.

"There are people your father instructed me to take you to. They have more answers than I."

Tempus took the two children by the hand and they left.

Chapter Twelve

The General

Stepping out onto the rustic cobbled street, Tempus and her friends were greeted by an instant warm glow; the sunshine was both relaxing and infinitely welcoming.

Jonny Jagger, a street musician, played his guitar, a collection of oldies from Children of the Stones' greatest hits. Arran watched in wonder as he played his way through a particularly impressive song, "Jimmy Jack Flash Drive."

Arran had always wanted a guitar, but his father refused to pay for lessons or to buy him an instrument, claiming the noise would drive him crazy. That alone was enough to stop Arran asking for one—in his eyes his father couldn't get much crazier.

Jonny's guitar had fifteen strings which controlled not only the traditional rock guitar sound but also that of the drums, bass, orchestra, and backing vocals.

"He is amazing," said Arran.

"Why can't I hear him?" asked Molly.

As far as she could see, Jonny Jagger was doing nothing but miming.

"That will be the Tempus network, I imagine," said the Professor. "Am I correct in assuming you are not a fan of rock music?"

"Yuck, that's not music; I'd rather hear Batsy sing."

The Professor gave an acknowledging nod. "The Tempus network knows that and keeps the noise from entering your ears. It takes certain annoying or unpleasant sounds and silences them in your own personal environment."

"Cool," said Molly. "Do you think it'll work on Arran's voice too?"

Arran was so transfixed by Jonny; he didn't pay any attention to his sister.

Jagger stopped playing and looked at him. "Hi there," he said. "Thanks for listening. You like it?"

"Like it? It's amazing."

Jonny pushed a button on the bottom of the guitar and a tiny green disc, the size of a penny, came out.

"There you go, enjoy," he said, handing the disc to Arran.

"No thanks, I don't have a CD player this small."

Jonny was confused. "A what? I may be playing oldies, but even I don't go that far back. Here, place it between your thumb and first finger and squeeze."

Arran pushed the disc between his fingers and was amazed to hear the "Jimmy Jack Flash Drive" song playing in his ears.

"Wow, am I the only one who can hear this?"

"Yeah, you are now your own personal stereo. If you want the music to go louder, change tracks; whatever you want just think it."

Arran increased the volume and began dancing and singing along, that is, until he turned to see Molly laughing at him. *STOP*, he thought and the music stopped.

Jonny smiled. "Now any time you want to hear the album, simply press it between your fingers for three seconds, then release it. Pop it in your pocket or something. The rest you can do with your mind till you tell it to stop."

"Thank you!"

"No problem. Just keep listening and push me up the charts."

Arran pushed the disc into his pocket.

"Where to, Professor?" Molly said.

"Grombit?" the Professor asked.

Grombit started walking. "Follow me; we need a taxi." After a couple of steps, he stood still, almost petrified. A high-pitched and piercing warning sound filled the street. *Not the general,* he thought. *In the middle of the day?*

"Stop and put your heads down, children—look away quick."

Grombit was clearly no expert on children, well, Molly at least. Telling her not to look up made her very curious indeed, but he clamped his eyes shut and whispered to the children.

"After Jhonas Spletka disappeared, one of his generals took over the Clan, and he has been terrorising the good people of the City ever since. You are safe as long as you keep your heads down and, whatever you do, keep your eyes closed."

Molly began to scan the street for anything out of the ordinary. Everybody, as far as she could make out, was either looking down or closing their eyes tightly. She saw, in the distance, a middle-aged man. His hair was dishevelled and grey, his suit, dirty and torn. His face was drained, almost lifeless, as if the blood had been sucked from his body.

He slowly limped past the people and animals to see if any of them were curious enough to take a look. No one was. He continued to move forward, looking both left and right till he caught sight of Molly, who was staring directly at him. His face cracked into a smile; a grin so grotesque it made Mrs Anderson's look like something right out of a

Disney film.

"Professor, I'm scared," Molly said.

"Keep your eyes closed, child!" Grombit commanded.

"I can't stop looking at him. He's coming for me."

"Shut your eyes, Molly," Tempus pleaded.

"I can't! He's standing right in front of me!"

The man took out a small black box, almost identical to the one Grombit had used to take human form, and pressed it between his hands. The box disappeared and the man began slowly moving his head from side to side. Every head movement made his eyes turn darker, till they were entirely black. Molly began to feel incredibly tired but she was unable to move or look away.

Eight small black dots appeared around the man's eyes. His nose and mouth seemed to melt away, replaced with thick, black, bristly fur. Two razor-sharp fangs appeared where his mouth once was. Four arms started to grow from his side and change shape, looking more like eight oversized insect legs. As thick black fur grew on his legs, his body transformed into two oval shapes; a smaller body in front supporting a giant abdomen behind.

"Please help me, Professor," Molly gasped. "It's in my head. I can feel him!"

"Grombit, I have to do something!" shouted the Professor.

The creature's focus was interrupted by the mention of Grombit's name. It stopped and released Molly from its gaze. She fell to the floor, unconscious.

"Grombit," it hissed, "Professor Tempus's loyal companion."

"Yes, what of it?" Grombit shouted back, not daring to look up. He felt an icy-cold breath on his neck.

"We thought you dead, Grombit. Where is Professor Tempus?"

"I wish I knew. Even if I did, you'd have to kill me. I'd never give him up."

Grombit felt something move across the top of his head.

"Oh, we will. But not before you join us."

"The power you've stolen from the little girl isn't enough to make that happen, and you know it. Without Jhonas Spletka there's nothing you can do but kill me, so go ahead!"

"I can wait, Grombit. I can wait."

A few moments of silence passed. Grombit heard people talking and running about their daily business in the street as though nothing had happened. His pounding heart slowed and he opened his eyes, breathing a huge sigh of relief.

"Okay, everybody, open your eyes, it's gone."

Arran and the Professor were already tending to Molly, who lay unconscious on the street. The Professor glared at Grombit. "Fix her now! This is the twenty-second century. I imagine medical science has improved considerably since my time."

"It has, Professor, but her ailment is not biological; it's spiritual you might say."

Arran started to cry, brushing the hair away from his sister's face. "Look, you stupid hedgehog, I don't care what you have to do. Help my sister!"

"There's only one man who can help your sister now, and he's…"

"My father?" the Professor said sadly.

Grombit nodded. "I don't know why the creature didn't take her, but she's not safe here. Can you carry her?"

The Professor picked Molly up. "Where are we going?"

"The only place we can go. The Citadel. We need a ride; follow me."

Arran and the Professor hurried as fast as they could behind him.

At the end of the street, a broken-down, rusted, yellow and black car waited. It had no wheels and no doors. It looked to Arran like something which belonged in a scrap yard. He and Molly had played in similar vehicles near the village rubbish tip at home. Grombit paused outside the car and scanned the expressions of the passers-by. A few had started to take a minor interest in the foursome staring at the car.

"Do what I say and don't ask questions," said Grombit. "Get in."

Arran shook his head. "You've got to be kidding, in this heap?!"

"No questions, young man. Get in now…please!" A few more passers-by began to take an interest in them. Although she couldn't explain it, the Professor sensed that they should follow Grombit's instructions.

"Don't argue, Arran. Your sister will be fine, I promise, just get in."

Arran followed the Professor into the car. "Why is everyone looking at us?"

Grombit sat in the front, placing his hands on the dashboard.

"This is no ordinary car, young man; it takes us directly to the Citadel, which contains the living force behind this planet. If any of the Spletka Clan were to discover its whereabouts, the results would be catastrophic. It is only to be used in emergencies, like now."

"Till now," Grombit continued, "the Tempus network has disguised the car's appearance, making it unappealing to the masses, and it therefore went un-noticed. Once we took an interest in it, the perception filter was slowly lifted and others began to notice. It's just a matter of time before one of the Spletka Clan finds it now."

A crowd formed outside the vehicle, which was no longer a battered, broken-down taxi cab, but a sleek, metallic blue sports car, the likes of which had never been seen before. It uniquely combined all the elegance one associates with a classic sports car whilst having the aesthetic and mechanical attributes that would satisfy any wannabe boy racer. It was infinitely desirable. Men, women, children, and animals all stood, staring in wonder. A few reached out and stroked the bonnet.

"Take us to the Citadel," announced Grombit.

The windscreen interior turned black, and the face of Richard Tempus appeared in the centre, ghostly white and looking exactly the same as his daughter had seen him in her vision the night before.

"It's just a hologram," said Grombit.

"Name?" the figure said.

"Grombit fourth generation."

A red light emanated from the steering wheel and scanned him.

"Journey not permitted," the figure said.

"I don't understand," Grombit retorted. "I have full clearance. Take us to the Citadel!"

The warning alarm that had sounded earlier resonated through the streets again; the Spletka were on their way. On instinct all the admirers standing around or stroking the car either ran off or stepped back and covered their eyes.

"Professor, that sound again," shouted Arran. "That lunatic is probably on his way back to finish the job he started!"

The white figure repeated its earlier announcement: "Journey not permitted; please leave the vehicle."

"Father, take us to the Citadel," Professor Tempus pleaded, holding Molly tight in her arms and staring at the figure on the windscreen. The figure looked at the Professor. A similar red glow surrounded her.

"Rebecca?" It spoke this time in a softer, less authoritative tone.

"Please, Dad, I need your help."

There was a sudden bright light surrounding the car and they found themselves instantly transported from the town centre to the gates of what seemed to be a huge disused warehouse.

Chapter Thirteen

The Citadel

Armed guards waited to receive them.

"Grombit," one of them acknowledged as he stepped out of the car.

"And you must be Rebecca Tempus?" another said, looking into the back. "I'm deeply honoured."

Tempus gestured toward the young girl sleeping on her knee.

"She needs help."

"One of the Spletka Clan," continued Grombit. "The general, I think. She survived a death stare."

"Then she's very fortunate," said the guard. "I'll take her."

The Professor was reluctant to let Molly go, pushing the guard's hand away when he reached his arms in to take her.

"It's okay," said Grombit, "we can trust him."

The Professor raised her hands. "If anything happens to her…"

"I understand," said the guard. "We'll do what we can."

He lifted Molly from the car and carried her through the entrance, leaving the door open for Grombit, the Professor, and Arran to follow close behind.

The warehouse looked like an empty, deserted storage facility on a single floor, no sign of any staff, medical equipment, or even furniture of any kind. The place was unclean, dusty, and cluttered with cobwebs.

"You expecting bailiffs?" asked the Professor.

The guard carrying Molly looked confused.

"There's not much here."

He smiled. "Oh, I see. I wasn't told you were…" He paused.

"No matter. It's a security measure; in the unlikely event one of the Spletka Clan ever found this place, all they would see is the vacant lot you're standing in now. If you could see it for what it really is, without the layers of dimensional camouflage, it's the site of a castle. One of the oldest surviving castles in England. Built by William the Conqueror, I believe. A little before my time, of course."

The other guard looked disturbed and scanned the area for the second time. "I can't see anything, sir, but there's something not quite right here. I can feel it."

"Okay," Arran interrupted, "enough of this. I'm not one of the Spletka Clan, I can't see anything dangerous, and I don't care who built this place. My sister needs your help now, please."

The first guard nodded in agreement and ordered the second guard to stand down.

"Here, put these on."

He handed Arran and the Professor a black metal wrist band, then slipped one on Molly's wrist.

"Sorry, Grombit," the guard said, "here you must stay for now."

Grombit looked hurt by the very suggestion.

"Our transport detected something unusual on you. It's probably the human transformation hard light image, but we need to be sure. Someone will be here presently to have you checked out."

Grombit sat on the floor, resting his cheeks on his hands, sulking almost.

"Grombit's an old friend," said the guard. "I didn't like having to do that."

"I'm sure he'll be fine, said the Professor sympathetically as she took a brief look at Grombit, who was now scratching his head with one hand and resting his chin on the other. "Now, Molly?"

"Yes," said the guard. "Your father perfected the process of short dimensional transference in which different environments can occupy the same space without interfering with one another."

"What?" said Arran.

The Professor rested her hand on his shoulder. "I assume it means this room, though empty now, with one flick of a switch can become many different places."

"What?" said Arran, who didn't care for all the science talk and just wanted his sister to be well again.

The guard smirked and shook his head, looking at the Professor.

"Just like your father."

"So I've heard," she replied. "I wish he was here now."

The guard looked down at Molly and nodded. Tiny beads of sweat covered her face. "You and me both. She's burning up. We should go."

Arran rolled his eyes. "Gee, that's a good idea!"

"Now," said the guard, "grasp your wrist band till this room disappears."

After a moment they all found themselves transported into the open air, standing on the edge of a huge colourful field; not just because of the impressive array of flowers but also the grass, which changed colours as the warm, gentle breeze brushed across it, casually encouraging the individual blades to amble through the full rainbow spectrum at will. As unfamiliar and staggering as this sight was, a more imposing structure captured their attention.

The sun, acting like an obliging spotlight, shone its rays upon the huge stone castle, surrounding village, and moat that stood before them. Several flags fluttered in the breeze from behind the castle turrets, and one flag, which was bigger than the rest, proudly displayed an insignia of a single white dove wrapping its wings around a planet.

"What's the symbol?" the Professor asked.

"That's the United Flag of the Planet Earth," the guard answered, whilst taking a small disc from his pocket and pressing it between his thumb and forefinger. "We have Professor Tempus's daughter plus two children; one in need of medical assistance."

No sooner had he spoken the words than a huge drawbridge lowered itself from the Citadel entrance over the moat and lay at their feet.

"Come on." He walked forward. The others followed.

The Professor had never been completely comfortable in large crowds, and the hero worship being displayed by the inhabitants of the village as they made their way to the castle did little to alleviate her anxiety, particularly as Molly, supposedly under her protection, was clearly not doing so well. Her skin was no longer bright, but had turned an ever-increasing dull grey colour.

Arran looked through the window of one building en route and saw hundreds of children of varying ages all seated perfectly still with their eyes closed. He supposed they were meditating.

"That's the Tempus School for Special Abilities," the guard said as they passed.

Normally Arran would have had an array of questions but he was more concerned with getting his sister to some kind of hospital, so he said nothing and followed the others to the castle entrance.

The guard pounded on the big oak door. The resonating sound was so deafening it could be heard outside. Arran supposed anyone inside would probably be nursing their ears for months. The door swung open and an armed guard immediately saluted, recognising the authority of the officer in front of him. He silently stood to one side, allowing them passage into the castle.

They walked into a beautiful throne room which was a mixture of polished marble, gold, and stone. The room was full of people seated at wooden tables of varying shapes and sizes. There were two long tables which spanned the entire width of the room, surrounded by smaller, more intimate seating areas.

Food and drink just seemed to materialize in front of people when they sat.

"Each serving is engineered to cater for the patron's individual taste and hunger level." The guard said to Arran, who was looking curiously around the room. Pillars, which looked more like a precious metal than stone, were situated at various parts of the room.

One huge pillar stood proud, in the centre of the room. Tempus watched as a young lady approached it and knocked three times. A door appeared on the surface, which the girl then pulled open and walked inside. Once the door was closed, the pillar returned to its original state.

"That's where we are going," said the guard and they all approached it.

The guard thought for a second before asking the Professor to knock on the pillar exactly as the girl before her had done. After three knocks, not one but four doors appeared around the surface, each with a label signifying the intended destination. The Professor walked around and read the signs on each of the doors: Infirmary, School, Orb Room.

The fourth door had in small letters across the top: Professor Richard Tempus.

"Too much to hope my father is in there, I suppose?"

"I don't know," answered the guard. "The doors the pillar chooses to show are different for everyone, and they change all the time depending upon what you need. I've never seen that one before."

She tried the handle. "It's locked anyway." She shrugged. "I'd hoped he could have helped her but…the infirmary then."

She pulled the infirmary door open and walked inside, unsure as what to expect.

Chapter Fourteen

The Medical Unit

Arran thought the pillar to be an elevator of sorts before he stepped in, and was rather surprised to find himself walking right into the medical unit. A vast and heavily populated community of doctors were walking through corridors, and in and out of patient rooms, followed for the most part by holographic nurses dressed in matching white lab coats and carrying clipboards.

The receptionist directly in front of them sat at a bare silver desk, with no phone or computer that he could see, yet she was typing vigorously into thin air whilst speaking to people on her left and right; except there was no one there. Arran felt sure she was probably a mental patient herself.

"Visiting hours to be determined at the doctor's discretion" was written directly below the reception desk.

A smart young lady walked toward the guard, dutifully followed by a floating stretcher. "I received your message, sir. All is ready."

The guard placed Molly gently on the stretcher and it made its own way, levitating across the hall to a room labelled "recovery."

"If you could wait here for a moment," the lady said to the Professor, "we'll call you once we've done a few tests."

Arran made to follow the stretcher and the lady, regardless of her instructions, but the Professor softly placed her hand on his shoulder to remind him that his presence may be more of a hindrance than a help.

"Well, if you'll excuse me, Professor," said the guard. "I need to make sure Grombit has been cleared."

The Professor nodded and the guard walked back through the door.

"Rebecca Tempus and guest to recovery room two." The

announcement sounded twice.

"That wasn't over a loudspeaker," said Arran. "That was just like when I was listening to Jonny Jagger's music."

"I heard it too," answered the Professor, feeling rather comforted by the name of the room they were walking to.

Recovery Room. Maybe it wasn't as serious as they'd feared.

A doctor adjusted the intensity of the blue ray of light which covered Molly's body as she lay asleep on the bed. "She's resting at the moment."

"Will she be okay?" Arran asked.

"Yes, provided she's allowed the time to recover. It will take time, but her signs are strong. The nurse told me she survived a death stare?" The Professor nodded. "Then I may make medical history."

The Professor looked confused and gestured for the doctor to continue.

"She will be the first person in history ever to survive. I'm quite excited to see what impact this will have on her immune system. I might have known the return of Professor Tempus would herald a miracle."

"Well, I wouldn't say return; this is the first time I've been here."

The doctor simply smiled, clearly wanting to say something but thinking better of it.

"When can I talk to her?" Arran asked.

"Right now if you want to," Molly replied.

The Professor and Arran looked at one another in shock, then at the doctor.

Arran stared at his sister, who was still lying motionless on the bed. "That was Molly's voice."

"Yeah, do you think?" A ghostly image of Molly appeared in front of everybody in the room. She stood next to her sleeping body and looked down

"Hey, Arran, this is weird—not every day you get to watch yourself sleep."

Arran cried and made to touch her, but his hand just drifted through. "Molly, I love you. Please don't die."

Molly's ghostly image looked at him and shrugged. "Erm, okay."

"What's going on?" the Professor asked.

"Visiting hours," the doctor replied. "She may be sleeping, but through the Tempus network you can still communicate with her, and she with you."

"I am connected with you, Arran," Molly said. "The Professor too and Grombit downstairs, though he seems to be sitting down sulking about something. Perhaps I'd better not disturb him."

Grombit was indeed sulking, feeling very sorry for himself, and walking around the bare room, hands in his pockets, and grumbling to himself.

"There's a fine thank you. Take them all the way here and for what? To be left behind. Don't need Grombit now, do you? Not even a worm bar to chew on while I'm waiting."

An annoying itch prompted him to scratch his head. He leaned against the front door, looking out into the barren wasteland, internally recalling the events in the car from earlier. Grombit found it very strange that Molly had not been taken by the general and that he hadn't been killed either.

He'd been vigorously hunted ever since Professor Tempus and Jhonas Spletka went missing thirteen years ago, and the Spletka Clan were not noted for their fine sense of forgiving and compassion. At the very least he'd expected the general to try to prevent their escape to the Citadel. Something didn't add up. It was almost as if they wanted him to find his way here. He scratched his head again.

"Molly needs to rest now," the doctor instructed.

"Yes, I am a bit sleepy, but don't worry, Arran, I feel fine."

"How long will she be like this?" the Professor asked whilst stroking Molly's hair.

He explained that it was very much up to Molly. The blue light was a blanket of sorts providing pure positive energy, and as she improved, the blue would eventually fade away, leaving a clear ray, at which point she would be fit and well.

"And in the cases where it has not worked, what happens then?"

The doctor sighed. "That will be every case I've dealt with to this date; the light changes from blue to red. Some of the stronger-willed creatures fight it, but the result is always the same. The body goes on living for a while, but the soul, the energy inside, dies."

Arran and the Professor exchanged a mutual glance of concern before the doctor went on.

"Jhonas Spletka had the ability to use this transformation to turn each individual to his side, feeding off the good, stealing their abilities, and leaving nothing but an obedient drone to add to his vile collective. He hasn't been seen for years. Since he disappeared, everyone I have treated has died. Molly has the strongest life signs I have ever seen."

"I don't think the general had time to finish his work," the Professor guessed. "He was distracted by the mention of Grombit."

"Then it's fortunate he doesn't have knowledge of our whereabouts. If he did, Molly would be in great danger."

Chapter Fifteen

Aiysha

"Grombit, are you Grombit?"

A young lady, one would assume by her attire, from the medical department approached.

"My name is Aiysha," she announced, straightening her name badge and pulling her hair into a ponytail.

"Sorry about your wait. I've been on a twelve-hour shift; was just catching up on some sleep when I was called to tend to you."

Grombit felt sorry for the tired-looking young lady.

"You look worse than I feel." He scratched his head again. "Do you have any worms?"

Aiysha was a little taken aback by his question. "No, I'm in perfect health," she replied. "Thanks for asking though."

"I meant for me, to eat." He licked his lips.

"Oh," she said quite calmly. "No, that's disgusting. Place your finger on this scanner please."

He did as he was told. The image on the scanner appeared as a small hedgehog. Underneath, the words: "Grombit, generation four."

"I do apologise," said Aiysha. "I didn't realise you were a hedgehog. The earthworms, probably not so disgusting then; I'll see what I can do when we're finished here."

Aiysha opened the front door, pointed the scanner at the car, then read the display on her machine.

Driver log login Grombit generation 4. Attempted login failed foreign body detected.

Login Grombit generation 4. Attempted login failed foreign body detected.

Command override priority 1 login Professor Rebecca Tempus Destination citadel.

Grombit scratched his head again, this time with increased intensity. Aiysha looked up from her scanner, concerned by the look of pain on the hedgehog's face as he clawed at his head.

"Are you all right?"

"Yes, I'm fine, just this itch I can't seem to…" He kept scratching, wincing in pain as he did so.

"Let me have a look." She raised her hand to touch his head.

Without warning Grombit grabbed her wrist to stop her.

"I'm sorry," he said, quite embarrassed. "That wasn't me. I can't seem to let go." His grip on Aiysha's wrist tightened.

"You're hurting me, Grombit. Let go!"

"I can't!" He tightened his grasp.

His remaining free hand grasped Aiysha's other wrist and

locked his hold on her.

"It's not me; I think the general put something…"

Grombit blinked. When his eyes opened, they were jet black. Grombit spoke, but the voice was not his; it was the sinister whisper of the general.

"Yes, Grombit, I deposited one or two of my lieutenants on you. Now we know the location of the Citadel and our armies are on their way. Thank you, you've been most useful. The young girl who escaped me can't be allowed to continue, of course."

Grombit's stare paralyzed Aiysha; like everybody who had been caught in the field of the death stare, she was unable to look away. Every moment that passed, her already tired body grew weaker. Grombit closed his eyes, shaking his head from side to side furiously.

"Get out of my head!" he pleaded. "Fight, fight, fight!"

He finally collapsed on the floor, his firm grip still around Aiysha's wrist, dragging her down with him.

Aiysha, finally free from the death stare, struggled to free her hand from his grip but her weary body provided little support. Grombit was still. She lay down so she was practically nose to nose with him

"Grombit, are you all right?"

No answer. Was he dead?

Grombit's lower eyelid flickered. Aiysha managed a slight

smile.

"Still with us then?" she said tenderly. His eyelid flickered again.

"Don't worry, Grombit. If they don't hear from me soon, someone will be…"

A tiny spider crawled out from under his eyeball. Aiysha's petrified reflection burned in each of the spider's tiny black eyes. She screamed and tried with all that she had to free herself from Grombit's vice-like grip. She started to cry as more spiders slowly and deliberately emerged from every facial orifice.

There was a rustle of hair on Grombit's head before one final arachnid, slightly larger than the rest, almost marched forward, to take command. The silent orders were given and the spiders made their way from Grombit's seemingly lifeless body to take residence on a new host.

Once the spiders fixed themselves on Aiysha's head, Grombit's hands, having served their dreadful purpose, relaxed, allowing Aiysha to pull herself away from him. She scratched her head furiously, drawing a small fountain of blood; a vain attempt to free herself from Grombit's eventual fate.

Her mind began to fade in and out of darkness. *Must warn the others*, she thought. Through her momentary spasms she remembered that the scanner used earlier to take data from the car had a panic button. She lifted the machine from the floor and desperately tried to push the button, her body seeming to fight the action.

"Have…to…concentrate," she gasped.

With one final burst of conscious energy, she pushed the button down, causing the scanner to flash red. The reply from the Citadel was instantaneous.

"Aiysha, is there a problem?" Aiysha closed her eyes.

"Aiysha," the voice repeated, "is everything all right down there?"

Aiysha opened her eyes and smiled. "Yes, everything is fine," she said calmly. "Grombit is unconscious; he must have pressed the panic button when he fell."

Chapter Sixteen

Mike Hamblin

"So, we can visit her anytime we like?" asked Arran as he and the Professor walked from Molly's room.

"Well, as long as the doctor says it's all right."

"Yeah, as long as he says it's okay," added Molly, following close behind.

Professor Tempus spun on the spot to look directly at Molly's hologram. "I seem to recall the doctor telling you to rest. Off you go."

"You're no fun," Molly mumbled as she disappeared.

"So, you are the famous Rebecca Tempus?"

The Professor turned around. A senior resident technician extended his hand in greeting.

"And judging by the name on your badge, I assume you are Mike Hamblin."

Mike was, to Tempus's eyes, a pleasant-looking fellow: shoulder-length blond hair and slight stubble framing a hospitable smile. He wore a white lab coat, fitting in with the seeming department dress code.

He smiled, looking down at his name tag whilst pushing his glasses up so they rested quite comfortably on the bridge of his nose.

"You might be the first person I've seen this century to be wearing glasses," she noted, with more scientific interest than anything else.

Mike didn't need glasses, of course—medical advancements

were such that eyesight problems were diagnosed and cured in any corner shop medi-centre within minutes. To Mike they were more of a fashion accessory, one he now hoped Rebecca Tempus would find familiar, endearing, and attractive.

"You are something of a legend around here," he said, looking deep into her eyes. "Though I have to admit, meeting you in person, you're nothing like I had expected."

Mike blushed, though the Professor was not quite sure why.

"What did you expect, Mike?"

He laughed, brushing her arm with his. "A stuffy old academic mainly."

Her eyebrows rose. "Well, that's a fairly accurate description, if not a little blunt. I…"

"No, no," Mike interrupted quickly. "An academic you may be, but certainly not stuffy, or old. I mean older people are…nice in a platonic…but you are not platonic, I mean old, not too young or old for…some things."

Having mastered the art of bumbling his words completely, he eventually stopped talking.

"Are you a patient here?" the Professor asked kindly.

There was a moment's silence before Arran, who had been watching the interplay between them carefully, laughed.

"For such a clever lady, Professor, you have no idea, do you?"

Both the Professor and Mike turned to face Arran. Mike was clearly embarrassed. The Professor was merely looking for clarity.

"I was wondering really," Mike continued, hoping to salvage something from his previous attempt at a conversation, "not sure how to say…"

He paused and the Professor grew slightly impatient.

"Come on then, out with it, man."

"It's difficult," he said. "I'm clearly not used to asking."

The Professor rested her hands on his as though he were a small child. "Asking what?"

"Would you like a coffee?" he eventually said. "I mean I was going for one anyway."

The Professor smiled. "Ah, I see, coffee. Got there in the end, didn't you? No, I'm not thirsty, thank you."

"No, me neither." He walked a few steps in the opposite direction.

"What an odd man."

Mike returned. "Actually, I also wanted to mention something else."

The Professor sighed.

"Tea?" offered Arran playfully.

Mike raised an accusing eyebrow in Arran's direction. "It's possible that Molly will be resting for quite some time yet. Perhaps Arran might like to meet some other children his own age. There is a games room; children of families working at the Citadel often go there."

Arran didn't find the suggestion unappealing at all.

"Sounds good to me," he said. "Why don't you have a coffee with Mike while I'm gone, Professor?"

"But I already said I'm not thirsty."

"Yes, but Mike is, and you know how lonely he gets."

"Well, no, I hardly know him at all."

"Ah, a coffee will certainly remedy that, don't you think?"

The Professor shrugged her shoulders. "Oh, very well, Mike; let's go and drink coffee!"

"It would be my pleasure, madam," Mike said with a wide schoolboy grin plastered over his face.

She chuckled a little, then stopped as a slight tingling sensation registered itself in the very core of her mind. *There's something very familiar about him*, she thought.

Chapter Seventeen

The Games Room

The entrance to the medical unit had transformed back into the single pillar they had used when they entered the castle; and now that Arran knew how it worked, he raced forward and knocked three times on the surface. A door labelled *Games Room* appeared and he reached for the handle.

"Is there a PlayStation?" he asked.

Mike laughed and gestured for Arran to open the door. "Have fun, Arran. When you're finished come back through the pillar; it should take you directly to us."

Arran stepped through the door and found himself standing on a moving cloud, high in the sky. Standing next to him was a very posh man in a butler's uniform.

"Good day, sir." His deep and deliberate voice caused the cloud to vibrate a little. "Welcome to the games room. I am the help program. Would you like a tour?"

Arran looked down and saw nothing but clouds and blue sky.

He shrugged. "Well, it's my first time here."

"I know, hence my offering you a tour."

"What happens if I fall off?" Arran asked a little nervously.

"That would be clumsy now, wouldn't it, sir?"

Oh good, thought Arran. *Programmes have perfected the art of sarcasm here.*

"Am I actually in the sky or is this some sort of virtual reality?"

"Your mind is here, sir. We have literally a universe of games; enough to cater to your every desire."

"So, if this is all in my mind, where's my real body right now?"

"This is not supposed to be so much a question-and-answer, sir—more I show you things, and you show a great deal of interest and amazement. But if you must know, you were scanned and sent to sleep the moment you entered the room. Your physical being is at this very moment sitting very comfortably alongside nine hundred and twenty-three other gamers. You can wake and return anytime you choose simply by thinking it."

The cloud, as though it were propelled by some sort of jet engine, suddenly sped off. Arran hit the dubiously fluffy floor and assumed a star shape, for fear he might fall into a deep abyss. The cloud raced forward, dodging left and right to avoid other clouds, then came to a sudden halt over the top of an enormous cloud with a diner on top.

"Are you tired, sir?" The butler watched Arran try to cling to his cloud.

Arran stood up and dusted himself off. "A little warning before you scoot off at ninety miles per hour would be nice!"

"One hundred and fifteen," the butler corrected, "but if you wish, I can let you know before we move."

"What is this place?"

"This is the Diner, sir. When you want a break from your game of choice, but don't want to leave the network, some gamers find it preferable to relax here and socialise. Would you like to go down?"

Arran shook his head. "Maybe later. I'd like to see some games first."

The cloud instantly sped off again, causing Arran to instinctively hit the floor. It came to rest amidst several other clouds. Some of them had passengers; others were floating quite freely. They all seemed to be partially connected to a larger cloud, above which rose the words in scarlet red "Beneath the Fall."

"I thought you were going to tell me before you made this thing move!" Arran said, rising once again to his feet.

"I didn't do that, sir. The moment you decided you wanted to go somewhere else, the cloud simply followed your command. This is a game, sir." The butler pointed at the big cloud.

Arran nodded, looking at the sign. "Yes, I guessed."

His desire to take a closer look resulted in his cloud moving nearer to it.

"It's called Beneath the Fall, sir."

"Yes, I can read."

"Once you have played it, sir, you can access the game directly from within your own cloud."

Arran watched as a young girl, wearing reflective shades and a baseball cap, stepped off her cloud and onto the bigger one; once there she simply sank down beneath the white fluffy mist. He half expected her to reappear underneath, but that was the last he saw of her.

Another three clouds pulled up alongside his, carrying three more gamers. Victor Graston, a fifteen-year-old troublemaker and self-proclaimed alpha male, stood on the cloud closest to Arran's.

He looked Arran up and down with an air of disdain before signalling the others to join him in the game. They stepped off, linked arms, and sank beneath the surface as the other girl had done before.

"If you want to play the game with others, there must be some form of physical contact before you enter the platform," the butler said, anticipating Arran's next question as to why they had linked arms before proceeding. "They are quite experienced gamers, sir. You may watch their progress if you wish."

"Yes, okay." Arran's cloud moved two inches to the right so it was touching Victor Graston's. Once contact was made, Arran sank down into his own cloud.

The mist cleared and Arran found himself sitting on a comfy

leather chair which was floating high over a waterfall that led to a turbulent river, populated by alligators and ill-tempered piranha which jumped in and out of the water, expectantly gnashing their needle-like teeth.

Victor and his two friends flew past Arran on hover boards, not even noticing his presence, and paused at the top of the fall. A three-second countdown sounded, accompanied by invisible crowd cheers. When the timer reached zero all three participants raced down the waterfall, screeching to a sudden stop when they reached the base— that is, except Victor, who continued down into the river and re-emerged with a piranha gnashed in between his teeth. He spat it out and raced toward the finish line, which had now appeared at the end of the river.

Just before Victor reached the finish, Arran let out a huge shout of approval followed by a clap of his hands. Victor, distracted, turned to look at him, then promptly fell off his board and into the water. His two friends stared at Arran, both with dumbfounded expressions of shock.

Okay, thought Arran, *maybe it's time I left*. Barely a second later, he was standing on his own cloud.

"Did you enjoy…" The butler was interrupted by Arran.

"Yes, it was lovely. We have to go now."

"Go?" the butler enquired. "But don't you want to try…?"

Victor and his two friends emerged from their clouds. Victor was rolling up his sleeves, followed by a definite clenching of the fist.

"Oh, perfect," said Arran. "When I'm not expecting it, you race 'round the sky without a hint of a warning. But now that I want to go, you decide that you fancy a chat!"

The butler looked a little perturbed.

"Very well, sir. Where would you like to go?"

Victor started to advance across his own cloud toward Arran, who now had to think very fast and blurted out the only place he knew.

"Erm, the Diner?"

His cloud raced off—closely pursued by Victor and his two friends.

Chapter Eighteen

Fight

Arran burst through the swing doors of the diner like a hapless victim seeking sanctuary from the dreadful nightmares of a horror movie; except this wasn't hallowed ground and his pursuer was not a vampire, or at least he hoped not. He needed somewhere to hide and quick.

Lucky for him, or so he thought, the place was simply bursting with activity; children, predominantly teenagers, and smaller animals sat in booths eating junk food whilst others danced and walked the aisles, chatting and laughing.

Meanwhile outside, Victor had jumped from his cloud and was racing toward the entrance. His two followers ran close behind, trying to keep up.

Arran dived into the crowd, seeking camouflage, safety in numbers. If he could find an unoccupied seat and keep his head down, his pursuers might just walk past, assuming he had simply slipped out.

The only free seat was at a small table where a small boy dressed in psychedelic knee-length shorts and a green T-shirt sat, desperately trying to drink a thick banana milkshake through a tiny straw.

Arran sat down and buried his head in his hands. The young boy, whose face had turned red due to the tremendous challenge the milkshake posed, jumped back, a little startled. "Do I know you?" he asked.

Arran popped his head up and considered the question. "No."

Then he put his head back to continue his ineffective attempt at concealment.

All too quickly the happy chatter in the diner suddenly stopped. The deafening silence yelled in his ears:

Guess who's found you!

He glanced up and stared at the young boy, who was clearly petrified, his attention firmly focussed on an approaching bully. Victor Graston had made up several reasons over the years to beat him to a pulp and now, there he was, standing at his table.

Arran slowly stood up and turned around. He would have been nose to nose with Victor but the bully had a few inches on him. He picked Arran up by the scruff of the neck, then levitated so he was practically touching the ceiling.

Arran's movement was limited, but he was able to glance down and see everybody's suspenseful face staring up at him.

"I don't know how you hacked into my game," Victor shouted, "but you're gonna pay for that."

"Sorry," Arran replied timidly.

"You will be."

He released his grip and Arran fell, crashing first onto the table, then the floor, eventually covered in the young boy's banana milkshake. There was a roar of laughter in the diner as Victor glided back down to the ground till he stood towering over Arran.

"H… H… How did you do that?" Arran hoped the answer would be verbal and not a swift kick to the stomach.

"It's my special ability," replied Victor. "What's yours, getting on people's nerves?"

Joss Minton, Victor's girlfriend, stepped forward and glared at him. Arran recognised her as one of the gamers who had stared so strangely at him when he caused Victor to fall in the water.

"He's called Arran," she said.

Arran was beginning to feel quite threatened. What were these people?

"Before you ask," she continued, "I can read minds. That's just *one* of my abilities."

"Guess what, Vic, Arran has no abilities." She laughed.

"He has the ability to get in my way when I'm playing."

"Look, I said I'm sorry." Arran stood up and wiped banana milkshake from his brow, trying to conserve what little self-respect he still had left. "I'm not going to say it again!"

Victor sneered at him. "Pretty brave for a DOA, aren't you?"

Arran shrugged and put on a brave face, though he was trembling inside.

"What's DOA then, Mr Brave Man who needs his girlfriend around to look hard?"

Victor pushed Arran backward onto a holographic chess table, disturbing the intellectual battle in which two hamsters had been engaged. "Devoid of Ability, stupid."

"Look, the DOA tripped." Joss laughed.

Victor snarled at Joss and she clamped her mouth shut.

"Come on then, DOA, just you and me!"

Arran steadied himself, then inched forward to square up to him.

"I'm not scared of you!"

That was a lie. He couldn't have been more scared if he was being chased by a rabid dog whilst trapped in a burning building.

"And what do we have here?"

Both Arran and Victor turned to see an old gentleman dressed in a black ceremonial gown and carrying a cane.

Victor snorted and sighed. "Nothing, Headmaster Dews. Me and him were just talking, isn't that right, DOA?"

Arran said nothing.

"Safe to assume your conversation has come to an end then, wouldn't you agree?"

Though he towered over the headmaster too, Victor would never dare confront him. Not only would he face expulsion from the Tempus School of Special Abilities but his meagre talents were no match for the damage the headmaster could inflict, were he of a mind to do so.

"Come on," Victor said to his friends. "Let's go." Just before he left, he turned. "Oh, and DOA, stay out of my way."

The headmaster smiled and winked at Arran before wandering back off the way he had come.

Chapter Nineteen

Rudolph

"Hi, I'm Rudolph," said the young boy, offering Arran a serviette to take care of the leftover milkshake. "That's one way to get it out of the cup," he joked, hoping to lighten the mood. "I was having no luck with the straw."

Sensing there was nothing left to see, everybody else wandered off and continued with their activities.

"Don't worry about him; he does that to everybody new."

Arran was clearly shaken up by what had just happened, but decided to put it out of his mind. He had more important things to worry about with his sister still in critical condition.

"Just one thing," said Arran. "How is it they have superpowers?"

Rudolph looked confused. "You mean their abilities?" Arran nodded. "Wow, that fall must have really done something to you. Nearly everyone has abilities these days. They change from person to person. Not many people haven't any at all, and those are nicknamed…"

"DOA."

"Yeah," said Rudolph. "I have enhanced hearing. I can hear a cricket landing on a leaf from over a mile away. In school I'm learning to filter sounds so I can pick out just the ones I wanna listen to."

"That's great, congratulations."

"Pardon?" Rudolph cupped his hand against his ear. "Just joking, I actually heard you."

Arran said nothing, sighed, and shook his head.

"What did you say your name was?"

"Rudolph."

"Rudolph. You mean like the…?"

"Donkey? Yes, I get that all the time, the old story of Mary, Joseph, and Rudolph the red-nosed donkey."

Arran laughed. "You may have your history a bit mixed up there, Rudolph. I'm Arran, pleased to meet you."

"Wanna play a game?"

"Yeah, sure." Arran shrugged unenthusiastically.

They walked out and Rudolph jumped on his cloud, spoke the word "lobby," and sank beneath the mist. *When in Rome…* Arran jumped on his cloud, mimicked Rudolph's actions, and drifted into his own cloud.

When the mist cleared Arran found he was standing in a completely empty space around the size of a tennis court. The walls, floor, and ceiling were completely white; there were no doors or windows.

He touched one of the walls and a message appeared before him.

Red Rudolph wishes to join your game session. Accept or decline?

"Accept," Arran said.

No sooner had he spoken the words than Rudolph was standing in the room with him.

"Like what you've done with the place," Rudolph mocked.

"Sorry, this is my first time."

"Ah, okay." Rudolph slapped his hand on the wall. "This is your home space, which you can decorate any way you like, with a single thought. Last week my home space looked like my bedroom. I was feeling a little homesick. Yesterday I fancied a relaxing time, so my home space became a lovely sunny beach, complete with picnic and clear warm water to swim in. Try it. All you have to do is think it."

Arran was incredibly excited at the prospect. The first place that came to mind was the restaurant in the Animal Kingdom hotel when he'd visited Florida a couple of years ago. His father had purchased three tickets, and then backed out of going at the last minute, asking the Professor to take his place, which she gracefully did.

Less than a second after visualising the place in his mind, he was standing right in the middle of the restaurant with Rudolph. The waitresses and chefs were hard at work, making breakfast to order whilst guests were milling around planning their days in the parks. He sat at the table overlooking the swimming pool outside, astounded at how real it all felt. Rudolph joined him.

"How is this possible?" Arran asked "I can feel, touch, hear, and smell everything here. It's just as I remember it."

"I didn't invent it." Rudolph laughed.

"I wish the food was real. I really miss those scrambled eggs."

"Go ahead. Order something."

With everything Arran had experienced since arriving in this century, it wasn't such a huge stretch of the imagination to think he would be able to taste the food as well.

Approaching the food counter, he marvelled at the intricate detail displayed before him. The chef was wearing blue and white striped trousers, a white chef's hat, and a blue top with a miniature picture of Mickey Mouse embroidered across the breast pocket.

He offered Arran the warm, friendly smile Arran remembered so clearly from his holiday there before speaking in a Canadian accent:

"Hi, Arran, great to see you again. Can I get you anything?"

"Scrambled eggs please."

"Coming right up." He handed Arran a plate of the most

delightfully delicious eggs. "There you go. Have a magical day."

Arran took his breakfast back to the table to join Rudolph, who had already filled his plate with waffles, blueberry and chocolate muffins, maple syrup, and a Spanish omelette.

"The food here is really good," Rudolph said. "I gotta come back; can I copy the location from you?"

"Sure." Arran shoved a fork full of eggs into his mouth. As he chewed, he became quite emotional. He'd wanted to go back to Disney World ever since he left, and this food, the restaurant, everything was like the long-awaited return without the ten-hour flight.

"I wish my sister was here to see this. She's in the medical unit."

"Is she in a recovery room? What's her name?" asked Rudolph.

"Molly—she's in recovery room two."

"Request access, patient Molly. Recovery room two."

Once Rudolph had spoken the words, Molly appeared before them.

She looked around curiously before poking an unsuspecting guest in the nose.

"Okay, I'm dreaming that I'm back in Disney World," she finally said.

"Well, yes and no," said Arran. "I'm dreaming I'm back in

Disney World and I invited you along."

"But you can't invite someone into your dream!"

Rudolph tried to help. "It's not exactly a dream, it's the Tempus Network. Arran used it to create his own world; once created he can invite who he likes. At this very moment you are still ill in recovery room two." Molly just stared at him. "Oh, I'm Rudolph, by the way."

"Rudolph, like the reindeer?" Molly laughed.

"Poor girl, your mind's all mixed up," he replied.

They spent the next half hour laughing and reminiscing about their previous experience in Disney World, and all the things they had encountered since arriving in the thirty-first century.

Rudolph thought for the most part they were pulling his leg; all this talk about time travel was very fanciful but clearly had no basis in reality.

"Maybe one day," he said.

Chapter Twenty

Aiysha's Alter Ego

"The young girl Molly. What is her condition?" Aiysha asked, speaking into her communicator.

"How do you know of Molly?" the controller answered.

She looked at Grombit, unconscious on the floor.

"Grombit told me. He is concerned for her. I'd like to be able to give him an update."

"I thought you said Grombit was unconscious," queried the controller.

Aiysha began to get irritated. "I know what I said! He asked me earlier." She spoke again with a softer tone. "I'd like to give him some good news when he wakes."

There was a pause whilst the controller checked. "She's stable at the moment. Only time will tell."

"I'd like to see her."

There was another pause.

"Sorry, Aiysha, you're to stay there with Grombit for the moment and wait. We're sending someone down presently to make sure you are both comfortable."

Chapter Twenty-One

Quiet Reflection

Tempus sat in the dining room sipping on her coffee, deep in thought.

"A credit for your thoughts?" Mike said.

The Professor looked at him. "I'm just concerned." She placed her cup down on the table.

"I haven't seen my father since he disappeared thirteen years ago. I know practically nothing about him, then find out he's been living one thousand years in the future. I come looking for him, only to discover he's missing, presumed dead, and I've walked into an active war zone. Not only that, Molly is fighting for her life after barely surviving something called a death stare, from which, to date, there hasn't been a single person infected who hasn't died or had the living soul sucked from their body. Then there's you."

She rested her chin on her hands and stared at him.

"Apart from this nagging feeling that I've known you for years, which I know is impossible, I mention I have time travelled a thousand years in a time machine and you don't bat an eyelid. I may as well have told you that I like coffee for all the reaction I got. So many questions and as yet, so few answers. I suppose I just feel helpless."

"Come with me." Mike smiled sympathetically. "Perhaps I can help fill in a few blanks."

Chapter Twenty-Two

Street Fighter

"What do you say we play a game, Arran?" Rudolph suggested after the food and the conversation was exhausted.

"Yeah okay, what you wanna play?"

"It's your construct," said Rudolph. "What games do you like to play?"

"I was pretty good at the Street Fighter game."

"Pretty good at getting your bum kicked by me," Molly added.

Arran concentrated and the game cartridge appeared on the table which he showed to Rudolph.

"Oh this?" Rudolph said, quite excited. "Yeah, okay, I played this before. I'll be Sagat."

Arran decided upon Bison, and Molly wanted to play as her old favourite character, Chun-Li.

Before Arran had time to focus on materialising some hand controllers and a TV set, Rudolph stood up and transformed himself into the giant game character Sagat, a huge man with red shorts and a lightning scar across his chest. He laughed mockingly.

"They call me the king for a reason!"

Molly, suddenly shocked and scared, hid behind her brother.

"Rudolph?" Arran enquired hopefully.

Rudolph, who now towered above them, looked down, oblivious. "You wanted to play, right?"

"I meant with hand controllers and a TV set." Arran paused. "Though this does look like more fun."

He clenched his fist whilst concentrating on the character Bison, and within a flash he was a living representation of the PlayStation character. The magnificent image, with flashing blue hands and a deep red Army uniform, stared down at Molly.

"Molly, this is cool. Just concentrate and think 'Chun-Li.'"

Molly didn't take much in the way of prompting; in a flash she was a giant computerised Japanese warrior with two Princess Leia buns on either side of her head.

Once they were all transformed, it was agreed they would take turns choosing the platforms upon which they would fight. Rudolph went first.

The Animal Kingdom restaurant disappeared around them and was replaced by an abandoned airfield. Crowds gathered, Sagat and Bison faced one another. Holographic numbers appeared between them:

3

1

Fight!

Sagat knelt down and shouted the word *tiger*. As he did so, a glowing fireball emanated from his hands and rapidly made its way to Bison. Arran watched it travel, in complete fascination—that is, until it hit.

"Ouch, that hurt! Why can I feel this?"

"Your mind makes it real," Rudolph answered. "Don't worry, there are safety parameters built into the network. The pain goes as quick as it arrives. No serious damage can be done."

Arran looked above his head. The impact of the fireball had caused a little of Bison's energy bar to dissipate.

"It's on now," he shouted, relishing the challenge.

Sagat rushed forward. Arran leapt into the air, his body glowing bright blue as he flew across the platform right through Sagat, knocking him to the ground. When he landed, he was pleased to see a quarter of Sagat's energy had been taken in that attack. The crowd cheered and Arran's body glowed blue again, preparing him for another attack.

"Spammer!" Sagat shouted as Bison's blue flame knocked him to the ground yet again.

Molly as Chun-Li jumped up and down in support of her

brother. "I want a go!"

Bison stepped back and Chun-Li jumped into the air and turned herself upside down. She began to spin clockwise, her legs horizontal with the floor. She then attacked Sagat with a helicopter spinning kick before depleting the remainder of his energy with a well-placed uppercut.

"We did it!" Arran applauded.

"Lucky you weren't fighting me," his sister joked.

"Is that so? Let's go, little sister."

"Since we're the same age, I can only assume that was a mean comment on my height. Prepare to lose, BIG brother."

Sagat stepped back to join the crowd as the siblings faced one another. The holographic timer began to count down as before:

3…

2…

Before the timer could complete, Molly's image began to fade.

"Arran, I don't feel so good." Her image faded out entirely.

Arran glared at Rudolph, who could only shrug his shoulders in reply.

"I need to help her. How do you get out of this?"

"Just tell yourself to wake," Rudolph said.

Chapter Twenty-Three

The Orb Room

Mike and the Professor stood in the lobby, facing the single pillar that had transported them to the medical facility, then the dining area. She knocked on the hard surface as before, and he walked her to the door entitled ORB.

"Beyond this door is the life force behind the entire planet, together with a living history of everyone and everything contained within. It also holds information on the seven planets discovered and inhabited since the twentieth century. There's a separate control room where we monitor and effect smaller changes where needed, but…" He smiled. "…the real power and genius of the world is in here."

She stared once again at the door adjacent.

PROFESSOR RICHARD TEMPUS.

"I'd love to think he's behind that door, drinking tea and reading H.G. Wells."

Though Professor Tempus's memory was fragmented, she did recall his fondness for books, especially those of Jules Verne and H.G. Wells. When she was a child, he had joked that Wells' design for the fictional time machine in his story had originally come from him.

"He told me they were great friends for a while," she said, looking dreamily at the door handle. "Can you open it?"

Mike shook his head. "Actually no one can. No one except your father and…" He paused. "Jhonas Spletka!" Mike almost spat the name out. "He was an evil man."

"Yes, I've heard," she replied whilst trying the handle. When the door didn't budge, she shrugged her shoulders. "Well, it was worth another try."

Mike motioned toward the ORB room. "Shall we?"

Resigned to the fact she wasn't going to gain access to her father's room, the Professor agreed.

Chapter Twenty-Four

Back in The Medical Unit

Arran's eyelids sprung open like an overeager roller blind, hungry for the overdue breath of sunshine. The virtual games platform was gone, existing now in Arran's mind as a vivid and fantastical dream. He jumped to his feet and paused; no dizzy spell, no time to stare in wonderment at the hundreds of children in deep sleep, blissfully unaware of his presence, not even time to search out Victor's resting body and give it a sharp kick in the leg as he walked past.

He found the pillar and knocked repeatedly till the door to the medical facility appeared. He yanked it open and rushed inside.

The atmosphere in the medical unit was one of complete tranquillity; there was no sense of urgent panic as Arran had expected. Doctors went about their daily tasks calm and relaxed. Two holographic nurses stood in the corridor not far from Molly's room, speaking of their off-planet holiday plans—apparently Mars Minor was hosting this year's planetary song contest for the third year running, and they had front row seats.

The door to Molly's room was locked so he peered in through the glass window. She lay, peaceful and content. An orange light surrounded her. Must have been a problem with the game interface rather than his sister's failing health, he thought. He turned and took a few steps back toward the game room before coming to a sudden stop.

It was just a matter of memory but he was almost sure the doctor said the light would be blue, gradually turning clear as her health improved. This light was orange. He rushed to the front desk.

***

Perhaps I should check on Arran and Molly before we go in, the Professor thought.

Mike, who was in front of her and facing the door, said, "Don't worry about it. There's a time displacement system in place once we enter this room. We could be in there for a week and when we return only a few seconds would have passed."

Confused, she tapped him on the shoulder. He turned to face her.

"Why did you just tell me that?"

Mike shrugged. "You said you wanted to check on them. I was just trying to help. I'm sorry, I didn't mean to…"

"No," said the Professor. "My concerns about the children were internal; I didn't speak them… I *thought* them."

"I'm sorry, I thought you spoke out loud. I sometimes get confused." Clear that this wasn't explanation enough, Mike continued. "We all have gifts, Professor. One thousand years have passed since your time. The human race has evolved. There are schools now where children, adults, and a few other species learn to nurture their natural gifts. We have one here."

Never able to resist a dig at Professor Richard Tempus's arch enemy, Mike continued:

"Jhonas Spletka had the capability to take the natural talents of others; unfortunately, to do this he needed their full cooperation. As you can imagine this was never willingly given, so he developed the ability to drain people's self-worth, leaving them very compliant.

Everything good and humane was removed from their soul, making them susceptible for the transfer of positive energy, life force, relevant memories, and of course their abilities. What was left when he had finished was an empty shell, a Spletka drone, carrying out his every desire and operating purely to please him."

"And he went missing the same time as my father," the Professor mused as she entered the ORB room.

Mike followed.

Chapter Twenty-Five

Back at Home

Just when she was beginning to think nothing else in the thirty-first century could surprise her any more, the Professor was faced with something which almost made her question her own sanity. Before entering the ORB room, she had pictured in her mind's eye a huge space full of advanced machines and technicians turning dials and on-screen monitors linked to satellites surveying the planet from above. She was not expecting to walk right back into her own laboratory at home.

"Welcome to the centre of our universe," Mike said with an expectant grin on his face.

"My house?" the Professor said, running her finger across the desk and looking at the empty space in which the time machine had stood.

"This is much more than a house," Mike said. "It contains the living energy of the planet and not just this planet either; it is with that energy that your father was able to create, among other things, the Tempus Network.

"Every thought," he continued, "every prayer, every deed good and bad, every time someone falls in love or suffers a loss, every time a baby is born, it draws upon energy both positive and negative. Your father was able to pinpoint the central location of this energy—passed down from years of research from his predecessors—then travel back in time and build this place. Your father said that the energy 'chose' to join with him and even helped with the construction. Just as you have a body that hosts your eternal spirit, this house can be seen as the body in which the energy of the universe resides.

The Professor, feeling a little weak at the knees, sat at her desk.

"Are you telling me this house is alive?"

Mike nodded. "This house has been looking after you your entire life."

Chapter Twenty-Six

Reception

"Excuse me."

Arran stood in front of the reception desk, watching the lady typing furiously into what he assumed was a holographic keypad which only she could see.

"Can I help you?" the receptionist eventually said, looking to her left.

"I'm over here." Arran waved his hands in front of her.

"No, I'm afraid you can't," she said. "The doctor will be around presently. Please be patient."

She then faced front and continued to work on her keypad.

"She won't be able to hear you, I'm afraid."

Arran turned to see Rudolph standing at his side.

"I need to see a doctor about my sister. Her light's turning to red, which isn't good."

"Hang on." Rudolph ran down the corridor only to re-emerge a moment later with the same doctor who had been tending to Molly earlier.

Instead of approaching Arran, he walked directly into Molly's room. Rudolph and Arran followed. The doctor placed a device on her head and ran his fingers across a silver panel; gradually the light changed from bright orange to blue.

"Rudolph tells me you invited Molly to play a game with you in the games room?" Arran nodded and the doctor continued to scold. "It is not without reason I told your sister to rest. Her condition is not physical as such. It is dangerous for her to spend energy doing anything other than recovering."

Rudolph looked away, knowing part of the guilt was his own. Arran felt ashamed.

"Will she be okay?"

"She's stable," the doctor answered. "But she needs rest."

Chapter Twenty-Seven

Where Is Aiysha?

"Mr Grombit, I'm Commander Abigail Williams and this is my assistant, Daniel. Can you stand?"

Grombit sat on the floor, head in between his hands, opening and closing his eyes as they adjusted to the light. Daniel grasped Grombit's arm, helping him to his feet.

"Oh my head," he said. "Could I get some worm and parsnip sloop? Light on the parsnip if you don't mind."

"I'll make a call," Abigail said. "Did you see what happened to Aiysha? She was supposed to be down here with you."

Chapter Twenty-Eight

A Brief Trip into the Past

"Well, I never thought I'd be asking this about my own house, but how does this thing work?"

Mike stood up and walked toward the library. "Come with me."

Professor Tempus joined him, and there they stood, facing a five-tier bookshelf crammed with volumes on physics, advanced mathematics, robotics, and astronomy.

"Are you going to tell me what we're doing here or do you want to test my knowledge on stars and their place in the universe?"

Mike laughed. "I wouldn't presume to challenge your knowledge on any subject, Professor. You see anything out of place here?"

"Okay, I'll play along." She did not appreciate Mike's smug tone. "Let's see, shelf one, yep, all in order here; shelf two, yep, all's fine here. Shelf three…" She stopped. "I've never seen that book before."

Right next to *The Relative Theory of Dimensional Transference in Einstein's Universe* was a small pink volume simply entitled *Rebecca*.

"It's always been there," said Mike. "The house knew that you weren't ready to see it till now."

She smiled. "You know, I'm going to be very disappointed if this ends up being a Daphne du Maurier novel."

She took the book from the shelf and opened it. Except for the first two pages, every page, which probably totalled five hundred, was completely blank. The first page was titled:

Professor Rebecca Tempus. Time Travel Diary.

The Professor studied the text. "This is my handwriting."

"That's because you wrote it."

"I don't remember doing this."

"You will," Mike answered. "That's the trouble with time travel; you don't follow the same linear line the rest of us do."

The Professor was beginning to understand. "So, I leave myself clues?" She turned the page, and the text read: "Take the letter from under the floorboard and replace with blue clip-on earring."

A wave of realisation washed over Professor Tempus.

"The earring—so that's how John didn't find the letter?"

Mike shrugged. "I know nothing of this. It's your personal history, documented by a literal mental note which then finds its way to your diary. If you want to take a look, simply concentrate on the time in question. You'll see it happen around you, like being a spectator on your own timeline. I can close my eyes if there's anything private you don't want me to see."

"No, it's okay." She focused her attention as directed.

Instantly Rebecca found herself standing a few feet from John and her earlier self as they spoke near the floorboard containing the envelope that her father had placed there.

"Hold that image!" shouted Mike

"And how do I do that?"

"Just think it!"

She did and the two characters froze.

"Mike, I can hear your heartbeat from here," she said, as he moved closer to the still image of John. "Are you okay?"

"You know this man?"

The Professor walked over to join him. "Uncle John? Yes, of course I do."

"You trust him?" Mike continued; his speech more reminiscent of a police interrogation now.

"I've been back and forth on that one. Why?"

"Because he is no uncle of yours, Professor. Quite the opposite. That man is Jhonas Spletka."

Chapter Twenty-Nine

The Unwelcome Host

The intruder, using Aiysha's body opened the door to the medical unit and stepped inside. *This is so easy*, she thought as she watched the staff and patients continue with their designated tasks, never sparing her so much as a single accusatory glance.

An unexpected voice from within her head spoke:

"What are you? You leave her alone!"

Shh, the intruder thought, *just go to sleep and let me be about my business. If it matters you can call me Lieutenant 452.*

"Help, somebody, it's not me," the inner voice shouted. "My body has been taken over by…"

They can't hear you, and kindly don't shout—you'll give yourself a headache. Now where is recovery room two?

"Ha, like I'm going to tell you that."

No matter, I'll find it. Is it over here? Perhaps here?

Aiysha's head slowly turned left and right as she walked casually past the rooms.

I'm sensing an emotional reaction to…this room here." The lieutenant peered through the glass window of recovery room two, watching Molly sleep peacefully under a bright blue light.

She tried the door handle, but it was locked. She pushed again; this time considerably harder.

"Those doors don't respond to brute force." Aiysha laughed. "Being a lieutenant in the Spletka Clan is clearly no measure of intelligence."

Yes, that's how we've managed to find your precious Citadel, the lieutenant jeered, *because we're stupid.*

Aiysha had no rebuttal.

A doctor approached her. "Can I ask what you are doing? I specifically ordered this patient was to be left alone."

With no power other than internal speech, Aiysha was unable to do anything but become an unwilling observer upon her own actions.

"Oh, I'm so worried about this young lady," The lieutenant said. "They say she was caught by a death stare. But she lives. I just wanted to sit with her." She then started to sob.

"Oh please, Lieutenant whatever your name is", Aiysha mocked. "You think the doctor is an idiot?"

"Yes, she's quite the miracle around here." The doctor smiled, looking through the window, "but no, I'm afraid she can't be disturbed."

Now there's a surprise, idiot lieutenant! Now get out of my body! Aiysha demanded.

"Please, Doctor, I won't disturb, just sit." Aiysha's eyes offered the doctor a very heartfelt glance as a single glistening tear formed in her right eye.

"Okay," said the doctor, unlocking the door, "but not for long."

What?! Are you crazy? Don't let me in! Aiysha yelled.

The inner voice was loud enough to momentarily disorient the lieutenant but the doctor naturally heard nothing. The door opened and in walked the Lieutenant . "Thank you, Doctor," she said as he walked from the room.

***

Grombit hung his head in shame, stamping his foot on the ground.

"Silly Grombit," he mumbled to himself. "Stupid, idiot, loony Grombit, your brain is so tiny, Wiggles the Worm could probably control it."

Daniel looked questioningly at Abigail.

"Grombit, do you know where Aiysha is?"

He shook his head. "She probably ran away scared."

Grombit told Abigail and Daniel the chain of events, from his unpleasant meeting with the general, to the mind and body control the lieutenant had used on him. He told them how he, for the most part a petrified spectator, had to observe as his hand clenched Aiysha's wrist.

The look of surprise followed by pain and fear on her face would probably stay with him for always. Grombit turned away from them before a sudden realisation hit him.

"Molly!"

***

The Lieutenant looked behind to make sure she was alone in the room before approaching the bed. The blue light was growing brighter; had they been any longer, Molly would have been fit and well. The general would not have liked that.

"Now, how is our patient today?" she sarcastically asked in a low whisper. Molly's sleeping body was naturally unaware of any threat.

"Leave her alone!" Aiysha shouted.

"*You should be happy, Aiysha,*" the creature answered. "*You are about to get your body back. This little girl is my mission.*"

There was a pause and a change in Aiysha's body state that made the creature chuckle.

"*Are you crying? What a wonderful sensation. If I weren't so busy, I might even be tempted to stay.*"

"Please do anything to me; just leave her alone."

Aiysha's pleas fell on unforgiving ears. The Lieutenant stroked Molly's hair before resting her hand on her head to allow the small army of spiders to release their grasp on Aiysha and provide a bridge for them to travel and rest on Molly's scalp. The moment they took root, the light around the bed to turned from blue to blood red. Aiysha, now released from their grasp and both tired and exhausted, struggled out of the room to find a doctor.

Chapter Thirty

Who is Jhonas Spletka?

"Jhonas Spletka?" The Professor laughed. "No, this is John Pentka and I've known him my whole life. He can be annoying at times but he's no evil dictator."

Mike was convinced that she was wrong, but his mind-reading ability also told him that the Professor truly believed that he really was plain old John Pentka.

"I'll unfreeze them," the Professor offered. *Then maybe when you hear him talk, you can get this crazy notion out of your mind.* She thought.

"I hope so," Mike said.

And stop reading my mind.

"Sorry."

The action resumed, exactly as the Professor remembered.

John crouched down to reach underneath the floorboard; then something occurred she didn't recall happening. The image of John and the Professor froze again. Mike looked confused.

"Why did you stop it?"

The Professor shrugged her shoulders. "I didn't."

There was a brief flash of light. Arran and another Professor

Tempus appeared, seemingly, from out of nowhere.

"Now there are three of me?" She looked to Mike for some sort of clarification but he was just as confused.

After a quick visual scan of the area, Arran reached ahead of John, took out the envelope from underneath the floorboard, and replaced it with a clip-on earring; they then crouched down, hiding behind the time machine, which was, at this point, still covered in a big green cloth.

Once they were safely hidden, the original Professor and John sprang into life, carrying on as if nothing had happened. John picked up the earring; then after saying a few words he left, followed part of the way by the original Professor. At that point time froze again, allowing the third Professor Tempus and Arran to put the letter back. Just before they left, Arran whispered into her ear. She stopped for thought, then pointed directly at her and Mike. Arran waved at them and they both disappeared.

The Professor stopped the playback, shaking her head.

Mike was almost speechless. "I don't really understand what just…"

The Professor held up her hand, cutting his sentence short.

"At some point in the future, Arran and I go back in time to make sure John doesn't find that letter, and apparently we have the ability to stop time. No doubt I'll find out about that in the future." She paused, considering the gravity of her next sentence. "Something troubles me though. It was just Arran and I. Does this mean Molly doesn't make it?"

"Professor, help me."

Molly's faint image flickered in front of her.

"Molly, are you all right?"

"There's somebody in my room."

"A doctor?" Mike suggested.

"She's in my head, Professor, like before. The creature I can't…"

Molly's image disappeared. The Professor took Mike by the hand and ran out of the room.

Chapter Thirty-One

Lieutenant 452

Arran was connected to the Tempus Network when Molly appeared again to him. He sat across the table from Rudolph in the Animal Kingdom restaurant, fiddling with the straw in his untouched banana and chocolate milkshake.

"We fight all the time but we…" He pushed the drink aside, trying to find the right words. "I'm just worried about her, Rudolph." His companion simply nodded in empathy.

All around him, holidaymakers were making the most of the ample buffet, but the exotic foods on offer held no appeal for him. One excited little girl showed off the badge she had pinned to her yellow Cinderella dress to the waitress, who upon examining it smiled, saying,

"Happy birthday, princess."

Arran remembered how fond Molly had been of her princess dress and how many compliments she had received, announcing to all the Disney staff that she was wearing a birthday badge.

It seemed she couldn't walk more than two feet without somebody stopping her and wishing her a magical birthday, or telling her how pretty she looked. As he watched the girl receive a free ice cream that filled half the table, a faint flicker of light that seemed to gradually grow in intensity obscured his view. An image appeared in the form of his sister.

"Molly!" Arran jumped to his feet, knocking his milkshake to the ground.

Molly was drifting in and out of focus. With tears in her eyes, she stretched out her hand to reach her brother.

"I have to hide; she's after me."

A dark figure began to take form behind Molly. Staff and guests panicked, most of whom screamed or fled the scene. Those who were left stared in disbelief as the form grew to three times the size of Molly. It was shrouded for the most part in a black robe reminiscent of the grim reaper himself. Its elongated facial features resembled drained watercolours of grey and white. Its black eyes housed the same petrifying terror that was responsible for his sister's illness.

From beneath its robe two skeletal arms reached toward Molly.

"Molly, run!" Arran shouted. "Don't look behind you."

Molly sought sanctuary behind her brother, as did Rudolph. Arran trembled with fear and had no idea what was keeping him standing. But he knew that whatever this thing was, it would have to kill him before reaching his sister.

The creature cocked its head slowly to the right and smiled, relishing the destruction it was about to impart.

A collective scream could be heard from all the remaining guests, just before they all dissolved into the air till there was nothing left.

***

The Professor and Mike burst into Molly's room. The doctor, who had already been alerted, was standing over the bed. The light was now a deeper, more intense blood red.

"Don't break the light," the doctor instructed. "If you do, she'll surely die."

The Professor stared at Molly, examining her from beyond the red light.

"What happened?" Mike asked.

"We don't know," the doctor answered. "One of our technicians, Aiysha, couldn't stay conscious long enough to tell me. Just that Molly was in trouble."

Professor Tempus noticed a strand of Molly's hair flicker.

"Is that a spider?" she asked, moving her head as close as she could to Molly without breaking the red light.

Both the doctor and Mike followed the direction of Professor Tempus's gaze.

"Spletka," they said simultaneously.

"I've got to put this place on alert." Mike dashed toward the door before briefly looking back at the Professor. "Good luck." Then he was gone.

The doctor stood by the Professor, staring intently at the spider on Molly's head.

"Somehow some of Spletka's lieutenants have managed to locate the Citadel. I don't know how. This has only happened once before and it meant the greatest war our planet has ever seen, ending with the disappearance of Jhonas Spletka and your father."

Ignoring the comments and questions that her scientific mind would naturally have asked regarding the war, or the one that had troubled her all her life regarding her father, the Professor simply said, "Is the spider bite fatal?"

"It can be," the doctor said, "but I suspect their mission is somewhat more sinister. The Spletka Clan, ever since Jhonas disappeared, have been searching for someone with the potential to nurture in the ways of evil and take over the Clan."

The Professor was shocked. "Molly? But she would never…"

"She survived a death stare. Only one other person in history has done that, and, well, he became the greatest tyrant this planet has ever seen. As I understand it before that, Jhonas Spletka and your father were friends. Jhonas, once upon a time, was a good man." The doctor made to stroke her head, then pulled back his hand, not wanting to break the beam of light.

"The Spletka are inside her head. The only way they can convert her is by breaking her spirit and effectively rebuild it using the Spletka code."

He looked down at Molly. Tiny beads of sweat fell from her brow, her breathing increasingly laboured.

"She's fighting it," he said. "We can only pray she's strong enough."

***

"Help me, Arran." Molly was visibly trembling behind her brother.

"Yeah, me too," said Rudolph, trembling and hiding behind Molly.

The creature could have rushed forward but preferred to slowly advance on the threesome, to Arrans eyes gaining more satisfaction, pleasure, and power by feeding on their combined fear.

Its whisper seemed to fill the room.

"Stand aside, little boy, we just want the girl. I can, of course, crush you on the way if you prefer?"

Arran was unwilling to move from his current position.

"Any suggestions, Rudolph, before we all die?"

Rudolph reluctantly moved from behind, to stand near Arran.

The creature's sinister laugh echoed in their heads. He had a sudden moment of inspiration. "Arran, we are all inside your head."

Arran looked confused. "Thanks for the geography lecture, Rudolph. Perhaps you can read it out at my funeral?!"

His sarcastic tone and quick wit made Rudolph chuckle slightly, despite the imminent danger as the creature advanced on him. The chuckle seemed to have a slight effect on the creature, and it temporarily stumbled back.

"It feeds on fear," Arran said to Rudolph. "Laugh again."

Silence.

Arran looked to his right. Rudolph was lying on the floor; the colour and life seemingly being drained from his body. The creature standing still was staring at him, clearly not willing to suffer any more setbacks in the completion of his mission.

Rudolph used the remainder of his waking energy to give Arran some advice.

"We are in your head, Arran, remember, Street Fighter. Remove the safety; the body can't survive without the spirit."

Rudolph closed his eyes and lay still on the floor as the creature moved its gaze from the sleeping boy back to Arran, advancing again toward him and his sister.

Arran tried so hard not to look into its eyes as it inched ever closer. *It's my head,* he mused. *It's in my head?*

He desperately struggled to make some sense of Rudolph's final statement.

"It's my head!" he yelled. "Of course!" He concentrated. "You're in my world now."

The creature seemed unperturbed by this revelation but did realise that he had turned the safety off. "Congratulations, little boy. Turning the safety off only means that when I kill you in here, you will die outside too."

"It also means if you die here, you die outside too." Arran's shouts were accompanied by tears and fear. The creature laughed.

Arran concentrated on the creature's legs. He closed his eyes, then opened them. Almost instantly iron shackles and chains bound the creature. It stopped, looking in amusement at Arran's attempt at incarceration. The shackles melted, as though they were made of Cornish ice cream, then fell to the floor.

"Is that the best you can do?"

It moved slowly forward again. Arran concentrated again and a huge brick wall appeared, blocking the creature from the children.

"How are you doing that?" Molly asked frantically.

"Something Rudolph told me; I just figured out what it meant. We can stop this thing if we work together." Molly shook her head, offence not fitting in with her "run and hide" strategy.

It didn't take the creature long to scale the wall. Its razor-sharp claws cut through the brick and held like a grappling hook, an action it repeated, steadily advancing up toward the top. Within a few seconds its body was entirely over the other side and it began crawling down the wall toward them.

"What can I do?" cried Molly.

"Just do what I'm doing. We need to fight this thing *together*!"

"How?" Molly said. "This is your head. I can't control anything."

"Yes, you can if I let you. Imagine you are player two on the PlayStation game."

Molly glared at her brother. "Yes, but if you fight on a PlayStation, you don't die in real life!"

Arran nodded and shrugged. "Yeah, well, let's not die."

The creature was now at the bottom of the wall and only a few feet from the children.

"My turn," it whispered, raising its arms in a grand ceremonious gesture.

Arran and Molly looked at one another, not quite sure what to expect. From within the creature stepped out another, a perfect replica of the original, then another and another; each with the same black eyes, the same deathly stare, and the same Machiavellian grin plastered across its face.

Within a few seconds there were literally hundreds of them all standing in a perfect circle around them, chanting and banging canes on the hard surface.

"A few of my friends. I hope you don't mind if they watch" came the ghostly whisper.

"Don't look at their eyes, Molly!" Arran shouted.

"How?" she said. "They are everywhere."

Arran closed his eyes and concentrated, and when he opened them, the ground beneath each of the clones disappeared. Molly watched in glee as they fell and disappeared from sight. She raised her hands in triumph.

"And Dad said playing computer games was bad for you," she joked.

Arran's conjuring had done more than kill off their unwanted audience; the environment upon which they stood was completely transformed. They were, each of them, standing on a huge single stone platform. Rudolph lay sleeping at their feet.

A black, empty, bottomless pit lay in wait for anyone, or anything, not surefooted enough to remain on the platform. Out of the darkness red flames rose, enough to make the creature realise that its task was going to be far from easy. Arran, Molly, and the creature stood in silence, preparing for battle.

The creature struck first, blowing an icy breath over Arran; as it did so he felt the frost consume his body till he wasn't able to move. The extreme cold was affecting his concentration, which was the creature's intent. It was all Arran could do to stabilize the environment they were in.

"Now for the scared little girl," the creature hissed, moving behind Arran to confront Molly as she moved backward—the creature in front mimicking her footsteps and moving closer with each step she made backward till they reached the very edge of the platform.

The intense heat from the flames made her feel faint; her back and neck felt like they were burning. The creature stopped and held out its hands.

"I don't want to kill you, girl. I want you to join us."

"I will never join you!" Molly looked over toward her brother. "I'm sorry, Arran," she said before stepping off the platform and falling into the flames.

The creature let out a piercing cry of anger before turning its attention on her still-frozen brother. It glided backward with such speed that its short journey was but a mere blur. It faced Arran.

"Your sister has decided not to join us, but I suppose you will do." It reached out a hand to touch him but a sudden explosion behind diverted his attention.

"Hey, Boney, leave my brother alone!"

It looked up to see Molly rising up above the flames, dressed in a black suit, top hat, and tails.

"How did you survive?" the creature shrieked.

"This is my brother's game." She laughed. "And he would never hurt me."

Arran's internal smile warmed his body.

She let out a piercing cry which stunned the creature, temporarily knocking it to the ground. Molly took the opportunity to land next to her brother, placing a glowing hand on his shoulder which melted the captivating ice block. He turned and hugged his sister before stepping back and looking her up and down.

"And who are you supposed to be?"

Molly lifted her top hat and did a curtsy. "You can call me Sultana."

Arran laughed affectionately. "That's *Zatana*, stupid," he said, realising she was going for the famed female comic book heroine.

Molly shrugged. "Whatever."

The creature got back to its feet, snarling, black blood dripping from its mouth as huge spider-like fangs grew from its mouth.

Molly nudged her brother. "Shall we?"

"Let's get it."

With that she levitated high in the air, looking upon it from above. The creature's eyes grew in size and attempted to catch Molly in the death stare. Unable to stop looking at it, Molly stayed in the air, transfixed and helpless, feeling her power drain.

"Stop looking at its eyes!" Arran shouted.

"Oh, good one," she shouted back, "I never thought of that!"

He sat cross-legged and closed his eyes in pure concentration. All of a sudden a huge pair of dark shades appeared on the creature's face. The barrier the glasses formed released Molly from the death stare grasp.

As expected the glasses melted from the creature's face. Arran's imagery was ready; once the glasses were removed it looked up to re-engage Molly, but a huge finger was waiting, levitated above its head, which instantly and violently poked it in the eye. The creature turned and squealed in pain.

Molly's laughter at the sight echoed around the room. She slowly landed, opening and closing her hands as she did, shaking her head from side to side.

"Arran, I feel different."

His concentration broke as he glanced over toward his sister.

The creature, not being one to miss an opportunity, knew it needed Arran out of the way long enough to take control of Molly. Its fingers glowed sickly green before releasing a venomous gas which, almost as if it had a mind of its own and sense of direction, encompassed Arran, making him slowly fall to the ground and close his eyes.

"Now, little girl," it hissed, "it's just you and me."

She looked at her brother, then back at it. "Fine by me!"

The green mist left Arran's sleeping body and encompassed her, but seemed to have no effect. She moved closer to the creature and grinned.

"How are you doing this?" It locked eyes, hoping to capture her in the death stare once more and complete the task it came to do— except that didn't work either. Molly continued advancing on the creature, her own eyes shining bright blue. Her stare now was beginning to have more of an impact on the creature. It backed away toward the edge of the platform. Molly stood in complete defiance. It grasped her wrist, then watched in horror and dismay as its arm slowly disappeared. Molly didn't remove her stare from the gaze which was focussed directly into its eyes. It tried to look away but could not, and as had happened with its arm, its entire body began to disappear.

"No, this is not possible!" It screamed in pain.

Molly didn't say a word; she simply watched as the creature disappeared entirely.

Once gone, she turned to see Arran and Rudolph standing, conscious and aghast, mouths open. She laughed at them.

"You two look like goldfish at feeding time. Shall we go?"

Moments later Rudolph and Arran woke in the games room.

They got up and ran toward Molly's room just in time to see her wake. She jumped from her bed, embracing her brother and the Professor, who had been sitting by her side.

"Thank you," she said.

"You are better, *much* better now," the doctor said. "Though to be honest I can't explain how you…"

Molly laughed and nudged her brother. "I had a little help, and may even have developed my own death stare."

"Death stare?" the Professor queried.

"Just something we did in Arran's computer game. Wish we could do it in real life though. I'll tell you about it later, Professor."

"I'd like you to rest up here in the Citadel for a couple of days, go over what happened in this computer game," the doctor interjected, "and there's some tests I'd like to do if that's all right with you."

Molly nodded.

"I suspect you are all quite hungry, Professor. I was going to get something myself; would you and the children care to join me?"

"I'm famished," said Molly, leading the way out of the medical

bay.

Chapter Thirty-Two

Bridget Fondue

"Table for four?"

Bridget Fondue smiled warmly as she welcomed Arran, Molly, the doctor, and in particular Rebecca Tempus into the smaller Citadel cafe.

"It's an honour to meet you, Professor Tempus. Your father was a great man."

The Professor shook her head and sighed.

"There goes that WAS word again."

Bridget attempted a half curtsy. "Do excuse me. I didn't mean to offend. Your father and I were great friends. I miss him terribly."

The Professor smiled, sensing that they shared a mutual understanding.

"Me too," she calmly said. "Well, you have me at a disadvantage."

Bridget raised her right hand to her brow and laughed.

"Oh, where are my manners? My name is Bridget, Bridget Fondue."

Molly laughed. "Like Fondue's Fanciful Fancies?"

"Yes." She directed the foursome to their table. "Fondue's

Fanciful Fancies is my shop." She shrugged in resignation. "Though many of the fast-food outlets have taken a significant part of my business. Still, I have my loyal clientele."

Arran tugged on her white chef's overall. "I love your Turkish delight cake, Bridget."

"Thank you, young sir. Would you like another?"

Arran nodded eagerly. "Yes, please."

"And for the young lady?"

Molly stroked her chin as though she were an aging male Professor herself, fiddling with a goatee beard. "I don't know. Is there a menu?"

Bridget laughed. "Simply press the silver disc in the middle of the table."

Molly's eyebrows rose. What could this be? What she saw didn't disappoint; a mini holographic menu appeared in the centre of the table. Molly tapped a picture of what looked like Disney's Magic Kingdom. The 3D image enlarged and moved toward her, complete with soundtrack.

Rediscover the magic of the Magic Kingdom with our four-layer pyramid of hazelnut, chocolate caramel, and honeycomb ice cream, exquisitely finished with strawberry and orange fireworks.

"Wow, that sounds great!" she exclaimed. "I want that." The

Professor raised a disapproving eyebrow. "Er…please," Molly added.

"Not to sound too much like a mother here, Molly and Arran, but shouldn't you be eating something a little healthier? Too many sweets are not good for you."

Arran and Molly both looked a little deflated. They respected the Professor too much to argue with her.

"Oh, I wouldn't worry about that, Professor," said Bridget. "Food in the twenty-second century is rather different. It analyses exactly what nutrients, vitamins, and minerals the body needs and provides those. It keeps the taste without any of the calories or teeth-rotting ingredients and so on."

The Professor happily submitted and the children cheered. She began thumbing through the extensive menu of desserts, typical junk foods, as well as extravagant dishes from around the world.

"So you are telling me I can order anything from this menu and it won't put any unwanted weight on at all?"

Bridget nodded. "That's right. It was one of your father's side projects; he had a fondness for old-fashioned custard tarts but not the cellulite."

"Incredible," the Professor exclaimed.

"So what can I get you?" Bridget enquired.

"Oh…coffee please."

The doctor laughed. "I'll have a coffee too."

The Professor took a sip from the coffee cup, placed it back on the table, and looked at the doctor. "Do you have a name or should we just keep calling you doctor?"

"Sebastian Matthews. Sorry, I thought you knew."

"Why would you think that?"

The doctor seemed surprised at the question. "Well, because of your gifts."

The Professor did not reply and gestured for him to continue.

"Well, as you may be aware, the human race is significantly more advanced than it was in the twenty-first century…"

"Yes, yes." She cut his sentence short. "Mike filled me in on all that. People's special abilities are enhanced and made stronger for the betterment of mankind."

"Yes, couldn't have put it better myself. It's part of the school curriculum: telekinesis, mind reading, advanced déjà vu, a whole host of subjects depending on the individual's gift."

Arran nearly spat out his Turkish delight pudding. "I want to go to school here, Professor!"

The Professor decided not to answer Arran, instead pursued her previous line of conversation. "And you think I have gifts?"

"I know you do, Professor; if you hang around enough people

with special abilities, you begin to see them in the individual without the need for any demonstration."

The Professor nodded. "And mine are?"

"Well, mind reading for sure, but I'm guessing others too."

"So why can't I read your mind right now?"

The doctor held up his hand to hide his obvious amusement at the question. "Well, firstly I have the ability to block anyone from reading my mind. Much of what I know could be dangerous in the wrong hands, and secondly you haven't been in this century for very long. It will take a while for that ability to surface fully."

"Do I have special abilities?" Arran asked.

The doctor nodded. "I'm sure you do; we need to access a day pass for the school tomorrow to find out for sure. If that's all right with you, Professor?"

"We'll see tomorrow," she answered cautiously.

The children hadn't been in this century long either and already, Molly had fallen prey to the planet's evil militia.

"How about me, Doctor, do I have special abilities?" Molly asked, with a piece of ice cream Magic Kingdom tower stuck to her left cheek. The doctor nodded, trying not to laugh.

"Yes, sweetheart, you do." He drained the contents of his coffee mug in one big gulp before announcing that he had to get back to work.

"It's been a pleasure, Professor. We have rooms prepared for you once you have finished your meals. Bridget will help you find them."

****

Mike sat in the control room watching Grombit on the holographic transference screen speaking with Abigail and Daniel. He was already up to speed with everything Grombit had said and had ordered him to the medical department, once Abigail and Daniel were sure he was no longer a threat to the Citadel. Mike feared that as part of one collective consciousness, the Spletka Clan's lieutenant's may have relayed the whereabouts of the Citadel to their general. If that were the case, it would not be long before they had their forces assembled and poised, ready for an attack.

Chapter Thirty-Three

Tribble

It was raining on Judean Street and the surrounding blocks. That area, unlike the rest of the city, was surrounded by darkness, illuminated only by the waning moon and the faded streetlamps.

A tiny mouse emerged from a drain and sheltered under the street kerb. After a cautious glance both left and right, he scampered up the street and scuttled in through a tiny crack in the wall at number 39.

Once inside, he waited, staring expectantly at an empty room and a closed door, through which he could not enter without special invitation.

The door opened and out stepped a uniformed guard, heavily built, with a fresh scar on his right cheek. His stare was almost vacant. The mouse bowed his head respectfully.

"The general is expecting me."

The man stood to the right, allowing the rodent safe passage into the room. Cautiously he walked in.

Up in the ceiling rafters a kestrel ruffled its feathers and watched with hungry eyes as the mouse leapt onto the long table in the centre of the room.

The mouse nervously glanced upward, he did not have the gift of mind reading, nor did he need it to know what was on the kestrel's mind. That same bird had made light work of his sister when he had refused to work with the Spletka Clan three months ago.

At the head of the table sat the general with two other people, one of whom he had met before. In his current condition the general did not look like the same arachnid type of imposing figure into which he had transformed earlier that day in the town centre. The wispy greying hair and pale skin on his face made him look like the sick, zomibified victim of an apocalyptic war. If it wasn't that the mouse knew what evil he was capable, he could almost feel sorry for the tired-looking old man.

To his right, Bellonta. She was the general's wife. Bellonta was an aesthetically attractive, yet imposing character with long black hair which covered half her face and did little to mask the sheer evil resident in her darkened eyes. She had the gift of telekinesis, aptly demonstrated at that moment as she willed a razor-sharp hunter's knife to slowly rotate in front of her, boring a small hole into the table.

To the general's left, Emma Crowdon, a primary schoolteacher, sat shaking and snivelling. The weary eyes of the general regarded the mouse steadily as he spoke.

"Tribble, did you arrive here unnoticed?"

Tribble the mouse nodded; his momentary glance at the kestrel made Bellonta smile.

"My family thinks I have gone scavenging for food," Tribble squeaked.

"Please, Mr General, sir."

Emma Crowdon's soft tone melted Tribble's heart instantly, though he was sure that no degree of sympathy would save her now.

"I promise I can work harder; please don't…"

The general put his finger to his lips before standing and gently touching the top of her head.

"Shh, I'm conducting business."

She remained silent. Her head bowed and her tears fell silently to the floor.

"Tribble, I want you to perform a task for me."

"Yes sir, General," the mouse replied obediently.

"We now know where the Citadel is, but to gain access to the upper levels, I'm going to need your help. If you are successful, your son will be freed."

The general coughed and stumbled forward, resting his hand on the table for support.

"Excuse me for a moment," he said, raising his hand almost apologetically for the interruption.

His stare at the schoolteacher was almost empathetic.

"Miss Crowdon, is that what your students call you?"

Emma raised her head to meet his gaze.

"Yes, Mr General."

"I'd like to thank you for your loyalty." He sighed. "It is a shame you couldn't perform the task I set you."

Emma Crowdon became caught in his stare and couldn't look away. The general's eyes turned a familiar black as he drained the life from her body.

Bellonta's joyous laughter was the last thing she heard. Once he was finished, the schoolteacher's lifeless body collapsed onto the floor and the general stood a little taller, with a little more colour in his own cheeks.

He returned his attention to Tribble.

"As you can see, you were not our first choice for this assignment, but she sadly declined. I trust I can rely on you?"

Tribble nodded.

"Good, I'll call on you when you're needed."

The general sat down. His wife stood and kissed his forehead before walking out of the room.

Chapter Thirty-Four

The Fallen Spies

"These are the creatures we took from Molly's head."

Brian Grospin, assistant technician, placed a glass box in front of Mike containing five tiny spiders.

"They seem to be alive but..."

He shrugged, trying to think of a technical term, and simply came out with: "Paralysed."

Mike rotated the box slowly, looking at his captives.

"So these are the general's lieutenants?"

Brian nodded. "Should we, I dunno, kill them?"

"No. Jhonas Spletka's death stare turned anyone he came into contact with into an evil drone." He lightly tapped the box to illicit some sort of response. "They have been the victim of something else. Molly has greater power than she knows. Twice she has fought the Spletka Clan and twice she has emerged unscathed—that's unheard of. You never know, with Molly's influence they might even reject Spletka and fight on the side of good. These little spiders are worthy of further study."

Brian nodded and turned to leave the room.

"Oh, Grombit has been cleared of any threat; he's in recovery room six for observation."

Chapter Thirty-Five

Mrs Tribble

Tribble lived with what was left of his family, beneath an old oak tree on the outskirts of the town centre.

"Where were you earlier?" His wife nudged him comfortingly

with her nose.

Tribble couldn't even make eye contact with her. They had been together and completely committed to one another for three years, nearing four; for a mouse, that would be the equivalent of fifty strong human years and nearing a silver wedding anniversary.

"What do you mean, dear? I was looking for food."

"I realise times are tough," she said. "And there is a food shortage for us, and you are dealing with the disappearance of our son but," she paused, "there is something more, something in your eyes."

He turned his head away, not favouring the direction that the conversation was heading.

"There is nothing more."

Though he spoke the words, they lacked the conviction she was so used to hearing in her husband's voice. She placed her paw on top of his.

"You are trembling, dear. Oh, what are you not telling me?"

She tried to move in closer to comfort him.

Though every fibre in his body yearned for that comfort, though he wanted to take his family and run, he pulled away. There was nowhere safe; his son's life depended upon his following the general's orders to the letter, without question and in complete secrecy.

His wife paused, dreading her next question.

"Is there…someone else?"

Tribble turned to face her. "No, dear, I could never betray you."

There was no conviction in those words either, not because he had forged a life with another but because his work for the general betrayed his own moral code between right and wrong. His choice to keep this work from his wife was in itself a type of betrayal, one which he would never be able to forgive himself.

"Please, dear, leave me here, go to bed. I have a headache and can't sleep now. I'll join you later."

Unsatisfied and deeply concerned, his wife reluctantly left Tribble alone to contemplate whatever was on his mind.

Chapter Thirty-Six

The Argument

"Well, these are your rooms." Bridget came to a sudden stop.

The Professor, Arran, and Molly stood in a corridor, rooms either side of them, rather like a hotel.

"Do we not get our own rooms, Professor?" Arran asked, noticing the room door he was facing had "Arran and Molly" written on a plaque.

"I'd feel better," said the Professor, "if you both shared a room tonight. I'll just be next door if you need me."

The children walked into the room, followed by the Professor and Bridget.

For the most part it looked like the premiere suite of a high-class hotel; two king-size beds, drawers in which to put clothes, and a writing desk. The north side of the room was tinted glass from ceiling to floor.

"Right, children," said Bridget, clasping her hands together. "Let me show you around. We've tried to make this room as familiar to your own century as we can, but there are a few minor exceptions which I think you'll like."

She walked toward the glass window.

"You can have any view you like from here. It's a bit like changing the desktop view on your computer at home. Here, let me show you." Bridget touched the glass window and said, "Change view, seaside."

Instantly the children found themselves looking out at Marsden Rock Beach, a place they had spent many a happy hour when they were younger. It offered a calming retreat where they could escape the terrible temper their father often displayed. Children and families were playing on the velvet sand, which greeted the calm sea as it came in.

In one corner of the screen a red-faced and disgruntled dog owner was getting rather annoyed whilst attempting to get his canine to stop sniffing other dogs' bums and return to him immediately. The dog clearly had other ideas.

Molly laughed. "Pity those dogs can't talk like they can here; we might hear him tell his owner to…"

"Anyway," said Arran, touching the screen and changing the subject.

"I want a turn. Change view, Call of Duty game."

The children were now faced with a war-torn street; soldiers crouching behind burning cars and dilapidated buildings, slowly advancing through enemy gunfire.

"Most definitely not," said the Professor.

Arran shrugged and gestured toward Molly, who then changed the view to her favourite SpongeBob SquarePants cartoon.

"And you can change the volume simply by touching the screen and saying the word 'volume,'" Bridget said. "When it is as loud as you want to make it, simply tell it to stop."

Molly settled down, cross-legged, to watch her cartoon.

Arran was clearly not interested in this. "Well, that's Molly set for the night."

Molly nodded in agreement, her eyes firmly fixed on the screen.

Bridget walked Arran over to an area with a sink and a bench, in the middle of which was a silver plate.

"Just like the restaurant," she said. "You get hungry or thirsty, press the silver disc and a menu will appear. Just choose whatever you want and a plate will appear with, well, whatever you have ordered."

"Cool," said Arran. "And can I log onto the Tempus Network and play games and stuff?"

Bridget nodded. "Yes, provided you have a blue disc, you can access it remotely from here. There are some spares on the writing desk; just sit down, place it in between your thumb and first finger, and…"

"It's okay, I know how these things work," Arran said, remembering the disc Jonny Jagger had given him earlier that day. He glanced over to the desk and saw two pens, a writing pad, and three blue discs.

"Oh, one more thing," Bridget said as she made her way toward the door. "If we need to contact you, it will be through the screen."

She pointed at SpongeBob as he rode on a bubble which was bouncing on Patrick's head.

"And if you want to contact any of us, simply touch the screen and say 'Call,' followed by the person's name; even if they are asleep they can still answer you, though if they are anything like me, they may get a bit grumpy having their dreams disrupted, so don't unless you have to."

The Professor hugged the children. "Good night, you two, and remember I'm just next door. You can call me on that anytime you want."

Bridget and the Professor stood in the corridor. Traditional British etiquette would suggest that this was the time for Bridget to say good night and allow the Professor to get some sleep, but Bridget had something on her mind.

"What is it, Bridget?" the Professor asked, watching Bridget idle in front of her, shifting uncomfortably from one foot to the other.

Bridget thought for a moment before answering. "Nobody has ever survived a death stare that I'm aware of, Professor. Molly has now. Twice!" She gasped. "I see something in her now; an ability stronger than any I've encountered since your father."

"What sort of ability?" the Professor quizzed, her desire to get to sleep placed on momentary suspension.

"That I don't know, but if the Spletka are on their way here, she could be our last line of defence."

The Professor stepped forward, almost threatening.

"I will guard that little girl with my life, Bridget. If there is to be any battle, she is not going on the front line, you need to understand that."

Bridget sighed, taking a small step back. "I am just a simple cook, Professor, and certainly not privy to such information." She gently smiled. "She is a wonderful child; they both are. Your concerns really should be taken up with Mike."

"And they will be!" The Professor stormed into her room, slamming the door behind her.

It had started out as a juvenile game between them: Arran touching the screen and saying, "Change view, Professor Tempus and Bridget."

The idea being they would overhear the conversation and have a laugh about it the following morning. What they heard was certainly no laughing matter.

"I'm scared, Arran," Molly said. "I can't fight the Spletka Clan."

"I know," he said. "I'll look after you, and so will the Professor."

He handed her his bowl of chocolate ice cream. She wasn't hungry but accepted it anyway, grateful for the unselfish gesture and the deeper meaning behind.

The Professor's bedroom looked identical to the children's in every detail except there was only one bed, which she lay on gratefully, fully clothed, and tried to rest. Her eyes were closed but her active mind was preventing her from entering anything like a dreamlike state.

Aware she was fighting a losing battle, she ordered a coffee from the self-service bench, then wandered over to the window, stretching out her finger to touch the glass.

"Change view, Professor Richard Tempus."

She wanted to look at a picture of the man she had travelled one thousand years into the future to see.

The screen flickered. A moving image came into focus, slightly obscured by white static mist. Her eyes squinted so that she could make out the image of her father behind the haze. He was slumped over the time machine, his body, bruised and bloody. Another man in a tattered suit lay sleeping (or dead) on the floor. This man, she assumed, was Jhonas Spletka; the uncanny resemblance to her own John Pentka was quite eerie.

Her father coughed and Jhonas stirred, rising slowly to his feet. He looked at the flashing green button on the machine, knowing he had to get to the Professor before he had time to push it.

"Good-bye, old friend," the Professor wheezed, watching with sad eyes as Jhonas dashed toward him.

One push of the button and it was over. The Professor vanished, leaving Jhonas Spletka standing, stunned in a piercing silence. He composed himself, straightened his tie, and walked from the room.

The static filled the screen. Just as Rebecca Tempus thought the disturbing home movie had come to an end, her father's voice sounded in her ears, repeating the words from her vision the night before:

"Find me, Rebecca."

Chapter Thirty-Seven

First Line of Defence

Arran and Molly were unusually quiet at breakfast the following morning. For a while this had gone unnoticed, as the Professor told Mike of her previous night's visions.

"I was there," said Mike sympathetically. He shrugged his shoulders. "For some of it at least. The Citadel was under attack. By the time I got to your father, it was too late. Jhonas was nowhere to be seen."

He shook his head.

"What happened?" she asked.

"Jhonas and your father fought. A powerful meeting of the minds if you like. The energy that surrounds this planet—the same energy that runs through your house—was at stake. If Jhonas were to win, it would have been his to control. He spent so long collecting negative energy, moulding dark spirits to give him enough power to challenge your father. I don't know exactly what happened, but clearly he didn't succeed. We all believe the good Professor gave his life so Jhonas would fail."

The Professor drank what was left in her coffee cup before turning her attention to the children.

Molly hadn't ordered any food and Arran was picking at the multi-coloured selection of toast and preserves in front of him.

"Molly wants to go home, Professor."

Molly bowed her head to avoid the eye contact both adults were trying to make with her.

The Professor reached across and touched her shoulder. "What's wrong, sweetheart? Did something happen last night?"

Arran answered for her again. "We heard what you and Bridget were talking about last night outside our room. She's no soldier; she's my little sister."

The Professor looked toward Mike. "How's the mind reading?"

He looked into her eyes. Images from her conversation with Bridget flashed into his mind before he finally turned to Molly. "You don't need to worry. No one has any plans of sending you out on the front line if there is a battle with the Spletka."

Molly raised her head to look at the Professor.

"Promise?" she said.

The Professor nodded. "I won't let anything bad happen to you."

"Anyway," Mike interjected, his voice slightly more upbeat, "I was told you two might like to visit the school today, meet some of the other kids."

A flash image of Victor and his gang appeared in Arran's mind before he dismissed it and turned to Molly.

"School in the future could be fun?"

Molly smiled. "Yes, it did sound fun when the doctor was telling us about it. Okay."

"Excellent," said Mike. "Shall we go?"

"I'll just stay here and have another coffee." The Professor pressed the disc in the middle of the table. "I have some thinking to do. I'll see you two a little later."

The children waved good-bye and walked off with Mike.

Chapter Thirty-Eight

The Tempus School for Special Abilities

Mike escorted the children to the front of the building that they had passed earlier in the courtyard when they first arrived at the Citadel. He gently slapped Arran on the back.

"This journey will be rather reminiscent of the one you took to the games room."

"What does he mean?" Molly asked.

"Just follow me," Arran said, pushing the door open and stepping inside.

Almost instantly they found themselves standing at the gates to the Tempus School for Special Abilities. The letters TSSA hung high above the high iron railings. The gates automatically creaked open and they cautiously stepped onto an a big play yard where hundreds of children ran around playing or stood talking to their friends; all waiting for the school day to begin.

One girl who had already run half the yard stopped beside Arran and Molly to catch her breath. "Have you seen...?"

There was a fierce gust of wind before another girl with spiked hair appeared out of nowhere, then slapped her on the head. "Tag!"

"Hey, no fair," the first girl yelled. "No using your abilities!" She gave an unimpressed snort before running off.

Hide-and-seek was played too but with a slight difference: Instead of hiding behind dustbins and lampposts, the children simply transformed themselves into dustbins and lampposts. One child changed himself into a small spoon which, as soon as the seeker had passed him unnoticed, sprouted little legs and tootled off to the den, where he was safe from discovery.

Molly became bemused by what appeared to be a game of telekinetic volleyball, in which two people stood either side of a net and controlled the movement of a huge pink ball using only their minds.

One young child sat in the middle of the yard waving his arms and singing; Arran recognised the song from the Jonny Jagger album he had been given the previous day.

In the bottom corner, a group of boys kicked a ball around.

Molly shrugged. "No difference from our time."

Arran laughed. "You can say that…"

His sentence was cut short when he noticed an advance of children walking in his direction. "Oh no."

"Hey, DOA. I thought I told you to stay out of my way."

Arran shook his head.

"Who are these guys?" Molly asked.

"Nobody, troublemakers. Just ignore them."

Arran and Molly turned to walk in the opposite direction and were quickly pursued by Victor and his gang.

"Hey, don't ignore me or it'll be worse for you!"

Arran turned around to face him. "What do you want, Victor?"

"Who's this, your girlfriend?" one member of his gang mocked, looking Molly up and down. "Is that the best you can do?"

His entire group laughed.

Another shouted, "Hey, darling, why don't you come with us and leave this loser on his own?"

Molly stood side to side with her brother. "You're the only loser I can see here."

Joss Minton stepped forward and looked at her. "She's his sister and…"

She put her hands to her ears and began to scream, "Stop, you're hurting me!"

Victor and his gang took a small step backward. A crowd of children began to form around them.

Molly's eyes had turned a bright blue and she was staring right at Joss.

"That's right, I am his sister. And if you don't leave I *will* hurt you." She broke eye contact and Joss collapsed to her knees, hands on the floor, physically and mentally exhausted.

"I will. I'm sorry, please stop."

Molly's eyes returned to normal and Joss slowly stood, tears streaming down her face.

"As for you," Molly said, turning to Victor, "any clever, witty remarks you'd like to share?"

Victor, trying to keep his cool, simply cocked his head to one side and spoke to his gang.

"Come on, let's go. He needs his little sister to protect him."

They walked off, with only Joss taking the occasional glance back in Molly's direction, her face a picture of surprise and fear.

"There you go." Molly laughed, clapping her hands together.

"All taken care of."

Arran sank his hands into his pockets and began walking across the play yard, his head bowed down.

"What's wrong with you?" Molly asked, running to catch up.

"I can fight my own battles."

"Yeah, you were doing a bang-up job before I stepped in!" she snapped.

"He has abilities. Everyone has abilities here…except me." He stared at her, looking for the right words. "Even you!"

"That's not true. When that lieutenant was after me, you did loads of stuff to her, or it, whatever, and she was far tougher than those idiots over there."

Arran shook his head. "That was different; we were in the Tempus Network."

Molly looked around. "Well, I'm no expert but isn't that where we are now?"

The school doors opened. A voice rang in Arran and Molly's ears:

Arran and Molly, please make your way to reception room three.

Chapter Thirty-Nine

A Moment of Reflection

The Professor sat alone for a good half hour, drinking coffee and drifting helplessly in a wild sea of thoughts. She had all but made her mind up to take Arran and Molly home once they were back from the school. She wanted so much to find her father, but the children's safety had to come first, and that was simply not something she could guarantee.

Bridget sat silently beside her. Her eyes dreamily searched the room, looking for the right words, perhaps some sort of apology concerning her remarks the night before.

The Professor spoke first. "You said my father and you were quite close."

Bridget nodded. "I love your father a great deal, Rebecca." She paused, thinking it unwise to get too familiar. "Oh, I'm sorry. I mean *Professor*."

"That's all right," she said, feeling somehow comforted by Bridget's voice. "I like it when you use my name. Nobody ever does."

"Your father did."

The Professor looked at her quizzically. "How do you know?"

Bridget stammered slightly before continuing, "Well, he is your father; he's hardly going to call you Professor, is he?"

Unconvinced, she nodded. "No, I suppose not."

"For what it's worth, I don't believe your father is dead."

Bridget rose to her feet. "He's just missing; I'm sure if anyone can find him, you can."

With that she walked toward the entrance, arms outstretched as a family of diners came in to delight in the day's special delicacies.

The Professor repeated her father's words, over and over:

Find me, Rebecca.

Find me, Rebecca.

FIND ME, REBECCA!

Chapter Forty

Send in the Troops

Mike sat in the control room, staring at the paralyzed spider lieutenants in the glass case. The largest one seemed to have developed a slight twitch, its two front legs raising a couple of centimetres, then crashing down to the floor again before it repeated the action, again and again.

What is it doing? he thought. A REM sleep, maybe? Or was it something more? He was distracted by a voice on the intercom.

"Sir, you might want to have a look at the city map, centred around Judean Street. We are detecting an unusual build-up of negative energy."

Mike pulled up the map on his holographic display. "Okay, let's see what you are up to, Spletka minions," he murmured as he tried to zoom in on the image. He saw nothing but dark static. After a couple of unsuccessful attempts, he spoke on the intercom:

"Why can't I get close enough to this image to find out what's going on down there?"

"I don't know, sir. Somehow they are blocking us from seeing what they are doing."

That must be taking an enormous amount of combined energy,

thought Mike.

"Shall I send a patrol in, sir?"

"Yes," said Mike. "Just observe and report back. I think their general is planning something."

"Yes sir, they are on their way. I'll report back when we have news."

Chapter Forty-One

First Day at School

The children filtered across to their respective classrooms, leaving Arran and Molly (within thirty seconds) standing in a deserted visitors reception area. Three vacant chairs were pushed up against a wall which faced a single white desk with a silver round disk in the middle. On the desk were the words:

Reception One.

Arran shrugged his shoulders. "You think we should just wander till we find reception three?"

"Suppose so," said Molly.

Before they could decide on an agreed route, a teacher with long, flowing black hair, wearing a brown business skirt which contrasted quite nicely with her bright blue blouse and shocking pink knee-length socks, ran up the corridor toward them.

"Arran and Molly?" she gasped, brushing her overtly lengthy fringe away from her face.

"Yes, that's us," said Molly.

"Excellent!" the teacher exclaimed. "Sorry I'm late. Was taking a bath." She straightened her hair again, then announced:

"My name is Eve, Eve Monovich." She paused. "But I don't give out my first name, being a teacher and all, so don't ask. You can call me Miss Monovich, or simply Miss; choice is yours."

"Hi Miss Monovich," both children said.

"Oh, please just call me Eve."

"Are you a new teacher?" Molly asked.

"Why yes, how did you know?"

"Just a guess." Molly sniggered.

"I'm the art teacher. Your regular teacher, Miss Crowdon,

didn't turn in this morning and Headmaster Dews asked me to step in till she returns. Now I'll be doing your induction and evaluation this mooning."

Arran shot a look in her direction. "Did you say mooning?" Molly laughed.

"I did. You noticed?" the teacher exclaimed. "It's all the rage with the children nowadays; they're all saying it."

"Perfect," said Arran. "A school of Mollys."

"No, no," Eve replied earnestly. "There are many more names in…"

She didn't finish what she was about to say, instead stood in front of them fast asleep, snoring very loud, her head turned up so it was looking up toward the ceiling.

Arran and Molly both chuckled.

"Miss Monovich!" Arran finally shouted.

The teacher immediately woke, yawned, and glared at them, her eyes nearly as wide as her mouth.

"Yes, mooning. Can I help you?"

"You said you were doing our induction, then fell asleep," said Molly.

"What a splendid idea," Eve replied directly. "Induction. Now we need to find a free room."

Molly shook her head. "How about reception room three?"

"Another splendid idea—are you sure this is your first day?" the teacher replied, slapping her thigh triumphantly.

She tapped the silver disk in the middle of the table three times. The children felt a brief moment of dizziness as the room became a blur, an indistinguishable mass of colours and shapes moving at super speed all around them.

Once the cloudiness disappeared, the room was exactly as it had been before, except the desk was now purple and had the number three on it.

Slightly disoriented, the children both sat down.

"Beats walking, I suppose," said Arran.

Eve joined them and studiously looked both children up and down.

"Now, which of you is Molly?"

Arran looked at his sister.

"Either you look like a boy…"

"Or my *big* brother is a little girl," finished Molly.

Arran kicked his sister in the leg. "I'm Arran and this is my sister Molly."

Eve jumped up from her seat excited and sat down again. "Mooning!"

"Mooning!" Molly laughed. Arran simply sat, arms folded. *Of all the words to catch on*, he thought.

"Now, children, one at a time tell me about yourselves: your likes, dislikes, and of course, any special abilities that you want to work on."

"Well, mine will take less time," said Arran. "I like computers and science, don't like idiot bullies and…" He stopped and considered his next sentence. "I have no special abilities."

Eve looked shocked. "None? None at all? Not even a smidgen of a tiny little ability?"

She closed the distance between her thumb and fingers so they were very close to touching and waved them in front of Arran's nose. Arran, irritated, jumped up from his seat and shook his head.

"No!"

"Are you sure?" She extended her middle finger and stuck it in his ear.

"Hey, get off!" he protested.

Molly fell about laughing.

"Sorry, Arran," the teacher said. "Just checking, young sir. Yes, you do have abilities; you just have some work to do to fully realize them."

Arran beamed. "I do? I have abilities? What are they?"

There was no answer. Eve had fallen asleep again.

Arran looked disbelievingly at his sister, who simply smiled and shouted: "Miss Monovich!"

She woke again. "Now, Molly, I believe?"

"Hey, what about me?" Arran insisted.

"Manners, young sir. Ladies first, now Molly."

Arran raised his hands in the air. "Okay, I guess I'll find out eventually."

Molly folded one leg on top of the other, mockingly stroking an imaginary beard on her chin before answering.

"Well, I like acting, singing, and animals. I don't like things that aren't acting, singing, and animals, and I seem to have the ability of the death stare."

Eve instinctively closed her eyes.

"Is she going to sleep again?" Molly asked.

Arran shrugged.

Eve shook her head fervently. "No, no, no, the death stare is impossible unless you belong to the…"

"Spletka Clan?" finished Molly.

"Yes, yes, yes," she repeated with escalating vigour. "Stay away from me!"

Both children laughed and Eve opened her eyes, avoiding all

visual contact with Molly.

"That is not funny, young madam; joking about such things is entirely against the Headmaster Dews' rules."

Eve stopped and stamped her foot on the ground.

"I realise you are new here, but the headmaster will have to be informed."

She clapped her hands twice and a brightly coloured orange door appeared in the back of the room where once there was a bookcase. It swung open as she walked nearer to it. She gestured for Molly to join her. Both children stood.

"No, not you, Arran, your timetable will be along soon. Your sister will join you presently."

Molly forcefully folded her arms in protest.

"But I didn't do anything…"

She couldn't believe she was being told off already. *Not unlike my other school,* she thought. *Probably be suspended before the day is out.*

Once they had both walked through, Arran sat down and watched the orange door transform once again into a bookcase.

Arran, please make your way from reception room three down the corridor to History room three.

Aware he was the only one who could hear the announcement,

he stood and made his way to the classroom.

There was a lone two-seat sofa chair outside Headmaster Dews' office, upon which Molly and Eve sat. Molly slumped down, still annoyed at her perceived injustice.

The walls were covered in awards and pictures. Molly was particularly drawn to the framed newspaper clippings of a young blonde girl, Sophia Tal Grasto. The headline read "World Chess Champion at Thirteen." The picture was of her receiving an award whilst Kirspotin Kaspano, the former world champion, stood crying at the scene of the most famous chess victory in history.

As Molly's interest in the story increased, she found herself being transported into the picture itself. Barely a second later, she was standing alongside an admiring crowd who were cheering Sophia in her monumental victory.

"I'd like to thank Headmaster Dews, for your support and encouragement," Sophia said, standing at the podium and addressing the crowd. "I don't want to thank my parents or offer commiserations to my opponent, who has told me that he has plans to throw himself head first into a skip before the day is out."

Once the speech had ended, the crowd's cheers faded into a dull echo and Molly was sitting once again outside the headmaster's office. Eve sat next to her, avoiding all possible eye contact.

Headmaster Dews' office door slowly opened and Eve stood up, straightening her hair. She marched through the door and motioned to Molly to do the same, which she did.

The cream-coloured room was quite empty when they walked in, except for a large cardboard box which was pushed up to the back wall. *Okay, not quite what I was expecting,* thought Molly.

"Headmaster? Yoohoo, Headmaster Dews, where are you?" Eve called out.

"Come in. Come in."

The elderly male voice came from inside the box.

"Headmaster Dews, are you in there?" Molly moved cautiously closer to it.

They were both startled and took a step backward when the top of a head popped out from the inside of the box, followed by the rest of his body as he levitated out and stood in front of them carrying a paintbrush in one hand and a hammer in the other.

"Excuse me," he said apologetically as he placed the tools back in the box. "Was doing a little remodelling, didn't want to get the office dirty."

Though he was wearing paint-splattered white overalls, he struck Molly as quite a neat, formal man with perfectly sensible brown hair and a little goatee.

His facial expression and very demeanour were quite unlike Mrs Anderson's when she was trying to impose her superiority upon others. He was a man whose very presence, though authoritative, seemed to invite feelings of respect and honesty.

This was unfamiliar ground for Molly, so thought she would save her customary bad temper, reserved for teachers she did not like, until he accused her of something she did not do.

"Hello, Eve." The head teacher smiled. "It's very nice to see you again."

Eve blushed. "Oh please, call me Eve."

Molly sniggered, which captured his attention and he looked at her as though he was looking over the top of a pair of glasses even though he wasn't wearing any.

"And who do we have here?"

Here we go, thought Molly.

"This young lady is called Molly," Eve said scornfully. "And she seems to delight in scaring the living beanpoles out of teachers by making up stories."

"I see," said the head teacher without altering the direction of his gaze. "Well, we encourage stories and an active imagination, Miss Monovich, but I sense this is something more?"

"Yes, Headmaster Dews. Molly claims she has the ability to

perform the D.E.A.T.H. stare, which we all know to be impossible unless you are in with the Spletka."

Feeling like she had been quiet for far too long, Molly spoke up.

"I can, too, do the death stare! I can show you if you like?"

He calmly shook his head and stroked his beard.

"No, that won't be necessary. Miss Monovich, would you leave us for a while please? Miss Monovich?"

Eve Monovich had fallen asleep and began snoring rather loudly where she stood, her head tilted back again toward the ceiling.

"Sorry about Miss Monovich; she does that, which you are no doubt aware by now."

Molly was confused; this was not the telling off she was expecting.

"Er, yes I've noticed."

"I have to say you don't look like you are in league with the Spletka Clan; quite the opposite in fact."

He calmly walked around her, finishing in his original position right in front of her.

"There are tell-tale signs and a bio signature which I normally pick up, and yours is most interesting. Why don't you take a seat?"

Molly looked around the empty room, raising her eyebrows, wanting to avoid voicing the obvious statement that the room was completely empty.

"How silly of me." The headmaster reached into the box and pulled out two tiny chairs that looked like they were hijacked from a dollhouse.

He gave one to Molly and placed another on the ground in front of him. As soon as it touched the carpet, it grew in size till it reached the appropriate height and he sat down. Molly placed her chair on the ground also, and it grew, though not as tall as the head teacher's, but was the perfect height for Molly.

She sat opposite him. Eve continued to snore beside them, twitching her nose and smiling as though she was in the middle of the most wonderful dream.

"Now, Molly, open your eyes wide, if you would be so kind."

Molly complied and the headmaster examined them.

"Interesting. Mike gave me a little of your background before you arrived this morning. That, combined with your antics in the play yard with young Joss Minton, led me to believe that you do have an ability not unlike the death stare."

Molly bowed her head in shame.

"I'm sorry about her, Headmaster, you see, she was picking on my brother and…"

"Yes, I know what happened and would appreciate it if you

could control that particular ability in the school."

"Yes, Headmaster."

"Which leads me to my next question. Can you control it?"

Molly shrugged.

"Perform the death stare on me, if you would."

Molly looked shocked. "Well, no, I don't want to hurt you."

"Your concern is welcome and added proof, not that any is needed, that your ability, though it may be the death stare of sorts, is not a replica of the Spletka stare. Compassion is a word they have no regard for. But please," he continued, "perform the stare on me, and stop if I ask you."

Molly agreed and stared at the headmaster. Her eyes did not turn bright blue and nothing happened. After several attempts she started to sob.

"I wasn't lying, Headmaster. It did happen before."

The headmaster rose and touched her on the shoulder. "I'm sure it did, Molly, but the conditions, I suspect, were rather different."

Molly dried her tears, looking confused.

"When you have used it in the past, can you describe your feelings at the time?"

"Angry and scared mostly."

"As I thought," the headmaster replied. "You do have the

power. But power without control, particularly yours, can be rather dangerous. Normal classes will be with the rest of the children, but enhanced ability classes will be with me directly. Yours is an ability that standard teachers are not trained to deal with, okay?" Molly smiled, nodding her head. "And if any other teacher or student asks, keep that particular ability to yourself, and no more demonstrations."

Molly agreed.

"Now let's wake Miss Monovich."

He clapped his hands; the resulting sound echoed around the room and was reminiscent of a small explosion. Startled, Eve Monovich woke, blissfully unaware of anything that Molly and the head teacher had spoken of.

"You see, Headmaster." Eve continued as though no time had elapsed since she fell asleep. "She's telling *you* big fibsquiggles now!"

The headmaster winked at Molly. "Is that true, young lady?" He spoke in a make-believe authoritative tone. "Can you really do a death stare?"

Molly played along. "No, not at all. I never said that. I said a breath stare. That is, I can stare at people who, er, breathe."

"Well, I don't see any harm in that." The headmaster laughed.

Eve looked very embarrassed.

"Oh, I'm so sorry, young Molly, my ears played tricks on me.

Come, let me take you to your next class. Sorry to have wasted your time, Headmaster."

"Quite all right. Now why don't you take young Molly here to join her brother in history room three?"

Chapter Forty-Two

History Class

As soon as Arran had walked into the classroom, the teacher standing at the front pointed to an empty desk at the back of the room.

"Welcome, Arran. I'm Miss Dongle. If you could take your seat, the class are sharing their homework assignments on the twenty-first century."

Arran sat behind his assigned desk, and a young ginger-haired boy walked to the front and faced his peers.

"Hello, class and Miss Dongle. My name is Benjamin Liddle and this is my presentation on food in the twenty-first century:

"Mummies and Daddies in the twenty-first century didn't let their children eat cakes and sweets; instead they went to shops in secret and exchanged big silver coins called credit cards for chocolate and put it in the coldest place in the house. This was usually a high-up cold cupboard called a fridge. When the children were asleep, they would eat the chocolate. Because they had been so secretive, they were punished, and their bellies and bums got bigger.

"They didn't want their children to see them looking so grotesque, so they ran away every morning at eight o'clock, hoping that whilst they were running their big bellies and bums would return back to normal.

"Children in the twenty-first century were made to eat food their parents had painted green which they called greens and which tasted like socks. Sometimes the children were promised chocolate if they ate the sock food."

Miss Dongle raised her hand to her mouth to disguise her smile. Arran's response was not quite so subtle: his laughter, uncontrollable, filled the room.

All the children turned to look at what was indeed so funny.

"Arran, would you care to share the joke with the class?" his teacher said sternly.

"No, Miss," he replied, at which point his sister walked into the classroom.

Sensing the tense atmosphere, she simply sneaked in and sat on the seat next to him.

"You getting into trouble without me?" she whispered so as not to direct any more attention to her.

"I didn't mean to laugh," Arran whispered back. "But you have to hear these homework history reports on the twenty-first century."

"Okay, thank you, Benjamin," said Miss Dongle. "Can we hear from Joss Minton next?"

Joss looked across at Molly, unwilling, perhaps afraid, to get up. It was clear she didn't even like being in the same room as her.

"Can I just go next time, Miss Dongle?"

Miss Dongle shook her head. "Joss, Joss, Joss. I know it sounded like a question, but apparently sounds can be deceiving. These reports form an essential part of your overall history grade, to which your parents have both suggested a keen interest in you performing well, so I will 'ask' one more time."

Reluctantly Joss rose from her seat and walked to the front of the class.

"Hello, Miss Dongle, hello class." Joss's weedy voice lacked her usual confidence and was barely loud enough to make the first two rows.

"Speak up, Joss," Miss Dongle said.

Joss nodded. "Today my presentation will be on." She cleared her throat. "That is, my presentation will be on…"

Molly smiled and gave her a cheeky little wink.

Joss looked down, afraid that Molly might repeat the same stare she had done in the play yard earlier. She started to cry, shaking her head side to side before turning to the teacher.

"Sorry, Miss Dongle, I can't." With that she ran, crying, from the classroom.

Arran felt sorry for her, despite the undeniable fact that she was a bully and had probably reduced more children to tears than Headmaster Dews and his entire staff would probably ever dare to venture a guess.

Molly tried not to show any compassion, folding her arms and grumbling under her breath, "She deserved it. It's her own fault if she's scared."

The rest of lesson, though tarnished by the incident with Joss, couldn't help but to amuse both Arran and Molly as they heard a constant stream of various misplaced facts about the history of the twenty-first century and before.

They found out that Santa was an evil hoarder, who once every year visited every child in the world, dumping all the rubbish from his house into theirs, usually under a tree which grew in every living room. He then proceeded to eat all their mince pies and drink their milk before raiding a cold cupboard called the fridge and eating whatever was in there.

One child had asked, "Did he never need the toilet?"

Molly was surprised to hear the teacher answer: "Well, Timothy, if you'd done your research you'd know that if he ever needed the toilet he would go, but," she waved her finger, "not one child has ever been reported as waking up in the middle of the night and seeing Santa on the loo."

Arran found it amusing also to learn that the way children were punished by their parents was to visit a land called "Fairground." The idea being that children would learn what is fair and what is not, and they would be placed on machines that propelled them at great speeds in all directions till their behaviour changed.

Chapter Forty-Three

Judean Street

"Team leader unit six. I'm outside Judean Street now. It all seems deserted." The scout clicked his radio. "Over."

Instantly a crackled response came back from his captain.

"Maintain your position, scout; we'll be there in a moment."

"Copy that, team leader; I'm on the corner of Judean Street outside the disused bookstore."

The scout's eyes wandered nervously, taking in his surrounding environment. The raindrops fell like tiny darts and stung like acid as they touched his skin. This was a place where it was always dark, without so much as a streetlamp to light the way. This was the place in which the bitter wind bellowed, forever lost in a perpetual search for someone to torment. In short, this place was the last stronghold of the Spletka Clan.

"Hurry up, sir." He rubbed the sides of his arms with the opposite hands to keep warm.

In the few moments since he had arrived, he could swear the temperature had dropped at least five degrees. And it wasn't particularly warm to begin with.

The street looked deserted. Not so much as a field mouse could be seen, yet the scout felt hungry eyes on him from all directions.

He closed his eyes and listened. One of the scout's special abilities was his enhanced hearing. As he concentrated he was able to focus upon the faint but definite sound of a young girl crying.

He could see nothing to qualify the message his ears delivered but was able to pinpoint, from sound alone, exactly where the cries came from. He looked ahead to house number 39. His ears hopelessly searched for any sign that his companions were anywhere near. They were not.

He pushed the button on his radio, bringing it up to his lips.

"Team leader unit six. I can hear a young girl crying. Should I check it out? Team leader, do you copy?"

He hoped his captain would tell him to stay put, safety in numbers and all that, but there was no reply, just radio static. He repeated his former statement. Radio hiss still the only reply he would receive.

I'll just stay here. They can't be that much longer, he thought and hoped. *Heaven alone knows what's beyond that door.*

He paced back and forth on the spot, all the time becoming increasingly worried about the young girl whose screams and crying seemed to have intensified. He no longer needed the special ability to hear her.

He glanced at the defunct radio.

"Perfect," he muttered in a very dissatisfied tone. "You know you're probably running into a trap, but then again…"

A final howl of pain from beyond the door of number 39 broke his internal mutterings and spurred him into action.

As he ran down the darkened, rainy street, he felt sure he could hear a thousand tiny voices all laughing mischievously at what was probably to be a failed rescue attempt. Shaking his head, he simply dismissed this as paranoia.

"So far, so good," he said, feeling that if he spoke the words aloud it would at least give the impression that he was not acting alone.

The door to number 39 was slightly ajar. Peering into the small crack that led into the house, he saw only darkness.

"Please help me, someone."

The little girl's whimper was followed once again by helpless cries and sniffles.

"It's a trap, it's a trap," he whispered to himself, wanting nothing more at that moment than to flee the scene.

Knowing that he could never live with himself abandoning someone less fortunate and all too aware that his sworn duty was to protect the innocent from all wrongdoers, he outstretched a hand, gently pushing the door, which offered no resistance. Instead it gave a huge creaking sound as it opened fully with enormous force, then hammered onto the wall behind.

It made him jump a little. Though the door was wide open, he still could see nothing. It was as though a thick black sheet had been placed at the entrance, obscuring any vision.

Reluctant to walk in, he spoke. "Hello, little girl. Can you hear me?"

The girl's crying stopped. "Please help me."

"Just walk toward my voice." The now petrified soldier's statement seemed more like a delicate suggestion than a reassuring command.

"I can't move. I can't see you, please help," she sobbed.

The scout took once last hopeful glance up the street for his companions before realising, for the moment at least, he was on his own.

As he stepped through the threshold he could still see nothing, but felt the hard of wood beneath his feet, which seemed to echo with every step he made closer to the sound of the young girl. As quickly as it had opened, the door slammed shut behind him. He had half expected this to happen.

He resisted the urge to turn and open it, knowing full well that if he did, he would be out of that house like a shot, without the girl. He proceeded slowly forward, sensing more and more that it was very unlikely he would find a young girl at all, but something far more terrible.

Above his head he heard an electrical crackling, like the sound of two opposing charged wires as they prepared for battle. When the scout looked up he noticed a tiny flicker of light. Almost instantly a dirty electric bulb appeared and hung loosely from the ceiling, swaying gently from side to side. The feeble light that emanated from it made the scout think of it more as a low-energy candle.

There wasn't enough power for the scout to clearly see his surroundings but he was able to make out faint outlines from furniture and more importantly the outline of a small girl crouched in the corner, snivelling.

Before moving toward the girl, he instinctively looked back to check the door was still where he remembered it being. *Stupid*, he thought. *Of course it's there.*

He walked toward the outline that was the girl.

"Can you stand up?"

"I don't know," replied the girl weakly.

"Here, take my hands," he said, crouching down and stretching out his arms.

The young girl grasped both his wrists.

"Now, try to stand up."

"No," she said gently.

Confused, he replied, "What?"

"No," she repeated, this time with a little more vigour in her voice.

Her grasp on his wrists tightened to the point where it caused extreme pain when he tried unsuccessfully to pull free.

The lightbulb, which had been more of a dim suggestion before, began to burn so bright that the scout had to squint. The little girl, who he could see quite plainly now, stood before him. She had long, wet black hair covering for the most part a pale, lifeless face; a face that was as white as the elegant and aged bridesmaid-style dress she wore.

She stared at him with eyes that were blue and then turned jet black. The scout's struggles could do nothing to counteract the strength of the entity which now had a firm grasp on him. From the corners of her eyelids, six tiny spiders emerged, crawling down her face and across her arms, making their way to the scout's head.

The little girl spoke, this time in a low, sinister whisper. "A gift for your soldier friends. Now go welcome them to the Spletka Clan."

The very moment the scout stopped struggling, the little girl released her grasp and collapsed to the floor in a heap. The scout simply smiled, rose to a stand, turned, and walked out of the house to meet the expectant soldiers outside the old bookstore.

Chapter Forty-Four

Holographic Tempus

After history class, Arran and Molly walked from the classroom to see Rudolph waiting in the corridor. Molly curtly smiled in recognition. Arran was somewhat more welcoming, outstretching his hand and slapping him on the back.

"Rudolph. What are you doing here?"

"Evolutionary studies next, then PE, but that will be cancelled with the Tempus Games being on. Headmaster Dews asked that I help you find your way around; big place this."

Rudolph walked into the classroom next door to the one they had just vacated.

"In here."

Molly sniggered. "Yeah, lucky you were here, Rudolph; we could have been lost for hours."

They sat at a small round table either side of Rudolph; there were several such tables around the room, each with mini armchairs levitating around them.

"Ooh, that is nice," Arran said as he sank into his chair.

The chair seemed to know exactly what to do to make sure he was sitting upright and concentrating yet experiencing the most extreme relaxation he had ever felt.

The rest of the class filled the room, sat at their assigned seats, and waited for the lecture to begin.

An orb of light shot through the door and hovered in the centre of the room, giving the children enough time to become aware of its presence and to settle down and stop talking amongst themselves.

The orb made its way around the room, taking the scenic route to the front of the class, milling around the children, dropping intermittent comments as it did so:

"Good morning, Joss. Coat off, Stephanie. Patrick, levitate pencils on your own time please."

Once at the front, the orb transformed into a holographic image of Professor Richard Tempus. It spread a soft yet friendly glow throughout the class. He ran a hand through the dishevelled mess of hair on his head; no chance at all of neatening his hair up, thought Molly. *The biggest danger there is that he loses his hand.*

"Well, hello class."

The Professor's voice was, as well as being the poshest voice Arran and Molly had ever heard, as warm and welcoming as the soft glow that radiated from him. It made them both feel instantly at home.

"I realise that many of you will be eager to get out of this class and participate in our annual Tempus Games."

There was a hushed air of excitement and anticipation around the room.

"So the sooner we get through the essential information for today, then off you can pop to the main hall, where I believe Alfie the sports teacher will be waiting for you."

"What's the Tempus Games, Rudolph?" Arran asked.

"Only like the coolest thing in the world," he replied. "All the schools in the world compete for one student and one school to be crowned Planetary Champion. What we do today will decide which of the students in this school will be put forward. Wouldn't get your hopes up though; Victor wins it every year. I'm sure he's got the Tempus

Network rigged somehow."

"I could always death stare him, give someone else a chance," Molly joked.

Arran didn't reply; he still hadn't fully forgiven her for embarrassing him in the school yard earlier.

"Oh, I'm so sorry…" said the Professor, looking directly at Molly, who shrugged, unsure as to why he was apologising, though his sarcastic tone should have given it away.

"There you were, sitting outside having a good old chinwag with your friends and then some inconsiderate buffoon builds a school around you."

"Sorry, Professor," she replied.

"Quite all right," he said and turned his attention to the rest of the class.

"Today we will be focussing on the human brain, its potential and its magnificent journey throughout the ages."

He pointed at a young girl with shoulder-length blond hair who was sitting at the front, looking very smug. She regarded her teacher with complete admiration. Molly recognised her as Sophia Tal Grasto, the young chess champion whose picture had been displayed outside the headmaster's office.

"Young Sophia here is an excellent example and perfect

embodiment of the evolutionary process of which I speak."

The teacher flexed his hands and ten shiny orbs shot out from each of his fingers and moved rapidly around the class, eventually levitating above a silver disc at the centre of each table. Each orb transformed itself into a holographic human brain.

With the exception of Arran and Molly, who thought the spectacle was the most impressive thing they had ever seen in a school, all the children looked upon the brains as though they were badly drawn sketches from an old textbook.

"I wish our school was like this," said Arran.

"We have, as you will recall," continued the teacher, "discussed the origins of the human brain and the associated theories ranging from the early belief that we are evolved from primitive apes, to the theory that we are—and always have been—an entirely different species that shared apelike qualities, to the more recent opinion that our existence is more of an eclectic mix of different species from Earth and its neighbouring planets, beginning in the land that used to be known as Egypt."

The teacher pinched himself on the hand and a tiny red light shone out from a small section of each brain.

"The brain is, and always has been, intimately connected to the body and the emotions that govern our decisions. The skills we have adapt to our surroundings; as these have changed over the years, so, too, have our abilities."

One-third of each of the floating brains began to glow red.

"This is how much of the brain the average human being had access to for many thousands of years. There were a few notable exceptions of course: Albert Einstein, William Shakespeare, Alfred Pennyworth the Second, and of course, though modesty should prevent me from saying it, me."

The teacher looked searchingly around the class.

"Can anyone explain what caused the massive increase in our brains' capacity over the last thousand years?"

Sophia's hand shot up into the air, but the teacher decided to pick on another less willing student. He pointed at Victor Graston, who simply shrugged and laughed, and when it became clear that the teacher wasn't going to take that for an answer said, "You?"

The teacher, though just a hologram, blushed a little.

"Flattery will get you everywhere, my boy, but no, not I. I may have been responsible for the remarkable and very exciting discovery that the human spirit was as tangible and real as our physical bodies, and furthermore instrumental in establishing on-going relations with our neighbouring planets, but it was those increased relations, together with the significant changes to our environment—which I also had a hand in—that prompted our brains to grow.

From the earliest times, the need for survival and the desire to adapt to our living environment have required that our brain perform the appropriate action; multiply that exponentially over hundreds of years, in which our wants and needs have increased and so, too, has our brainpower."

He thought for a moment.

"So yes, I suppose, taking into account my research and achievements, in a sense you are right, Victor. Well done me."

The class laughed.

"Well, at least he's modest about it," said Rudolph, casually running his hand through the floating brain, which now glowed red in its entirety.

Once the class was over, Rudolph jumped from his seat and a smile formed on his face, so wide it looked like he had just placed a coat hanger in there.

"Tempus Games, follow me."

Chapter Forty-Five

The Assembly

"I heard what your sister did to Joss in the play yard this morning," Rudolph said to Arran as they walked to the sports hall.

"I'm right here, you know," Molly interjected.

"Yeah, sorry. Please don't do a death stare on me," Rudolph joked.

Molly shook her head, unamused.

They stepped into a huge hall. Long wooden benches had been provided on both sides, upon which the children sat. Light streamed in from the glass ceiling, illuminating the portraits of previous Tempus Games winners, which adorned the walls, as though they too were expectant spectators.

All but the sports teacher, Alfie, seemed to be wearing matching uniforms. Though the design slightly changed to accommodate each child's personal taste in dress, everyone had a black stretchy T-shirt and trousers, with a silver and purple sash flowing from the waist. Interwoven on the front of each uniform was the school emblem with "TSSA in the Heart of the Game" embroidered over the top.

The same emblem and message was also superimposed in the middle of the room as a holographic display, hovering over a silver trophy, out of which flew blue and purple fireworks. The image rotated like an overly confident fashion model who knew that all who gazed upon her would simply stare in admiration, which to its eternal credit, they all did.

Alfie caught Molly's eye. He was unlike the bad-tempered sports teacher she had been used to. His beaming smile was only superseded by his almost cartoon-like big green eyes and the disorganised spiked hair of blue, white, and black, which helped to complete the electric shock look he was clearly going for.

He was dressed very smartly in a stylish suit and tie which displayed the school crest. He also had a robe, that flapped behind him like a wannabe superhero's. Noticing they were not in the appropriate attire, Alfie approached Arran, Molly, and Rudolph.

"Hello, sir," Rudolph said. "This is Arran and Molly."

"Hello, and mooning, children," he announced.

Molly liked him already. "Mooning, sir."

Arran simply shook his head.

Alfie quickly looked them up and down and pointed toward a glowing blue square in the ground.

"Now, children, we are about to begin, but before we do, if you could go change into your uniform. Just stand in the square."

"It's not very private!" Molly protested, looking at the glowing square in full view of everyone.

Rudolph sniggered and shrugged. "I'll go first."

Once he was standing firmly on the panel, the blue beam began pulsing, covering his whole body. Rudolph's clothes, from head to toe and in that order, changed from the multi-coloured shorts and shirt he was already wearing, to the designated sports uniform.

"Excellent, excellent!" The sports teacher clapped his hands.

"Now, you next, young man, step on the square."

"Go on," said Rudolph encouragingly. "It's quite safe."

Arran looked a little confused. "I'm sure it is, Rudolph, but if we're in the Tempus Network, why do I need the blue square? Can't I just do this…?"

He closed his eyes and after a brief flash of light, he was instantly wearing his own brand of the sports uniform, only on this one the silver sash was woven into the shape of a lightning strike. Rudolph and the teacher looked aghast.

"H… H… How did you accomplish that, young Arran?" Alfie asked.

Arran shrugged. "We're in the Tempus Network; you can do what you like here."

The teacher shook his head fervently. "No, no, no… I mean yes, but no. The school has restrictions placed upon it. No child," he paused, "or staff member for that matter can simply do as they please. The system was designed by Professor Tempus himself, the greatest mind in history."

For the first time, Arran began to feel quite special. *It's about time I did something out of the ordinary,* he thought. Of course "out of the ordinary" in this time was very much a relative concept. He also felt a little deflated; people in this time could levitate, read minds, or do death stares. He was able to change clothes without standing on a blue square.

Although Molly was pleased that Arran was finding his ability, her sibling rivalry could not prevent her from trying the same.

"I don't need to change in the square either." She closed her eyes whilst the others waited eagerly. She concentrated hard, hoping to open her eyes and accept the same revered comments that Arran had received a few moments earlier. When she opened them, however, all she did receive were three sympathetic smiles from Arran, Rudolph, and Alfie. Her hoped moment of triumph had not happened and she resigned herself to have to trundle over to the same square Rudolph and every other child had done to change into her sports clothes.

Once they took their seats, Rudolph, Arran, and Molly watched as Alfie moved to the centre of the hall directly under the hologram. He raised his hands and the general chatter came to a halt.

"Welcome to the Annual Tempus Trials. The winner of these games will determine the one—yes, one single person—who will represent this fine school and, we hope, eventually take the planetary trophy!"

Rudolph nudged Arran and whispered, "Every country on the planet has one person chosen by their school to take part in the games. The winner gets that." He pointed at the trophy. "And is crowned planetary champion for that year."

The sports teacher continued. "Our congratulations to Victor Graston, who has been selected for the past three years to represent the school." He coughed politely.

Victor was sitting on the opposite side of the hall, staring directly at Arran, whilst a group of his friends and followers patted him on the back, smiling and offering words of encouragement.

"And jolly bad luck," the teacher continued, "that Victor wasn't able to take home the planetary trophy. Let's put our hands together and hope that this is the year of Tempus School for the Special Abilities England!"

There was a thunderous applause, populated with joyous laughter and cheers.

"Without further ado, it is my distinct pleasure to say: Let the games begin!"

As though on cue, the sunlight streaming in through the windows dimmed; at the same time, save the rotating trophy, the hologram disappeared too.

The trophy grew to four times its original size. A trumpet fanfare could be heard, whilst a voice not unlike that of a typical game show host called for everybody to stand.

Once they were on their feet the cup melted, floating momentarily in mid-air like a deflated moon before falling to the ground like millions of tiny silver raindrops.

Once on the floor, the raindrops took shape, forming themselves into tiny discs, each with a different name inscribed upon it. Out of the darkness, where moments before the trophy had proudly stood, appeared a huge florescent screen upon which a man with a neon coat, neon bushy eyebrows, and pink and silver hair that looked like a giant exploding bonfire. His booming yet slightly effeminate voice was accompanied by an orchestral arrangement, not unlike the *Star Wars* theme Arran remembered from his own century.

He called for people to take their positions, and every child walked onto the platform.

"Contestants, welcome!"

He laughed heartily and clicked his fingers.

The silver discs rose high in the air and began to sparkle like tiny stars in the night sky.

"Pretty, aren't they?" he said. "One of these coins has your name on it. All you have to do is find it, place it between your thumb and first finger, and sqeeeeeze. Sounds easy, don't it?"

The screen disappeared.

One by one the lights embedded in each of the coins went out, leaving the room in total darkness; save for one single shining coin. Every child's attention was drawn directly to it.

Like all coins that Arran and Molly were accustomed to seeing, it had an image on it, an image of someone's face, but who they could not quite make out; that was, until it grew to the size of a cinema screen. The children instantly recognised him as the holographic teacher who had taken their previous class.

The image smiled, scratched his head, then rubbed his eyes.

Clearly unaccustomed to speaking in public, he coughed and stammered before he was able to utter his first word.

"Emm, er…I, er…hello." The man coughed before continuing. "My name is Professor Tempus."

Molly nudged Arran. "You think he's related to our Professor Tempus?"

The image glared down at her "Of course I am; now kindly don't interrupt."

"Sorry, Professor," she answered in typical primary school fashion.

The image then smiled sympathetically at Molly, which confused her.

"Quite all right, my dear." He then gathered his composure and addressed the crowd. "Now where was I? Oh yes… My name is Professor Tempus, founder of this school and of course inventor of the Tempus Network. This is a recorded message, so try not to ask too many questions, for my responses in this form are rather limited, and by not too many questions I of course mean none whatsoever. We learn in part by doing. As for the rest please pay attention."

Over on the other side of the hall, Victor rolled his eyes. *Every year the same*, he thought. *When will that babbling fool just get on with it?*

The image contemptuously looked out of the corner of his eyes at Victor before continuing. *Sorry, Professor*, Victor thought.

"Now the coin you must find is like a puppy, forever faithful and, truth be known, wanting to be found by only its owner. There are a few rules and things to look out for. Firstly, if you find a coin that is not yours, leave it alone. Do nothing to bring attention to it, for if you do pick it up, it will call out to its owner, like this."

An image of a young boy creeping up upon a coin could be seen by every child in the hall. The face on the coin, once it was picked up, turned bright pink, then beetroot red and emitted a beacon of light. The mouth then opened wide and let out a piercing scream before biting the young boy on the finger. The boy dropped it of course and popped the sore finger in his mouth.

The image disappeared and the Professor continued to speak.

"Now the young boy who picked up the wrong coin has not only spoiled it for himself, as he is ejected from the games, but for everybody else as the beacon is bright enough to be seen by the coin's owner. The cry that the coin lets out will not stop until the owner and the coin are re-united."

Victor found this amusing. The only reason he'd won the games three years running was not because he possessed a superior intellect or keener sense of where his coin was, but purely because he'd gently persuaded others, through the medium of a clenched fist, to look for his coin in favour of their own. It was understood that should they find their own coin, they must under no circumstances pick it up. All Victor had to do then was sit down, relax, and wait for the beacon guiding him to his coin.

The Professor pushed his little round spectacles further up the bridge of his nose.

"There is an initial challenge before you will be allowed to enter the games of course. We can't just let anyone in, can we? This will be a test of intellect and must be completed entirely on your own. Thank you for listening. Now, before I pass you back to our fine sports teacher, may I say good luck. Stay close to your beliefs and prove that I am not mistaken in mine."

The hall went dark.

The sound of a huge heartbeat filled the room. Alfie the sports teacher spoke up.

"Say good-bye to your friends, people. When the lights come on you will be on your own in a strange land. All you have to do is find the doorway out. Good luck!"

"Wonder what that means," Molly said.

It was still pitch black so she could not see Arran but expected some sort of vocal acknowledgment from her brother. There was none; in fact she could not hear anything at all, save the heartbeat which rang out in her ears like a drum.

"Don't worry, Molly. If you get into trouble, I'll help," Arran said after hearing the announcement.

Like Molly he heard no reply apart from the beating heart.

Rudolph and the rest of the crowd had done this before, so knew better than to waste their energy. Instead they waited for the challenge that was to befall them.

Chapter Forty-Six

The Forest

The heartbeat faded and Arran felt the warmth of sunlight on his face, accompanied by a fresh breeze and the sweet sound of birds singing their morning song. He was no longer in the hall, but alone in a vast forest; thousands of trees spanned out in all directions as far as he could see.

At first Arran was rather excited to be entering the Tempus Games; he'd always loved the challenge that computer games posed, and this, without a doubt, was bound to be the greatest challenge he'd ever faced.

After walking for a while it became apparent that no obvious doorway was going to jump out, no matter where he turned—all that presented itself was the same old tired scene he'd experienced when he entered the games; tree after tree after same old boring tree.

He stopped and looked up at the blue skies. *Maybe if I climb up I'll see something*, he thought. It occurred to him that maybe the doorway did not look like the type of entrance he was used to seeing; the doors in the Citadel, after all, were big stone-like pillars. There might be the ruins of some old temple somewhere, and embedded in one of the pillars would be a door with a welcome mat at its feet. This thought gave him a little hope as he mounted and began to ascend the nearest tree to him.

His expectant triumph was dashed the moment he reached the top, however. No matter where he looked he saw nothing but the tops of trees. He guessed there were millions of them. He glanced up at the sun whilst mopping the sweat from his brow, wondering if someone had turned up the heat.

Once he was back on the ground he started to walk again slowly through the foliage, but couldn't help the new and uneasy feeling in his gut, like he was being watched. He stopped to look around but saw only the gentle sway of the leaves and branches as they moved in harmony with the wind.

"Hello?" he called.

There was no verbal answer, but a sudden and thunderous vibration beneath his feet made him jump back. He looked on in wonder as, on the very spot he had been standing, an enormous oak tree sprouted up. Carved on the bark were the words KNOCK THREE TIMES, which he eventually did with some initial hesitation.

As soon as the third knock had sounded, the front face of the tree opened like a huge door and out stepped…Professor Rebecca Tempus. Arran was lost for words, not knowing what to expect but feeling instantly safer at the sight of one of his best friends.

"Hello, Arran," the Professor said curtly.

"Professor, how are you…? That is… Why? Well… What are…? Er…"

"All fascinating questions, Arran," the Professor replied. "I do look and sound just like your Professor Tempus but I'm not. I have been furnished with enough information to replicate in many ways her personality. But the truth is I am your angel. In this section of the game you can call on me three times when you need help and if I can, then I will help you. Everyone in the game has their own chosen angel who will help their candidate according to their own abilities."

"So I can call on you three times?" Arran sounded a little more relieved. The Professor shook her head.

"No. You have just called me, which leaves you with two."

"That's not fair!" Arran protested. "I didn't know I was 'calling' on you."

The Professor chuckled. "Well, we learn by doing, don't we? It's quite funny; your sister called upon me as her angel too and has also made exactly the same mistake, thinking she still has three wishes, so to speak. You're not twins by any chance, are you?"

Arran nodded.

"Interesting!" The Professor rubbed her hands together. "It is said that a twin's psychic connection is stronger in this place."

Well, you certainly sound like the Professor, Arran thought. "Does that mean I can talk to Molly?"

The Professor laughed giddily. "Oh, this is simply wonderful. Your sister just asked me exactly the same question."

"Fascinating." Arran was a little annoyed that the mock Professor wasn't being overly helpful. "What is this place? And please don't tell me Molly just asked you that too."

The Professor, very probably about to say just that, stopped in her tracks. "Oh, okay, spoilsport. This is the forest!" She raised her hands proudly, as though she were a great tree herself.

The same chain of events had also happened in Molly's version of the game. She sighed at the Professor.

"Can't I get you on Mastermind, Professor? Special subject: the screaming obvious. I can see it's a forest. What more than that?"

The Professor twitched her nose slightly. "This is the beginning. Look around you, every tree is a doorway. To gain access, simply knock three times."

She leaned up against one small elm.

"Some doors will be the way forward."

She knocked three times on the bark. A small door appeared which was in turn opened by a smaller red squirrel wearing a mini chef's hat and an apron.

"Halloo, wonderful to see you," squeaked the squirrel. "Come in, meet the wife, I'll pop the kettle on."

The Professor closed the door on the squirrel's face.

"And some will be a tremendous waste of time." She paused. "Though on the plus side squirrels do make wonderful tea and crumpets."

"Professor, there are thousands of trees here," Molly exclaimed. "How am I supposed to know which leads out?"

The door to the Professor's oak opened and she stepped backward through the entrance.

"Now if I told you that, then there would be no challenge in the game. It's all about knowing yourself and controlling your gifts."

The door slowly closed and the tree disappeared in the ground from whence it sprang.

"Now remember," her voice echoed, "you have two lives left. And if you wish to leave the game simply say 'End game.'"

With that the Professor was gone. Arran and Molly were once again alone.

Arran wandered the wood, looking for some sort of clue. In truth he was probably looking for a tree with the words: THIS WAY TO THE EXIT. He had no such luck; all of the trees were, to his eyes, more or less identical.

"Know yourself, control your gifts," he repeated to himself. "But how?"

He eventually made up his mind to sit down right where he stood and not move till he could think of something a little more constructive than to amble through the forest, aimlessly pounding on barks of trees. To his mind he could die of starvation before finding the right one.

Molly's tactic was rather different. She spent the first thirty minutes tiring herself out by knocking on every tree she could, but received no indication that the pathway out lay ahead. She did, however, receive two invites to tea from a family of field mice, see a sign which said certain death this way, and meet a disgruntled badger waving his fist and moaning at how he was on nightshift and that she had just disturbed the most perfect dream.

She then walked for hours, randomly knocking on trees, feeling lost, clueless, and alone. She had never given up on anything in her life, but strongly considered speaking aloud the words "End game" and taking the easy way out.

After kicking another tree in frustration she sat down and began to sob. Arran, who had not moved and was now sitting cross-legged, in contemplation, heard her cries and looked around. Though he could not see her, he felt her anguish. *Molly, I wish you could hear me*, he thought.

Molly looked up and glanced around. "Arran, are you there?"

Arran heard that too. *Yes, I'm here*. His internal messaging system seemed to be working remarkably well. *Are you still stuck in the wood too?*

"Is this what the Professor was talking about with us being twins?" Molly asked.

Arran nodded his head, then reminded himself that she could not see him. *Yes, I think so*, he answered in his mind.

Molly stood and began walking randomly through the trees again, brushing her hands on them as she passed.

"I'm stuck," she admitted. *"I can't see my door for all these stupid trees. There's too many!"*

Arran thought for a moment. *"Remember the thing the older Professor was saying about the coin, how there was only one coin for one person and it wanted to be found by its owner?"*

"Yes," Molly said, kicking a stone into an unsuspecting oak.

"Maybe it's the same with the trees. You know one tree for one person, practice for when we get into the games. Our Professor said it's about controlling our abilities. Maybe we have to use our abilities to find it?"

"Okay," answered Molly impatiently, *"I got that, but how?"*

Arran shrugged. *"I dunno."*

"Well, thanks for nothing then. What are you saying? Use my death stare? On a tree!?"

"I don't know," Arran replied. *"Was just an idea."*

"Well, it was a stupid one. Whoever heard of doing a death stare on a tree?"

"Oh, like you're the expert! Up until yesterday you'd never heard of doing a death stare." Arran retorted. *"Who's to say that if you have your own personal tree it won't respond to the death stare?"*

She shook her head unconvinced.

Molly's heightened state of frustration, given the situation, made it quite easy for her to use the death stare if she wanted to. Arran's recent revelation made no sense to her; if anything, she found it very irritating.

She stood in the densest part of the forest and took a couple of deep, controlled breaths. Her heart rate gradually increased as her eyes glowed blue, shining like an imposing beacon. She was angry, frustrated, and wanted nothing more than to be out of there.

On impulse every tree in the place mirrored the human response to the death stare and took cover in the ground, each rapidly disappearing from sight till there were none left.

"Perfect!" She collapsed onto the ground. *"Now instead of trees there are miles and miles of empty fields!"*

Just as she was about to give up, the Professor's voice and that of Headmaster Dews rang out in her ears, slightly overlapping one another:

Control your abilities.

Power without control, particularly yours, can be dangerous.

Can you control your ability, Molly?

She stood again. "Okay, I'm ready," she said. "You can come out now." The trees, like frightened children, slowly and cautiously re-emerged, growing once again to their full height.

She filled her lungs with air, looking both left and right; her eyes turned bright blue, only this time not with the same dangerous intensity. Molly was concentrating and searching for the tree that "felt" right.

Almost instantly every tree in the forest turned a charcoal black, all except for one elm, which seemed to grow bigger, with multi-coloured light dripping from the skeletal branches like the first melted icicles of spring.

The tree glided slowly toward her.

Thanks, Arran, she thought as she knocked three times on the bark. The door opened and she was greeted with a handshake by Alfie the sports teacher.

"Congratulations, Molly, you are progressing to the next level. Come with me."

She followed him inside and the door closed behind them.

Chapter Forty-Seven

The Train Platform

Molly stepped onto on a grey cobbled train platform. There was no train and apart from a few metres of track, which spanned the length of the platform, no train tracks either. There were no birds in the sky, no sky even. It seemed there wasn't even ground underneath the platform.

It was as though she and the sports teacher had walked into an artist's canvas, which had been waiting for him to return and finish what he had started.

To say the place was deserted or lifeless would be a vast understatement.

Molly edged past Alfie and closer to the platform edge, curious to see if the tracks and platform were indeed floating in mid-air, or mid-canvas.

"I wouldn't do that, young lady; I wouldn't want you falling in."

"Into what?" Molly asked, shrugging her shoulders. "There's nothing down there."

"Quite so, young lady, would you like to fall into an endless and bottomless sea of nothing?"

"Good point." Molly stepped back; she was curious, but not so much that an endless trip into oblivion was worth the effort. "Where are we?" she asked.

"The platform," Alfie replied matter-of-factly.

Ask a stupid question, thought Molly, *and receive the most obvious answer invented*.

"Okay," she said, changing tact, "where will the train be taking us?"

Alfie laughed. "Very funny, Molly."

She simply shrugged. "Well?"

Alfie looked up from his pocket watch and a wave of realisation hit him. "Of course!" He slapped his brow. "You're not from here, are you? Headmaster Dews told us you and your brother were from out of town. Do excuse me."

I only want to know where the train is taking us and when it will be here. Fairly standard questions really, Molly thought.

"The platform is how we travel around in the Tempus Network, but there is no train. If we are travelling to London, for example, then we send a request using this." He held up his pocket watch. "And London comes to us. No need for a train or any other form of transport till we actually get there."

"What do you mean London comes to us?"

"It's a bit over my head, to be honest; it's like space can be folded in on itself. Imagine two points on opposite ends of a piece of paper. To bring those points together you can either take the long route and travel from one end to the other or you can just fold the paper till the two points touch. We are one point; our destination is the other."

"Clever. Does it work outside of the Network?"

"Yeah, right." Alfie laughed. "I don't even think the great Professor Tempus can do that; imagine if you could though." He looked up at the absent sky. "What would be next, time travel?"

Molly said nothing.

She may be wandering around in a land that her own imagination would have denied as mere fantasy, but, even here, she had knowledge of something that no one else did. Time travel was possible.

Bad luck, old Professor Tempus, Molly thought. The time machine had been discovered and built by her very own Professor Rebecca Tempus.

"Shouldn't be long now," Alfie said, staring again at his pocket watch.

Molly glanced over his shoulder. Written on the watch were the words "Shouldn't be long now." *Dare I ask?* "Your watch isn't very specific," she said.

Alfie looked almost hurt, closed the watch, and placed it back in his waistcoat pocket. "It's very accurate actually."

"*Shouldn't be long now* doesn't sound very accurate to me."

"Well, it wouldn't, would it? This is my watch, not yours, and what it says is very accurate to me. If you were lucky enough to own a watch, which you don't, the Tempus Network would make sure it expressed itself in a manner more in keeping with your particular sensibilities. It's all very individual 'round here, you know."

Molly shook her head. "Okay, what does *shouldn't be long now* mean to you?"

"It means three, two, one; look over there."

He pointed at the blank canvas sky to the right of the platform. There in the distance, a single starling flew slowly toward them. Each flap of its wings brought with it something so beautiful and unusual, it nearly drove Molly to tears.

Like a painting being born, the blue sky began to form around the bird, clouds too. Another flock of birds, a variety Molly had never seen, flew past. One landed briefly on the platform, then after a brief rest took to the sky again. The sun shone upon the newly formed trees, houses, and fields, illuminating the most beautiful-smelling flowers and the city that surrounded them.

A single ship could be seen in the distance surrounded by a vast and peaceful ocean. It was as though Molly and Alfie had been standing in a paint-by-numbers scene, which was then seamlessly completed around them.

Once the city parked up in front of them, a man in a blue conductor's uniform and little blue cap stepped off the street and out onto the platform. He tipped his hat in recognition of the sports teacher.

"Afternoon, Alfie."

"Bert," he acknowledged. "One for the second stage of the Tempus Games, please."

"Ah." Bert crouched down to look at Molly, who smiled back politely. "So you've made it this far, young lady? Jolly good luck in retrieving your coin."

"Thank you, Mr Bert," Molly replied with a polite curtsy. "I'll do my best."

"What a charming young lady," Bert said to Alfie, standing upright again to speak with him. "Ship, is it?" pointing into the distance. Alfie nodded. Bert took Molly by the hand and they walked toward a rowing boat tied up by the water's edge.

Molly looked around just in time to see the platform and Alfie disappear and be replaced by a row of shops and a middle-aged man who was walking alongside his dog. She was too far away to hear anything, but from the body language it looked as though they were having a bit of an argument.

Bert rowed Molly to the bottom rung of a ladder that led directly to the ship deck.

"Safe journey, young lady." Bert waved her off the boat. Molly thanked him and climbed the ladder.

She spent much of the boat ride wondering if Arran had made it out of the forest and tried to establish some sort of psychic connection with him.

Chapter Forty-Eight

Arran's Journey

Arran wandered the forest, relying on pure instinct to tell him which tree was his. He must have walked past fifty or sixty trees before eventually stopping at a silver birch; its leaves were browner than the rest, almost rusted, and had a variety of colourful flowers growing on the ground beneath its branches. He couldn't explain why, but this *was* his tree.

Before he knocked, he decided to put his own ability to use just in case his choice was wrong.

He closed his eyes. When he opened them he had multiplied. Thousands of Arrans, all part of the same collective consciousness, stood next to a different tree, spanning every tree in the forest. The Arrans all knocked three times in perfect unison.

The forest seemed to momentarily come alive, with thousands of doors being opened from within. The responses from the inhabitants ranged from warm and welcoming, to informative, to crude and threatening, but none of them led out of the forest.

"Well, if this doesn't work it's back to the drawing board."

His other selves disappeared and he knocked three times on the bark of the birch.

In the doorway an image began to materialise. Victor Graston propped himself up against the doorway.

"I wouldn't come through this one if you know what's good for you, Arran."

Victor's biting remark was nicely complimented by the twisted, scornful, and threatening look on his face.

Arran hesitated, stepping back slightly, entertaining the thought that his initial theory may have been wrong; maybe this wasn't his tree after all. Something kept him from moving away completely, however, despite the barrage of threats Victor had begun to hurl in his direction.

"I warned you, Arran. Stay out of my way; your little sister's not here to protect you now."

Tiny beads of sweat fell from Arran's brow. He wished he wasn't but he was scared.

Help came in kind from his sister's voice.

"You were right, Arran, trust your instinct. This game knows you as well as you know yourself."

"Well," Arran said finally and firmly, "if that really is you, Victor, then the one thing I would never do is trust you, and since you are telling me to back away…" He paused for slight contemplation. "I'm going to move ahead."

Arran took a giant step toward the doorway and the image

instantly changed from that of Victor to Alfie the sports teacher. He had made it through.

Chapter Forty-Nine

The Spletka Scout

"Team leader, there you are, me old mukka."

The scout quickened his pace to join his colleagues, but not so fast as to raise any unnecessary alarms.

"Why did you move from your position?" the team leader asked.

"Thought I heard something; was just about to check it out." He shrugged. "Think we should? I do." His playful bravado in such a dangerous place unnerved the rest of the men.

The team leader stood, arms folded, looking decidedly unimpressed. "Sir?"

The scout looked at him. "What?"

Through gritted teeth the team leader elaborated, "When you are speaking to a superior officer, the sentence should be: 'Do you think we should check it out, *sir*?' And while we're on, try substituting the word 'investigate' in place of check it out!"

The scout, though he apologised, was clearly as far from sorry as one could ever be. In fact, he seemed quite amused.

"Sorry, SIR. I heard a scream, SIR, a little girl, SIR, in that building over there, SIR. I thought it prudent we…investigate, SIR. But you are the sir, SIR."

Had this confrontation been on more neutral ground, the scout would have faced immediate disciplinary action, but seeing as they were standing in the middle of one of the most dangerous places in the city, the team leader and captain decided to finish business here, then deal with his oddly behaving colleague later.

"Lead the way, scout."

"Certainly, sir. It would be an honour and a privilege."

The scout smiled as he walked, almost skipped, completely fearless with his hands behind his back toward number 39.

The patrol of six men behind followed very carefully, despite the overt boldness of the scout.

Outside the door, six distinct voices could be heard, children crying. The scout's eyebrows rose as he slapped his captain on the back. "See. I told ya. Tell you what, you guys stay here and I'll go in and see what's wrong with the little cherubs."

"You stay here!" the captain commanded sternly. "I don't know what's come over you, but I'm not risking you going in there."

"Okey dokey," the scout replied.

"The rest of you with me." The captain led his men inside.

Once they were all through the entrance, the door slammed shut behind them. The scout put his ear to the door and smiled. The children's cries were very quickly replaced by screams, the screams of six grown men who were about to become undercover agents for the Spletka Clan.

Chapter Fifty

The Door

After knocking three times on the pillar the usual doors appeared and the Professor motioned toward the orb room. Before she had time to push the door, something out of the ordinary caught her eye.

The adjacent door, marked "Professor Richard Tempus," was slightly ajar.

My father's returned? Her first thought was quickly displaced by a second. She remembered Mike mentioning the name of the only other person who could open that particular door: Jhonas Spletka!

She wondered if it was a coincidence that this was the only time she had approached the pillar without company. Maybe whoever was in there wanted her on her own. It crossed her mind that she should go get Mike, maybe a couple of guards too.

For two minutes she simply stood and stared, looking to see if anyone would leave the room or if she could hear anything. The place was silent.

"This is stupid," she said to herself. "I shouldn't do this alone." The moment she took a step away from the door it clicked shut.

Scientific curiosity compelled her to turn and face the door again. Completely on cue, the door opened slightly. Someone or something was definitely extending an invitation. How sinister or friendly that invitation was, the Professor did not know but it was clear it wanted her to enter.

She walked in and the door closed slowly behind her.

Chapter Fifty-One

The Tempus Games

Arran and Molly stood on deck with around one hundred other children, including Victor Graston, his girlfriend Joss, and the rest of his gang, all of whom were looking directly at Arran. One boy clenched his hand into a fist and punched the open palm of his other hand. Arran looked away and Victor sniggered; any action taken to intimidate his new victim would always be met with approval.

They were on board what looked like an old-fashioned pirate ship which was battling with the elements to take them safely to their next destination. The city was far behind them and what was once a tranquil ocean had become more enraged, rocking the ship from side to side, perhaps reminding all aboard that courage and tenacity were needed if they were to succeed.

Alfie appeared on deck and began to speak with a young girl, Annabel Summer, who was crouched down on the floor, head in between her legs. She quite obviously did not like the sea and felt rather scared and nauseous.

Victor, egged on by a couple of his friends, took a step toward Arran, who instinctively took a step back. Molly on impulse jumped in between them. "You sure you want to go there?" she shouted.

Victor let out a nervous laugh. "I was only going to wish the DOA good luck," he lied.

Arran placed his hand on his sister's shoulder and spoke softly. "It's all right, Molly. I've got this." Reluctantly she stepped to one side.

Victor was visibly surprised by this sudden act of bravado, even if it was delivered in an unconvincing way.

"What do you want, Victor?" Arran asked.

"Like I said to your protector, DOA. I just wanted to wish you good luck."

Arran glanced at his sister. "She's not my protector. And any problem you have with me can be settled with me and me alone, after I have retrieved my coin."

Victor and all of his gang (except Joss, who still found it hard to make eye contact with Molly) let aloud a huge, thunderous roar of laughter.

"You don't actually expect you will get your coin, let alone before me, do you?"

Arran stayed silent, but nodded his head.

"Fine. I'm going to enjoy humiliating you and your protector. Pity your other weedy friend isn't here to see it too."

Arran scanned the deck of the ship. No Rudolph. He felt sorry for his newly found friend.

The twin psychic connection must still have been strong because Molly sighed before answering her brother's thought with one of her own:

Yeah, I know. Don't worry, we will get through this. Victor needs to be taught a lesson. From now, I'm not looking for my coin. I'm helping you.

Thanks, he thought, smiling and glancing quickly at her.

Her next psychic communication made Arran smile too. *Way to go standing up to that bully. I'm proud to be your sister.*

Alfie marched to the centre of the deck and addressed the crowd. As soon as he started to speak, the ship's movement together with the sea and the seagulls in the air completely ceased.

"Can I have your attention please?"

Annabel stood weak-legged beside him, her head hung in shame.

"Young Annabel here has opted out of the game, which leaves space for one other to join our merry crew. Well done, Annabel, for making it this far and better luck next year."

The teacher clapped his hands together. Annabel disappeared and in her place Rudolph stood with a rather surprised expression on his face.

"Congratulations, Rudolph." Alfie shook his hand. "You are still in the game. You may join the rest of the crew." Arran and Molly both clapped in approval as he walked over to them.

The ship, the birds, and the sea began to move once more. Victor stepped in and blocked the path between Rudolph and Arran. Rudolph simply stood still, not wanting to give his aggressor an excuse to beat him to a pulp.

"Going somewhere, Donkey?"

"Get out of his way, Victor, save it for the game."

Victor was surprised once again that this command was

delivered by Arran.

"If your sister and Alfie weren't here…" Victor started, then stepped back when Molly smiled and gave him a wink. "We'll settle this later, DOA. Just me and you."

Victor and his gang turned and walked to another area of the deck, all except Joss.

"What do you want?" Molly snapped.

"Look, I know you have no reason to trust me," Joss said weakly, "but I'm sorry. Truly, for what I did to your brother, and I don't know…" She started to cry, then quickly wiped her tears. "I don't know what you did to me, but the pain of everybody—and I mean everyone I've mocked and hurt—has been haunting me ever since." She tilted her submissive face for the first time to look Molly in the eyes. "I just want it to stop."

Molly had no reply. Her rehearsed answer, "Get out of here, go join your boyfriend before I do a death stare on you!" seemed now to be wildly inappropriate.

"It's okay, Joss," Arran interjected kindly. "No hard feelings."

"Thank you." She joined Victor and his gang, ignoring the "What were you doing over there with the DOA?" and "Did you tell him we would get him?"

Joss said nothing but turned once more to exchange a brief look of grateful understanding with Arran.

"What happened to you, Rudolph?" Molly finally asked.

Rudolph shrugged. "I think there's a time limit. Those who are left, don't make it out of the forest till the game ends. I found my tree just too late. That was until someone who had already made it decided to leave the game. Who was it by the way?"

"Some girl called Annabel Summer."

"I don't know her," Rudolph replied. "But you'll have to remind me to thank her later."

A seagull, perched on the main sail, yelled in a voice so ear-splitting that all aboard could hear: "Land ahoy!" He then ruffled his feathers proudly as Alfie addressed the crowd.

"Very soon we will be arriving on the island and I will be leaving you. From here the game is very simple: you must be the first to find your coin. There will be helpful clues and some designed to be less than helpful. You are not permitted to touch any coin that is not your own. That will mean instant disqualification. That being said, all is fair in love and war, and you may use whatever tactics and abilities you have to throw your opponents from their trail."

Three miles from the island the sea calmed and the ship stopped.

"This is where the ship stays, people. Remember, each and

every one of your coins *is* on the island. The time has come for me to say farewell. Good luck one and all."

Alfie clapped his hands and disappeared from the ship deck.

Chapter Fifty-Two

Rebecca Learns the Truth

The Professor, surrounded only by the darkness of the room and an eerie sense of familiarity, listened carefully for any sign of movement. The only sound she could hear was that of her own heart and breath…and something else.

Her natural scientific curiosity, together with the will to find her father, prevented any thoughts of escape to take prominence in her mind. She was no robot of course; feelings of fear and trepidation continued to pass through her in regular waves.

"Too much to ask for a little illumination?"

A blue light to her right instantly switched itself on; its origin was unclear but it shone down on a bed, upon which lay a sleeping body, somebody whom she recognised instantly. She cried as she moved toward him.

"Well, I'm here, Father."

She sat on the chair by his bed and touched his hand. It was ice cold, but he couldn't be dead. His dirty shirt and buttoned tweed jacket moved gently up and down in time with his sleeping breath.

She stroked his hair. "Am I too late?"

There wasn't so much as a flicker of the closed lids of his eyes.

She knew there would be no response. That would be too easy. Her words were choked with emotion as she softly spoke.

"It's a forlorn hope but I'm here now, you can wake up."

Tears fell gracefully on his hand, before rolling onto the bed.

"Please wake up, Dad."

She sat motionless, not sure what to think, cursing her own intellect for not providing a solution. This was her father's sleeping body, of that there was no doubt, but his living spirit was absent, she could feel it. Her head began to throb. Trying to come up with an answer without having access to all the facts was a near impossible task.

Surely her father would have intended her to come before he ended up in this catatonic state. But the date on the letter he left—3021—was quite specific. The thought occurred that maybe there was something wrong with the time machine and she was in some future date.

"I just don't see why you had me brought here now if you're..."

A sharp pain on the back of her head made her wince and spin around.

The rest of the room was still dark but there were definite sounds, footsteps followed by a door slam. Before she had time to focus on whose footsteps they were and where they came from, she heard another set of steps, then another, then another, and so it continued till soon it began to resemble the sound of a busy train platform in the dark.

A ghostly, glowing figure of a lady walked through the closed door to stand directly behind her. Still sitting, the Professor spun around to look her in the eyes. She was astounded to see she was looking at herself. The figure was dressed exactly the same and looking, not at her but right through her at her father.

Her ghostly double began to speak. "Father, I'm here," she said softly, before turning to face the back wall.

All of a sudden another voice from the opposite side of the bed spoke. "I'm here, Father. What should I do?"

The voice came from yet another ghostly replica of herself.

As she looked around the room, she saw many different versions of herself appear, all unaware of each other's presence. Some were silent and pensive, some paced in frustration, whilst others stood still in contemplation.

None of the apparitions noticed her. Some of them would stop and say things like:

"Father, I need your help" or "Please, I can't do this alone."

One stood on the other side of her father yelling into his ear.

"Wake up. I need you now. The children are trapped!"

After the constant barrage of noise and movement, the Professor watched as one at a time, as if they were late for an appointment, each of the apparitions ran from the room. Though the closed door did not move, each exit was accompanied by the sound of a door opening and closing. In one case, the sound of a door being slammed shut.

Time travel, the Professor thought.

Rather than jumping to the conclusion that this had been nothing more than madness, or an optical illusion, she supposed that each of the apparitions was another version of her living self, caught in a perpetual time loop. Why they all seemed to converge here and now, she was less clear on; perhaps her father made it possible for her to see them. But why? To avoid the mistakes her other selves had made?

The difference was, this time she could see all her previous attempts play before her eyes. Did this mean she was on the right track?

"You are the only constant here," she said to her father. "Unchanging throughout an otherwise evolving environment, yet somehow guiding everything. But to what end?"

The blue orb of light that had shown Rebecca her father moved down so it was level with her head, almost staring into her eyes. She was not scared or nervous; in fact she felt more relaxed than she had been in some time. She reached out her hand and touched it.

Once contact had been made, the room exploded in a blinding

light. She felt no danger in this and had no urge to cover her eyes. Instead she watched as the room around her transformed into her father's laboratory.

Her father sat at the desk, scribbling into his notebook, whilst a young girl of perhaps six or eight sat playing in the time machine, pretending for the most part it was a horse and carriage.

Like an unseen ghost, the Professor crouched down to see the innocent face of her younger self as she pushed a button on the machine and spoke.

"Is that Eloi command? We're coming in to land. Morlocks approaching. We'll be there in a few minutes."

I remember this, the Professor thought and laughed a sentimental laugh. She turned around to face the basement door. *And I think I remember what happens next.*

The basement door opened and a man, almost identical to her uncle John, walked in. He had long black hair and was dressed in army black material attached to a flowing ceremonial robe.

The young Rebecca Tempus exited the machine, ran up, and embraced him. "Uncle Jhonas!"

Jhonas patted her on the head before directing his attention toward Richard Tempus.

"How's it going, my old friend?"

Richard rose from his seat, shaking Jhonas by the hand, his face as giddy as an expectant child on Christmas Eve. "The Tempus Network is self-sustaining! The energy behind this planet and its neighbouring celestial bodies now runs directly through this house."

He placed his hand on Jhonas's shoulder.

"I am honoured to have been gifted control of it. At my request, old friend, you will be charged with safeguarding this as well as our precious Citadel. You must understand, in the wrong hands this energy could be disastrous. Positive energy can be converted to negative."

"What energy?" Jhonas shrugged. "And gifted from whom?"

"That I am not permitted to say. Suffice to say, the human race has evolved to a point at which our destiny is well and truly in our own hands. I monitor the balance and make necessary adjustments, if and when they are needed." Richard Tempus studied his friend's blank expression. "You have a question?"

Jhonas walked to the bookshelf and ran his fingers slowly left to right along the tiers.

"Look, Richard, you are my oldest friend, and my employer. If you want me to help protect something, then of course I will." He paused and scratched his head before continuing. "You say there's a universal energy that runs through this house. I don't see it; you're asking me to protect something without having any concept of…"

The Professor smiled, walking over to join Jhonas by the bookshelf.

"I will allow you to see the world momentarily through my eyes."

The Professor stood toe to toe with Jhonas, whose impressive build and size meant that he towered over him. Tempus raised his hands and placed them on Jhonas's temple.

"Close your eyes, old friend. When you open them, you will temporarily see just what it is that you are protecting."

Little Rebecca Tempus stopped playing in her time machine. The look on Uncle Jhonas's face had become far more interesting.

His eyes were wider than she had ever seen them; it was as though he was using them for the very first time. The wonders his senses beheld were obviously beyond compare.

"Are you okay, Uncle Jhonas?" The young girl noticed that his eyes had started to water.

He slowly turned to face her, opening his palms toward the heavens. A multitude of emotions ran through his body, making him want to laugh, cry, shout, and sing, all in one breath.

He reached out and touched the Professor's desk, then gasped as an overwhelming feeling of renewed positive energy ran though his veins.

"The power," he said. "I've never felt so...alive."

His attention turned from the house to the Professor himself. "It's in you too, Professor, more than anything. I can see it running through your veins. I can feel it!"

To say he could now see his old friend in a new light would be an understatement. The Professor's body was glowing bright blue and radiated such wisdom, compassion, knowledge, and command.

As quickly as the words were spoken Jhonas witnessed his environment return to that which it had been before. Feeling a little lightheaded and weak at the knees, he sat down.

The Professor sat on the corner of the desk to face him. He took his hand. "Now you see?"

Jhonas nodded in agreement.

Richard smiled. "In effect, my old friend, to protect this power, you **will** be protecting me."

"With your strength and power you don't need protecting, Professor. You could annihilate anyone who stood in your way."

"My strength comes from the conscious decision that I would never do that."

Jhonas, finally feeling his rational mind return ever so slightly, asked: "If you have control over the energy of the planet, why don't you just banish all negative energy? People and animals would be nice to one another, there would be no murders, no burglaries, no unnecessary violence, no…"

"This is a living energy, my friend," the Professor said calmly. "I believe it has chosen me because I understand that good cannot exist without evil, and to take away people's right to choose to be good or indeed bad would be nothing more than an endorsement for all that is evil in the world." He stared at a book on the shelf. "A great man once said: 'When I despair I remember that all through history the ways of truth and love have always won. There have been tyrants and murderers and for a time they can seem invincible. But in the end they always fall. I have faith, my friend.'"

He turned to face Jhonas once more. "For the most part the human race must be allowed to choose their own destiny, I just give it a helping hand."

"Can your power be taken?" Jhonas asked.

The Professor shook his head. "No, not whist I live. I can gift the power to another."

"And if you were to die, what then?" Jhonas asked cautiously, not knowing how the Professor would react.

For the first time Jhonas saw his old friend as a more imposing creature than himself.

"I really don't know, Jhonas," the Professor sighed. "It is

fortunate I can count on your protection."

The vision ended and Rebecca Tempus opened her eyes. She watched as her father slept just as he had done before. His gentle voice spoke from within the light.

"Go back to the beginning."

The closed door clicked open and after one last look at her sleeping father, she stood and slowly walked from the room. The door closed and locked itself behind her.

Chapter Fifty-Three

Preparing for War

The general raised his hands as though he was surrendering to the sky and fell to his knees. A bolt of lightning pierced the clouds, striking him in the heart. The assembled crowd of loyal Spletka followers were silent, watching in perfect love and admiration as their leader rose to his feet, unaffected, perhaps even a little stronger. Thunder crashed above and he took a deep breath before addressing his army.

Bellonta stood behind him. She bowed her head dutifully, in respect of her husband; an action which was followed by the rest of the crowd.

"People, animals, and earth elements that have wisely joined with us, our time has come. Our wait to yield the eternal power that Professor Tempus selfishly had claimed as his own for so many years is at an end. We now know the location of the Citadel; and more than this," he bellowed, clenching his fist and snarling.

"The good Professor's own daughter, the one he had hidden

from us for so long, has returned. Control of her will gain us the obedience of the Citadel and ultimately control over the greatest life force ever to be seen by any living entity since the dawn of time. Today, people, is the day of the Spletka!"

The crowd's chanting started as a low murmur and steadily grew to a sound so loud that its echoes could be heard on the outskirts of the city. "Spletka, Spletka, Spletka!"

The general looked toward the seven soldiers he'd recently enlisted. They stood guarding the crowd perimeter, to make sure there was no uninvited guests. The general, though he was an imposing character, was still not in full health, his face still white and gaunt, his body still weak.

His recent visits to the middle of the city had not salvaged enough spiritual energy; the few victims he had managed to capture in his death stare were not enough to restore him to his former glory. A brief nod from the scout, indicating that all was as it should be, told him that it was safe to continue.

"The late Professor has passed an energy to his daughter, an energy which I shall take great delight in prying from her dying corpse. This energy, my friends, shall transform me back to that which I once was. This energy will once again herald the return of Jhonas Spletka!"

The crowd's applause once again filled the city. Joy to the loyal supporters and terror for anyone else unfortunate enough to hear the deathly cheer.

The tired eyes of the leader looked toward his wife Bellonta, who, sensing her leader's fading energy, took him by both hands.

"I am ready," she said with complete devotion and loyalty.

He began to take deep meditative breaths in and out. Bellonta's breathing mirrored that of her husband. His eyes turned that familiar jet black as he drew life and energy from her body. Slight colour returned to his cheeks as she grew paler and paler; tears snail-trailed down her face till eventually she let out a piercing scream, at which point the general broke physical contact with his wife.

Bellonta, weak and unsteady on her feet, was led away from the crowd by two of the armed guards. The general turned one last time to his followers.

"Our time for skulking in the shadows is over. Those among you who have your assigned tasks, go now. As for the rest of you, combine your skills, abilities, and loyalty to the Spletka Clan, for on this day we take the power and our rightful place as rulers of this planet!"

Chapter Fifty-Four

Back to the Beginning

"Go back to beginning," Rebecca Tempus mused as she stood outside the entrance to the Orb room.

There was little doubt in her mind as to what her father meant by that; she must go back to when she was a child, the time when her father showed Jhonas the wonder of the house, back to the time of the vision. For that she would need the time machine, which was hidden back at her house. *I'll need to call Mike and arrange transport to take me back*, she thought.

The door to the Orb room gently clicked open. The Professor smiled. *Maybe not.* She walked inside.

The room was still an exact replica of the laboratory she had left the time machine in, but it *couldn't be* the same room, could it? She fished around in her right pocket and retrieved the green button which, when pressed, would take the machine out of camouflage. When she pressed it, the button began to glow. She waited, standing on the spot where the time machine should be. Nothing happened.

Schoolgirl error, she thought. *The time machine is not going to materialise if I'm standing in its way.* She took a step back and the machine appeared. She touched the aluminium frame with her hand, silently welcoming it as though it were a long-lost friend.

She paused to consider Arran and Molly and whether she should wait for them before embarking on such a journey.

"I have a time machine," she said to herself. "I could be gone for hours, days even, and mere seconds would have passed by the time I return." Her mind was made up.

Once in the driver's seat the Professor ran her fingers across the dashboard.

"Okay," she pondered. "Not quite sure of the year; I was around six in the vision. I'm thirty-four now, which means I was born in 1991 and I was six in 1997. This should be interesting."

A sudden and unpleasant realisation struck her. The time machine was limited in its backward time travel capabilities. Without a photograph taken by the time machine at the correct time in 1997, she had no way of getting back there.

She banged her fist on the same dashboard she had been caressing only moments earlier.

"How could I be so stupid?"

There was a rustling of paper from within the inside pocket of her tweed jacket which prompted her to reach her hand inside and pull out an envelope containing her father's letter and the three photographs. The top photograph was a picture of the laboratory. On the reverse side, in tiny blue ink, was etched the numbers 1997.

"Oh, Father, you are a clever fellow." She smiled as she placed the photograph face down on the empty panel display in front of her. She fixed the green button back in its assigned slot and when it started flashing, she pushed it in. The machine began to vibrate as the outside environment faded from view.

Moments later she was in a laboratory nearly identical to the version she had left in 2021. She left the machine, nervous and aware that she was about to speak, face-to-face, with her father. Of course she would need to persuade him that the thirty-four-year-old woman he would be confronted with was in fact his six-year-old daughter and not some unlikely burglar with a similar dress sense to the proprietor of the house.

The laboratory was empty, not a soul in sight. She instinctively thought she should venture upstairs to search for her father. This was her house after all, though it would be some years before she could lay any validity to that statement.

The sound of someone coming down the stairs and into the laboratory made her quickly crouch behind the desk and out of sight. It occurred to her that the footsteps, now in the room, could be those of Jhonas Spletka, and so she decided to stay hidden.

They approached, and then stopped. This put the Professor on edge. Was she discovered? Her increased heart rate and anxiety disappeared as quickly as it had arrived, however, when the owner of the footsteps began singing, and by singing we speak in the loosest sense of the word:

"The sun will come out tomorrow, bet your big fat bottom that tomorrow, there's be a sun big, bright, and bouncy…"

The Professor bounced out from behind the desk. "Bouncy, er, I mean Batsy!" she exclaimed with her arms open.

"Ahh!" Batsy fell to the ground and shot her hands in the air, flinging the dusters and array of bottled cleaning products she had been holding around the room.

"W-W-Who are you?"

The Professor looked at her quizzically. "Batsy, for Pete's sake, it's me, Professor Tempus. The time machine must have got it wrong. I mean I'm supposed to be in 1997, but I'm right back here."

Batsy struggled to move her tubby frame to a standing position, then in complete amazement circled the Professor.

"Can it be true? Is it really you, Professor?"

"Yes, yes. It's me, Batsy. This is truly a unique experience for me. I'm actually pleased to see you."

"Why thank you, Professor." The cleaner offered a small curtsy. "Though I imagine the fact that you are a woman now must be slightly unique too."

The Professor was suddenly lost for words, clearly confused, yet not altogether surprised. She'd never thought of Batsy as being one blessed with anything more than a single brain cell.

"I've always been a woman, Batsy. The fact that I don't adorn myself with fine jewels and short, revealing skirts is hardly an indication that I am, in fact, a man."

"But, Professor, you were a man last week when you came to visit?"

Though it was very tempting to revert to her old habits and throw a shoe in Batsy's general direction, the Professor sensed a genuine concern in the housecleaner's voice. It occurred to her that if the time machine had done its job properly, Batsy would have no recollection of any lady going by the name of Professor Tempus, not yet anyway.

"Just who do you think I am, Batsy?" she asked carefully, studying the expressions on her housecleaner's face. She was searching for something more than the usual out-of-order sign.

"Why, Professor Richard Tempus of course, except he's a man and you... Well, you're not."

The Professor nodded. "It's a bit of a giveaway really, isn't it? My name is Rebecca. Professor Rebecca Tempus. Richard Tempus is my father."

The Professor was ready for Batsy to be still further confused, for the Rebecca Tempus to whom she was probably acquainted was no more than six years old at this point.

For the first time for as long as she could remember, however, the housekeeper genuinely surprised her.

"Then you'd better come with me, Professor."

She turned and walked from the laboratory and up the stairs into the dining room. After a short, stunned silence, the Professor followed her. Once inside the room, she was asked to sit and offered a cup of coffee, which she accepted.

"Okay, you have my attention."

Batsy took the seat across the table from her, pouring herself a small cup of Earl Grey. She twiddled with her fingers a moment in contemplation before speaking.

"Please forgive my earlier antics, Professor. I needed to be sure you were who you said you were. I know that you know me but I don't know you." She stopped. "Well, not yet anyway."

The Professor shook her head. "You don't know me as a thirty-four-year-old woman, but you do know me. By my calculations I am, in your time, a six-year-old child."

The housekeeper laughed. "No, I am not familiar with the Professor's daughter and only found out recently that he had a daughter, who may pay me a visit."

"Does my father not live here in this house?"

Batsy nodded. "Indeed he does, but not now. Your father is not of this time." She stirred her cup of tea, with teabag still present. "He was born a thousand years from now."

"How do you know of time travel?" the Professor asked her.

"Oh, Professor." She chuckled. "I may not be as smart as your father, or as you probably are, but I have my gifts; chief among them, good, old-fashioned, honest loyalty. Your father and I are great friends. He asked me to look after you. Both now and later in my future, which by now I assume is in your past."

The Professor thought back to all the times she had insulted Batsy, threw shoes at her, and generally credited the average amoeba with more common sense than she, and began to feel a little ashamed.

"Before I say any more, Professor, I must ask you a question. Why are you here?"

"A message. My father left me a message saying I must go back to the beginning. Clearly this is not it. I had a vision, a memory maybe?" She shrugged. "Clearly I was mistaken."

"No, you weren't mistaken." The housekeeper reached into the pocket of her apron and pulling out a photograph which she handed to the Professor.

"This is when it all began. Your father said you'd know what to do with it and asked me to tell you that when you arrive in this time, it will be exactly five minutes after you, Jhonas, and your father have left the room. You are to collect something."

The Professor pushed her coffee cup to one side and looked into the cleaner's eyes.

"Collect what?"

"Your inheritance," Batsy answered.

Chapter Fifty-Five

The Hatchling

Grombit lay on his bed, staring blankly at the ceiling. He had been there alone in that room for a little longer than he was comfortable with. A polite cough to his right made him turn.

"Hello, Grombit," Mike said, pulling up a seat beside him. "How are we feeling?"

The hedgehog turned. "Oh my worms, you startled me, Mike."

Mike put his hand on Grombit's shoulder. "Sorry, I didn't mean to…"

"Quite all right. How is the young girl, Molly?"

"Fine, fine." Mike nodded with a satisfied grin on his face. "Better than fine actually; there have been a few surprising side effects which we are still trying to understand."

"And everybody else, Arran, the Professor, the young Doctor Aiysha was it?"

"Aiysha's resting, and we'll know more soon. The Professor and Arran are fine."

"Can I see them?"

"I'll ask them to stop in. You have to stay put for the moment as we still have a few tests to run on you."

"Oh, Worms preserve us," Grombit complained. "I was hoping to get out of here. I can't seem to connect to the Tempus Network by the way. Not only that, my human hard light seems to have stuck. I can't turn back into myself."

"Yes, I know." Mike rose to check the display on the side of his bed.

"The spider's lieutenants, when they took control of you, did so when you were in human form. For the moment it has frozen you like this; we feared it was because one of the lieutenants had evaded our initial search and was exercising some sort of control over you or the Tempus Network, but we got them all, don't worry."

"That's a relief." Grombit pondered, screwing up his face. "And disgusting too. No offence of course, but I couldn't stay like this forever. I've just started dating my future Mrs. Grombit. She's even eaten my homemade Worm Wellington, without complaining. She'd have a turn if she saw me like this."

"Worm Wellington?"

"Oh yes, quite delicious, it's worms, served from a Wellington boot."

It was now Mike's turn to screw up his face. He wished Grombit a restful few hours, then left the room.

Grombit lay on the pillow and closed his eyes.

Behind his left ear a microscopic egg began to hatch, and out crawled a tiny lieutenant spider, which, with absolute military precision attached itself to his scalp and sinking its fangs in good and deep.

This was the connection Spletka needed to capture Molly. Using Grombit as a host, it wasted no time in hacking into the Tempus

Network, providing a direct doorway into the Tempus Games.

Chapter Fifty-Six

Sharks

The ship was parked three miles from the island.

Jennifer Connolly, a fifteen-year-old gymnast with enhanced swimming capabilities, confidently shrugged the challenge of how to get to shore by standing on the ship's edge and diving into the water.

"Come in, it's fine," she shouted, waving to some of her friends.

Just as they were about to jump in, one child pointed at something moving toward Jennifer at tremendous speed. A large dorsal fin emerged from the water. Jennifer, upon seeing this, swam as fast as she could to shore, chased by the ill-tempered and evidently hungry shark.

Jennifer was more thankful for her special ability than she had ever been. Even at her tremendous speed, the pursuing shark was very close to ending her chances in the games and perhaps even her life.

Arran turned to Rudolph. "What on earth was that?"

Rudolph was stunned.

"Rudolph, that thing could have killed her!"

It seemed from the faces of every child on the ship that this was not something they were used to. The Tempus Games were meant to be one of discovery, not survival.

One small boy started to cry. "I can't do this anymore," he wailed. "End game!"

According to the rules, simply speaking the words should have been enough to make him disappear from the ship deck and wake up in the school, but that didn't happen.

The boy who did not disappear spoke again, this time much louder, whilst wiping snot and tears from his face.

"End game, end game!"

Two bolts of lightning shot from the sky, which had turned a scarlet red, and seemed to electrify the sea, inspiring the calm waters to frantically move in all directions. There was no shelter either from the heavy rain that started to fall like tiny bullets upon the ship's deck.

As the little boy, whose fruitless cries of "End game" had aptly demonstrated, there was no escape.

Chapter Fifty-Seven

Till Next Time, Batsy

The Professor sat in her time machine, and Batsy stood by her side. She placed the picture Batsy had given her in the hollowed-out hole, and the green button began to flash. Batsy smiled down at her.

"Have a good trip, Professor."

The Professor thanked her and before pressing the button added: "When you do see me again I will have no knowledge of ever meeting you. Actually I will have very little knowledge of anything. I have been suffering from amnesia these past thirteen years, but do forgive my treatment of you. I have always been fond of…" She paused. "If my father is not of this time, then how is it I am of this time?"

Batsy smiled. "I'm sure you'll work it out, Professor. As you said, you have suffered amnesia. How sure can you really be where or when you come from?"

The Professor nodded, turned to the display, and pressed the button. The machine was gone.

Batsy ambled upstairs, poured another cup of tea, and like the weary traveller, began the long wait for the Professor's return.

Chapter Fifty-Eight

Tribble Makes a Choice

Tribble's wife was rather shocked to see two armed guards standing at the entrance to their rundown home and demanding to see her husband.

"What do you want with him, Officer? He is a peaceful soul, never done no wrong to no one."

The scout pushed in front of the captain and grinned; a failed attempt to ease her concern.

"Of course he hasn't, Mrs Tribble, I assume?" Mrs Tribble nodded. "We just need to," he paused, "ask him a few questions."

There was something she really didn't like or trust about these men, but they had all the correct documentation. There was no denying that they were who they said they were.

Resigned that these men were not going to leave without speaking to her husband, she begged them wait a few moments whilst she woke him up.

As it happened, waking him wasn't necessary. He was all too aware that he had unwelcome visitors and no form of escape; the fact that he was hiding under the bed, shaking like a three-year-old child in the middle of a thunderstorm, was very likely an impulse reaction.

"Are they gone?" he asked his wife, well, he asked his wife's feet, which were all he could see from his limited view from beneath the bed frame.

She crouched down so they were nose to nose and facing one another.

"No, dear, they are still here and I suspect here they will stay till you go out and speak with them."

She gently stroked his snout, something they had often done to one another as a reminder of the enduring love, affection, and trust they both shared.

"Is there something you wish to tell me?"

Tribble thought for a moment. He couldn't face his wife learning of all that he had done, nor could he risk his son's life, but he knew that were he to stay in the room a moment longer, the temptation to tell her everything may be too great.

Tribble didn't feel that courage was one of his greatest assets, but decided the lesser of two evils was to go outside and lie to the guards about whatever intel or connection they may have discovered between him and the Spletka Clan. He would then come back into the house and give his wife an even more pathetic and feeble lie about their reason for calling, which of course she would never believe.

"I'm sure it's nothing, dear. I'm sorry about this cowardly

demonstration," he said, feigning an unconvincing smile. "I'm just a little on edge these days, pressure and all."

He slid out from under the bed and dusted himself off.

"I'll go see what they want, my dear. I shan't be long."

I hope.

Tribble made sure the door was closed and his wife was not in earshot before looking at the blank, expressionless faces of the guards.

"W…W…What do you…that is, how can I help you, Officers?"

The scout sighed. "You may as well admit it, Tribble, we know about your connection with the Spletka Clan."

Tribble tried to hide his shock and dismay. How did they know?

He buried his head in his hands, avoiding all eye contact, considering what he should say next.

Hate wasn't a strong enough word to describe his feelings for the general and the Spletka Clan but he daren't say anything; his son's life depended upon it.

"I don't know what you are talking about, Officer. I've heard of the Spletka Clan of course, but well, who hasn't?"

"Tribble!" said the scout in the accusatory nature he'd used so often in interrogations, when he felt the need to superimpose his authority on unsuspecting captors in the past.

Tribble wanted so much to tell the guard everything he knew, and the scout's overwhelming influence over him served only as an added incentive, but he half-heartedly said, "No, I don't know what you mean. Your information is wrong."

Satisfied, the scout lifted him into the palm of his hand, which he raised till he was finally eye level with the defenceless mouse. He regarded Tribble carefully before smiling.

"Good. The general sends his greetings; and because you didn't crumble under pressure from me, your son's life has been extended, though I imagine the general's pet vulture will be a tad disappointed."

Tribble shot him a surprised look, to which the scout simply winked.

"Your services are now required. Make whatever excuse you like to your dear wife and come with us."

Tribble nodded, jumped from the scout's hand, and scampered back into his house.

Chapter Fifty-Nine

The Inheritance

The time machine stopped and the Professor stepped out. *Déjà vu*, she thought, *back in my lab again.* She tiptoed to the door and listened.

Exactly as her father's message had detailed, he, Jhonas, and her six-year-old self were upstairs.

"Sweetheart, put everything back when you are finished with it," she heard her father say and felt a grin of remembrance emerge from within.

She knew that her younger self was busy taking the grandfather clock upstairs apart to see how fast she could rebuild it.

"Come for my inheritance?" she pondered, collecting only her thoughts and wandering her all-too-familiar environment. "What inheritance?"

The Professor didn't have long to wait for that particular question to be answered. The time machine began to vibrate on its own, causing the floor beneath her feet to shudder.

Strangely, considering what she had been through already, this seemingly inconsequential event caused her an unusual amount of concern.

That should only vibrate when I tell it to do so.

She walked toward it and the machine began to glow a variety of colours. The vibrant spectrum flowed from it like a river and covered the whole room: the walls, the floors, the bookcases, the scientific equipment, and the forever aging objects on the shelves. Absolutely everything was transformed and so full of life.

As the colours intensified, so her concern disappeared and seemed redundant. The room in which she stood had become so inviting, so welcoming. Her natural scientific curiosity was placed on hold as she, for that moment, knew that this was not a time for questions, rather one to receive answers.

The colours surrounding the room began to rise like excited heat vapours and fill the room, slowly at first, then with increased vigour. Green, blue, red, and bright white auras formed and, as though they had a mind of their own, circled the Professor almost as if they were studying her.

Finally, they settled mid-air, right in front of her, and simply observed. An increasing urge to touch that which had initially found her so interesting overwhelmed her. She took a small step forward, extending her right hand, a gesture which could have quite easily doubled as one for friendship. The auras floated back a few centimetres, for the moment denying contact.

"It's all right," she whispered. "I won't hurt you."

As it had no definable form, the Professor could not *see* the aura's hospitable smile, but she certainly felt it.

She had never experienced anything like this before, but the aura felt so natural and so familiar, almost as if it had been there all along and for as long as she could remember, even taking into account her amnesia.

The Professor took a deep breath inward and as she did so, the auras followed and joined the passage of air which entered her body. The life force ran through her veins and joined with her beating heart, making her feel such love as she had never done before. Tears of joy fell from her eyes and formed a multi-coloured puddle as they fell to the floor. She felt blessed with something more than knowledge and power, but truth and empathy in their greatest degree.

She laughed.

"This is my inheritance?"

She opened her hands and watched as energy shot from her fingertips, flying out in all directions.

"Something I can truly never own. Nor would I want to."

"You can experience, you can influence the greatest and purest energy this planet has ever seen. That is ownership enough. You now have knowledge of all that is, all that was, and all that could ever be.

You see both good and evil, and though you can banish evil with a thought, you must keep a balance, for one cannot truly exist without the other."

Upon hearing the words, the Professor spun around to see her father standing propped up against the frame of the door. The colours and auras faded from sight, perhaps sensing that she craved a little privacy.

"Hello, Rebecca."

Surprised there were any tears left, she found herself crying once more.

"Father?"

His arms opened out in front of him, gesturing for her to come closer.

"You have your mother's eyes."

He took a brief look in the direction of the upper levels of the house, where his six-year-old daughter was in bed, sleeping underneath a sea of teddies and leftover grandfather clock parts.

"Then again you always have had."

Not risking the possibility that this was any type of illusion or for some unknown reason she, or he, would suddenly disappear, she ran to his open arms and hugged him for all she was worth. He returned the warm sentiment and the embrace. There they stood for at least two minutes without speaking a word; no sound from either apart from Rebecca's crying and the sniffs from her running nose, which she instinctively wiped on her father's shoulder.

"Sorry," she said, slightly embarrassed.

The elder Professor took a handkerchief from his pocket and wiped his shoulder.

"Quite all right, my dear; glad to see some things don't change."

A sudden wave of realisation.

Rebecca's eyes opened wide, and her mouth also craned open in a perpetual look of shock, searching for the right words

"Father. Oh my goodness," she finally said. "I know the future. I can tell you, and you can..."

"No, absolutely not!"

Her father's stern answer was accompanied by a contradictory and comforting gentle squeeze of her hands.

"You are a time traveller now; what has played out for you in your own time stream or is yet to play out for me is fixed. Just think, if you tell me what you want to and it influences my decision-making process, would you even be here now? Would I? Can you guarantee that the new future you create will be a better one?"

Rebecca paused, considering her father's words. "But..."

"Look inside yourself, my little girl, and within the new energy that flows in your veins. Let it be your guiding light. After all, it will be with you now until the day you die."

He stopped.

"Unless you willingly give it to another, but remember, you were chosen for a reason. And not just because you are my daughter."

She wanted to say so much, to thank him or whatever power it was that had chosen her. More than this, however, she wanted to save her father's life.

Instinctively she thought to look in her diary, the one she found in this very laboratory many years into the future when she was with Mike. Page two now had writing on it, again scribbled in her own handwriting, though it read like something her father would say:

The road less travelled, for the time traveller is sometimes the right one. There are no shortcuts here. Don't create unnecessary ripples, and trust in your abilities. There is more at stake than your father.

This inscription left her with an undeniable feeling that to say anything to her father about his possible demise at this point would be a grave mistake. She at least wanted to warn him about Jhonas, but anything she said, no matter how innocent she made it sound, would be instantly detected by her father, thereby changing the future. She bowed her head in resignation.

Her father broke the silence.

"So, do you have any children now, a husband?"

Rebecca shook her head politely, not used to speaking of such things, but she supposed of all the people in the world, her own father certainly had the right to ask.

"No husband, no time for…you know." Raising her eyebrows slightly and shrugging, she continued. "I do have two children, well, in a manner of speaking. They aren't mine in blood but we are close. I would adopt them in a heartbeat."

The very fact that she even let this enter her mind meant that she had absolutely no intention of returning Arran and Molly to their father, especially while there was still the possibility that he was Jhonas Spletka, which, if it were true, raised a whole new set of questions, chief among them being what he doing was living back in the past. If he were Jhonas, however, it perhaps answered one which she had often wondered before she first set off in the machine, regarding the sale of the house in which she was standing.

"Father, I don't feel it would betray future events to say one day I will own this house. What would happen if I were to sell it?"

Her father looked shocked. "That you must never do, Rebecca. This house is at the very centre of the universe and home to more than just you. The sun's rays can be felt and appreciated from thousands of miles away, but they are at their strongest from within the very core. We are standing on the spiritual core, if you like; it's now part of you." He pointed toward the time machine. "It's partly what makes my machine work and the reason why only I or one of my chosen bloodline can use it."

"But what use does the universe have for a legal document saying I have sold the house to another? Such a peripheral date-stamped concept surely holds no weight in the universe!"

"Indeed it doesn't, but selling the house will change something in you. Resigning yourself to the fact that you are leaving this house to another, especially now knowing what you do of the energy held within, will be seen as you willingly separating yourself from this gift, and in part at least, that gift will belong to another - provided they know of its existence, which thankfully few people do. At the moment it is known to just the two of us and my chief of security and long-time friend."

Jhonas Spletka, Rebecca thought.

Just at the point she thought she should at least warn her father not to trust the loyalty of his "long-time friend," something happened. She sensed the faint smell of the sea, heard children crying, and above all heard Arran and Molly shouting:

"Professor Tempus, we need you now!"

She looked to her father.

"I have to go, those two children I told you about…"

"No need to tell me." He kissed her on the cheek. "Your abilities will tell you where you are needed. Remember, the quickest path is not always the correct path. Safe journey, my daughter."

***

"Professor Tempus, we need you now!" Arran and Molly shouted amid the panicked shouts and screams of the children on the ship.

Arran crouched down, holding his sister close in an attempt to protect her.

The sea, like an ill-tempered child in the middle of a tantrum, lashed and threw its mighty weight against the hull of the ship, which rocked helplessly from side to side. Sharks leapt in and out of the water as though they were graceful dolphins, grinning their razor-sharp teeth at the children as they did so.

Chapter Sixty

Safety Off

Mike's door swung open and Alfie ran in.

"Forgive my intrusion, sir, we have a problem."

Alfie was shaking and sweating as though he had just seen or been the victim of a horrific accident.

"Sit down; what's your name?"

"Alfie, sir, sports teacher T.S.S.A.," he spluttered after releasing a few coughs to clear his throat.

Mike handed him a cup of water, which was taken and drained almost as soon as he had received it.

"Okay," said Mike, "calm down, start at the beginning."

Alfie took a deep breath and proceeded.

"The annual Tempus trials are in operation. After we gathered all those who had made it past the preliminary stage, the successful children were placed on the ship simulation, ready for the island— ready for the true trials to begin."

He coughed again and was handed another cup of water, which he only sheepishly sipped before placing it down on the bench.

"Thank you. Anyway, I left the simulation. Barely moments after I had got out, our monitors began to fade. I saw rogue elements in the program; things we did not put there. Almost as if some outside force was hacking the system. The sea turned wild. Loads of children started to cry 'end game' as their ship struggled to stay afloat, but we weren't able to bring them back. Then the safety was switched off."

Mike jumped up. "What do you mean the safety was switched off? Bring them back!"

"I tried, sir, we all did. When our persistence continued, we were locked out of the Tempus Network altogether. We can't even get into the school; everything's dead."

Mike took a couple of collective breaths. "When you say the safety has been switched off, does that mean…?"

Alfie nodded. "If we can't do anything, every child's life on that ship is potentially at risk. The only one who stands a chance of survival is the one who finds their coin—that is if the coins haven't been removed too. As for the rest…"

Mike sat down and buried his head in his hands before a disturbing thought seeped into his mind; this time he spoke slowly and calmly but with utmost determination.

"Were Arran and Molly on that ship?"

Alfie nodded "Yes, sir, I'm afraid they were."

Mike rose to his feet and ran to the door. "I need to find Professor Tempus."

Alfie looked confused. "But isn't he…?"

"Not him, Alfie, his daughter, Rebecca. Excuse me."

Chapter Sixty-One

The General's Plan

Though there was nothing out of the ordinary about the enormous oak table upon which Tribble was standing, he couldn't help but think of it as an elaborate excuse for a chopping board, with him auditioning not to be prepared as the main course. He humbly bowed his head.

"I didn't expect to see you so soon, sir."

The general's eyes, though worn and tired, emanated an almost victorious glow.

"Things are moving faster than I had anticipated, Tribble. One of our agents has managed to hack into the Tempus Network and, for the moment, restrict access."

Tribble raised an eyebrow; the world of computers was one of his gifts, and he knew first hand that hacking into the network was no easy task.

"He's good," the general continued. "But, well, how can I put it? He's not you. Our control over the network is not indefinite, and in time, the great Professor's daughter, if she now possesses the power, may work out how to free the souls we have trapped in there.

"There is one individual in particular we are interested in, a girl called Molly. If she can be persuaded to join us, then our arms would be insurmountable. If not," he pondered, then shrugged his shoulders, "so be it. She will die alongside every other child currently connected to the network."

Tribble was horrified at the thought of being potentially responsible for the deaths of hundreds, possibly thousands of children, but weighed up against the life of his own son, he reluctantly agreed.

The general sensed Tribble's unease and looked up to the rafters. His vulture stepped out from the shadows and took to the air, landing with a resonating thud at the general's side. It regarded the mouse with a greedy intensity that sent a deathly shiver down his spine.

"Of course you don't have to, Tribble; we could simply shake hands." The general stroked the vulture's head; it responded in kind by moving its body in and out of his palm much like an affectionate cat. "And my friend here can have an unexpected snack before lunch."

Tribble reverently shook his head. "What would you like me to do, sir?"

Satisfied, and somewhat amused, the general spoke on.

"Combined with your technical genius, you have a particular gift for illusion and mind manipulation, a gift for which I have a particular need. The young girl in question has not been in this land very long and should be easily fooled by your pathetic parlour tricks. Once we break into the Citadel you must enter the network and appear to the children as the good Professor's daughter, Rebecca Tempus. Once you have persuaded her to commit a few shameful acts and help our cause, we will have a new recruit and you can go home with your son."

He sighed a disparaging breath.

"Please don't fail me, Tribble, If Molly does not join us, your son and you will be of no further use to us. That would be a shame."

Chapter Sixty-Two

Arran Has an Ability

"Rudolph, what is your special ability?" Molly asked, grasping his arm with one hand. The other was being used to suck her thumb whist she huddled beneath her brother.

All through her life she had never been a fan of thunder and it was coming down with the same portentous persistence as the torrential rainfall.

"I'm just asking because if you can fly or something, it would be pretty handy about now."

"Advanced echo location," Rudolph answered solemnly. "I can close my eyes and find my way around quite easily; kind of like what bats do, but I feel vibrations."

"Oh good, that's useful." Arran's sarcastic snap was met with an apologetic shrug from his friend. He turned his full attention to his sister. "You okay?"

Molly didn't answer; she just sat head in between her knees praying for the nightmare to end. She didn't have long to wait to be reassured that her prayers were, for the moment, falling on deaf ears.

The continued sound of terrified screams from all the children was suddenly overpowered by a dark and menacing laugh which resonated from within in the psyche of every living soul aboard the ship.

The sensory overload became too much for Rudolph, who could hear not only the screams but the heartbeats of everyone aboard. His ability to block out unwanted sounds was, in his own heightened state of panic, redundant. He looked wildly in all directions for a safe haven and refuge. There was none.

"End game."

His feeble words barely registered in his own supersensitive ears and, as had been the case for every child who had spoken those same words, they went unanswered.

He fell to the floor, assuming a foetal position at Arran's feet.

For Arran, everything started to happen in slow motion. Muffled sounds and cries drifted through his numbed ears as though they were all happening underwater. His initial thought was that alarm and stress had combined forces, causing a temporary deafness. He was soon to discover that this was not the case when Rudolph yelled his name.

The high-pitched and crystal-clear tone rose above the bed of underwater sounds like a military jet plane. He reached down, pulling Rudolph up to a kneeling position.

"Something's wrong," Rudolph whispered.

These words had no trouble in reaching Arran's ears; though his response at this rather obvious statement was delivered with both sarcasm and anger.

"Really? You think so?!"

His sharp answer seemed to have no negative effect on his friend.

"No, you don't understand," Rudolph continued. "There's something under the ship, like a huge pointed iceberg. It's travelling at great speed." He placed his hands on the deck of the ship, closing his eyes. "It's coming fast; once it hits, this ship will go down."

Joss Minton was standing by Victor and his gang on the opposite side of the ship, too far away to hear what Rudolph was saying. But her reaction to what she had just read in Rudolph's mind was crystal clear.

She looked to Arran, who simply nodded in affirmation of Rudolph's last words. She whispered into Victor's ear, who ran across the deck to confront Arran.

"Hey, DOA, is what Joss said right? Is this ship going to sink?"

For the moment, Arran and Victor's fraught relationship didn't even register in Arran's mind as a concern. His survival instinct, together with the need to protect his sister and friend, was all he cared about.

"Yes, Victor, it's true."

Victor put his arm around Joss and pulled her close.

"Well, we'll be all right!" he shouted as a huge wave rose high above the ship then crashed down, soaking everyone on board. "I can levitate to the island."

Arran looked hopelessly at the many hundreds of children on the deck who clearly had no chance of escape.

"You've got to help them, Victor. How many people can you carry at once?"

Victor let out a piercing laugh. "Help you? Not a chance. I can carry two more, Joss and one other. Sorry, DOA."

Joss panicked. "Vic, you can't just leave them here to die."

"Watch me."

"Victor, please!" she shouted.

He opened his mouth to deliver yet another biting remark before slowly raising an eyebrow as a malicious thought took form in his twisted mind.

"Tell you what, DOA. I'm doing one trip only. If you like I'll save you and Joss, but you have to leave your sister and that behind to die." He pointed at Rudolph, who was snivelling on the floor. "You and me have a score to settle."

Molly looked up at Victor. He took a small step back, worried she would use her death stare on him before realising she had no such intention. There was only fear in her eyes. She turned to her brother.

"Go, Arran, there's no point in both of us dying. Save yourself; do it for me."

There wasn't even the tiniest fraction of a second upon which Arran would have considered this a realistic option. He shook his head.

"I'm not leaving her behind, Victor." He then sent a telepathic message to his sister: *And I don't want to hear any argument from you!*

The whole ship began to vibrate when a huge pointed iceberg tore through the ship's deck as though it was paper, throwing two children overboard and at the mercy of the sharks.

"You sure?" Victor laughed as he watched the sharks feed on the capsized kids.

"Take Molly instead," Arran pleaded.

"Yeah, right," said Victor. "See ya, DOA."

With that he levitated six feet into the air, clutching Joss with one arm, and floated safely to the island.

Molly didn't even bother asking her brother why he didn't go with Victor. If the roles were reversed, she would have done the same.

Sharks continued to expectantly swim the circumference of the sinking ship. Their perpetual grins could no more mask their intent than if they were holding a knife, fork, and an empty serving plate in each fin. Molly slowly stood and watched in horror as one more child was thrown into the water and devoured instantly.

She turned to her brother.

"What do we do?"

Arran cautiously poked his head over the side of the ship, looking for any sign of lifeboats, of which there were none. *Why am I not surprised?* The ship was slowly sinking and unless something was done, he knew they would all perish.

High up in the scarlet sky, a thick black cloud moved swiftly toward them, growing vastly in size as it approached. It stopped directly above the ship, as if controlled by an electronic remote. Molly and Arran gaped at the looming figure now hovering above them.

In the past, on days when Molly and Arran had been involuntarily excused from class, they occasionally sat on the high grassy hill not far from their school, basking in the sun and admiring the sporadic cloud formations overhead, pointing out the strange shapes they seemed to form.

Molly's love for the animal kingdom and her desire to hold close all things that were cute and cuddly meant most cloud formations to her resembled little dogs with droopy eyes, or fluffy bunny rabbits playing with one another.

Being the typical big brother, Arran would, in her eyes, always spoil her visions by introducing a third more troublesome element, perhaps an arrow making its way for the doggy's head or a bubbling pool of lava beneath the rabbit's feet, just waiting for the right time to cook them alive.

He didn't have a cruel bone in his body and would never advocate such happenings in real life, but he did enjoy on occasion, winding up his sister.

The cloud hovering above the ship had transformed itself into a shape unmistakable to both children. They seemed to be looking at a cloud formation of a death mask. Arran had always found the idea of death masks fascinating, from the moment his history teacher had told him the stories of how some famous people like William Shakespeare had plaster casts made of their face once they were dead, in the hope that a part of them would live on forever.

What once was a rather morbid fascination had become very worrying to both children, as the death mask was an exact replica of Grombit's sleeping face, which was easily, in its current form, the size of an impressive apartment block. Molly and Arran instantly felt a stab of deep remorse for their friend.

Grombit's sleeping face floated gently to the deck, and children screamed and ran, wading through water on deck to flee from it. A few feet from the floor the mask stopped, towering over Molly, Arran, and

Rudolph.

The figure's mouth slowly started to open till it covered the entire length of its face. From within the darkened depths of the face, a low, guttural sound resonated, at first indistinguishable, then recognised by all children as one single word:

"MOLLY."

Molly clung to her brother for protection. She considered, for a moment, using her death stare but knew within her heart it would have no effect. To her eyes this thing was already dead, and even if it wasn't, its eyes were closed.

Water lapped at Molly's feet as the ship grew ever closer to the surface of the sea, and the guttural "Molly" echoed once again.

Some children, forgetting the dangers that lurked in the waters below, jumped overboard once the huge mouth of the mask opened, much to the delight of the ravenous sharks who were greedily waiting for the ship to go down so they could enjoy their main course.

The death mask called Molly's name a third and final time before taking a huge inward breath. Molly felt her body being pulled toward it, as though she were trapped within the air flow of an enormous vacuum cleaner.

Surprisingly none of the other children seemed to be physically affected by this but her relatively weak body couldn't resist and she was propelled with great force toward the gaping mouth.

Arran quickly grabbed her hand and with his other arm wrapped himself around the wooden railing which ran the inner circumference of the ship. "Do not let go!" he commanded.

His sister did not reply but began to feel the inevitability of her terrible fate approach. The tight grasp he had on his sister's hand began to loosen. The Grombit-shaped death mask was winning. The siblings looked one another in the eyes.

Molly, please hang on.

I can't, Arran, it's too strong. It's…

Molly released her grasp, helplessly watching the desperate look on her brother's face as her heels scraped against the deck, providing negligible resistance to the pulling power of the death mask as it dragged her backward.

On impulse Arran closed his eyes and concentrated hard. When he opened them a huge mattress appeared out of thin air, blocking the path between Molly and the death mask. Instead of being dragged into the open mouth, she was propelled at great speed into the mattress before landing rather surprised on her behind, scratching her head.

"Of course!" he yelled. "I can do this!"

He was now not just thinking of Molly's safety, but was confident he could help every child on board. Arran's self-congratulatory celebration was put on hold, however, as the death mask rose up into the air and tilted its gaze in his direction.

"Okay," Arran bellowed, "let's see what you got!"

Of course he was thinking, *Please don't hurt me or my sister, Mr. Mask*, but he put on a brave face.

He waited a good three minutes, with the water still rising till it reached his knees, simply staring in defiance at it. The mask did nothing, content to simply watch the sinking ship fall.

Though he was scared, this was one thing he had no intention of letting happen.

"Thanks, bruv."

Molly rose to her feet and stood alongside her brother, whose recent actions with the mask had attracted a great deal of attention and hope from the surrounding passengers.

In a ship of frightened, chaotic souls, he was not just the only one who stared danger in the eye and fought back, but was outwardly the only calm, collected person in proximity. Inwardly this was certainly not the case of course. He was shaking like a leaf.

Children who sought salvation and protection now gathered 'round Arran. Not used to this, he shied back a little, only to be pushed forward by a smiling Rudolph. "They're looking to you now, mate."

Arran could almost feel their combined energy; the estranged look of hope had returned to their faces and was now directed at him.

"Pity we don't have the time machine, eh?" Molly said. "We could fly them all out or, I dunno, go back and tell people not to come to school today."

Arran carefully considered what his sister had said, recalling the many things that had happened since Molly first persuaded him to take a ride in her 'high-tech hovercraft.'

"Hovercraft!" he shouted. "Well, maybe we don't have a time machine, but how about a high-tech hovercraft?"

Molly laughed nervously. She wasn't quite sure whether her brother was joking or had gone quite mad. What he did next possibly indicated a little of both.

He pointed his arms rigid by his side, then slowly raised them in the air. As he did so, the sinking ship rose up above sea level. Encouraged by the cheers of every child, he pointed his hands straight ahead toward the island, and the ship made its way there, this time floating upon a river of air and over the top of some disappointed sharks who were going to have to survive without their afternoon meal.

Rudolph took a look back at the death mask. Though its expression and position had not altered, it was, in his eyes, simply dumbfounded. A few of the children who were feeling a little cocky and a lot more confident waved good-bye to the sharks as the ship left them behind.

Once they were safely docked on the island, Arran created, out of thin air, a stairway between the ship and dry land, which the children gratefully walked down onto the sandy surface.

"Now you're just showing off," Molly said.

Arran shrugged it off but with a satisfactory smile, the only visible indication that he was, at that moment, feeling better than he ever had.

Chapter Sixty-Three

Outside the Network

"Where have you been, Professor?"

Professor Tempus closed the door to the Orb room and barely even registered Mike's question.

"It doesn't matter, Mike. I had a vision. Arran and Molly are in trouble."

"That answers my question on how I break the news to you. Nice to know your abilities are surfacing, Professor."

"Mike! The children—what on earth is going on?"

Mike raised his hand to his temple, wiping away the many beads of anxious sweat that had begun to surface in the past twenty minutes since he began searching for her.

"We don't know exactly," he replied as they walked into the cafeteria. "We can't get into the Tempus Network. Something is stopping us. Ironically the only person who might have created an opening is trapped in the network itself."

The Professor glared at him. The tears in her eyes were a mixture of anger and regret.

"Molly?"

Mike sat at a table.

"No, Arran. Both children have extraordinary abilities, Professor, and Arran's lies in the world of computers; he is able to deconstruct the Tempus Network like no one we have ever seen, making of it what he will."

A coffee mug appeared from the top of the table in front of him which he grasped with both hands as though it were a hot chocolate and he was sitting amid the mountains of the cold Swiss Alps. He took a sip.

"Have you always known of his ability?" the Professor asked, annoyed that she was finding this out for the first time now.

Mike shook his head. "Actually while I was waiting to hear from some of my soldiers about a disturbance just outside the City, I did a little research on Arran and Molly's exploits in the Tempus Network, before communication was cut off of course.

"He's done things that, well, to be frank you shouldn't be able to do. Only one other creature to my knowledge has ever come close to his abilities. Like his sister he's turning into a bit of an enigma. All I can think is that if they are both children of Jhonas Spletka, then maybe their own abilities are quite powerful. Before him, the death stare was practically unheard of. Certainly not to the level he uses it."

He paused, remembering the horrors the people of the City were subjected to under the temporary rule of Jhonas Spletka many years ago.

"Or at least he used to, before he disappeared into your time."

If it even is my time.

Mike knew what she was thinking and nodded in agreement.

"Who is the other creature you spoke of? Can't he or she get us into the Tempus Network?"

"'Fraid not," Mike answered. "The creature was a timid field mouse called Tribble. He died not long after his son disappeared, stress, I suppose. Your father missed him terribly."

"Sir, we have news back from the patrol we sent to Judean Street. You are not going to believe…"

The message was directed straight to Mike's ears and was heard by no one else. He raised a hand apologetically to the Professor.

"Excuse me for a moment; I've been waiting on this call."

The Professor gestured for him to go ahead. She ordered a coffee and sat patiently sipping at the rim of the cup whilst Mike spoke.

To her ears Mike seemed both relieved and worried at the same time. She did her best to make sense of the disjointed conversation.

"Tribble?

But that's impossible.

But where did you?

Prisoner?

A disturbance in the Tempus Network?

Of course I do.

Send him here at once."

Mike returned his attention to the Professor, except she offered her own interpretation, to save him the effort of having to explain.

"Tribble is alive and well, your guards have found him, and as he's the only one who can hack into the Tempus Network, rather conveniently, I might add, you're asking him to come over to the guarded and sacred Citadel as fast as his tiny little legs and procured transport can carry him?"

Mike was almost speechless.

"Well, yes, that's about the size of it, but to be on the safe side I've asked the guards to accompany him here."

The Professor drummed her fingers lightly on the table top.

"The same guards you asked to check on the disturbance?"

Mike didn't see any problem with that and didn't like his judgment being questioned, even by the daughter of Richard Tempus.

"Yes, well, they *were* the ones who rescued him. They are loyal to us, Professor. I can vouch for them personally. I'd have thought you would be relieved."

Before the Professor could say another word, something quite sudden and unexpected happened. She noticed what looked like a blue flame rising out of Mike's head and burning bright. He was quite unaware of this, but also couldn't help but notice the direction her curious gaze had taken.

He brushed the top of his head with his hand, thinking maybe he had something on there that shouldn't be, or there was a hair alarmingly out of place, sticking up and looking like it had taken on a personality of its own. The flame continued to burn, unencumbered by Mike's hand. As his interest increased, his whole body seemed to emanate a yellowish glow. She smiled, thinking this a rather beautiful albeit unusual development in her abilities.

"What?" he asked, feeling a little self-conscious.

"Nothing." She could tell he was trying to read her mind; there was of course the intense stare shot in her direction, but beyond that a more obvious indication. A yellow aura seeped out of his body and she could see it moving toward her own head. She waved her hand though the aura as it approached, which broke the path and it returned to its owner.

Mikes eyes widened, startled.

"How did you do that?"

"What, from your perspective, did I do, Mike?" The Professor rested her head on her hands, studying the colours that Mike was turning.

The yellow was now accompanied by a little red fireworks display in his body.

"Something only your father could do. I was reading, or trying to read your mind but…you stopped me."

"What were you feeling," the Professor probed, "when I stopped you?" *When the fireworks display started*, she thought.

Mike shrugged. "Don't know, surprise, shock."

Interesting. On impulse she decided to take out her diary to see if there were any new writings. The middle of page three had just two sentences.

The living energy from the house now runs through your veins. You can see life in its entirety.

Quite sure that she was destined to be every bit as secretive as her father had often been, Mike rose from his seat. "I have to go to the control room and wait for Tribble. Would you care to come along?"

The Professor, still feeling anxious about Tribble's sudden appearance, stood up and walked alongside him as they left the room.

The Professor picked up the glass case in the control room, peering in at the spiders and taking a particular interest in one which was perpetually locked in a repeated movement. Its two front legs banged on the glass floor with the regularity of a ticking clock. Mike stood by her.

"The spiders we found on Grombit's head. All are paralysed, except that one."

Physically there was little to distinguish the spiders from one another, but the Professor saw something quite unusual on each one of them. The auras which filled them were a grotesque blend of green and black. Equally each one had a flame on its head of the same colour.

The intensity of the flame was nowhere near as strong as the one she saw on Mike's head; in fact it looked as though they were dying out, that is, apart from the only spider that was moving.

Its aura kept changing from bright blue, then back to the green-black mixture, and its flame rising and falling as if it couldn't decide whether to go out or burn brightly. As the Professor moved her face closer to the side of the case, the spider stopped banging. She felt all eight of its tiny eyes look up at her, and on impulse she pulled her face away. The spider followed and began to scrape on the glass wall that separated them.

The Professor placed the box down.

"All these spiders are going to die, except that one. Its fate and influence is not yet decided."

Mike sat down and considered trying to read her mind, then rejected the idea.

"Just how do you know that?"

The Professor didn't answer. She simply shrugged her shoulders and sat next to him and stared at the monitor which was focussed on the black mist surrounding Judean Street.

"How much do you know about the general?"

"Not much," Mike answered. "He rose to power and popularity amongst the Spletka almost as soon as Jhonas disappeared. We know him more by reputation than anything. Looks like Jhonas taught him the death stare before he left though; he takes the occasional trip into the city, to try to capture some souls, generally scare people, you know. We have an alarm system in place to warn people when he comes near. Other than that he keeps himself fairly well hidden."

"How's Grombit?" the Professor asked finally, almost as an afterthought.

"Fine, he's resting at the moment. Had quite a trying time."

Chapter Sixty-Four

Sophia Tal-Grasto Joins the Gang

The forest which surrounded the small beach looked both eerie and uninviting. Molly wasn't sure if it was an illusion brought on by the dreadful experience they had all been through, but she felt sure she saw one tree shake the leaves from its branches, leaving an army of bony fingers, which beckoned her to come close. She looked away and stayed put, sitting with her brother and Rudolph on the sand.

Arran looked up; the rain had at least stopped, but the red skies remained. The sea had turned a deep bloodred also; it was as though their intended environment had been mortally wounded—just a matter of time before it drifted away entirely.

Though the immediate danger had gone, he could tell everyone was still on edge. They were still trapped, waiting for an answer. Some seemed to be looking to Arran for that. Several children had already offered their thanks and said they were confident that if anyone could get them out of this, it would be him.

He had no answers to give, and really didn't like everyone's hopes resting firmly on his shoulders.

"You were very brave." Sophia Tal-Grasto approached him and paused for a second before deciding it was okay to sit with them. "How did you do that?"

"It's nothing special," Arran answered. "Just my ability. I can do stuff with computers."

Sophia laughed. "Yes, stuff no one else can do. And in this place it *is* something special. In this place it's like having superpowers or something."

Arran rejected her statement with a tired sigh. She extended her hand in greeting.

"I'm Sophia."

Molly, who had been trying to remember where she had seen Sophia before, tapped her forehead. "That's where I've seen you. You're Sophia Tel-Grasto, the chess player?"

"Yes, that's right. Chess champion, to be more precise." She shook Arran's hand, after which she offered it to Molly. "Are you Molly?"

Molly nodded and attempted a polite smile.

Sophia looked into her eyes as though she were searching for something. "So you are the one everyone was talking about in school, the one who can do the death stare? You scared the bejeesus out of Victor and his gang."

"A lot of good it's doing me now."

Sophia examined the red sky and then the frightened children on the beach. Rudolph, who had grown tired of waiting for his introduction, spoke up. "Hello, Sophia, I'm Rudolph, pleased you asked. I'm very happy to meet you too."

Molly laughed.

"Hello, Rudolph," Sophia quickly and formally answered, without so much as an acknowledging glance in his direction. She turned her attention back to Arran.

"So what's our next move?"

Arran glared at her, pure frustration directing his vocal cords. "I don't know, okay!" He lowered his head so he was no longer looking at her. "Sorry, I can tell everyone is looking to me for answers, but…I don't know. How would I?"

"Lucky I'm here then," said Sophia.

Arran was hopeful. "You know what we should do next?"

"No," she said cheerfully. "But like any problem in life, there are always answers. Once found, the problem dissipates and becomes an opportunity. I like opportunities."

She rose to her feet and paced back and forth.

"Let me see. This thing, whatever it is, has trapped us on this island and tried to kill us, well, most of us; judging by what I've seen, it seems to want Molly alive. At this point I can only assume it's after Molly's ability. Since her ability is unheard of in anyone not connected to the Spletka Clan, I can further speculate with a reasonable degree of accuracy that this is the work of the aforementioned Spletka Clan. My guess is they are looking for a new recruit to add to their cumbersome collective."

Arran, Molly, and Rudolph exchanged a worried glance before returning their attention to Sophia, who was in mid-flow.

"Then you made a mattress appear out of thin air, and then

moved the ship to save all of us?"

"Yeah, I guess," said Arran.

"Please don't interrupt. You are something the Spletka did not count on, and since it didn't kill you instantly, my guess is it can't."

She took an uneasy glance at the forest.

"Their leader is now a general, which would indicate that their next move will be drenched in military precision. They will want you out of the way, and since they can't do it directly, they will use whatever advantage they have."

"Which is?"

"Look around. Hundreds of children who will do anything to survive, even kill. I say we move into the forest before…"

As though it had been listening, the mask which had been left out to sea drifted inward. In no time at all it was floating directly above the sandy beach. Arran, Molly, and Rudolph stared in wonder, and every child on the island simultaneously looked curiously at the mask, then at Molly.

Sophia took a worried glance at the mask, then back to Arran. "The Mask is speaking. Here, take my hand and form a circle everyone. I'm guessing you can't hear this or you would have fled the beach by now."

They all joined hands and heard a voice which certainly wasn't

Grombit's. It reminded Molly of the lieutenant they had both defeated the day before, similar but not the same. It was commanding, sinister, and mockingly upbeat.

"You were expecting the Tempus trials. Well, we have a new challenge for you all. You'll note the safety is switched off, which means, except for one lucky individual, yes, just one, the rest of you are going to die. Your coins are gone too, so no escape there either." The mask sniggered. *"All you must do to stay alive is bring me the young girl Molly, alive. If her annoying brother tries to stop you, kill him."*

Molly and Arran looked around and felt a mixture of emotions emanate from the children, predominantly fear, which overshadowed for the most part the intense pang of guilt. Arran had, after all, just saved their lives.

Arran still had formidable powers, and Molly's death stare was nothing to be sneezed at. Even with this, some children seemed ready to pounce.

Molly stood and her eyes glowed bright blue as she stared directly at the mask.

The mask began to scream and gradually faded from sight; all that remained was a faded echo:

"Ah, the death stare! I can't handle it. I'm dyyying!"

Molly looked at Arran, surprised. "Well, that was easy."

Suddenly the mask popped back into plain sight, this time right in front of Molly.

"What gave me away? Was my death too over the top?" The mask laughed. *"You can't hurt me if you can't see me, little girl. You can no more perform a death stare on me than you could a remote control toy. Now, time is ticking and I want my sport. You have three minutes' head start before I send everyone after you…run!"*

Arran, Molly, and Rudolph didn't need a second telling. They fled into the forest, closely followed by Sophia.

"What are you doing?" asked Arran, stopping briefly on the sand.

"Coming with; that okay with you?"

"But if you do they'll all be after you too," Rudolph interjected.

"Ah, isn't that sweet, Rudolph is it?" Sophia spoke calmly, standing to face him. "Well, you are probably very right about that. Might I suggest we lay out a picnic blanket, eat sandwiches, drink tea, and discuss the merits of my decision? Or we could talk about this later and, I don't know…run?!"

I like her, thought Molly.

Me too, thought Arran.

"Thanks, you two," Sophia answered aloud. "Perhaps we can all sit and have a group hug when this is all over. Right, now let's keep running."

Molly looked quizzically at Arran.

Sophia continued: "Oh please, I didn't come to be the world's chess champion without having a magnificent brain. Joss Minton isn't the only one in the school who can read minds. By the way, Arran, I think she likes you."

Arran blushed and ignored the statement.

Rudolph, who couldn't hear Arran and Molly's thoughts, only heard Sophia's side of the conversation and thought her quite mad.

She's with Victor, thought Arran, *and I don't have time to think about that sort of stuff.*

"Very good point," Sophia answered. "I didn't notice him on the beach by the way."

"What are you talking about, Sophia?" said Rudolph.

"Look out for that tree stump!" Sophia shouted.

"Stop saying random things!" Rudolph yelled. Then he tripped over a tree stump.

"Warned you," Sophia said smugly, extending her hand to help Rudolph to his feet, which he dismissed, swatting it away like a persistent fly.

"I can get up on my own." He kicked the stump once he was on his feet again.

Molly stopped and turned to Arran.

"Exactly where are we all going?"

He shrugged his shoulders. "I dunno, away from everybody else."

"What about up there?" She pointed to the top of a tree, which was easily fifteen times bigger than they were.

She looked again to Arran, who, taking the hint, closed his eyes. When he opened them, a huge ladder stood reaching to the upper branches.

"Nice," Rudolph said.

"You're still a show-off," joked Molly, being the first to begin the climb, closely followed by Sophia, then Rudolph.

Finally, Arran climbed the ladder to join them on a little wooden platform lodged in between the branches. He made the ladders disappear just in time to avoid being seen by six children wandering below.

"What do we do if Molly does that death stare thingy?" one child asked.

"Death stare? As if. That's just some stupid rumour. No one can really do the death stare," another replied.

"Besides, she can't do the death stare on all of us at once. Someone will just have to creep up from behind."

They continued to talk strategies till they disappeared from sight.

Molly was worried.

"They're right, you know. I don't think I can do a death stare on more than one person at a time. They could get me in a rush."

"You have people here who can stop them," Arran answered.

"Yeah, Sophia, see if you can distract them with a game of chess," said Rudolph flippantly.

Sophia shook her head. "We all have our abilities. Even him." She pointed at Rudolph, who grunted.

"But let's not forget this is the Tempus School for special abilities, and each and every person down there has special abilities. Some can run faster, some can hit harder, some can…"

"…Hear better?" came a shout from the bottom of the tree. "I hear you, Sophia Tal-Grasto. Come down with your friends and no one gets hurt. Or do I have to come up there and get you?"

"I very much doubt your enhanced hearing ability is accompanied by Spiderman's powers too, so yes, why don't you come on up here, Donald Mousley?"

Donald, who was standing alone at the foot of a tree, knew he'd never be able to climb.

"I'm not alone down here," Donald lied. "I'm with Victor,

Arran's bestest friend. He can just float up there and get you."

Molly looked at Arran, worried. *If that were true, then why didn't he speak first?*

Yeah, I think he's lying; besides, if he is you can just death stare thingy him, Molly.

"Victor's not down there," Rudolph whispered in Arran's ear.

Molly overheard. "How can you be sure?"

Rudolph turned to face her. "Are you kidding me?" His voice was still in a low whisper. "I can pinpoint a moving iceberg travelling at great speed using sound vibrations alone and you don't think I can hear someone a few feet away?"

Molly was a little defensive and apologetic. "I wasn't saying— sorry, I just…"

"Well, Donald," shouted Sophia, "I have absolutely no doubt you heard those whispers. So what do you want to do? We're not coming down!"

Donald punched the side of the tree in frustration. He pulled his hand back quickly; if he had any doubt before, his poor hand now knew that the tree was stronger than he.

"Do you not care about anyone, Sophia?" He rubbed his sore hand. "Well, I know you couldn't care less about me, but if we don't bring Molly to that thing, everybody on this island is going to die!"

Sophia couldn't believe what she was hearing.

"Of course I care and if you're fool enough to believe what that thing told you, then it only confirms my initial decision about us was right."

Rudolph nudged Arran. "Lovers tiff, I think."

"You've known me for many years, Donald. How many times have I been wrong about…anything? The only reason we are not all dead right now is because for some reason that thing wants Molly, and Arran is standing in its way."

"Er, hello?" interrupted Rudolph, slightly offended.

Sophia sighed. "Oh very well, only Arran, Rudolph, and I are standing in its way."

"He's starting to walk away," said Rudolph with his palm placed gently beneath him on the tree.

"And before you decide to warn someone else, Donald," Sophia shouted, "since you're gullible enough to believe what this thing tells you; remember: It said only one person will be saved, the person who brings Molly to it. Everybody else *will* die. I'm sure Victor is giving enough to allow you the victory."

He didn't reply but as he skulked off into the distance, he thought about what Sophia had said. He wasn't the toughest one in the school by any stretch of the imagination, so didn't fancy the idea of fighting anyone for Molly and if it came to it, a one-on-one battle with Molly wouldn't be good for him either. She'd just do the death stare on him.

"Soo… What did he mean, Sophia?" Rudolph asked. "When he said that he knew you couldn't care less about him, his blood pressure and heart rate increased too."

Sophia shook her head. "Went out for a short time, then I decided that he may be good to speak to, but we didn't have the intellectual connection. So I finished it."

Rudolph laughed. "The famous intellectual connection, yes, of course. Romeo, Romeo, would you mind taking a quick math test before I decide whether or not you're the type of person I should be associating with?"

Sophia didn't grace him with any sort of answer.

"Are we safe from him, Sophia? Will he tell anyone?"

Sophia shook her head slightly at Arran. "I don't know, but I don't think he'd give us up. He still has feelings for me even after all this time, and wouldn't want to place me in danger."

"How long since you two have been a couple?"

"One and a half days," she answered earnestly.

"And he's still bothered about it?" Rudolph joked. "Some people don't know how to let things go."

"Nice to see everyone knows about mine and Victor's differences," Arran said. "Actually, come to think about it, I don't remember seeing him on the island."

"Me neither," said Molly.

Chapter Sixty-Five

Meanwhile Victor Receives a Visit

Nearly half a mile away, on a small grass clearing, Victor and Joss sat, considering their next move. Joss, though she was grateful to Victor for saving her life, was finding it near impossible to come to terms with how easily he had condemned everybody on that ship to die. She hadn't spoken to him since arriving on the island.

"Sure is a lot of trees." Victor grunted. He picked up a stone, threw it, and narrowly missed a bird nest on one of the branches of a nearby oak.

Joss broke her silence. "Hey, quit it. Not happy with killing everyone on the ship, you're trying to kill the wildlife on the island too!"

Victor grinned and closed his eyes, lying back on the grass.

"Dunno what's come over you lately. Besides, saved your life, didn't I?"

"Victor…"

"Shut up, Joss; preferred it when you weren't talking. I wanna get some sleep."

"Er, Victor…" She thumped him on the side of his leg, to get his attention.

"Ow!" He sat up and glared at her. "I may not have the same death stare of the recently deceased Molly, but you'll regret that!"

Joss wasn't looking at Victor, but at a dark figure standing right in front of them, at least she thought it was standing. It had no legs or feet that she could see from beneath its black hooded robe. It was floating and reminiscent of the Grim Reaper.

Victor turned to face it and was taken aback, momentarily startled.

"Just who on earth are you?"

He was scared, but male bravado taught him never to show his true feelings, and boys don't cry, ever.

The hood of the creature tilted to the side. There was an empty space where the face should have been. Joss cowered and Victor stood up, putting his shoulders back and tilting his own head back as he did.

"You don't frighten me. I'm Victor Graston and I don't get frightened!"

From the darkness of the hood, a skull emerged with spinning fireballs in place of eyeballs. The creature raised its right arm and pointed it at Victor. A skeletal hand emerged, holding a green and black fireball. The creature snapped its hand open, releasing the fireball, which shot like a bullet through the air, landing on Victor's forehead and sending him crashing to the ground. The energy from the fireball seeped through his body, feeding on what little remorse and compassion he had, till there was none left.

Victor lay flat, unable to move so much as a finger.

"What do you want with me?"

The creature seemed not to notice Joss, who had backed away from both it and from Victor.

"We will help you, Victor."

The same deep, guttural sound that Arran and Molly had heard on the ship was speaking.

"To do what?" Victor replied.

"To liiive."

Its resonating reply echoed and amplified in Victor's head. The remaining dark flame on his forehead sank beneath his skin as though it were water. Once absorbed, it visibly caused a high degree of pain in every part of his body. Victor looked to Joss as though he was being electrocuted, without the need for an electric chair.

"What do you want from me?" Victor yelled, tears streaming down his face.

The pain stopped and the creature spoke. "Of all the pathetic souls on this island, you are the only one worthy of joining us."

"He's one of the Spletka," Joss said, though once she spoke the words, she began to wish her stupid mouth had remained closed.

The creature didn't look at her but the guttural sound "Jossss Minton…shhhhhh." was accompanied by a singular skeletal finger pressed against the place where its lips should have been.

Victor sat up and Joss moved toward him for protection. She placed her hand on his. He quickly snatched his hand away; male bravado still ever present.

"Excellent!" The creature's resounding voice caused vibrations in the ground beneath them. "Arran saved the girl Molly and brought everyone to the island. We want her, alive. You are going to lead everyone else in an effort to bring her to me. Kill anyone who stands in your way, especially her brother, which should please you. Fail me and you die."

Victor, who had become enraged at the thought of Arran still being alive, nodded and the creature disappeared. He rose to his feet and felt one pulsating wave of pain pass through his body as he heard the words:

"We'll be watching you."

"What are you going to do, Victor?" Joss asked, secretly relieved that Arran and the other children were safe.

He sank his hands in his pockets and walked back into the forest, muttering:

"I'm gonna get Arran; you coming?"

Joss reluctantly followed.

Chapter Sixty-Six

A Not So Friendly Incentive

The death mask spoke. No child could see it, but its chilling message was heard and understood by all.

Attention, everybody. It has become abundantly clear that you need an incentive to move a little faster, so every half hour, completely at random, I shall hunt down and kill one of you. That is until Molly is brought to me. Have a nice day!

"We probably shouldn't stay here, Arran," Sophia said, looking over the forest. Her vantage point gave her quite a view from over the tops of the trees and something else beyond.

"What's that?" Molly squinted her eyes, then shrugged. "Unless any of us have advanced super-vision I'm guessing no one knows."

"Well," answered Sophia, "I was actually talking to Rudolph. If he can do what bats can do, then…"

"Oh, I'm privileged," answered Rudolph. "Sophia has spoken."

Sophia was unimpressed. "Without the sarcasm?"

Rudolph took a couple of deep breaths followed by a long exhale, closing his eyes.

"It's a building, like a bungalow. There's one person inside, an adult, the owner, I suppose, and a dog."

"What do you think?" Sophia asked Arran.

Molly and Rudolph exchanged an anxious glance.

"Well, I know I wasn't asked," interrupted Rudolph, "but I vote we stay here. You said that guy wouldn't rat on us!"

"That was before," Sophia said. "If this maniac is going to start randomly killing people, my dear ex-boyfriend might well think he's doing a public service by giving us up."

Sophia nudged Arran.

"Well, we can discuss this till somebody comes, or you can make a ladder materialise out of thin air and we can make our way to this bungalow."

"How do we know we will be any safer there?" Molly asked.

"We don't," Arran said. "But as Sophia said, we're not safe here anymore."

He closed his eyes and when they opened, the top of a silver wooden ladder lay before them, which stretched to the grassy ground at the foot of the tree.

"Ladies first," Arran said; Rudolph, who was about to dismount, stepped back and allowed Molly and Sophia to pass. Rudolph was next. Just before he stepped foot on the ladder, Arran placed his hand on his shoulder.

"You are the scout now. You're going to know if anyone is

around before any of us do."

Rudolph attempted an encouraging smile, and then followed the girls down.

Chapter Sixty-Seven

Victor Gathers His Army

"Hey, Duck!"

Donald, still sulking, was sat beneath a blue elm tree when Victor and Joss approached him. He naturally recognized the toughest boy in the school standing over him.

"Hello, Victor."

His reply was meek, though there was a sense of resigned recognition that no matter what Victor could do to him, it would never be able to match the sheer terror facing him and every other child on the island.

"You seen Arran, or that stupid sister of his?"

Donald thought for a moment, then shook his head.

"He's lying," Joss said.

"No, I'm not," he retorted. "I haven't *seen* them."

"A formality," Joss said. "He has spoken to…" She paused, staring into his eyes. "…Sophia Tal-Grasto. So she's helping them, is she?"

Donald clapped his hands over his ears as if that was going to stunt Joss's ability to extract the thoughts from his head. Victor reached down, grasped Donald by the neck, pulled him to his feet, and pushed him against the hardened bark of the elm.

"Why are you lying to me, stupid!?" The mention of Sophia's name seemed to annoy Victor nearly as much as that of Arran's. Donald avoided looking into Victor's eyes for fear he would read such an action as one of defiance.

"He wants to protect…Sophia," Joss said. "I think he's in luurve."

Victor laughed and released his grasp, allowing Donald to fall back to the floor. Victor, never being one for compassion, was also very cunning. He knew if he got his hands on Arran, he would need the combined efforts and abilities of everyone on the island, with him as absolute leader of course.

"Sorry, Donald." Victor extended his hand to help him to his feet. His tone was much softer and friendlier. "You heard the announcement from that thing. We need to find Molly. I'm going to need your help to gather as many people as we can."

"It's no use," Donald said, fooled by Victor's false impersonation of friendship. "Only one person can deliver Molly to the…whatever it is. Everyone else is going to die."

Victor looked at Joss, then smiled.

"Not if you're with me, Donald. I was visited by that thing separately. It said I was to form a gang. Those who fight with me are to be spared."

This was of course a lie and Joss knew it, but she simply nodded her head in agreement.

"What about Sophia?" Donald asked.

"She'll be fine," Victor said with a sympathetic smile that could win an Oscar for its believability. "If you can persuade her to give them up and join us then she'll be spared too."

"What about Arran? I mean he saved all our lives on that ship. Will he be saved?"

No amount of false compassion could disguise Victor's feelings toward Arran.

"No! Absolutely not!"

He then collected his tormented emotions and lowered the volume of his voice.

"That is, the thing that wants Molly delivered also wants Arran dead. Unfortunately, he has left this unpleasant task to me."

Victor and Joss both sensed the conflict in Donald.

"Besides," Joss added, "Molly is his sister. He'd probably welcome, you know."

Victor nodded in agreement.

"Yes, in a way, we'd be doing him a service."

Joss hated herself for what she was saying but for the moment could not see any way of saving Molly and Arran except to somehow persuade Arran to give his sister up. This was perhaps an impossible task, but to stand any chance of doing that, they must first find them. And unfortunately, Victor was her best chance.

"Now," said Victor, flicking one of Donald's ears. "First we are going to go to where you spoke to Sophia, and if they are gone, you are going to help me find my old gang and everyone else on this island to form an army to track them down, okay?"

Donald nodded and led them back through the forest.

Chapter Sixty-Eight

Steph Garbil

"What you goin' t' do if you find them?"

Steph Garbil, a teenage gymnast, sat with her friends Joseph and Matilda, watching the black clouds slowly pass the deep red sky above them. Joseph picked a little wax from the inside of his left ear and examined the contents, as though he were considering his next meal in case there was no sign of food within the next few hours.

Matilda seemed deeply disturbed by this and stood, burying her hands in her pockets and kicking a loose branch against a nearby tree.

Unencouraged by the lack of response to her question, Steph sighed, shaking her head.

"We can't do anything to them, can we? I mean that boy, Arran, he saved our lives. Not much of a thank you."

"Yeah, like we have a choice!"

Matilda had picked up the branch and began twirling it in the air as if it were a baton.

"Unless we bring Molly to that scary face thing, then we all die. Besides, it's not Arran we have to get, is it? It's his sister."

Having finished contemplating his proposed lunch, Joseph wiped the wax on his T-shirt and decided it was up to him to point out the screaming obvious.

"Okay, first off, Molly can do the death stare, and you might say, hey, that's fine, we can get her in a rush or something; you also gotta think they are helped by the cleverest girl in the school or maybe the planet, Sophia whatsaname! And as if that wasn't enough, their other friend has bat sensory hearing and he'd hear us coming from miles away; but wait, that is still not enough. Arran earlier today was able to fight that mask thingy and lift a ship up out of the water all on his own. Who's to say he won't produce another ship out of thin air and drop it on our head just for trying? As you said, he's her brother."

Matilda considered what Joseph said, sitting back down next to them.

"We all have special abilities. Arran and Molly aren't the only ones. If we club together we could get the better of them. What's the difference? If we don't we'll die anyway."

Joseph sighed and nodded in agreement. "I suppose so."

They both looked expectantly at Steph.

"No," Steph said. "I'm not doing that to someone who just saved my life, nor should you. We should be trying to help him and his sister instead of planning their execution."

Matilda stood and gestured for Joseph to get up, which he did.

"Well, if you're not with us, Steph, I guess you're against us.

We're going looking for them. Let us know if you change your mind."

Steph looked hurt that the two people she had considered friends were able to diminish that friendship in a matter of moments.

"You have no conscience either of you. If I have to die it will be doing the right thing, rather than stay alive and succeed in betraying everything I believe in."

Joseph and Matilda walked off further into the forest, leaving Steph to sit alone.

Chapter Sixty-Nine

Enter the Spy

A dark cloud centred over the citadel as the general and his armies arrived on the outskirts.

Bellonta took great joy in leading the way, skipping playfully across the multi-coloured grass which seemed to rot away and die as her diseased aura, like a ravenous virus, passed through it.

The general and Tribble followed close behind her. He picked up the small field mouse.

"This is as far as we go for now, Tribble. You know what you have to do?"

Tribble nodded. The temporary control which the Spletka had over the Tempus Network meant that, for the moment, they were undetected.

Chapter Seventy

Craig Stamfordshaw

Craig Stamfordshaw had incredibly famous parents; parents so famous, in fact, that their jobs meant they rarely had the time to see their eight-year-old son.

They had become extremely popular as tube stage entertainers and travelled the world doing guest appearances, talking on chat shows, and producing their truly unique holographic tubular stage show.

To appease the male and female fans their marriage was kept secret, as was Craig. He spent most of his days alone in his parents' mansion, coming out only virtually, when he connected to the Tempus Network to go to school.

The children knew Craig simply as Stammers, a mocking nickname that made reference to the vocal stutter he had developed at a very early age. His few and futile attempts at communicating with other children at the school had been met with laughs and jeers, enough to make him retreat into his own personal space.

Most of the children were at the school to learn how to enhance their special abilities. Craig's as yet unexplained ability was one the school needed to suppress.

Craig was able to take and use the special abilities of any person he touched. The effects on him varied from person to person and were never permanent, but usually left the victim in a never-ending state of paralysis. So far only the headmaster seemed immune to Craig's touch.

He walked alone, his eyes red with weeping. The sporadic bolts of lightning which gave the trees a fleeting neon glow made Craig cower, and he buried his head in the long scarf that was his replacement for the security blanket he had used in his formative years. Only his green eyes and thick black spiked hair could be seen of his head.

"Hey look, it's Stammers!"

Victor walked toward him, followed closely by Joss and Donald.

"Whatcha doin', Stammers? Where's all your friends?"

Victor laughed, only too aware that he had no friends. Most of the children considered him a freak and gave him a wide birth. The only reason Victor had not administered a physical beating to date was because he knew of Craig's ability and wouldn't want to risk losing his power of levitation.

Victor looked down at Craig's hands to make sure he was wearing gloves before extending his hand as a false gesture of friendship. Craig was confused by this bully's behaviour.

"W… W…wha…d'y…w…w…wa…wa…?"

Victor interrupted, feeling that one sentence from Stammers

could easily last a lifetime.

"What do I want, Stammers? Same as you, not to die, and if we don't work together we will. You know that, don't you?"

Craig's bright green eyes seemed to dim slightly as he nodded reluctantly.

Speaking to other children had always seemed alien to Craig, but aligning himself with the worst-tempered child in school seemed ludicrous, however necessary it may be.

"Good, Stammers!" Victor slapped him on the back. "Now we need to find Arran and Molly, then give Molly to that mask thing. Donald was just leading us there. Come on, Duck, keep walking."

Donald turned and punched Victor in the mouth before telling him he was a bully and the time had come for him to pay for his cruel nature… Well, that's what he wanted to do, but he simply shook his head, grunted, and continued to lead the way.

"This is it. It's the tree Sophia and the rest of them were up," Donald eventually said, whilst leaning up against the bark.

Victor looked toward Joss, who with a simple nod of the head confirmed that Donald was speaking the truth. "Can you hear anything?" he asked.

"No, I think they're gone."

"Let's have a quick peek, shall we?" Victor pulled Craig

Stamfordshaw close as a human shield against Molly's possible death stare. To his mind, Molly was the only perceivable threat, having not been witness to Arran's earlier heroic deeds. "Now Stammers, if Molly is up there and she pulls that death stare thingy on me, you will have to touch her, got it?"

Craig nodded and removed his gloves. Victor placed his hands under Craig's armpits and slowly levitated.

"And don't you dare touch me with those, Stammers, if you know what's good for you."

Once at the top they found nothing but an empty platform. The Spletka influence in his veins meant that if Victor hadn't needed Craig past this point, he would have simply and without any remorse dropped him to the ground to continue his search, rather than carrying him safely back down to the ground, which he did.

"Right, we keep going. Stammers, the gloves go back on and you walk alongside me. The rest of you, come on. Donald, you got the super lugs, so you go up front and take us in the direction of voices; we will either find them or others to join our merry little crew. Get going."

Donald's ability didn't disappoint. In just twenty minutes he sought out and helped enlist thirty-three different students. Some had been wandering alone, others they found in groups, as well as three members of Victor's existing gang who heartily embraced their leader before learning of his plans to kill Arran and deliver Molly.

Barney, a stocky and not so intelligent but incredibly strong member of Victor's gang, was the only one who even questioned the potential implications of killing Arran.

"Kill him, Vic? I mean, don't mind beating on him for you, but to kill him? Headmaster Dews isn't going to like that, might even get suspended from school or detention or something like that."

Victor simply shook his head. "Just do as you're told, Barns." He was beginning to like his new position of power. He'd always been the head of a gang, but now it felt as though he had control of a small army, an army of individuals with special powers, a super army.

I'm good, he thought as he marched through the forest, *and these idiots bought that garbage I was spinning; if they stuck with me their lives would be spared.*

Each and every child on that island was destined to die, except for him of course, and Victor loved it.

Chapter Seventy-One

The Spletka Sacrifice

A huge resonating gong sounded three times. The sky turned from red into an enormous monitor which began flickering grey and white. The mask that had terrorised them earlier faded into view on the screen.

"The Spletka are not ones for empty threats and we do like our entertainment. As you have, so far, not delivered the girl known as Molly to me, one of you is going to die. The rest of you have the unique pleasure of watching."

The mouth of the mask looked as if it were attempting a smile before fading from view.

Every child's gaze was fixated on the monitor as a multi-sided die appeared and slowly rotated. On each side not a number but a picture of a living, breathing child who was trapped in the forest. Victor's face was not on the die; also absent were the faces of Arran, Molly, Sophia, and Rudolph.

"I don't get it," said Arran. "If that thing really can do what it says, what's to stop it from killing Molly?"

Molly diverted her attention from the screen for a brief moment to shrug and look helplessly at her brother. "I'm not complaining."

The sound of a clock ticking played alongside the rotating deathly die, which gave way to the sound of a heartbeat as the die gradually slowed, then stopped, showing its first victim. The heartbeat continued.

As well as being cruel, the Spletka Clan, it seemed, also had a taste for the theatrical.

"Oh no." Rudolph stared at the image of the girl selected by the mask. "I know her; she doesn't deserve this."

Steph stood, wide-eyed, looking in horror and disbelief at the die, which was a perfect and ominous mirror image and moved exactly as she did. The heartbeat stopped and the mask spoke:

"Stephanie, I understand that you have already said good-bye to your friends; this is fortunate."

All the children on the island watched in dismay as Stephanie sobbed, shaking her head reverently, and then she briskly wiped the tears from her eyes and glared at the screen.

"We all know why you picked on me, because I won't hunt down Molly and Arran, the boy who saved us all. And nor should any of you watching this. What kind of people are you, that you'd simply submit to a bully whose cowardice is…?"

A sharp pain in her stomach made her double over in pain. Her face, which became increasingly red and strained, glared at the screen. The power had gone from her voice, but she was going to get the words out even if they were her last.

"Go on then, do it, kill me. At least I'd die as myself, not a servant of the Splet…of the Splet…Spletkaaaaa!"

The name Spletka resonated into a piercing howl of pain as her body rose in the air and was stretched out in all directions for all to see.

Her tears turned red as her eyeballs rolled back, indicating that life had left her. She stayed in mid-air, body twitching sporadically till the force which was keeping her airborne released its grasp and she fell to the ground, lifeless and still.

Matilda and Joseph stared at the screen, which was flickering between the image of the death mask and the still body of Stephanie. A single tear emerged from the corner of Matilda's eye and paused as if respectfully pondering a thought, before it made its way, slow and deliberate, down her cheek to finally settle on the ground below.

Joseph placed his hand on her shoulder. She neither welcomed nor rejected this gesture. She was simply stunned.

"I'm sorry, Matilda." Joseph was not used to being comforting and had trouble finding the right words. "You know, had she agreed to find Arran and Molly, she probably wouldn't be dead right now. Shows we made the right decision."

He feigned a smile.

Matilda slowly turned to look at Joseph. Her burning expression was a clear indication that words of comfort were definitely not his strong point. She clenched her fists and Joseph thought he was about to receive a sound beating for his comment. Instead she quietly spoke three words before raising her fists in the air and yelling into the screen above.

"Hey, mask, you still hungry? Because I'm not playing your insane death game anymore. You may as well take me too. Come on, you coward, come on!"

The air was still and clear; unconcerned and unthreatened by Matilda's outburst. The screen remained unchanged. She dropped her hands by her side and repeated the same three words that she spoke earlier.

"I'm sorry, Steph." She then sighed. "You're on your own, Joseph."

She walked defiantly into the forest. The screen disappeared and was replaced again by that same bloodred sky, a stark reminder to all that opposing the Spletka Clan would not be tolerated.

Chapter Seventy-Two

Tribble's at the Door

As Tribble and the guards traversed the drawbridge, there was little in the air to suggest that only a few hundred yards away, hidden, lying in wait, was the most terrible danger.

Bellonta kissed the general's cheek. He turned and ran his fingers through her thick black hair, watching as the two guards and the small mouse were escorted through the entrance.

His army remained deathly silent. Black clouds gathered and blocked what little light there was, doing their best to keep the Spletka Clan's presence a secret.

The signal would soon be given and they would advance, destroying everything good and pure in their path.

Mike's monitor bleeped before an image of Charles Plumber, the citadel's chief security officer, faded into view.

"Tribble and the guards are here, sir; do you want me to show them up?"

"Yes, thanks, Charles, rush them through security. We need Tribble's help now."

"Yes, sir."

The screen went blank. The Professor's concerned look began

to annoy Mike a little.

"What is it, Professor?"

"Do you not think this is all just a little bit too easy?"

Mike sighed and scratched the back of his head.

"Just what is easy about this, Professor? Is it that the Tempus Network is down? Or maybe the fact that we have half the school trapped in there. Or perhaps, just thinking on my feet here, but could it even be that there is no safety in the network, meaning anything could be happening to each and every child, including your precious Arran and Molly!"

The Professor looked undisturbed by his outburst, well aware of the current situation. She noticed a tiny flicker in his life force flame before it returned to normal.

"Be careful, Mike. I suspect you have a heart problem, and outbursts like that won't help."

Mike was taken aback. "How did you...?"

"We all have our gifts."

There was a knock at the door followed by the entrance of Tribble, then in turn by the two guards.

"You have your father's look, Professor." Tribble smiled as he jumped up onto the bench and extended his paw nervously in greeting.

The Professor shook his hand and returned his smile but her

attention was much more focussed on that which only she could see, emanating from the guards and Tribble himself.

The flames of the two guards were strong, but burning jet black. Tribble's flame was not strong at all, flickering in colour between bright yellow, blue, and dark grey.

With each colour change the flame died a little.

"Are you all right, Tribble?" she asked. "You don't look well."

Tiny beads of sweat ran from his brow, down his snout, and dropped from his nose.

"Oh yes, thank you," he replied. "Just not a great traveller and I must confess to being a little nervous meeting the great Professor Tempus in person. I'll be right as rain in no time."

The Professor glanced at Mike, who for the moment seemed to share the Professor's concern. All attempts at reading the mouse's thoughts or that of the guards were unsuccessful. The guards' minds seemed almost blank and the only image Mike could get from Tribble was that of his son.

"You two wait outside."

Mike waved his hands in a shooing motion toward the guards. They reluctantly complied and left the room, but were clearly aggrieved at having to follow the directions of some inferior individual.

They did take solace, however, in the fact that he would be dead soon enough.

Chapter Seventy-Three

Joseph's Discovery

"Surprised we haven't run into anyone yet?" Arran said to Molly, the trees and foliage seeming denser with every step. "You sure you can't hear anything yet?" he called to Rudolph, who was walking a few feet ahead, taking his new responsibility very seriously.

"Sh" came the reply. "How am I supposed to keep watch if you keep talking all the…"

Rudolph stopped and raised his right hand, a silent gesture indicating that everyone behind him should shut up and stop moving.

What do you think? Molly psychically asked Arran.

"Dunno," he replied out loud before realizing his mistake and covering his mouth with his hand.

Molly sighed and shook her head. Their heartbeats increased slightly in anticipation.

Rudolph turned and concentrated, as he tried to separate their combined heartbeats, which were pounding in his head, from the other sounds.

"Something is walking this way."

Barely a moment later there was a rustle in the tree ahead of them and out stepped Joseph. He froze when confronted by the foursome, his heartbeat now joining the percussion band in Rudolph's mind.

If it weren't for their combined special abilities, Joseph may have had a chance on taking two or three of them in a straight-up fight, but four of them, one with the death stare and another with a power to…well, he wasn't quite sure, but what Arran did on the ship was very impressive.

"Are you Molly?" he asked, clenching his fists more out of nervousness than anger, and took a small step forward.

Rudolph, who had been standing at the front, decided to be a gentleman and give Arran, Molly, and Sophia a clearer view, so he stood behind them; besides, he didn't want to be punched in the nose.

Joseph's strength, though not the greatest in the school, was enough to earn him a certain degree of respect, even from Victor, who generally would not pick on anybody if there was a chance he might not win.

"Are you alone?" Molly replied.

Rudolph's head popped up behind Molly's left shoulder. "Yes, he's alone."

"You're Joseph, aren't you?" Sophia asked. "I've seen you around school. You were friends with that girl; the one who was murdered moments ago, in front of everybody."

"Her name was Stephanie!"

He began breathing deeply, reminiscent of a bull readying itself for the charge. "And she was a fool, an idiot, and you!" He pointed at Molly. "Every moment you're alive you condemn every one of us to the same fate. I'm not going to allow you to…"

He took a determined step forward and Molly's eyes began to glow bright blue; she was almost snarling at him. Anticipating this move, Joseph turned his head away and covered his eyes with his arm, in an almost mock Shakespearean actor pose; though his other fist, which was swinging blindly in front of him, destroyed the classical image somewhat. He looked more like a cross between a circus clown, Mr. Bean, and a mime artist trying to swat flies. Sophia tried her best to cover her smile.

Deciding enough was enough, Arran concentrated, and before Joseph had time to swing his fist one more time, Molly was sporting a very large pair of unfashionable dark glasses and Joseph was strapped into a chair, unable to move and looking directly at the foursome in utter astonishment.

"Well, this is getting us nowhere," Arran said.

Joseph was about to speak and was silenced when Arran simply put his index finger to his lips. Considering his predicament, Joseph thought silence may be the best way forward for now.

"Where was I? Oh yes," Arran continued. "Molly, as you may be aware. can do the death stare, meaning your special ability, unless it's the anti-death stare, probably won't stand a chance, and as far as I can make out, the results are fairly permanent."

Molly took off her glasses and threw them to the ground; her eyes returned to normal, though she was clearly not happy with her brother. "That wasn't funny!"

"Was a bit," whispered Rudolph; his head popped up behind Molly's other shoulder.

"And you stay out of this!"

Rudolph sank his head back down. "Sorry."

"Now Joseph, was it?" Arran continued.

He nodded slowly, but remained silent.

"Molly is my sister and even if you were able to catch her unaware, I'll always be here, and I have a few tricks up my sleeve too. I can do much more than strap you to a chair, believe me."

Joseph finally spoke, his voice calm and collected.

"You can do what you want to me and maybe that would be better than that mask thing killing me." He looked at Molly, almost inviting her to turn on the death stare. She didn't comply. "But if *you* don't kill me, I will never stop trying to capture you and will rally whatever forces I can find to take you down. One of my best friends has been killed because she didn't have the guts to stand up to you. I have nothing against you and your brother—well, I'm sorry, he saved all our lives, but we have no choice. Can't you see that?"

Rudolph eventually piped up and stepped out from the cover of the others. Joseph was strapped in good and tight, so the chances of anything happening to him were fairly minimal.

"So let's get this straight, you are telling the girl with the death stare that you are going to hunt her down?" He nodded before continuing, "You sure you don't want to walk up to Victor Graston and tell him he talks funny too?"

Joseph grunted, shaking his head. "Shut it, weedy, brave behind your big friends."

Arran smiled. "Clearly you're not talking about Molly there then?"

Molly laughed. "Hey, shut it. You got the height, I got the beauty; that's what Mom always said."

A sudden hot flush ran through her body, followed by a single mental image; a flash of white light followed by an explosion, then another of a lady, her back turned to Molly, weeping.

She hadn't mentioned or even thought of her mother for as long as she could remember. A short look in Arran's direction indicated that the same realization and vision had also hit him, almost as if their mother had not exactly been deleted from their minds, but suppressed, bypassed, ignored. The trouble was the more they tried to remember, the harder it became to recall even a single picture of her in their minds.

Sensing that there was something quite off topic going on between Arran and Molly, Sophia felt that a little interjection of common sense was needed.

"Okay, Joseph, you are either incredibly brave or very, very stupid. I'm inclined to believe you are a little of both. Arran is never going to let you near Molly, and for what it's worth, neither will I. With his strength and mine," she tapped her forehead, "getting by us will be, well, not impossible but pretty close."

Rudolph spoke up. "Hello, I'm here too, y'know. You'd think my special power was invisibility," he muttered to himself.

Sophia shook her head and Rudolph plonked himself down at the foot of a tree stump and sulked.

"Sorry about that, Joseph. Where was I? Oh yes, and if by some miracle you or your rallied forces got by Arran and me, Molly's death stare would sort you out instantly."

"You don't know that it would work on loads of people at the same time," Rudolph grunted.

Sophia sighed. "Thank you, Rudolph, you've just gone from

practically useless to completely pointless. I was hoping to keep that little gem of uncertainty from him."

"Whatever." He snorted.

Rudolph's resentment toward Sophia and her supposed superiority was evident. "Well, Arran, what are we going to do?"

Arran and Molly knew there was a discussion to be had regarding their mother but they also were aware that this was not the right time. Arran looked at his captive. Joseph didn't say a word; his mouth may as well have been welded closed. He had said all he was going to say and his opinion was not going to change.

They clearly didn't have the time to waste. If Joseph was here, it wouldn't be long before others came.

"We haven't got time for this, Arran."

Molly stood directly in front of Joseph and took a deep breath, preparing to administer a rather large, lethal dose of her death stare.

"Molly, stop!" Arran stood between them.

"Get out of my way, Arran. I do this, or he tells other people where we…"

"We could be ages away by the time anyone else arrives; besides, I'm not just going to let him go, am I? Rudolph, is there anyone else near?"

Rudolph listened for a moment. "There is a rather large

gathering of people, but they are moving in the opposite direction to where we are going."

Molly was resolute. "Move, Arran. I have to."

"No!" Arran shouted back. "You start doing this and what separates you from the Spletka Clan?"

"He's right," Rudolph said. "We're not the killers, they are."

Molly spun around to face Rudolph, who, afraid that she would turn the death stare on him, ducked behind Sophia.

"Oh get up, I'm not going to hurt you, stupid."

She sighed and turned back to Joseph and spoke in a calm, deliberate manner.

"Fine, I won't hurt you either!" She paused for thought. "For now. Nor are we going to let you go, so here you must stay!"

Joseph remained silent.

"Come on, you guys, let's go. Which way, Rudolph?"

Rudolph felt rather proud of himself; he had persuaded Molly not to hurt Joseph and now he was showing them all the path to sanctuary. "Well, if we keep walking that way, we should hit the building I spoke of earlier."

Sophia jabbed him in the elbow.

"Hello, mouth! A simple 'that way, Molly' would have done. Sure you don't want to shout it out so Donald and everyone else can hear it too?"

The foursome walked off, leaving Joseph sitting still bound and strapped to the chair.

A few minutes later a thought occurred to Sophia. Almost as soon as it had, she received a thunderous headache, as an unwanted idea forced itself into her head.

"Rudolph, that boy Joseph, the one strapped to the chair."

"Yes?"

"Do you happen to know what his special ability is?"

Rudolph shrugged. "Dunno, but I'm guessing it's not Houdini's power of escape. He looked pretty helpless strapped to that chair."

"I have a terrible feeling, something I should never have overlooked; that's why he was so quiet. We must hurry."

Rudolph's pace quickened and the rest of the party followed suit.

As well as being very strong, Joseph was gifted in the art of telepathy; so gifted in fact that he could transmit a thought to multiple recipients at any one time, choosing to exclude whomever he chose. His cry of help easily bypassed Arran, Molly, and Rudolph. Although Sophia did not receive the full message that was sent out to everyone else on the island, her advanced intellect was able to pick up a fragmented echo.

Help

Trapped.

Molly.

This.

Follow.

Building.

Hurry.

Chapter Seventy-Four

Mike Changes Tribble (and Not for the Better)

"Pleased you're here, Tribble, though I have to say, rather surprised."

Mike picked up a crystal coffee cup and gently passed it from one hand to the other in a constant and repetitive movement. He had no intention of drinking the contents; he merely wanted to distract Tribble.

Mike had attended the Tempus school for special abilities as a mature student six years ago and very quickly mastered the unique power of understanding and command of the mind, both human and animal. He was able to build up an empathetic connection with any individual over which he wanted control.

On a subconscious level, they very quickly developed a complete trust of him and the previously guarded doors to their minds were gracefully swung open, allowing him complete, unencumbered access. He was of course a man of great morals so had never misused this ability for his own gain.

He could clearly see Tribble was troubled and he needed to be sure that whatever was on his mind could not and would not interfere with the work he was about to undertake.

Mike moved the cup so the murky brown contents that half-filled it could be seen by everyone in the room, particularly Tribble. He reached into his pocket with his free hand and took out a dropping pipette which he lowered into the cup. After squeezing and releasing the rubber nozzle at the top, he extracted some of the liquid and started to fill the small cylinder. Tribble watched, more interested than hypnotized at this point; so, too, was Professor Tempus, though she guessed what was to come.

Tribble's eyes met Mike's, who smiled before slowly lowering his gaze to the pipette positioned a few centimetres above the cup. A slight squeeze of the cylinder prompted a tiny teardrop to fall into the centre of the liquid. Concentric circles flowed outward from the point of impact. He ran his fingers around the rim of the cup, creating one rather sweet and melodious tone. The auditory accompaniment made the circles appear to move slower than they actually were.

A second drop of liquid into exactly the same place gave the circles increased vigour and depth. Subsequent drops made the circle's colour change, moving subtly though the rainbow spectrum.

Mike spoke:

"Relax, Tribble, notice how easily your breath flows, in perfect harmony with the circles. You can feel your stress lifting as they move outward, slowly but surely, eventually fading away to insignificance."

The Professor smiled. Mike assumed it was because Tribble

looked almost comical. His whole body was swaying ever so gently left and right, in rhythm with the concentric circles. The Professor's subtle expression of pleasure was not so superficial; she could feel the field mouse's worries evaporate.

Tribble's flame was burning bright yellow. His life signs were much stronger.

Mike continued. "I need you to focus on my voice; can you do that, Tribble?"

"Your voice, yes" came the gentle reply.

"All problems, all stresses do not exist in this room; you are relaxed."

"Relaxed…"

"Good, Tribble." Mike smiled, satisfied. "I am going to count backward from five, and when I reach zero you will focus entirely on the reason you were summoned here today. No outside pressures can or will prevent you from performing your duty."

Tribble nodded, though if Mike had any idea that he was in the process of helping transform Tribble so he could work for the Spletka with a clear conscience, he would have stopped immediately.

"Five. Four."

Tribble's flame, which was still as strong, had changed slightly, the yellow colour darkened.

"Three."

The flame grew darker still and now resembled the colour of a banana which had been left untouched for a month.

The Professor looked anxious. "Mike, are you sure this...?"

Mike raised his hand to silence her and emphasised the point by pushing his finger to his lips.

"Two."

The flame was now entirely deep dark brown.

"But, Mike, I really don't..."

He turned his head and shot her a look which said, *Will you please be quiet? I know what I'm doing!*

"One."

The flame was now jet black and burning strong. Something was very wrong. The Professor couldn't explain what it was but she didn't feel comfortable trusting the children's safety to this mouse.

"Mike, you should stop now. I can see..."

"Zero."

Tribble suddenly stopped swaying, and his eyelids sprang wide open, no longer feeling heavy and sleepy.

"Well, Professor, Mike. I understand you need my help and who am I to refuse? May I have access to your personal log-in details to the Tempus Network?"

Mike looked at him quizzically. "Why mine, Tribble?"

"Tut, tut, tut." Tribble shook his head. He jumped up on the bench directly in front of them and touched the screen. The prompt asked for log-in details

"Because this network no longer knows or recognises me, Mike. What I need to do requires top level access. Namely yours."

He stopped and beamed a grin that wouldn't have been out of place on any rodent toothpaste commercial. Mike was quite stunned by the remarkable change in his demeanour. Tribble looked at his own wrist, a sarcastic mime intended to tell Mike that he didn't have all day and could he kindly get on with it. Mike spoke into the monitor.

"Allow Tribble voice print."

"Voice print sample?" the computer responded.

"Halloo, good morning and let me in," Tribble said, much in the same way Professor Tempus would imagine the big bad wolf from the fable speaking, whilst requesting access into grandma's house.

"Access level?" the computer again responded.

"Full, unrestricted access." Mike spoke again, though this time with noticeably much less confidence. "Now we need to fix the Tempus Network and rescue the children. What do you need, Tribble?"

The mouse smiled and chuckled, looking Mike up and down as though *he* were the small insignificant rodent.

"Oh, Mike, you are funny." He closed his eyes, touched the screen, and shuddered with excitement. "I can feel them all in there, but they are not alone. There is a Spletka already in there, so I'm not sure why I was needed. He seems strong enough to do what he wants. He could even…"

He took a slow and pleasured gasp for air.

"What do we have here? There are two elements here, two people who do not belong."

"Arran and Molly," the Professor interjected as she slowly made her way toward the closed door; her intuition told her that this was no longer a safe room to be in.

"Arran and Molly?" Tribble repeated. "Oh, but she is good. I can see why the Spletka want her—and the boy. Her brother, no? He can do things in there which… Ah, that is why I am needed. Quite right too."

Mike, get him off that machine! The Professor telepathically commanded.

"Tribble, I think perhaps you better let me…"

Tribble shot a glance in Mike's direction. "Mike, please do forgive me. I should deal with you now. Doors open."

The closed door unlocked, swung open, and in walked the guards.

"Just so you know, I'm not doing anything at the moment, well apart from restricting your own access to the Tempus Network, letting in some of my, we'll say friends and turning your precious Molly over to the Spletka Clan."

"Guards, arrest that mouse!" Mike shouted.

The guards lifted their guns and pointed them at Tribble. They took a step closer and Tribble raised his hands in the air, a shocked look now plastered across his, what was until now, smug-looking face. The guards glared down at him, then across at each other.

One smirked, then the other; then the first one, no longer able to control himself, burst into fits of laughter, dropping his gun.

"You laughed first," said one guard.

"Did not," replied the other.

Tribble lowered his paws. "You guys," he exhaled under a huge sigh of relief. "Had me going there for a minute."

"Sorry, Tribble," the head guard replied. "You should have seen your face though, ha ha."

Simultaneously, both guards turned and wiped the smiles from their faces. Mike stood up to protest and was immediately persuaded to sit down when he found himself nose to nose with the business end of a gun barrel.

"Do sit down, Mike, and try not to cause a panic. It would be a terrible shame to have to kill you." Tribble's voice was instantly serious and monotone.

Mike sat and Tribble's voice changed again, suddenly reminiscent of something one may expect to hear from a children's presenter as he hopped up and down.

"Actually it wouldn't. It may even be fun."

What have I done? thought Mike.

Tribble spun around to see the Professor inching ever closer to the open door.

"With you in just a teeny tiny moment, Professor. Do me the courtesy of not leaving; we have barely had enough time to get to know one another, and besides, if you try to leave I'll have you shot in the head." He turned again to Mike. "Sorry about that. Now where was I?"

He tapped his head, a mocking gesture indicating that he had a memory like a sieve. Nothing could have been further from the truth.

"Oh yes, you must make an announcement that we will be having some visitors and they are not to be treated as hostile, okey dokey?"

"You must be mad!" Mike shouted.

"I'm furious!" returned Tribble. Then he chuckled. "Not really. But if you could do that now, I won't have to shoot you in the leg."

The guard standing above Mike lightly tapped him on the

forehead with the butt of his gun.

"Jus' in case you're wonderin'. I'm the one be doin' the shootin'."

There was an expectant silence. Tribble raised his eyebrows and shrugged, not so patiently waiting. "Tell you what," he said. "These new-fangled guns are a mystery to me. From what I understand it emits a green light ray which melts; is that the right word? We'll say *melts* away anything in its path. I'd like to see it work."

The guard pointed the gun to Mike's trembling right leg. Tribble placed his paws to his ears and told the guard to fire.

Confused, the guard spoke to him. He saw that Tribble was blocking his ears and therefore could not hear, so he spoke again a little louder. Finally, Tribble removed his paws. "Yes, what is it?!"

"Er, the gun not make any noise; Tribble not need t' cover the ears."

Tribble sighed. "I know. It was for dramatic tension." The guard shrugged. "I'm sorry about him," Tribble said to Mike. "Not too sure who's sharing the family brain cell at the moment, but he's a good aim; and has a wonderful singing voice too, or so I've been told."

The guard smiled and took aim again.

"Tribble, you don't have to do this." Mike's voice was both pleading and frightened. "I saw an image in your mind." He gasped,

"Your son. Whatever is happening I can help."

In an instant the Professor saw Tribble's flame turn to a weak yellow before returning to the darkened deathly colour characterizing the dramatic personality change from the meek little mouse that had entered the Citadel.

"No you can't," Tribble said flatly. "Fire!"

The guard pulled the trigger and a green light ray left the gun shaft, illuminating a perfect circle of green on Mike's right lap. At first, nothing happened. Mike was relieved, he thought the gun must be faulty. Two seconds later he let out an anguished cry of pain as the perfect circle seemed to hollow into and slowly through the leg, leaving blood and bone remnants as though they were painted with dripping oils, as part of a Salvador Dali masterpiece.

On impulse, his leg sprang up, kicking the bench and knocking the glass case containing the spiders to the floor. Though cracked, the case remained intact.

The Professor lunged forward to cover Mike's leg and was instantly blocked by the other guard.

"So eager, Professor." Tribble laughed as the first guard turned off the power from the gun, making the light disappear. "It's not your turn yet. But soon, be patient."

The flame on top of Mike's head was flickering as he fought to remain conscious.

"Okay, the other leg please…aim."

The guard aimed.

"Stop!" shouted the Professor. "Can't you see you're killing him?"

Tribble looked confused and replied calmly and matter-of-factly, "Well, yes of course I can. I'm no expert but I don't think he'd do what I wanted if I bribed him with cake, or gave him a big sloppy kiss."

"And he can't do it if he's dead or unconscious, can he?!"

The guard holding the gun pointed straight at Mike's other leg, waiting for the command to attack; he was almost dizzy with excitement and clearly enjoying the situation, deriving some sadistic, sick pleasure from seeing Mike suffer so.

The other, more intelligent guard moved from the door entrance to speak with Tribble.

"This isn't what we were told to do. We are supposed to let the others in and you were to gain control of the Tempus Network. You're not…"

"I'm not what?!" Tribble shouted back, stamping one of his tiny paws on the desk. "I'm doing what needs to be done. And I have control over the Tempus Network. I got that the second I touched the screen. Mr Melty Leg over here gave me his log-in authorisation."

Mike, though he was in extreme pain and sweating profusely, managed to give Tribble a defiant look that said, *You can kill me, but we're not going down without a fight.*

"And unless you want me to tell your boss that I could not complete my task because the incompetent henchmen he sent to help decided that following instructions was too much for them…"

"I wasn't saying that, Tribble. It's just…" The guard paused, almost expecting to be interrupted before simply nodding his head. "Sorry."

"Well, that's better, isn't it?" Tribble replied, once again upbeat; then he muttered under his breath but loud enough so everyone in the room could hear: "As if I haven't got enough to do, break into the Tempus Network, capture Molly, kill Arran and his friends. I mean a mouse's work is never done. Wonder what I'll have for tea. I bet they have a great canteen here."

The Professor was standing right next to the open door. It had crossed her mind that she could easily overpower a mouse; the two guards, however, posed somewhat more of a problem. They would have shot her long before she came within grasping distance of Tribble. It also crossed her mind that he could hear everything she was thinking, because as soon as the thought had formulated in her mind, Tribble smirked, raised his eyebrows, and shook his head.

"You can try, Professor, but I reeely wouldn't advise it."

Her second thought was rather more fleeting, self-preservation, literally a fight-or-flight reaction. Before the guards or Tribble had time to react, she bolted through the open door and ran as fast as she could.

Both guards stared blankly at one another before looking to Tribble for some sort of instruction.

"Well, get after her then!" he yelled. They both ran from the room, leaving the mouse and Mike.

"Really sorry, Mike. Can't get the staff these days, can you?" He glanced down at the puddle on the floor. "How's the leg?"

The room containing Richard Tempus was open. Rebecca stole a glance down the corridor at the two advancing guards before ducking in and slamming the door shut. She crouched down, her back resting against the door, and listened, unsure if they had seen her dive into the room. She was equally unsure if a flimsy door was going to be of any use in shielding her from two highly trained army soldiers.

On the other side the guards came to a standstill. The entrance had disappeared and was replaced with the single stone pillar.

"Did you see where she went?" one guard asked rather impatiently.

"I coulda sworn she came in through a door here," the other answered.

"Oh she did?" snapped the other. "I find that pretty unlikely, given that there are no doors here!"

"Well, I thought…"

"You thought you thought!" The Professor heard what she thought to be a sharp clip across the ear, followed by a 'yelp' from the less bright guard. "Thinking's never been your strongpoint, has it? What you thought you saw was obviously an optical illusion. We were warned that stuff like this might happen."

"She musta went in another direction."

The suggestion was met with another clip of the ear. "Yeah, good thinking." He stamped his foot in frustration. "C'mon, let's get back." They marched back to Tribble and the ailing Mike.

The Professor's heart rate—which upon the guards' approach was like a flock of overzealous woodpeckers at feeding time—had slowed to a more normal speed to resemble someone who was merely frantic and worried.

She stood, clueless. Not a state she was used to being in. Her father lay still. She expected no less. A soft glow from the blue orb illuminated his resting body.

"What do I do?" She spoke softly, with little hope of any reply.

She walked to the opposite end of the table and knelt down next to his body and placed her hands together as if about to pray. A few tears began to form at the corners of her eyes. She smiled slightly.

"I don't think I've cried so much as I have done these past few days."

She touched his head as if to wipe the sweat from his brow. There was none. Aside from the fact she could see he was breathing, one would have assumed he was dead. His skin was still cold to the touch. There was no pulse to speak of.

Her mind raced through a million and one images. All the terrible things that were happening, the evil people who were about to storm the Citadel and destroy everything good and pure her father had built, and more importantly, the one element which outweighed all the rest, Arran and Molly.

She had brought them here; she was showing off really and she knew it. She had an invention and wanted the two people closest to her in the world to be there, to share it with her. She never meant to, that is, she never considered for a moment that any danger would, that is...

"Father! I don't know what to do. Wake up! I can't do this alone; I need your help. Arran and Molly are in danger."

She slammed her fists on the table next to her father's head before stopping to look at the empty chair on the other side of the table.

She recalled her previous visit to this very room. She had been sitting in the empty chair, looking at the ghostly images, and one of those images had been acting exactly as she was now.

She had assumed that all the ghosts were past images of herself, of past unsuccessful timelines. But maybe, being a time traveller, the images of past and future were combined.

The room once again filled with the same entities as it had done before.

This time each in turn walked up to and stepped inside the Professor's body. She did not resist, instead felt a renewed understanding of all the possible futures she could encounter.

She knew what she had to do, and the sacrifices that could mean.

Going outside was not first on her list of favoured options but she trusted her own instincts. The guards were gone for now, and she had work to do.

Chapter Seventy-Five

An Old Friend Returns

"Sorry, sir, she got away." The first guard walked into the room, his head bowed in shame. The next followed behind.

Tribble was not amused.

"She got away?" He rolled his eyes and shrugged.

The guards remained silent.

"Well, I'm a forgiving mouse. I really am. I am confused though. I mean two strapping, seasoned soldiers such as yourselves, outrun by a little girl. What happened, did you pass a shoe shop on the way and had to stop for a little peruse?"

The not-so-bright guard spoke up, scratching his head as he did so. "She disappeared, like she was there, then like she was not there." He was then clipped again across the ear by the other guard.

"He knows what disappeared means."

Tribble did seem rather disturbed by this news.

"What do you mean disappeared?"

"Oh well, maybe he doesn't know what it means." The second guard shrugged.

The more intelligent of the two decided to speak up. "She was running down a corridor, then seemed to duck into a room in a stone pillar, but by the time we caught up with her, she was gone. There was no room, no door, nothing."

Tribble closed his eyes and concentrated. Within a matter of moments, a map of the corridors closest to the room in which they were standing was on the screen.

"Point to the place you lost her."

The guard did as he was told and Tribble zoomed in on the stone pillar. "There is another, perhaps more familiar force at work here. Though I can't work out how that is possible. The pillar *is* the door. You'll see it when you return, I'll make sure of it."

Tribble knew now that the guards were not outrun, and there was something very powerful in the Citadel with access to the Tempus Network.

"No more games. I'll have to work fast."

He looked at the guards and pondered for a moment before telling them to go capture the Professor. "And do not return till you have her."

The guards nodded and walked out of the room.

He looked to Mike, whose head was bowed. His eyes were clamped shut as he struggled to cope with the pain. Tribble contemplated his next move, then nodded his head decisively and touched the screen.

An image formed depicting the general patiently waiting outside the Citadel, supported by his vast army. The general spoke.

"Tribble, very pleasing to see you."

Tribble immediately lost his cocky attitude. The general was still able to scare the little mouse to his very core.

"The defences are switched off, sir. I'll release the drawbridge. Just follow my signal to the main control room." He paused for thought. "The two children, sir, they will soon be trapped. I'm doing what I can to slow them down, but I suspect Professor Richard Tempus is here somewhere. He still has some control over the network."

Rather than being worried the general simply nodded his head.

"As it should be, Tribble. Get inside the network, remember the plan."

Upon hearing the voice, Mike raised his head and stared at the screen

"Impossible!" he gasped. "It can't be."

The general smiled upon hearing this voice.

"Hello, Mike, my old friend. How are you?"

Chapter Seventy-Six

Hedge

A tiny pane of glass fell from the panel, pushed out by the previously paralysed spider. Had Rebecca Tempus been witness to it, she would have seen a fading blue aura surround it. The spider was no longer Spletka and it had a new mission. It cautiously stepped out and traversed the floor, creeping silently under the closed door.

***

"Just up ahead."

Rudolph pointed at the huge hedge in front of them which stretched both left and right as far as the eye could see.

"There doesn't appear to be a way past it," Sophia mused.

"Yeah," said Rudolph. "It's really thick, no gaps at all."

Without warning, he charged into the leaves and branches, which immediately drew closer together upon impact, giving him a small electric shock in the process.

He fell back, dazed.

"Not sure how I know this," said Arran, "but that hedge has just been placed there. I think someone is trying to slow us down."

"Makes sense," said Sophia. "They don't know exactly where

you are, but if the Spletka intercepted Joseph's last message, they know where we *were*, and thanks to Rudolph, they know where we are going."

Rudolph turned his head in shame.

"Remind me not to do the Tempus games next year," joked Molly, looking at the enormity of the hedge. "You can get past this though, Arran…right?"

Arran shrugged. "Probably. I'll take a quick look overhead first."

Arran, who had the power to do pretty much anything he wanted to in this place, decided the easiest option would be to simply levitate and make sure everything was safe, then airlift everyone to the other side.

He closed his eyes to focus. When the lids slowly opened, he was the perfect picture of concentration. He took a deep breath and raised his hands. Rudolph gasped in astonishment as he watched Arran float up into the air.

"That's just so cool."

"He's a show-off," added Molly.

"It's only levitation," said Sophia. "Twelve point two seven percent of the students in this school can do it."

"How can you have point two seven percent of a student?"

Rudolph asked, rather sarcastically.

Sophia didn't grant him a verbal response, but she did reach inside her jacket and hand him a pocket mirror.

Arran's levitation worked fine, in the sense that he rose up as high as he wanted to go. Unfortunately, seeing over the top of the hedge was somewhat more problematic.

The hedge grew at an alarming rate, and the higher Arran climbed, the more it grew. Arran's three friends watched as he sped up as fast as he could. The hedge matched his every move till he was but a tiny speck in the sky to the others on the ground.

Arran's return was less graceful than his earlier self-confident ascent. The frustrated crash with which he landed made the earth move.

"Not so wise, Arran," Sophia said. "There are people who can feel and track vibrations in this school. By now many of the children will have worked out that their best chance of finding us is by working together."

"It's this stupid hedge," Arran said. "Touch it and I get electrocuted, and flying over it... Well, I can't."

Sophia stared at the hedge. After a moment she smiled and reached out to touch a leaf.

"No," shouted Rudolph, "you'll electrocute..."

It was too late. Her hand touched the leaf, and if she was being electrocuted, she was taking it rather well. She didn't flinch once.

"I'm not a threat." She looked 'round at Rudolph. "You charged at the hedge, and it saw you as a threat, hence the electric shock." She stroked the leaf as though it were a puppy. "Even if the Spletka did place the hedge here, it is still a hedge, a living organism. I think it senses that all I want to do is communicate with it."

Arran looked confused. "How do you communicate with a hedge?"

"I was rather hoping you could do that actually, Arran; more than anybody here, you operate on a level closer to the base code of this environment. Come here. Give me your hand."

Reluctantly he approached with his arm outstretched.

"Now stroke it, say hello."

His first attempt was met with a tiny electric current which passed through his fingers. He stepped back.

"It feels your confusion," said Sophia. "Try again; think of it as a small defenceless animal."

He touched a leaf, gently running his fingers around its circumference. "I'm doing it!"

"Good," said Sophia. "Now the part I can't do. Explain to the hedge, using the same telepathy as you do on Molly, why we need to pass. If my presumptions are correct, and your abilities are stronger than whatever entity placed it here, it should grant us safe passage."

Arran placed his hands flat against the hedge, his fingers pulsing, his eyes closed as he telepathically told the story of how they had come to be here and of the evil making its way toward them.

Mother Nature, it would seem, has eyes and ears everywhere, even in the Tempus Network; no sooner had Arran stepped back than the leaves and branches began to rearrange themselves and an enormous archway stood in front of them, providing clear and easy access through the hedge to the other side.

"It says it will close again once we are all through," Arran said to the others.

They all gratefully stepped to the other side, and as good as its word, the hedge's leaves and branches filled the empty space until the archway was no more.

The deathly gong resonated and the screen filled the sky.

Wandering on her own, deep in the heart of the forest, Matilda came to a standstill. Tears filled her eyes when the die stopped and she was shown who the next victim of the Spletka would be.

Chapter Seventy-Seven

Craig Takes off the Gloves

"Well, you took your time!" Joseph shouted as Victor approached.

His continued struggles at the straps which bound him to the chair were fruitless. Victor was rather surprised at Joseph's apparent lack of respect. But rather than be annoyed he simply laughed.

"Yeah, I'm sorry, mate. Tell you what, put her there." He raised his hand, offering a friendly shake. Unable to move Joseph simply stared at him silently. "Oh, I forgot. You can't, can you? It's a lovely little ability you have there, helped us out a lot. We were walking in completely the opposite direction."

"Well, that's a fine way of thanking me!" Joseph yelled. "Now do me a favour and let me out!"

When the gong sounded they all looked to the skies at the rotating die. When the final victim was selected Victor, rather surprised, took a step back to make sure it wasn't him and was pleasantly surprised to see that he was only standing next to the intended target.

Joseph couldn't believe it, his head a lethal mix of anger, sorrow, and fear.

"What?!"

He looked around at everybody else, who said nothing and tried not to make eye contact with him; all except Victor, who simply shrugged. "Sorry, mate."

"I did my best. I tried! Why me? What did I do?"

Though the image on the screen remained focussed on Joseph, the sound of the death mask could be heard.

"Joseph. You are talk without actions. You could have captured the young girl; instead you wasted time and allowed them to escape, allowed them to bind you to this chair."

Joseph couldn't believe what he was hearing.

"I didn't have much choice in the matter, did I? I'd like to see you try to…"

The mask interrupted as though Joseph had never spoken.

"Victor, you lead this army. Are you all talk and no action?" Victor shook his head slowly. "Use what resources you have and dispose of young Joseph here."

Joss glared at Victor. "You can't, Vic."

Victor smiled. "Yeah, I can. Stammers, come here a moment and take off your gloves."

Craig Stamfordshaw walked through the crowd, which instantly parted like the biblical Red Sea as he passed, not one student daring to risk even the slightest touch.

When finally he stood in front of Joseph, a collective gasp of eager anticipation could be heard. Murmurs passed in waves of panicked confusion.

"What's he going to do?" asked one child.

"I've heard he can take your abilities and leave you burned to a crisp," said another.

Victor raised his hand to silence the crowd. "Now I'm not quite sure what will happen here, Joseph." Victor spoke softly. "Well, I do know you will have no powers or special abilities anymore, but beyond that, I simply have no idea."

"Victor, please don't. I've done nothing to you."

For all the response he got he may as well have been speaking to the death mask, which, though it could not be seen, was as present as the unseen monsters that lurked in the darkened shadows of the deserted alleyways of Judean Street.

Craig meekly spoke. "Victor, I don't w-w-want t-t-t-to d-d-d..." He stopped.

"I bet you're a hit with the ladies," Victor joked.

There was a flash of lightning and the mask, huge and imposing, appeared above all of them.

"Do it!" it bellowed.

"S-s-sorry." Craig reached out his hand to touch Joseph, who was struggling fruitlessly to avoid any contact.

Craig placed a finger on Joseph's forehead.

Craig showed no bodily change, but Joseph started uncontrollably shaking as if a thousand volts were hungrily racing their way through his body. He gasped for breath and his mouth and eyes snapped open as if pleading for release.

Release came, but not the one he hoped for. Pulse weakened, he slumped forward, not moving except for his mouth, which was opening and closing. Tiny drops of saliva fell to the floor like a mini, slow-moving waterfall.

"Eughh," Victor said, looking at Joseph. "That's gross. He's not dead?"

"May as well be." Joss looked on in utter disgust. "He's lost his mind, there's nothing in there."

Victor shrugged. "Oh well, that's what happens when Stammers touches you. Least now I know. Put the gloves back on, Stammers."

He turned to the crowd. As though they were one giant body, they all took a cautious step backward. Victor smiled and took in a huge triumphant breath. The feeling of power was unlike anything he had experienced before.

The mask faded from the sky and Craig Stamfordshaw put on

his gloves, crying his eyes out and unable to forgive himself for the terrible thing he had done—perhaps afraid for the disastrous things he would be asked to do later.

"You have Joseph's telepathic ability now, do you?"

Craig did not answer, his grief the only outward display.

"Oh for goodness sake, Stammers, do you or do you not have his ability?"

Though he did not move his lips, every child heard his deafening response cry out in their ears.

YES!

Victor shook his head, unprepared for the emotional response.

"All right, all right. I just asked, jeez."

Craig wiped the tears from his eyes. "W-w-why did y-you…?"

"Don't blame me, Stammers; you saw the mask. I said I could save you all, but my orders come from the Spletka, can't argue with them."

Craig was unconvinced.

"Now I hate to have to ask you this, mainly because I could die of old age before I get a response, but how does this work? If you touch somebody else, do you get their powers as well as Joseph's?"

Craig shook his head.

"Wow, concise. I like it. So the moment you take somebody's

powers the new power replaces the old one?"

"Y-y-y…"

"Just nod your head, Stammers, much easier."

Chapter Seventy-Eight

The Advance

The general turned and looked at the mostly blank faces of his army, each and every soldier willing to lay down their life in protection of their precious general and in the fulfilment of his orders. Most of them once good, honest people, transformed into mindless drones by his own death stare. The others among them willing volunteers in pursuance of the Spletka dream.

The Spletka mission was simply domination, a dictatorship that would eventually grow though the planet like a ravenous cancer till everything good and pure was consumed.

The General knew that his death stare was the key, and to his mind the only one who could stand in his way now was Professor Tempus's daughter.

He would walk into the Citadel, which would be easy to do with the perception filter Tribble had placed over them during their last communication. It would take effect once he entered the network. The guards wouldn't notice the danger till it was too late.

From there he would take by force the inexperienced Rebecca Tempus's power and enlist the services of Molly; if she would not yield, then he would kill her.

Made no real difference to him.

His excited heartbeat almost brought a touch of colour to his cheeks, making him look less like a walking corpse and more like a terminally ill man.

His soft, gravelled voice, which struck intense fear into anyone outside the Spletka, seemed to soothe and excite both Bellonta and the army.

He stroked Bellonta's cheek with his bony hand, his elongated fingernails releasing an energy that burned very slightly, leaving an indentation as though she was being branded. She did not move away, nor did she flinch; in fact she seemed to be enjoying it.

"Shall we, my dear?"

Bellonta's loving eyes flashed in admiration before him.

Their time had come.

Chapter Seventy-Nine

Tribble Enters the Network

Mike was almost unconscious, which annoyed Tribble, who was trying to conduct a deep and meaningful conversation about politics, food; oh, and why he was picking up traces of Richard Tempus.

"Look, Melty Leg."

Which was now Mike's new nickname.

"It's not that I don't admire your self-restraint, but I'm kind of on the clock here. I don't think the good General will be quite as understanding as me when he finds out all you have done is made a sickly puddle on the floor, without giving me any useful information."

Mike stared at the blank screen on which the general had appeared only moments before.

"He can go to hell."

Each word he uttered took a tremendous amount of concentration and effort.

Tribble laughed. "I think he's been; in fact in about five minutes I suspect hell will be coming here."

Tribble then turned to look at the blank monitor. He touched the screen.

"And I suppose that's my cue to enter the network."

Mike watched in confused amazement as Tribble's form changed. He was transforming into something but…how…?

"Professor Tempus?"

Mike was barely conscious but there was a tinge of hopefulness in his voice. Tribble was an exact replica of the good Rebecca Tempus. He turned and smiled before lowering his head so he was eye level with the ailing Mike.

"Nope, still me. Gaining the children's trust may need a spot of deception. Wish me luck."

He waited, savouring the moment of unspoken rage coming from Mike before continuing.

"No? Nothing? Oh very well, I'll be seeing you. Say hello to the general when you see him."

He turned, touched the screen, and vanished.

Bellonta marvelled at the magnificent Citadel as it gleamed in the moonlight.

"What are we waiting for, husband of mine?"

Almost on cue, the huge drawbridge lowered itself, laid out like an unguarded royal welcome mat.

"Oh, that." She grinned.

"Yes, that, my dear."

The general casually advanced on the Citadel, followed by his army, while guards stood at their posts all around the Citadel, blissfully unaware of the approaching danger.

Chapter Eighty

Lady Profeta

"Maybe your ex-boyfriend was right," Molly said to Sophia, whose clenched fists and piercing stare at the empty space where the screen had been underlined her own rage eloquently.

"I hate him. He's a bully," she answered. "And you sacrificing yourself won't change that. If anything it will mean that the Spletka, with no further need for us, will kill us all the faster."

They turned to take in their new environment.

The old lady quietly tending the roses in her front garden was perhaps the last thing the children expected to see once they reached the other side of the hedge, but there she was, a sweet silver-haired dear, dressed in a long, flowing, floral gown which almost seemed like an extension of the garden itself.

There was no grass; every inch of soil had been used to accommodate every rare and exotic flower imaginable. The floral display was subtly broken by a cobbled stone path which led from her back door and spiralled around the whole area, making sure all the plants were within arm's reach.

"Rain, would you be so kind?"

Her sweet voice seemed to soothe the flowers and charm the

elements into doing her bidding.

"My roses need a little drink and the retenfalifa buds too."

A tiny shower came from the sky and fell to the soil, but only on the two plants the lady mentioned. The rest of the garden remained bone dry and basked in the glorious sunshine.

"Wow," Molly said, momentarily forgetting the imminent danger from which they were all running. "That is beautiful."

The old lady, who was kneeling on the path speaking to a daffodil, slowly turned at the sound of Molly's voice to see the four children staring in wonder on the outskirts of the garden. She smiled, and with a little effort rose to her feet.

She brushed the soil from her clothes and it fell to the path, then got up and walked back to the base of the flowers from which it came.

"Okay, I didn't expect that," said Rudolph.

"Come in, children, the kettle is on. I imagine you are quite hungry too?"

The lady didn't wait for a response and hobbled happily down the spiral path and in through her back door, which she left ajar.

Arran looked to Sophia. Though he remained silent, the question on his face was evident.

Well, you're the brains here. Is it safe?

"I don't see why not." Sophia led the way into the lady's house, taking care not to step on any of the plants on the way.

The children followed. Rudolph was quite unnerved by some of the flowers which turned their multi-coloured heads to watch the children as they passed. Arran saw this also and his gift triggered another sensation; he felt sure that if he listened closely enough he could actually hear the flowers speaking to one another.

"She said they'd be right over."

"Yes she did, didn't she?"

"Which one do you think is Molly?"

He brushed it off as his overactive imagination and continued on into the house.

Sunlight beamed in through the windows and illuminated the quaint kitchen. In the centre of the room, five chairs were placed around a large oak dining table with a steaming teapot, a small jug of milk, and a bowl of sugar cubes. Five place mats, five plates, and five cups and saucers had been positioned opposite each chair, patiently awaiting the children's arrival.

The lady opened the oven, and the inviting aroma of freshly baked bread wafted around the kitchen. The children sat as the lady, wearing floral oven mitts, carried the food to the table. Once there, she sat down, removed the oven gloves, and rested her chin on her fingertips, which were held together as though she was about to pray.

"You're just in time. I'm Lady Profeta. It's very nice to meet you all in person."

Arran looked at her quizzically. "You know us?"

Miss Profeta smiled and nodded her head, looking not at Arran but directly at Molly.

"Yes, I know all about you." She then opened her hands in a welcoming gesture. "All in good time; now, please eat."

Rudolph looked greedily at the large loaf. "Do you have a knife?"

Sophia shook her head, a resigned shake that said, *What must it be like to have so much space inside your head?* "I don't think we need one. Miss Profeta, if she lives up to her name, old Spanish, I assume? Anyway, she probably knew we were coming before we did, hence this elegant table layout. Just the right number of plates, chairs, cutlery and I'm guessing food and drink ready, bang on time for us as we entered her house. I suggest we reach for the bread and see what happens, because she is right. I am famished!"

"Not sure about famished, but you're certainly a know-it-all," Rudolph retorted as he reached and touched the loaf. The instant his fingers made contact with the food, a single slice separated itself and fell into Rudolph's hand. He took a huge bite. "Mmm," he said out loud as he chewed. "Banana cake, this is gorgeous, just like my mom used to make."

Arran sighed. "Oh, I'm not over keen on banana."

"Then might I suggest you don't have banana, Arran," Miss Profeta replied. "But please do take a slice." The bread fell into Arran's hand just as it had done for Rudolph and he took a small cautious bite.

"Lasagne, French fries, just a hint of salt. One of my favourites too, thanks."

Molly was next; unsurprisingly she went for the chocolate fudge cake. Last to take a slice was Sophia.

"What does yours taste like?" Molly asked.

"Freshly baked bread and butter."

"But doesn't it change into something you like?" Rudolph asked.

Sophia shrugged. "I like freshly baked bread. Why ruin the aesthetic with an uninvited taste?"

Arran was first to get to business, half-eaten lasagne still in his mouth. He looked at the woman who was busy pouring the tea. "So, Miss Lady Profeta." He paused to consider the most delicate way to ask, "Who are you?"

Miss Profeta took a sip of tea, savouring its taste.

"Perfect."

Arran waited patiently as did the other children, very interested in what she had to say.

"A friend…to you and aid to all who ask the right questions, even the ones who are approaching the hedge as we speak."

Rudolph glanced behind toward the still open door, then back at Lady Profeta.

"Hadn't we better get a move on then?"

"You are free to leave this house whenever you please…but to leave the network you must first embrace the network."

"You mean the coins?" Sophia added. "Our coins?"

The lady nodded. "It is the only way out of here, but be careful; one coin will lead one of you out, but the right coin will set you all free."

Which coin sets us all free?" asked Rudolph.

"If she was going to simply tell us that, there would be no challenge in the game," said Sophia.

"This is no game," said Arran. "Some very real people are on their way over here to kill us and capture my sister."

"I didn't say **I** found it to be a game, but this is the Tempus games platform, and like any computer game it can only operate by a pre-defined set of parameters; you should know that. Which means, we need the coin to get out of here, and there is only so much Lady Profeta can tell us."

Lady Profeta nodded. "Your young friend is quite correct; there are rules by which even I must abide."

"I thought that Spletka mask thingy said all the coins had been removed from the island." Rudolph thought back to his time on the beach with the rest of the students.

Lady Profeta smiled and reached over to touch his hand. "Do you find the Spletka to be a trustworthy sort?"

Rudolph shrugged and shook his head. "No, I suppose not."

"Then what can you tell us?" Arran wanted to get back to the matter in hand.

"I can tell you that Molly is one of the reasons you are still alive now. The Spletka have it in their collective mind that they can convert her over to their side. Arran's abilities have kept you all hidden from detection so far, but the Spletka could, if they wanted to, kill every living organism in the network. Unfortunately, that would include Molly."

She stared sympathetically into Molly's eyes.

"Are you sure you don't want to join them?"

"Course not," said Molly.

"Oh well," sighed Lady Profeta, shrugging and making her way down the corridor. "The correct coin is the one closest to the key. Please make your decision before you leave the house, and do use the front door." She swung the door open, but not one of the children dared to step outside.

"There's nothing there," said Molly.

"Yeah," said Rudolph, "just black. We could be stepping into a bottomless pit or something."

"I assume that's what Molly meant by 'nothing,'" added Sophia.

"We haven't made up our minds where we are going yet. I guess when we do it'll look different out there."

"Well, it's not much of a puzzle," Rudolph said. "Lady Profeta said only one coin will work on all of us and that Molly is the key, so we should go for Molly's coin."

Sophia looked at Molly. "Lady Profeta said that the correct coin is the one closest to the key. That does not necessarily mean that your coin is the one."

"Er, hello, supposed know-it-all," snapped Rudolph. "Course it's her coin; you don't get much closer to Molly than Molly."

Molly looked at Arran and smirked. "Yeah, you do. Given the choice I'd free Arran over myself. Which makes Arran's coin closer to me, and as I'm the key..."

"You sure?" asked Arran.

Molly nodded, as did Rudolph and Sophia. "We're all going for

Arran's coin please, Miss Profeta."

Miss Profeta embraced Molly.

"You have chosen wisely, my child; may the heavens go with you."

Chapter Eighty-One

Gemma

"What have we here, Stammers?" Victor asked whilst looking at the hedge; more because he liked the sound of his own superior voice than because he wanted an answer. Victor also knew he would be able to rudely walk away from Craig Stamfordshaw before he was able to reply.

"It's a h-h-he… It's a…"

It was too late. Victor was off looking for an entrance; he quickly noted that there was no visible entrance. He got the same electric shock when he touched the hedge and didn't bother trying to levitate over it. He couldn't be bothered with the effort involved in lifting everyone safely to the other side. He was a bully and was more inclined to destroy whatever stood in his way.

He turned to his private army.

"Okay, fellas, this hedge needs bulldozing because it keeps electrocuting me, and we need to be on the other side. Anyone good with electricity? Surely one of you freaks has some sort of electrical gift?"

Gemma Marsden stayed silent and looked down to her toes, even though five or six of the children were staring directly at her.

"Come on," shouted Victor. "Surely one of you can do something, or have you forgotten if we don't get Molly we're all going to die!?"

Marie, Gemma's best friend, nudged her forward out of the crowd.

Gemma, like many others in the school, had been extensively bullied by Victor and his gang when she first joined Tempus's School for Special Abilities. She was scared of him and didn't relish the idea of speaking up and drawing attention to herself.

Victor heard the murmurs in the crowd and looked toward Joss for an interpretation; she pointed at the frightened schoolgirl being gently ushered out from the crowd.

"It's her, Gemma, she has the ability to absorb electricity, oh, and to inflict a shocking amount of pain too if the occasion called upon it."

She chuckled at her own joke but clamped her mouth shut when she found she was the only one laughing.

Victor smiled, remembering his past encounters with Gemma. Most memorable was the time he and his gang attacked her with water bombs during her private ability enhancement session; at the time this was something that could very easily have killed her.

He was also aware that Gemma thought he was rather cute

when she first came to the school, but as a shy, short, ginger-haired kid with pimples and glasses, she had assumed there was no way Victor was ever going to reciprocate any romantic interest.

"Right, Gemma, come 'ere."

Gemma raised her head submissively to look at Victor, taking care not to look him directly in the eyes. Her parents taught her that to look another human being or animal directly in the eyes was a threatening challenge and, unless you were sure of backing the stare up with physical reinforcement, it was best to remain invisible.

There was no chance of simply fading back into the crowd unnoticed now though as everyone was looking directly at her.

"Gemma!" Victor shouted. "Get your shocking butt over here before I douse you in water."

A few members of Victor's gang laughed, but Gemma stayed put, like a rabbit caught in the headlights of an oncoming car.

Seeing he was getting nowhere Victor changed his tone, well, as much as a bully can.

"Perhaps I overdid it with that water thing, and the beatings and, well, all the other stuff too, eh?"

Gemma turned away.

Victor took a deep breath and sighed. Being nice was something he'd never had to do to get what he wanted before coming onto the island.

"I'm sorry, Gemma, but we have to put that all behind us. I'm trying to save us all, but I need your help to do it. Will you help?"

A few people in the crowd were taken in by Victor's show of false sincerity and a few random people egged her on.

"Come on, Gemma!"

"What's the holdup?"

"She's just standing there."

"I think she's on Molly's side. She wants us all to die."

The crowd was now, to Gemma, beginning to sound more intimidating than Victor. She walked toward him and they all cheered.

Victor raised his hand to shut them up, which worked instantly.

She stood and faced the hedge.

"Okay," said Victor. "How does this work?"

"I just touch it," she replied. "I never dealt with massive electric charges before. Headmaster Dews was trying to teach me to focus my energies to handle more charge, but said I needed to practice focus, or it could be dangerous for me."

Victor nodded, pretending to listen and care about what she was saying.

"Well, there's no time like the present, is there?"

Gemma turned her head, this time looking him in the eyes. To her mind he was basically saying give it a go, and if you die…you die.

Victor was no mind reader but the message in her eyes was clear enough:

Are you crazy? I'm not doing it!

"Gemma, I don't want you to die." He raised his hand and pointed at the crowd. "None of us do, but if you don't do it, we all will die."

She shook her head, trying to comprehend what she was about to do. This was not how today was supposed to go. By now she should have bowed out of the hunt for her coin and would be at Bridget Fondue's Fanciful Fancies, making her way through a tray of lemon and almond cream fingers with her parents.

She stretched her hand out and touched the hedge with her finger. A massive electrical charge passed from the hedge and into her body, making her jump back and fall to the floor.

Victor looked at her in surprise. "Well, I could have done that."

He let out a thunderous roar of laughter, accompanied by everyone in the crowd apart from Maria, who was quietly speaking to herself.

"Come on, Gemma, you can do it. Remember what Mr Dews told you. Focus. Now get up!"

Tears streamed down Gemma's face and she covered her ears to shield herself from the oncoming taunts.

She turned to see Victor, almost doubled over in laughter, and then something happened. Fear turned to anger. She breathed heavily and with renewed energy rose to her feet, marched toward the hedge, and grabbed a branch so tight a trickle of blood from her hand dropped to the ground from where a thorn had cut her palm. The crowd and Victor fell suddenly silent.

A rage of electricity raced through her body; she screamed a piercing cry and fell to her knees but she didn't release her grasp. Instead she slowly rose to a standing position. Her hair transformed from ginger to a red fire colour, then silver neon, the same colour her eyes were turning. She took three deep inhales and on the third shouted:

"DIE!"

At once she forced a massive electrical charge out of her body and back into the hedge. The branches and leaves turned bright red and burst into flames. Within seconds, the entire hedge was no more than pitiful piles of ash. The once doubting crowd began to cheer.

"Gemma, Gemma, Gemma."

She turned once more to Victor, who was visibly impressed and put his arm around her.

"Nice one, Gemma. I like the hair; it's a better look for you."

Gemma's face turned red again, this time not from rage. She was blushing.

Aside from the picturesque cottage surrounded by a floral garden, the area beyond the place where the hedge once stood was a barren wasteland as you would expect to see in an old western movie. There was even a tumbleweed that passed in front of them.

There is no way the entire crowd of children will fit in that cottage, thought Victor.

"Me and Joss are going inside; you lot wait here."

Joss walked up to join him as he opened the gate.

Although Joss kept to the path, Victor did not hesitate to trample the flowers, taking the shortest route to the open door. He couldn't hear the cries the flowers made, and perhaps that was just as well. Had he been able to hear them, he would only have stayed a while longer to inflict some more needless pain.

He and Joss stopped at the entrance and the door opened.

"I have a feeling we are expected." Victor looked back at the crowd. "Can't hurt to take a little protection, just in case." The child army stood patiently waiting for Victor's command.

"Stammers, Gemma, come with us."

The two children ran to join them. Gemma took Victor's lead and trampled as many flowers as she could on the way. The electrical residue she was still giving off wilted the flowers as her feet touched them.

All four children walked in through the open door together.

Chapter Eighty-Two

Help from the Father

"Oh come on, Rebecca Tempus, you have a high IQ. You can do this."

Talking to herself was not alien to the Professor; she'd often had some very frank and in-depth discussions with herself during the endless hours she'd spent working in her basement laboratory, whilst scribbling in her father's journal.

She took her own newly acquired journal from her pocket and turned a new leaf to discover a new inscription, which simply said:

"Invoke the energy."

"Oh, brilliant, invoke the energy. What on earth does that mean?"

She looked up and down the empty corridor, rather surprised that no one had come looking for her yet. She continued to speak out loud, searching her mind for some sort of...

"Wait a minute...what on Earth indeed. The earth, the power, the energy behind this planet."

She recalled her state of mind earlier in her laboratory, the rainbow energy that ran through her and everything she could see.

"Okay, I just need to concentrate; to open my mind, heart, and soul, to allow…"

She sat on the floor cross-legged and closed her eyes, attempting to clear her mind. She concentrated on her breathing, making her breaths slow and deliberate. Each intake seemed to arrive with renewed energy. It was as though she was taking into her body complete love and understanding; she even felt the living spirit of her father enter her consciousness, which made her weep.

She opened her eyes to see the rainbow tears once again fall to the floor, exactly as they had done once before.

She stood, head held high, arms by her side, palms open and inviting. Her environment was transformed; the walls, floor, doors all had the same multi-coloured energy flowing round and through them. The air itself populated and, if she was religious, she would say by spirits or orbs floating each in a pre-determined path. Some of them passed right through her, elevating her own spirit and mood each time it happened.

She took a step forward, then cautiously stopped. The colours at the far end of the corridor faded slightly in colour. As she breathed in, a sickly, damp, and mouldy smell entered her body, nearly enough to make her retch.

The two guards who were sent to seek out the Professor appeared at the top of the corridor and proceeded to walk slowly toward her.

She spun around. Her father's door was locked, no visible escape. The guards moved closer.

She stood motionless and frightened, no idea what to do. She considered calling for help, but that may only result in getting someone else as well as herself killed. The guards came to a complete standstill directly in front of her, then looked at one another.

The not-so-bright guard pointed his finger directly at her face.

"That door weren't there afore. That's where she went into."

"You sure?" the other answered.

"Yeah, am sure. Think she's still in there?"

The Professor's mood changed, from complete fear to utter confusion. Her father's voice resonated in her head.

"Don't say a word, baby girl, and take a side step to the right."

Unquestioningly, she did as she was instructed.

The brighter of the two guards tried the handle but the door did not budge.

"Can a try, sir? Am really good with doors an' that."

The first guard shrugged and stepped back, allowing the supposed door expert to do his magic.

The not-so-bright guard bowed his head and ran as fast as he could at the closed door. The door did not budge and the tremendous impact sent the guard crashing to the floor, nursing his sore head. The first guard shook his head disapprovingly as he stood over him.

"Very good, tell me, did you train as a locksmith?"

The other guard answered earnestly, "No, no, it's like a natural gift av got."

The Professor chuckled as the guard rose to his feet. Both guards' ears pricked at this sound and the Professor clamped her mouth shut.

"You heard that too, right?"

"Yeah, a did." He faced the door. "Oi Professor Whatsaname, we cun hear ya in there. Open the door and we'll kill you."

The other guard struck him across the back of his head with the palm of his hand.

"Trained negotiator too, are you? …Stupid."

He shouted through the door too.

"Come on out, Professor, we won't hurt you. You have one minute. If we don't see you then you can kiss good-bye to your friend Mike. Come on, Professor, we know you can hear us."

Professor Tempus's father's voice rang out in her ears again.

"They can't see you, my dear. Now go help Mike; you don't have much time."

Chapter Eighty-Three

Lady Profeta Meets Victor Graston

The interior of the cottage looked completely different than it had appeared when Arran, Molly, Sophia, and Rudolph had been welcome guests of Miss Profeta.

The room was dank and cold. Aging wallpaper peeled away from the walls, which were mostly covered in mould. Massive cobwebs in one corner framed an old lady who was crouched near an old mongrel drifting in and out of sleep.

If she weren't in the relative comfort of the cottage, you would swear she belonged on a street corner somewhere begging for scraps and loose change.

Victor was the first to move forward.

"Hey, oldie. You seen some kids pass through here?"

Miss Profeta raised her head slightly to look him in the eye. She may have looked aged and weak but her stare was somehow unnerving. Victor signalled for his three companions to join him.

Her feeble voice was barely a whisper.

"I have seen many children pass through this way over the years. The first must have been way back in…"

"I haven't got time for this," Victor interrupted. "Joss, look inside her head."

Joss was slightly distracted, her attention taken by the dog. She stepped forward to pat him on the head.

"Is he all right? He doesn't look that well."

Miss Profeta simply smiled, raised her hand, and stroked Joss's cheek. She spoke very clearly without moving her lips; a kindly, comforting voice that only Joss was able to hear.

You are not like the others here. You have a different purpose. It won't be long before you are discovered. You should join the others while you still can. They are headed toward the marketplace. Take a left at the crossroads. The others must not follow you.

"Er, hello, Joss. Today would be good."

Victor shook his head and put his arm around Gemma, who was only too happy to stand there and help make Joss feel jealous. The action did not have the desired effect. Joss's affections were elsewhere and this immature behaviour served only to make her feel more ashamed for associating with Victor in the first place. She stood up and walked to him.

"She doesn't know anything. All she is thinking about is that dog. It's not very well. I think it had a fight with a larger animal and…"

"Yeah, whatever, Joss; tell it to the Samaritans, will you?"

Joss shrugged her shoulders.

"Look, oldie!" Victor shouted, intending to threaten Lady Profeta. "Oh, what's the point? You ain't seen nothing. Do you at least know what's up ahead?"

Miss Profeta spoke one last time before drifting into a deep sleep. Her voice sounded decidedly croakier than it had been previously.

"There is a crossroads. Decide your route carefully because once you travel upon your chosen path, there is no way back."

"What do you mean by that, oldie?"

Miss Profeta murmured slightly but remained sound asleep.

"Hello, oldie?!" Victor shouted.

"I t-t-think she's as-as-asleep," Craig said, half covering his ears with his hands, an attempt to block out Victor's brash, loud voice.

"No, do you think?" he replied sarcastically.

"You won't get anything more out of her," Joss said.

Victor glared at her and marched out of the same door he came in, his arm still around Gemma, who grinned and flicked her hair in Joss's direction as they left the cottage.

Victor's army was waiting at the gate of the cottage when they left.

"Right, you lot, that woman was about as useful as a mouse hole in an elephant house."

Gemma laughed. The rest remained silent, patiently awaiting instructions for their next move forward.

"We're going to the crossroads."

Chapter Eighty-Four
Professor to the Rescue

"Hey, Mike."

The familiar sound of the Professor's voice, though it was only a whisper, was enough to stir him. She loosened the straps which bound him.

"Get away from me."

He looked around but could see nothing but the empty room and the blank computer monitor.

"I can't see you!"

Trying to make sense of it, he supposed his mind may be playing tricks on him. Whatever the case, his last recollection of Professor Tempus was that of an imposter; Tribble's cruel disguise designed to gain the confidence of Arran and Molly.

"Leave me alone. I know what you are!"

The Professor was confused and a little hurt. She assumed the sound of her voice and his impending rescue deserved an overwhelming show of gratitude, or a "hello" at the very least.

She knelt in front of him and concentrated hard, willing Mike to be able to see her. The cloak that was shielding her from his sight lifted and he saw the Professor's smiling face in front of him.

"Do what you want with me," he shouted—well, as much as he could. "I'll never help you get those children."

"It's me, Mike, snap out of it. We have to leave. Rather quickly would be good."

"Professor?"

"That's me."

"Let me inside your head. I have to be sure."

The Professor nodded. "Okay, but make it fast. Time is of the essence here."

Mike raised his head and looked into the Professor's eyes; three seconds later the corners of his mouth cracked a smile.

"Oh, thank goodness. We need to warn… It's Jhonas!"

"What do you mean it's Jhonas? Where? Mike, speak."

Mike was asleep.

The Professor sighed. "Oh, great, thanks, Mike; you've been very helpful…not."

She glanced down at his leg wound and shook her head. *Poor man,* she thought. *I'm not even sure the doctors in this century could do anything with that.* The congealed, watercolour mess of Mike's skin, bones, and blood dripped through the open, perfectly round wound in his leg. She touched it gently, wishing there was something she could do to help.

The Professor suddenly began to feel faint and violently sick. Her whole body started to convulse. She wanted more than anything to lie down. Her head throbbed as though somebody were pushing red-hot needles through her eyes from the inside.

"What's happening?" she gasped. "What's happening?"

She gasped again, this time with a different focus. Mike's leg was healing. Her very touch was somehow making the dripping oil colours re-form back into skin, bones, and blood. She wanted to let go. She was growing weaker by the second but refused to release her grasp till Mike was back to full fitness.

The skin eventually formed nicely over Mike's leg, and his eyes snapped open. Just in time to see the Professor fall to the floor at his feet. He knelt down and carefully cradled her head in his arms.

"Professor, are you okay?"

The Professor, weak, managed a small laugh. "Yes, I'm good, you?"

Before Mike had the opportunity to respond, it was the Professor's turn to faint. She lay on the floor, motionless.

Chapter Eighty-Five

Tribble Meets the Gang

Tribble, now walking in a body that was the exact replica of Professor Tempus, strolled the beach and stared up at the sky.

"How do humans cope with this appearance?" He brushed the tweed jacket with his hands.

"You can understand why they wear so many clothes. If I had a body and face this ugly outside the network, you wouldn't be able to see me for the layers of material I'd need for camouflage."

He looked up at the floating Grombit death mask that rose in the sky like a mummified sun. He allowed himself a wry, expectant smile before pursing his lips together. After a short intake he exhaled, whistling a long continuous tone. To the ordinary listener there was no sound at all, but the mask was no ordinary listener; its hollow, morbid stare angled itself down, looking angrily at the replica Professor.

The whistle continued, growing steadily in intensity till the mask took the bait and slowly dropped down from the sky and they were almost face-to-face.

"It's about time." Tribble offered the mask a courteous bow.

"A brave move and rather stupid move, attracting my attention like that, Professor Tempus," the mask said, its facial features still and motionless.

Tribble's eyebrows crossed, and he was momentarily confused before realising his voice and appearance would be the last thing the Spletka would either want or expect on this island.

"Oh, the voice and the clothes and this face. Repulsive, aren't they?"

The mask did not respond.

"Tough crowd," Tribble continued. "Anyway, don't worry, I'm here to find Molly and her brother Arran."

The mask glowed red, fire burning in the empty hollows it had for eyes. "That is something that will never be allowed!"

Tribble was not intimidated; in fact, he was rather amused. He raised his right hand and clicked his thumb and middle finger together.

A transparent helium balloon appeared around the mask and extinguished the glowing flame as fast as it had appeared. A single string dangled from the balloon which Tribble grasped and set off walking, almost skipping, further down the beach. Just one lady and her prize-winning balloon.

"Right, floaty, let's compare notes," Tribble joked.

This was the first time the floating mask's featureless face suited the situation and the one emotion the agent of the Spletka was now feeling...surprise.

"Firstly you can relax. My name is Tribble, asked by the Spletka to come in and tell you how to do your job properly, as you have not managed to capture, or even find for that matter, Arran or Molly."

The mask's bellowing voice replied, "But you look just like the…"

"Oh, that will never do," interrupted Tribble. "You sound like the voice of God and if anyone is going to sound like that, it's me."

He paused for thought, considering which voice to give the mask, and after chuckling slightly he clicked his fingers. "There, try that."

The mask repeated and concluded its previously attempted sentence; only this time the commanding boom was gone and replaced by a weak and feeble imitation of Mickey Mouse.

"But you look and sound just like the old Professor's daughter, Rebecca Tempus."

Tribble was laughing so hard at the vocal adjustment; he nearly released his grasp on the balloon.

"Sorry, you sound brilliant, and stupid. Don't worry, when you speak to the idiots inside the network you'll still have your intimidating Godlike persona."

He sat on a rock and casually bobbed the balloon up and down, tugging gently on the string and releasing.

"I have disguised myself as the children's faithful friend and ally, Professor Rebecca Tempus. I'm actually much more attractive than this." Then he muttered to himself, "Not that that's any great challenge; these humans are repulsive. Even you are more desirable."

The Mickey Mouse voice spoke once again. "How is it that you have the power to do this to me in this place?"

"Because I have much more intelligence and skill than your average Spletka drone, thank you. There are many things you can't do here, though credit where credit is due: I assume outside the network you are a spider hacker attaching yourself to Grombit's hard light image to allow me and Spletka passage into the network, and stop everyone else from getting out."

The mask nodded.

Tribble clicked his fingers together again and the balloon disappeared. "Well, as long as they don't know that you're there in the real world, we can go about our work. The reason you cannot find the children is because of Molly's uniquely talented brother Arran. He's good, perhaps the only one on the planet even more so than me. Luckily he has no idea what he can do or we'd all be dead right now, hence the forthcoming trickery on my part." He did a brief twirl.

"Tribble may have a hard time killing the boy, but the good Professor

Tempus, why, she's their friend and protector."

The mid-air nod from the death mask high in the sky could almost be mistaken for a show of joy.

"Arran has the power to mask their whereabouts, though I suspect he has no idea he is doing it. With him out of the equation all of our jobs are going to be so much easier, we can all go home and have tea."

"Long live the Spletka!"

"Well, there's something I never expected Mickey Mouse to say," Tribble said. "To be honest, I don't care much for the Spletka, or anything for that matter. Once my job is done I'm outta here."

"So what is our next move?"

"To begin with you're going to tell me everything you know, who's on the island, what skills do they have, who is on our side, and who do we need to eliminate? You killed anyone yet?"

***

Victor didn't have far to travel before he found the signpost; in fact it appeared, grew from the ground like an eager tree, right outside Lady Profeta's house almost as soon as he had made his mind up that he needed to find it.

It had multiple signs on it, each bearing the name of a child still contained within the Tempus Network.

Each sign pointed to a path which led to a gate, too many to count at a single glance.

"What now?" Victor asked, openly shrugging. The post with Arran's name lay to the left.

"You want to kill Arran," said Gemma. "Let's take that path."

All sense of morality had left her consciousness; she seemed only interested in pleasing Victor.

Joss knew that taking the path Gemma suggested would lead them right to Arran, Molly, and the other children.

"Victor, that doesn't necessarily mean that's where Arran has gone; chances are they stuck together and went down one of the other paths to throw us off the scent. They are not stupid. They've got Sophia Tal-Grasto with them. I reckon we should choose the path least likely; Rudolph's one perhaps?"

Chapter Eighty-Six

Milk Please

Arran, Molly, Sophia, and Rudolph, once out of Lady Profeta's house, found themselves standing on a short, gravelled path which led to a busy marketplace on an enormous circular grass field. Directly in front of them an old poodle lay sleeping, twitching his nose slightly at intervals as though he had found something particularly inviting in his deep dreamlike state.

"You think it's dangerous?" Rudolph asked.

Molly didn't care; it was a cute dog and needed to be petted immediately. She ran toward it, her arms outstretched. She knelt down and stroked his head, and to everyone's surprise the dog began to purr like a contented cat.

"I read a story like this once," Molly said. "It's about a dog who thinks he's a cat. He was born into a family of felines and much to the disgust of every dog in the neighbourhood, he tried everything to fit in with his new family."

"Coincidence," said Rudolph.

"I don't believe in coincidence," Sophia mused.

"So!" Rudolph rebuffed.

"Neither do I now," said Arran.

Rudolph shrugged. "Okay, whatever. You saying it's a clue of some sort?"

Arran joined the communal shrug and looked to Sophia, who was more interested in Molly's reaction to the dog.

"What did the dog look like in your story, Molly?"

Molly rested the contented sleeping dog's head on her lap and continued to massage behind his ears.

"Well, there were no pictures, but it was a cute white poodle. In my mind though, he had a pink collar and written on it was…"

She felt around the dog's neck. There was a pink collar attached to a heart-shaped tag. The writing on it made her a little lost for words. She looked to her brother.

"What is it?"

"Milk Please," Molly replied.

"I think when Arran said that, he was rather hoping for something that made sense," Rudolph said. "Or are you a little thirsty? Not have enough to drink at Miss Profeta's?"

He was a little sarcastic but also jovial, careful not to provoke her into using the death stare.

Molly didn't even grace him with a gestural response and continued to look at Arran.

"Milk Please. I never told anyone about that. When my teacher read the class the story, I imagined him to have a pink collar exactly like this, with 'Milk Please' written on it."

"In *your* mind?" Sophia stroked her chin as though she was a university Professor. "What happened, did you give the dog milk?"

Molly nodded.

"And?"

"Well, in *my* mind, not in the story, the dog spoke to me and became my bestest friend."

Sophia nudged Arran.

"Well, you're the one in this world who can make huge ships float and turn into hovercrafts. Think you can manage a bowl of milk?"

"No, not a bowl," Molly interrupted. "A glass with a big red curly straw coming out of it. If this happens as I imagine it, he will grasp the glass with both paws and drink from the straw."

Arran smiled.

"Only you. Yeah, okay, hang on a sec." Within seconds the glass was resting in Molly's hands. She placed it in front of the dog's nose. The children watched in wonder as Pluto the Poodle stuck his tongue out, then lifted his weary eyelids to reveal two deep burgundy-coloured eyes. His tongue felt around the top of the glass till it found the straw. He opened his mouth and closed it around the straw. In one big slurp the milk was gone and the dog was a very happy kitty.

Pluto jumped onto her and licked her face.

"Mmm, that was delicioso, Molly. I is your bestest friend. Would you like to play?"

Molly laughed, play wrestling with the dog.

"It's exactly like I imagined, even his voice. Ah, isn't he cute?"

"She could be here for hours like that," said Arran, pleased to see the smile return to his sister's face. "Sophia, I suspect you have some sort of explanation?"

"It's just a theory really, but I think the path marked Molly would have more things like that in it. It's a path to her mind. Maybe *this* whole marketplace is a map of your mind." She laughed at the ingenuity of it. "What better hiding place for something, like a coin, than in your own mind?"

"But this isn't her path," said Rudolph, "it's Arran's. What's Molly's dog doing here?"

"Echoes; this whole marketplace *is* Arran's really, but the very fact we are here means we will all see things which are familiar to us in this place. The problem is…maybe Molly shouldn't get too attached to that dog."

Molly stopped playing and jumped up. "Why not?!"

Sophia spoke to Arran and Molly together.

"In surgery, in your time, let's say someone gets an artificial heart or lung or something, and the body sometimes realises that something does not belong and actively tries to remove it. Would that dog be in Arran's mind had Molly not brought it here?"

Arran shook his head.

"No way, let one of Molly's cutsie dogs in and before you know it I'd be plagued with huge giraffes making gross daisy chains."

"You wouldn't hurt this dog, Arran…would you?"

Arran shook his head.

"Of course he wouldn't, not out in the real world, but in this one, well, look up into the sky." Sophia pointed out the unusual cloud formations.

"A psychologist would have a field day with you, mate," Rudolph said as he watched the innocent fluffs of cloud join together, rearranging themselves to form the cutest little bunnies and teddy bears.

Molly looked on in horror as the cloud animals, like lemmings, dove into a sea of cloud spikes. One little cloud rabbit walked, again and again, into a brick wall without the sense or inclination to walk around.

Arran laughed, though Molly's unamused face sent him crashing back down to earth.

"They're just clouds, Molly; I wouldn't really do that."

"Yeah, whatever. Just try it and see what happens."

Her eyes glowed blue, a condition which was quickly dissipated by Pluto winding his way around her feet like the affectionate cat dog he was.

"I is must saying I like it here in your head, Arran."

Molly shot Pluto a surprised look. "You know where you are?"

"Oh yes, Molly, tickly behind my ears, would you? It helps me concentrate." Molly obliged. "Mmm, that's nice," Pluto purred, "though it's just making me sleepy. You is stop now."

Molly, slightly offended, lifted her hand.

Pluto sniffed and licked his nose, removing a tiny droplet of milk that had somehow made its way there from the glass earlier.

"Is tasty. I know Arran who is no to hurt Pluto, so do not to worry, Molly. I am to expect two more friends."

The dog looked toward Sophia and Rudolph. "This is you, no?"

He made the closest impersonation of a smile that a dog can muster.

Rudolph was the first to speak up. "Hello, Pluto, I'm Rudolph."

The dog wagged his tail and for reasons that would soon be known to Rudolph, he trotted happily behind his new friend, then without warning walked forward, pushing his nose right into Rudolph's rear end.

"Pleased to meet you," the dog muffled.

"Hey!" Rudolph shouted, leaping forward in shock. "What do you think you're doing?"

Sophia laughed. "Dogs don't greet one another by shaking hands, Rudolph."

Pluto looked confused. "What's being up with him? I is just trying to be polite."

"Yes well," Rudolph retorted, clasping his bottom with both hands, "in future a simple hello will do just fine, thank you."

Sensing she was next to be graced by the canine greeting, Sophia spoke up.

"I think we can dispense with the formalities for now, Pluto. I'm Sophia, very pleased to make your acquaintance. We have to find a coin in a hurry. Can you help us?"

The dog shook his head enthusiastically. "Yes, of course I is help. This is why I am being here."

"Talk about your mixed signals," Arran said.

"It's his way," said Molly. "He shakes his head when he means yes and nods when he means no; and will only speak out loud once he has been given milk."

"You is to please look at the marketplace down there."

The marketplace looked like an old-fashioned carnival; a mass of stalls, manned by people of varying sizes and opposing personalities, from the instantly likeable to the downright repulsive. They were selling items or tempting passers-by into various games of chance.

A huge circus-like tent centred the marketplace like a monument. The whole area was surrounded by a tall iron railing, broken partway by a door with the words DO NOT ENTER etched in neon red.

"What do you suppose is behind that door?" Rudolph asked.

Arran shrugged. "Dunno, but I'm in no hurry to find out."

Molly pointed to a building on the outskirts of the carnival.

"Look, it's our school."

"A school is a nice safe place," Sophia said. "And the coin will be in the safest place in your imagination. Shall we try there?"

Arran dismissed that idea instantly. "School might be safe to you, Sophia, but not me. Besides, where there is school there is Miss Anderson, and I don't fancy running into her."

Most of the people who were milling about and enjoying the festivities seemed either instantly recognisable or vaguely familiar to Arran.

"You is finding your coin down there," said Pluto. "But you is to be careful, friends; some not very nice peoples is coming here soon. They is to stop you getting your coin and is to do horrible things to

Arran. Now, if Pluto friends will excuse, Pluto needs the sleep." The dog lay down, curled into a feline ball, and fell asleep.

The four children walked past the sleeping dog, down the path, and into the marketplace.

"Must be pretty weird for you, Arran."

Arran gave Rudolph a cursory glance. "What?"

"This place, your head, you know…weird."

"I suppose." Arran shrugged. "Considering what I've been through and seen already, my weirdo definition meter is already maxed out. Besides, being my head and all, at least this is a little familiar."

He glanced toward the Do Not Enter sign. "If not a little disturbing in places."

Chapter Eighty-Seven
Tribble Takes Charge

"Rudolph's path is quite out of the question!"

Tribble, apparently from out of nowhere, marched forward in long, confident strides toward Victor, Joss, and Gemma. Of course he was in disguise, so to everyone's eyes it was not Tribble approaching, but Professor Rebecca Tempus.

"Rudolph is a nobody, a nothing, an insignificant…"

"Then he has something in common with you, whoever you are, lady." Victor nudged Gemma, who instinctively burst into laughter at his unfunny witticism.

Tribble followed suit and mockingly burst into what seemed to be fits of uncontrollable laughter, quite over the top. Of course it was all fake. "Oh, oh." He doubled over, clutching his tummy. "You are too funny. My sides they are splitting. I'm surprised they haven't cracked."

Victor didn't like anyone poking fun at him and wasn't about to let this slide, certainly not in front of his newfound admirers.

"Stammers, take off the gloves and shake hands with our new comedian friend."

Craig removed his gloves and stood between Tribble and Victor, extending his hand. Tribble stopped abruptly and grinned, extending his own hand for Craig to hold, which he did, or at least he tried to.

Craig's hand passed right through Tribble's, who continued with his previous fit of laughter. Craig looked to Victor for some sort of instruction. When none came he replaced his gloves and stepped back.

Victor squared right up to Tribble.

"What are you then? A ghost? A hologram? Whatever you are,

you better get out of here or…"

"Please, dear, not in front of the children," Tribble replied, before punching him on the nose and knocking him to the ground. "Let's just say we have the same goal here, and without my help the young boy Arran will kick your scrawny behinds into next week before you have the chance to put Stammers here anywhere near him."

Victor rolled his eyes back, rising again to his feet.

"We must be talking about a different Arran then. The one I'm chasing is a pathetic DOA who couldn't fight his way out of a wet paper bag."

Tribble shook his head.

"Oh Victor," he said sympathetically. "Your sister got all the brains in your family, didn't she?"

"I didn't know you had a sister, Vic," said Joss.

He shrugged it off as though it were nothing and Tribble continued. He held out an outstretched hand toward the confused army of children.

"Remember bailing on these guys and leaving them all to die on that ship? Well, Arran managed to save nearly every single one of them."

He sniggered at the irony; now they were all following Victor and hunting down their saviour.

"The work of a DOA? I don't think so."

Tribble nodded his head in admiration of Arran's abilities.

"I can tell you there's not many people can pull off a stunt like that." He shrugged. "To my knowledge there are only two beings alive who can, and you're looking at the other one now."

Tribble stepped back and gave a grandiose Shakespearian bow, feeling that the revelation he had just shared was deserving of a round of applause, or at least a little admiration. He shrugged off the disappointing, stunned silence of the crowd before continuing.

"I will allow you to lead your band of merry idiots after them, and for the most part I am a guide."

He stopped and squared up to Victor, standing nose to nose.

"But make no mistake: you work for me, and my suggestions are to be obeyed, or I may get a little angry. You won't like me when I'm angry."

He stopped and pondered before shaking his head. "No, sorry, that's the Hulk. Still the message is the same. Obey me or else."

Victor stared defiantly into Tribble's eyes, certainly not used to being told what to do by anyone, and this was the second time today, now by a mere girl. He nudged Gemma, who on instinct raised her hands and shot a bolt of electricity at Tribble's head. The lightning passed right through without so much as moving a hair on his head, though he did raise an eyebrow followed by a slow and deliberate shake of his head.

"Can you swim, Gemma?"

Gemma was suddenly very afraid.

"H... H... How did you know my...?"

"Shhh..."

He clicked his fingers and within an instant Gemma was submerged in a glass case, completely filled with water. She writhed frantically and began to bang on the container lid.

Could she be drowning right there in full view of so many children, each too afraid to so much as lift a finger to help?

Tribble smiled and chuckled slightly.

"Can you swim? So sorry, Gemma, meant to ask if you could breathe under water."

Gemma's eyes were wide open, her mouth clamped shut as she banged on the glass in front of them. A tear ran down Joss's eyes. She appealed to Tribble.

"Please let her go, she won't cause you any more..."

Tribble raised his hand, a nonverbal "shut up."

"This is the best bit. In a moment her body's fight-or-flight survival instinct will take over. She will try to use her natural God-given powers to escape this, and you know what happens when electricity and water get together. It's shocking."

He opened his hand at his chest. A packet of salted popcorn appeared and he began to eat, looking eagerly at Gemma as she tried to resist the urge to use her power. He offered the packet to Victor, who, to save face and show he didn't care, dipped in his hand, took a fistful, and shovelled it into his mouth. Had Gemma not been completely submerged in water, everyone would have noticed the stream of tears rolling down her face.

Her eyes turned bright blue and her hands, no longer banging on the glass, trembled in front of her. Within an instant a bright blue bolt of electricity shot out from her fingertips, shattering the glass into a thousand pieces, but not before the hungry current rived through her body, rendering her quite lifeless. Soaking wet, she lay slumped on the floor. Everyone looked toward Tribble.

He had their obedience.

"Forgive the crude display. Everything I can do, so can your 'pathetic DOA Arran,' who knows, maybe more. It will be interesting to find out. The only plus side is, I have much more experience."

He pointed toward Arran's path.

"That is where they have gone. They are looking for Arran's coin. If they find it then they can all get out of the network alive and you lot will be left here to die. I can't see everything in this place; some of it is still somehow controlled by the old Professor Richard Tempus from the great beyond, but I see enough."

He sighed. "Speaking of which, I prefer more of an aerial view, so I'll be going." He cheekily raised his eyebrows. "You'll see me again, toodaloo. Oh and rest assured, I do have a plan so clever you could put a shirt and tie on it and send it to work. I'll be watching."

Tribble walked away from the crowd and disappeared as though he was the ghost of Christmas past.

Joss ran to Gemma's body and crouched down so she was kneeling beside her head. Gemma was not breathing. She felt for a pulse. There was nothing, well almost, though there were no physical life signs. She was able to look inside Gemma's mind, which was filled with cries of pain, despair, and just two words:

Leave me…

Joss stood and faced Victor, remorseful. She shook her head slowly and returned to his side. Victor didn't say a word, didn't give Gemma so much as a second glance, didn't seem to care.

He took Arran's path and was quietly followed by the child army.

Chapter Eighty-Eight

Mike to the Rescue

Alarms had been sounding all over the place, filling the air like an ominous claxon, superseded only by the screams and the gunfire as the Citadel guards tried to defend themselves against the oncoming onslaught of the Spletka drone army.

Mike knew they didn't have long before Jhonas would burst through the door in search of Rebecca Tempus; trouble was she was still on the floor, unconscious and in desperate need of medical assistance. To take her to the infirmary was risky, as the place may well be overrun by now. No safer than here, he thought, as he crouched down to pick her up.

"Excuse me, Professor," he said, as he hoisted her limp body into his arms. "Wow, for such a petite lady you certainly aren't carrying the weight of Tinkerbell, are you?"

He slipped out of the room and started to advance slowly up the corridor, till a very familiar voice boomed in his ears.

"Not that way, Mike. There are guards just up ahead of you. Turn around. I've placed a spiral staircase by the stone pillar. It will take you directly to the infirmary, but hurry. Others are coming."

Mike looked around but saw no one. There was no mistaking

that voice though.

"Richard, my old friend, is that you?" he asked, elated.

"Just keep my daughter safe. She sacrificed much of her own energy to bring you back from the land of the departed."

"Don't worry, Professor, I'll look after her."

Mike was confused, but comforted by the sound of Richard Tempus. A wisp of hair fell away from Rebecca Tempus's face. He thought she looked almost angelic as she lay sleeping in his arms.

"Don't worry, Professor, I'll look after you."

Two Professor Tempuss now, he thought, *could get confusing. Perhaps I'll call you Junior or something.*

She opened her eyes and smiled. "Don't you dare. Rebecca will do just fine."

Shocked, Mike dropped the Professor on the floor. He scrambled down to try and pick her up. She tried to look unamused but all she could muster was a slight chuckle.

"Sorry, Professor, Rebecca. Not used to people reading my mind; that's usually my gig, that and you were supposed to be out cold."

"Sorry to disappoint," she replied, weak but still laughing. "Help me up, will you?"

He held her hand and pulled her to her feet. She stumbled and nearly fell again but Mike caught her and put her arm around his shoulder.

"Still not a hundred percent," she said.

"Yep, I gathered. That's why we're going to the infirmary."

Alerted by the sound of the Professor's feeble laugh, the two guards who had been searching for them earlier appeared and began to run up the corridor toward them.

"Best hurry," she said.

"We'll never lose them like this, Professor."

With that he lifted her tightly into his arms and tried his best, but there was no way he could outrun the two seasoned army soldiers who could almost taste the victory in every step.

Mike stumbled forward, almost dropping the Professor to the ground again; his legs were growing tired. For all his brave intentions, he could have used a few more sessions in the gym to cope with this unexpected weight.

The Professor looked at the imposing figures drawing ever closer to them, and the smiles and looks of triumph on their faces made her a little sick. Her eyes glowed bright green; then she closed them.

The two guards suddenly stopped dead in their tracks, dumbfounded.

"Where'd they go?"

The Professor spoke telepathically. "We are invisible, Mike, but they can still hear us. Don't say a word, and get us out of here, would you?"

"You sound just like your father; you know that?"

"Why thank you, Michael," echoed Richard Tempus. "Now remember, the infirmary is up those stairs."

The Professor could also hear her father's voice, and was instantly thankful. She whispered to Mike, "We are invisible, not soundproof, so from now on telepathic conversations only."

Still invisible to the naked eye and completely out of breath, Mike burst through the entrance of the infirmary, the Professor still cradled in his arms. The lady on the front desk was startled at the door, which was, to her mind, moving of its own accord.

Though the gunfire and screams had been going on for a little while, she had refused to leave her post. Sick people still needed her help. She stood up, carefully surveying the area. When Mike's voice came out of nowhere and spoke to her, she nearly jumped out of her skin.

"We need some help here, a little pick-me-up for the good Professor here."

"Mike?" The lady clearly recognised his voice. "I can hear you but I can't see... Are you dead?"

"What? No. Professor, would you be so kind?"

The transparent mist that shielded Mike and Rebecca Tempus cleared and they were once again in full view of anyone who cared to look in their direction.

She looked quizzically at the Professor in Mike's arms and sniggered, thinking they looked rather like a honeymooning couple.

"You do move fast. Was it a nice ceremony, Mike?"

The Professor immediately understood the inference and stumbled to her feet out of Mike's arms, still a little dazed, and grabbed the reception desk for support.

"Is there a room free?"

The receptionist pointed to the room Molly had been in earlier.

"Thanks."

With Mike's help she made her way to the room and lay on the bed, breathing a huge sigh of relief as her body relished the restful comfort of the mattress. Mike flicked a switch and the familiar light scanned her body. He read the display.

"Nothing that a little rest won't cure, Professor. Not sure what happened to you, but your body is healing at an alarming rate; shouldn't take long."

He had a disturbing afterthought; her father's vitals were not unlike hers, following the first battle, and look where he ended up.

"We don't have the time. I need to…"

She struggled on to her side, only to be pushed gently back to her original position by Mike. Her weakened body didn't offer much in the way of resistance.

"You need your strength for what is to come. The best help you can be right now is to rest and get better."

Reluctant, yet resigned, the Professor nodded and closed her eyes.

Mike walked over to the door and stopped. "Thank you. You saved my life back there."

A micro expression of a smile appeared and left the Professor's lips.

You're welcome. Don't be long—the children need me.

Mike sighed. "I won't."

Within moments he was behind the receptionist's desk, donning her headset and mouthpiece. Warning all in the Citadel that they were under attack and trying to organise battle plans with the guards.

Chapter Eighty-Nine

Bridget's Appeal

Already inside the building, walking at almost a leisurely pace with Bellonta by his side and followed by the remainder of his army, the general could not help but laugh as Mike's battle commands resonated throughout the Citadel.

"Do you hear that, my dear? The children are making a little sport for us. Shall we play?"

Bellonta's eyebrows raised and her body tensed, excited at the potential promise of bloodshed and violence.

"Oh yes!"

Two guards approached holding weapons and commanded them to halt, unfortunately with all the authority an ant would have upon the approach of an oversized boot.

The general casually waved a hand in their direction and the weapons they were carrying melted out of their hands, leaving a sticky puddle on the floor.

"Oh look." Bellonta laughed. "The toy soldiers are still standing their ground."

"What bravery, my dear—that should be rewarded. They will make an excellent addition to our family, do you not agree?"

Bellonta nodded.

Unsure what resistance they could muster to stop such an unopposable force, the two guards stood tall and held out their hands as though they were trying to prevent oncoming traffic from passing.

"I command you by the authority of Professor Tempus and the United Federation of the planet Earth to stop, then leave this place in peace."

"Well, that's me convinced," replied the General flippantly, turning to look Bellonta in the eyes as he approached them. "Shall we pack up and leave?"

Bellonta joined in the role play. "I believe we could stay a moment longer, for tea."

The general agreed. "Sorry, gentlemen, I believe we are going to stay."

He smiled, then with a stern, determined face stared the two guards down. They both made the grave—and some would argue unavoidable—mistake of looking back into the General's eyes. They were both horrified as his eyes turned jet black. He seemed not just to be looking at them but reaching down and clutching at their very soul. They wanted more than anything to move, protecting the Citadel now playing second place to saving their own lives, but they were trapped.

"You won't die today, gentlemen. In fact, in a sense I'm setting you free, free from all the measly, mundane decisions you have to make day to day. Free to become a Spletka."

Soul-less, the two men simply saluted and fell into rank with the rest of the Spletka drones behind Bellonta.

Mike watched in horror on his monitor as hundreds more guards were captured in the same way.

"It's like taking lambs to the slaughter," he said quietly. "Only these lambs come back to slaughter their former friends."

He was at a total loss of what to do. The Citadel's defences were down and the General didn't even seem to need his army; his power was astounding. Surrender was out of the question, but what could they do?

Bellonta touched and stroked her lover's cheek the way he always liked it.

"I've never seen you with so much energy and power, my sweet. How are you doing this?"

"I am home, my dear, once cast out and now returned. The Professor tried to keep me from this place many years ago because he knew my return would herald a change. A new era. My era."

"Well, I think we've got everyone on this level. Shall we move up to the next?"

A drone, a faceless Spletka follower once known as Harry

Bartholomew, loving husband and father to three children, whose special ability was his sensitivity to vibrations in the air waves came forward from the army ranks.

"That is not all, sir. I sense 320 separate heartbeats dead ahead."

"I should know that already, soldier; your abilities are mine too. Interesting. Are they armed?"

"No sir, I think they are hiding."

"Oh goody, hide and seek."

Bellonta jumped up and down, as giddy as a child. "My great-grandmother used to tell me about this. That was before I killed her, obviously."

Directly ahead of them was a stone wall. A medieval torch was attached dead centre, the sole source of light for the room.

The general squared up to it.

"A lever of some description I should imagine," he said, pulling it down. The torch was no lever to a secret passageway behind the wall. It was simply a torch. The general tugged and the torch fell to the floor, setting his shoe instantly alight. He stared at the flame and it extinguished, seemingly excusing itself in the presence of something far more dangerous.

Now in complete darkness, the general sighed impatiently. He heard Bellonta by his side giggling.

"Spooky, ain't it, love? I like it."

"I don't," replied the General cautiously. "There's something else here."

"Hello, old friend."

There was no image, no physical form to identify the voice, but the general knew exactly who it was.

"Professor Tempus, mon ami. I thought you dead." He smirked. "We were just coming for your daughter actually and of course control of the Tempus Network. Thereafter, the whole planet; don't mind, do you?"

The Professor didn't rise to this. After a brief pause he simply said, "Good-bye, old friend."

The walls and ceiling glowed bright white, and an intense heat accompanied the blinding light. The general and Bellonta, though temporarily stunned, were otherwise unaffected. The Professor's voice spoke again.

"You know the rules, my old friend. The spirits of those you have taken will be returned to their rightful living owners until such a time as you have joined with the universal power."

The Spletka drones throughout the Citadel ceased their attack and shielded their eyes, tears streaming down their faces and onto the concrete floor as they screamed. Then the noise stopped and they raised both arms into the air as if reaching for something wonderful, reaching for their essence, their very souls.

Their arms dropped to their sides and their eyes transformed from jet black to their natural human form. Content, they closed their lids and slept, still standing; comfortable and at ease for the first time since they were turned.

"There they will stay, in stasis."

The General, for the first time, looked worried, a welcome change from the all-powerful smugness he had displayed on a daily basis for the past thirteen years.

The room returned to the state it was in before. The torch was once again attached to the stone wall, burning proudly.

"Why didn't I change?" Bellonta asked, walking around and examining the sleeping former drones.

"I didn't take your soul by force, my dear. Your loyalty and love for me have always been your choice. You are therefore permitted to be my ally on this quest."

He walked to her, caressed her cheek, then gently pulled her head to his, kissing her softly on her black velvet lips. Her resulting smile preceded a deep affectionate stare into his eyes. She had no fear, only admiration. All she wanted was her General, and realization of his dreams was something she would gladly give her life for.

The general pulled away suddenly, raising one finger to his lips. "Shhh."

He tiptoed once again toward the burning torch.

"It seems, my dear, that though I do not have my army or their living energies, I am still blessed with the abilities of our dear departed brothers and sisters. I can hear the heartbeat he heard earlier."

The general gestured vaguely into the crowd, not knowing exactly which of his drones had come forward earlier. They all looked the same to him.

"It gets louder the closer I get to this wall. Just about…"

He started to touch and feel each stone individually as though it were a Braille treasure map.

"Just about…."

He rested on the stone directly below the burning torch and pushed it gently.

"…Here."

The torch moved backward as though it were being absorbed by the wall, till it had vanished entirely. The whole wall began to glow that same bright torchlight before crumbling to the floor in smouldering ashes, revealing a staircase which led down into a darkened passageway, at the bottom of which stood another familiar figure from his past.

"Bridget Fondue... Is that really you?"

She turned her head away in shame.

"It is you! How long has it been? Oh yes, thirteen years, I remember. You left me to die."

"You're a murderer!" she spat under her breath. "You killed Professor Tempus and would have killed everyone else if...."

"...If I wasn't robbed of what was rightfully mine? Yes, I know. Besides, it seems the good Professor is not dead, only now he's slightly more ethereal. Still thinks he's God apparently. And people criticize me?"

Bellonta gracefully moved toward Bridget, half smile, half menace, waving her head slowly from side to side as she did, never once breaking eye contact.

"Who's Bridget, my sweet?"

She ran one of her exceptionally long fingernails across her cheek without breaking the skin.

"Is she a new toy for me to play with?"

Bridget was terrified but if it wasn't for her heart beating fifty to the dozen, the determined concentration on her face would have disguised her fear perfectly.

"Bridget's an old friend, my dear."

He regarded her and allowed himself a brief sentimental trip down memory lane, a place he had rarely visited over the years.

"More than that really, weren't we, Bridget?"

Bellonta stood back and looked on in disgust.

"Eww! You and this…woman? There's nothing special about her."

She sniffed the air around her head.

"You were a better person then," Bridget said, hoping to appeal to any shred of humanity that may still remain in his soul. "You can be again."

For a moment she thought that her plea had worked. The general pondered, bowing his head ever so slightly.

Bridget was about to speak again when the general raised his head and looked directly into her eyes.

There was a moment of complete silent understanding between them. A tear dropped from her eye. She realised the futility of her efforts. She also knew her end had come.

The general clicked a finger on his right hand and Bridget fell to the floor. Her heart stopped, dead.

"Come, my dear, we have a Professor to find." The general linked arms with Bellonta and advanced down the corridor.

Mike looked to his monitor and cried. He had just lost one of his oldest and dearest friends.

Chapter Ninety

The Power of the Mind

"I know everybody here. Even the people I don't know…I know," said Arran, looking ahead into the carnival.

"Oh good, that makes sense," Molly replied, moving to stand beside him, closely followed by Rudolph and Sophia.

"Look." Arran pointed into the crowd. "There's Ronald from school and there walking behind the school, chess club Pete, and over there, Jimmy."

"Jimmy from school?" Molly couldn't see him. "Regal Jimmy?"

All the kids called him Regal Jimmy because of the unconventional way he tended to greet people, a royal wave of his hand followed by an equally royal bow. Arran thought it was hilarious and for a while had taken to doing the same; that was until Miss Anderson had seen him and issued yet another detention slip.

"Where is he?"

"There, look, next to the cupcake stall."

Sure enough he was there and all the children saw him munching on probably his fifth cupcake. He turned to face them and bowed, rotating his right hand in an inviting royal greeting.

"Look. He wants us to come over."

"That or he's eaten too much and he's choking on a cupcake," Rudolph added.

Sophia laughed. "That was funny. Interesting," she said as she led the crowd toward Regal Jimmy.

"Very pleased to meet you." Sophia extended her hand in greeting. Jimmy simply stood motionless and waited for Arran to come to the front.

As soon as they were facing one another, they exchanged mutual royal greetings, culminating in a tip of an imaginary hat. They then stood and embraced. "Thanks for coming, Jimbo."

"Thanks for inviting me. This is your head after all."

"So all your own memories…?"

"Don't exist, not here. I am here because you remember me, and everything you remember about me exists here."

"So what do we do?"

"You tell me, brother. What do ya wanna do?"

"Well, we're looking for my coin—any ideas?"

Jimmy shrugged his shoulders, then pointed to a stall near the big circus tent.

"You tried the coin stall?"

As good a place as any, Arran thought and they walked toward the proprietor, who was an exact replica of the homeless man Arran and Molly had passed every day on the way to school. He liked the irony—back home the man spent most of his time begging for money, but here he was giving it away and still no one wanted to come near him.

"Novelty coins, get them here!" The seemingly uninterested crowd of passers-by gave him a wide berth.

Time and place seemed to have no impact on his popularity. He was visibly pleased and surprised when the children pulled up at his stall and spoke to him. He took a brief look behind, to be sure they were indeed speaking to him and not someone else.

"Afternoon, children. Can I interest you in a coin? We have a Victor, three-time winner of the games here. Very rare indeed."

He delved into one of the many buckets of coins haphazardly arranged on the counter and pulled out a gleaming coin which displayed a contented and smug grin plastered to the face of Victor Graston.

"No," snapped Sophia. "Not him!"

"We're looking for Arran's coin. Do you have that one?" Molly asked politely as she silently asked Sophia to control her temper.

He stared at Arran's face, for a while a little perplexed and disappointed.

"No, I don't think so, unless…"

He reached inside a bucket labelled "New arrivals" and pulled out a single coin with Arran's picture on it. "Here we are. Fresh in today. Are you collectors?"

Arran shook his head and opened his hand hopefully in front of the man to receive the coin.

Once the coin was in his possession Arran looked at Sophia. "Well, I have the coin. What now?"

Sophia sighed. "It's not your actual coin; it's a replica. At least you'll know what your coin looks like when you find it."

Sensing the disappointment in the air, Regal Jimmy spoke up.

"Well, that was fun, what next?"

"I'd like to get out of here before a big angry lynch mob led by Victor Graston comes to kill me and my friends," said Arran.

"Well, that certainly doesn't leave you with much time."

"How much time?"

"None, look."

He pointed up the gravel path. Standing next to the sleeping dog and looking out into the crowd were Victor, Joss, and the child army. Victor had not yet seen them, but a slight glance to the left by Joss put pay to that. She locked eyes with Arran, who shook his head, a pleading gesture.

Don't give us up.

She was happy to see him alive, and Miss Profeta's words gave her pause for thought. She didn't feel she would be welcome to join him and Molly, but if she could lead Victor away then they would at least stand a chance of getting out unscathed.

Get down, Arran.

Arran responded to the voice in his head by placing his hands on his sister's shoulders, gently pushing her to the ground. Sophia and Rudolph followed suit without question. There they stayed covered by the safety of the stall in front of them.

"Musical chairs, is it?" Jimmy asked without reply. "Did you all trip and fall at the same time maybe?"

"Get down," Arran finally said and Jimmy obeyed. "There's people out there looking for us. We don't really want to be seen. Understand?"

"Ahh. What kind of people?"

Arran remembered that as well as being funny, Regal Jimmy was also incredibly forgetful.

"Bad people," he said. "Well…" he corrected himself, "one bad person and a large collection of sheep."

"I see no sheep, Arran," Jimmy said, popping his head out into full view.

"He means a large collection of people who blindly do as they're told. You know, act like sheep?" Sophia grinned and turned to Rudolph. "Don't worry. I'll explain it to you when we have more time."

"Oh, she's soo funny," Rudolph retorted. "Don't know why I'm so afraid of Victor; my sides will have split long before they catch up with us."

Victor grew tired of scanning the area. "You see anything here besides a carnival of pathetic losers?"

Joss shrugged, electing to keep Arran's whereabouts to herself. "Nope."

"Big help, thanks!"

"Sorry. They would have had to pass here though. It's the only way in."

Another voice spoke.

"But not the only way out."

Both Joss and Victor spun around to see Tribble standing behind them, looking as before, like an exact replica of Professor Tempus.

Victor was the first to speak. "What do you mean not the only way out?"

"The coin, stupid; if you don't find them before they find Arran's coin, they get to leave and you are stuck here with your newfound friends, for the rest of your miserable little lives." He paused and smiled. "Which, on the plus side, wouldn't be for very long."

"Not that I don't enjoy tree hugging, well, grass hugging, but do you think they are gone yet?" Molly asked, spitting a piece of grass from her mouth.

"Dunno," replied Arran. "Jimmy?"

Jimmy looked confused. "What exactly am I supposed to be looking for?"

"A large collection of people who don't belong here, probably led by a tall idiot with bleached and spiked hair."

Jimmy spotted Victor instantly. "Oh, yes, I see them. Bleachy head is talking to some lady; now he's talking to a dog. Though I think I'd best stop staring at him."

"Why?"

"Because he's staring right back at me. I think he might come over."

"What? You idiot. Get down!" interrupted Rudolph.

Before Sophia had time to protest, Regal Jimmy was on the floor with the rest of them, out of sight.

Sophia shook her head.

"Well done, Rudolph, yet again you win the prize for most useless comment. Do you not think that looked a tad suspicious, Jimmy ducking down like that?"

****

"Anyway, your only way out of here is to find Arran's coin. It acts as kind of a gateway between the Tempus Network and real life."

Tribble paused and did the educated pacing that he seemed to enjoy so much.

"So you have two things to do here: First find Molly and her little band of happy wanderers, and two, find the coin, go home, and have tea and crumpets with your mummy."

With that, the Professor Tempus lookalike disappeared.

"Typical," said Victor, "about as much help as a one-armed man in a finger counting contest."

He looked at the dog sleeping at their feet.

"Well, if they came past here maybe the dog saw something. I'm assuming dogs can talk here too?"

Joss nodded.

"Hey, dog, wake up!"

Pluto's peaceful snores only served to infuriate Victor.

"Dog!" he shouted before crouching down and hitting Pluto's head with the palm of his hand. Still the dog slept, unperturbed.

"Maybe he will only wake at the sound of his name," Joss suggested, knowing full well that the name on the dog's collar was not his real name. Having an ability to read minds was certainly coming in very handy.

Victor felt around the dog's collar and tag and read aloud what was written.

"Milk Please." Victor stood up, looked at Joss, and shrugged. "What kind of stupid name is Milk Please?"

Joss giggled, not at the name but at Victor's stupidity.

"I know," said Victor, thinking they were sharing the same observation.

"Oh well, here goes." He turned to face the dog. "Milk please. Here, milk please, WAKEY WAKEY, MILK PLEASE!"

Of course the dog remained asleep.

"Stupid dog," snapped Victor. "Hey, who's he staring at?"

Standing behind a stall in the marketplace a boy just stood, looking directly at Victor. Barely ten seconds later, the boy disappeared from sight behind the stall.

"Well, the dog may not have any answers but I'm pretty sure I know who does. Come on."

"Er, guys," whispered Rudolph, "we need to get out of here now."

"No kidding, Sherlock. Isn't that what we've been trying to do ever since we arrived?" Molly snapped back.

"Yes, thank you, Molly. Let me put it this way: A large group of people is travelling at increased pace toward us. I can hear them. Or even another way, please, Mummy, I don't wanna die!"

Chapter Ninety-One

Rebecca's Dream

Professor Rebecca Tempus slept, but not as peacefully as she had hoped. Flashing images of dying and tortured children congested her mind; innocent people having their souls ripped from their bodies, unable to protest or even think for themselves as they joined an ever-increasing collective, emanating from a general who strolled carefree past them, growing stronger with every life he took.

He was of course joined by his equally seditious lover, Bellonta.

Amid the nightmare images the Professor felt sure she saw a spider enter her room, ponder for a while, then walk out, but she put it down to an overactive imagination.

More than this was the image that shocked her awake, in which she saw herself drive a dagger into Molly's heart from behind, then cry as Molly fell to the ground.

She jolted upright; her eyes snapped wide open and alert. For the moment everything was quiet. That wouldn't last long and she knew it.

Chapter Ninety-Two

The Surgery

The general walked the dark and dank corridor. The occasional droplet of water which fell from the brick ceiling echoed and amplified upon impact with the floor, sounding more like a mini explosion.

The only other sounds were that of his and Bellonta's footsteps. He didn't speak; concentrating hard and relying on his few remaining stolen abilities to guide him in the right direction. *I don't even need the army*, he thought. *Even with my limited power I can still take anything I like here.*

Bellonta let loose a laugh; she knew exactly what her lover was thinking and she had a ringside seat.

He stopped when he came upon a brick wall that seemed to be blocking his path.

"Oh, Professor Tempus, old friend, can you not do any better than that?" he mused, relishing the challenge. "Your mind games will not work on me now. Fool me once…" His statement harked back to an encounter with the old Professor some years previous.

He took Bellonta by the hand and marched full force, right through the wall. Being but an optical illusion it offered no resistance.

On the other side of the wall was a waiting room that wouldn't be out of place in any busy doctor's surgery.

The general recognised every soul in there and felt a deep chill creep slowly up his spine. Ghostly images of the dead; everyone he had attacked and consumed with his death stare. They wandered, lost and worried. Some sat on the leather seats and cried as they looked at pictures of the loved ones they had been torn apart from. Others paced frantically back and forth, occasionally banging their fists on walls or on the small table that centred the room, making the collection of unread magazines fall to the carpeted floor.

The general felt a momentary pang of remorse for the hundreds of lives he had taken in pursuit of his goal, before shaking his head and coming back to his senses.

"Is that the best you have, Professor?"

He waved a hand through one of the spirits who went about her ghastly business, not noticing.

"I get it. Show me all the wrong I've done and I'll simply say sorry, go home, and start making baby bottles for underprivileged children as penance. There's only one thing that could stop me. Hand over the power behind the Tempus Network and the planet, *then* I will go!"

A hatch opened at the other end of the room, behind which a young blonde receptionist spoke.

"General, the doctor will see you now."

Before he had time to protest or even demand an explanation, the spirit of a doctor, the first he had ever captured with the death stare, walked through a wall. He approached and stood toe to toe with the general, looking him directly in the eye.

The general recognised him instantly.

"Hello, Pete. No hard feelings?"

Pete's wife had reluctantly moved on and remarried since he was turned. His daughter had been killed by one of the Spletka drones six years ago, but not before she was forced into killing her own father to stop him capturing her mother and turning her over to the General.

Pete's ghost didn't answer, but his look of defiance and hatred said it all. He reached with both hands inside the general's chest. For the first time in as long as he could remember, the general began to feel real pain and fear, as every soul he had taken, one by one, was systematically extracted.

Bellonta tried to lash out at the doctor but her hands passed straight through his body.

As a last resort the general's eyes turned jet black; he attempted to catch Pete in the death stare. Pete simply looked at him, slowly shook his head, and smiled.

The death stare had no effect on the dead.

Once he had finished, Pete removed his hands and disappeared, like mist floating back through the walls and ceiling, alongside every other spirit in the room. The place was empty. The last image the general saw before he fell back unconscious into Bellonta's arms was a projection of Richard Tempus, who smiled sympathetically and spoke.

"When he wakes, tell him there will be no further need for bloodshed. The power he seeks cannot be taken by force. I shall create a direct path to the Orb room."

The Professor disappeared and a freestanding door stood in his place.

Chapter Ninety-Three

The False Tempus Joins In

Victor led the restless crowd past the dog, past the fruit stall, and right past the strange-looking man who was balancing on a pair of stilts, happily occupied juggling eight piping hot scones, intermittently catching one in his mouth and eating it, whilst simultaneously dipping a hand in his pocket and producing a replacement scone.

Passers-by seemed rather impressed. Not Victor though; he was on a mission.

"Well, where is he!?" he bellowed.

Victor spun 'round to face Joss, who, for the moment, looked just as confused as he did, though not for the same reasons.

"I saw them right here. How did they get away?"

The area behind the stall was completely clear; absolutely no sign of Arran or Molly, just a few empty popcorn cartons and a half-eaten toffee apple.

Joss looked inside Victor's head. He hadn't actually seen Arran or Molly; what he saw was someone who he thought may lead him toward them. His mind seemed to fill in the rest, thinking he actually saw Arran, but he believed it as sure as he knew his own name.

He stared intently at the vacant space, unwilling or unable to turn away, that was, until his concentration was broken by Joss's hand on his shoulder.

"Come on, Vic, there's no one here."

Victor reluctantly turned to face her.

"There's something not right here!"

He may have been a violent psychopath, but there was nothing wrong with his intuition.

Arran and his friends lay, crouched and silent, unseen, right where Victor had been looking.

Don't move a muscle, Molly.

I wasn't planning on… How are we doing this, Arran?

Arran and Molly were holding hands and concentrating very hard.

No idea, Molly. Feels natural though, doesn't it?

More of an instinct really.

Yeah.

This telepathy you two have is rather handy.

Hi Sophia, nice of you to join us.

Rudolph was not telepathic, but through Arran's quick thinking, he had the use of a floating chalkboard and a fat piece of chalk. The internal messages that passed between the children appeared on the board as they were spoken and, any time he wanted to communicate he rubbed the board clean, picked up the chalk, and wrote…

So, we're invisible right now? Rudolph etched on the board.

Not exactly, Arran answered. *People see more of what Molly and I want them to see and less of what we don't.*

I don't understand.

Like a perception filter, added Sophia. *Very clever; it's not that they can't see us, it's more like, with a little persuasion, they don't want to.*

I don't understand, Rudolph repeated.

For goodness sake, Molly said. *Arran and I are working together. I think I'm helping control their minds and Arran is changing the surrounding environment ever so slightly so as to make them think that there's nobody there, though this could all be Arran.*

Rudolph drew a single question mark on the chalkboard.

Sophia shook her head. *Oh, for the want of a brain cell! Rudolph, we are all invisible!*

Well, why didn't you say so?

***

"Oh no, not her again!"

About fifty yards behind Victor and the gang stood a lady dressed in a smart tweed skirt, boring blouse, and an equally boring tweed jacket.

"She's the most annoying woman I've ever…"

Victor froze still and stopped talking. He felt control of his entire body being taken away from him. He reluctantly began to move toward the lady as though he were a remote control toy. Joss and the army followed behind in the same fashion. Tribble looked rather disturbed and a little scared of the slow, deliberate advance.

"Don't speak, my little toy soldiers, just walk toward me," Tribble said quietly. "Look rather angry too if you would. We may as well put on a show for them."

The woman in tweed was exerting her authority yet again and thoroughly enjoying it.

"Professor Tempus!" Arran said quietly but out loud. "Victor and his gang are moving in on her."

"Please don't hurt me," Tribble said submissively. "I'm just looking for my two friends Arran and Molly. Have you seen…?"

"We've got to help," Molly said. "Take the invisibility off us and I'll death stare the lot of them!"

"No, they'd get you in a rush," Rudolph interrupted. "Then all of us too. Game over."

"What do you know!?" Sophia retorted. "That bully needs to be taught a lesson!"

"Shut up, both of you," Arran said. "Rudolph is right. We have no idea what they can do. We get out of here and rescue her later."

Molly didn't listen. She stood up and the invisibility shield was lifted. Victor and his crowd turned to face them.

Tribble disappeared.

Joss and Arran exchanged a look of silent desperation, broken only when Victor walked to the front and smiled an altogether satisfied yet resentful smile.

"Didn't think you could hide forever, did you, DOA?"

He paused, slightly reluctant to move forward as Molly took a step forward.

"Come on then, Victor." She inhaled a deep breath, ready to administer her own particular brand of the death stare when Arran placed his hand on her shoulder and stood next to her.

"I'll handle this, Molly."

She stepped back.

"Kick his bum then or I'll…"

"Not getting your sister to fight your battles then? At least you'll die like a man, albeit a pathetic shadow of a man, but the closest you'll ever get."

Sophia stood next to Molly and shook her head at Victor disapprovingly. She was unenthusiastically followed on Arran's right-hand side by Rudolph, who refused to make eye contact with the bully who had made his life at the school a complete misery.

Arran and Joss locked eyes for a moment and shared a moment of perfect understanding. She nodded her head ever so subtly so as not to arouse suspicion from Victor.

"Come on then, DOA, let's see what you got."

Arran crouched down, picked something up from the ground, clenched it in his fist, and then told everyone to hold hands, which they all did without question.

"What's that you picked up, DOA? You gonna throw stones at me, are ya, or is that just to make your pathetic punches stronger? Ooh, I'm scared."

Arran looked to his friends to make sure they were all linked.

"I'm not going to fight you, Victor."

He released his grip to show a glowing coin which he placed between his thumb and forefinger.

"Good-bye, Vic."

Victor lunged forward to try to knock the coin from his hand, but it was too late. Arran and his friends had vanished. With no Arran to break his fall, he was left sprawled out on the floor with a mouthful of dirt and grass.

He jumped to his feet, clenched his fist, and marched into the crowd, punching the first person he saw.

Sally Fielding fell to her feet, with her hand cradled over her bloodied nose, wondering what she had ever done to deserve that. A braver person would have launched some sort of protest but she stayed quiet.

***

"Neat trick," said Rudolph, propping himself up on an old disused garden shed as he watched Victor and Joss argue in the distance.

"Yeah," said Molly. "So you can teleport here too?"

Arran shrugged smugly. "Apparently."

"This is very good," said Sophia. "Now that idiot bully thinks we're out of the network, he won't be looking for us. Clever, using that coin you were given."

Arran was feeling rather proud of himself. "Thanks."

"So," said Sophia. "We need to find your actual coin. This place is supposed to be a mind map of your head. Where is the safest place to hide something here?"

Arran shook his head. "Sorry, I have no idea." He looked at the tool shed. "I mean, take this. I have no idea what it is. I've never seen it before. This is *my* head; everything is supposed to be familiar."

He shrugged again apologetically.

Sophia studied the shed and nodded slowly.

"I did say there would be tiny elements of *our* minds in this place too. The dog was from Molly's head, Rudolph's mind is probably empty anyway, and this," she tapped the shed, "this is mine."

"What is it?" Rudolph asked.

"It's a tool shed," Molly said.

"I know that," he replied, "but…"

"I used to live here," said Sophia.

"Not big enough to fit your head in, is it?" Rudolph said, and then laughed.

Nobody joined in. They could see the solemn, reflective look on Sophia's face.

"Oh, right," said Rudolph. "It's okay when she does it to me but…"

"Hang on," said Arran, cutting Rudolph's sentence short. "What is this place, Sophia?"

"My parents found it embarrassing to have a daughter with such a high IQ. They wanted a championship gymnast, a model, or a tennis star for their daughter. I was eventually banned from all books and reading material. They moved everything to this tool shed outside the house in the hope that I would become more like my idiot brother. The things in this shed provided more comfort to me than… They told me if

I wanted to study all the time it would have to be in here."

She peered in through the open doorway. "I slept here most nights."

She walked inside followed by the others.

The shed looked pretty much like any tool shed from Arran and Molly's time; they had half expected cyber shears or something. There were no books on the desk which stood in the centre of the small room, just an old-fashioned computer. Old-fashioned to Sophia and Rudolph, but to Arran and Molly it was a state-of-the-art modern laptop. On the screen was a flashing icon:

Tempus Network Hack.

Sophia sat on the only seat and moved the mouse over the flashing icon.

"This is how I found out about the Tempus School for Special Abilities. It was the first time I entertained the possibility that I may not be such a freak after all."

She attempted a laugh.

"I aced the aptitude and intelligence test online, faked my parents' permission slips, even faked my name and was invited to live at the school's halls of residence. I ran away from home to get here."

Rudolph, feeling a little ashamed now, thought to ask Sophia if her parents ever tried to find her, but from what she had said and the fact that she was at the school, the question seemed a little redundant.

"Even there, I felt a little like an outsider," Sophia continued. "If it wasn't for Headmaster Dews, who I'm sure could see right through my charade, I probably would have run from there too."

"You faked your name?" Rudolph finally said, feeling the need to fill an uncomfortable silence. "You're not really called Sophia?"

"No, that part's right. Tal-Grasto is a fiction. I didn't want people associating me with my bully of a brother."

A slow wave of realisation swept over Arran. "Graston. Your brother is Victor Graston?"

Rudolph instinctively took a step back. Sophia nodded, ashamed.

"Any way we could use that to our advantage?" Arran asked, placing a comforting hand on her shoulder.

Sophia shook her head. "No, we never speak. He's just as ashamed of me as my parents were." She looked at the screen. "We might be able to use this though," she said, more to deflect the focus from her and her unwanted sibling.

She thought for a moment.

"It was only ever designed as an interface into the Tempus Network. The most I could ever do was send messages and have a snoop, see what was going on in there. I was never able to literally jump in, physically, like we are now. Besides, what would be the point? We are already inside the network."

"Couldn't it be reversed so we could…" Rudolph started.

"Send communication outside the network?" Sophia shrugged her shoulders. "I don't know. It would be very like characters from a computer game escaping their boundaries and breaking out into the real world, because right now, that's what we are, avatars in a computer."

"Could we actually break out of the Tempus Network like that?" asked Molly. "Don't we need his coin?"

"Yes, to physically break out, but we may be able to send a distress call or something. At the very least find out what's going on out there."

Rudolph, Arran, and Molly exchanged a hopeful glance as Sophia clicked on the icon and began to frantically type.

Chapter Ninety-Four

Misdirection

"On a lunch break, are we?"

Victor looked up to see Tribble standing over him, tapping his watch and lightly tapping his foot.

He shrugged it off and took another bite from the fruit scone he had taken from the man on stilts; that same man was now on his knees, crying and trying to work out why the nasty boy had broken his stilts, sent him hurtling to the ground, and stolen his array of scones.

"Not much point now, is there? They have gone," Victor said nonchalantly, with half a mouthful of scone proudly displaying itself for all with enough stomach to look in his direction. "Arran found his own coin and they all disappeared."

Tribble laughed.

"Did I mention that your sister got all the brains in the family?"

"She's no sister of mine!" Victor spat.

His point was eloquently emphasised by the pieces of mashed-up scone of varying sizes which were propelled out of his mouth as he spoke.

Tribble wiped his tweed jacket. "Charming. Fooled by that little charade, were you?"

He fumbled in his pockets and produced a white handkerchief, which he proceeded to weave around his fingers, never breaking eye contact with Victor, like a true natural-born magician.

"Watch this."

He took a deep breath, then paused, sneezing into the handkerchief.

"Excuse me, that wasn't part of it." He opened it up and examined the contents. "Ew, must have been saving that for a while." He winked at Victor, who was slightly disgusted by Tribble's antics. "Here, catch!" With that, he threw the handkerchief at Victor.

Victor took a step back, not wanting a face full of Tribble snot. Mid-air, the kerchief changed form and moulded itself into a gold coin with Victor's image engraved on the front. It landed at his feet.

Tribble gestured for Victor to pick it up, which he did. The image on the coin became animated and began to snarl. Its mouth slowly opened to reveal several layers of pointed dagger teeth. Before Victor had time to say anything the coin sunk its teeth into his thumb, drawing blood instantly. He pulled his thumb free and threw the coin to the ground, where it transformed back to the original snotty handkerchief.

"The power of illusion, Victor the Unvictorious. Arran and his little band of misfits are still 'round here somewhere, and you were fooled by a simple optical illusion."

Looked real enough to me, Victor thought, still sucking on his thumb like Disney's Prince John.

"How do you know that? We haven't seen a single coin since we've been stranded on this death trap."

"Well, no, you wouldn't have. All your coins have been removed by order of my boss…and yours, I suppose."

"That means none of us can ever get out of here."

"Well, I say all the coins. There are certain parts of the Tempus Network I can't get access to, and those parts are keeping Arran's coin exactly where it is, as a permanent doorway for them to get out."

Tribble thought for a second.

"Unlike you, I can get out anytime I please. I'm just here to do my job, then go home and…"

Tribble pondered, thinking perhaps of his wife and his son. This reflective moment was much more reminiscent of the old Tribble, a frightened but warm-hearted field mouse who feared for the life of his baby boy, who wanted nothing more to have his family back together, reunited and happy.

He shook his head, wiped a single tear from the corner of his eye, and snorted a decisive breath.

"Right, to business; Arran, Molly, and the other two think they have the upper hand here. Collectively, they are a match, even for your little army of desperados. We are inside a graphical representation of Arran's mind. If the Tempus Network has accommodated his friend's personalities too, then there will be elements of the other's lives in this place, but for the most part you are wandering Arran's mind. Weird, eh?"

Different people can walk the same street and their perceptions can be as unfamiliar as if they had been in totally different environments. Victor scanned the vast landscape and saw elements the others had not really noticed:

A shabbily dressed clown stood by a pond, his pointed dagger like teeth gnashing into his bottom lip as he produced a toy boat from behind his back, inciting all the children currently playing in the water to stop what they were doing and slowly move toward him. His greedy, bloodlust eyes opened wider the closer the children got.

Not far from there, an old-fashioned and highly polished red Plymouth Fury stopped at intervals around the carnival. The heavy passenger side door swung open, allowing unsuspecting victims entry. Once inside, the door slammed shut and the locks automatically came down, trapping the people inside. Victor laughed as they clutched their throats, trying fruitlessly to prevent the poisonous gas seeping from the dash from entering their system.

Near the school, an army of black rats stood around a huge two-headed pink rat greedily gorging on a human foot. It looked as if he was their commander and was issuing battle plans in between huge mouthfuls.

Victor's eyes finally rested on the same "Do Not Enter" door that the rest of them had seen.

"I dunno what kind of books the DOA has been reading," said Victor, "but I like it."

Tribble instantly clipped Victor across the ear, spiralling him into a fit of rage; something he suppressed, having witnessed the devastating fruitlessness of any offensive action taken against him.

"Your clues as to their whereabouts and his coin are all around you," shouted Tribble. "Ask the right questions, torture the right people, whatever you like, and you will find them. You have a common goal at the moment. You are both looking for Arran's coin."

"If you know so much, where is his coin then?"

"Oh, why didn't I think of that?" Tribble snapped, sarcastically. "Do you think we'd be messing about here if I knew that? It's well hidden somewhere here. I don't know where, but for the moment neither does Arran. We just have to find it before he does. Your task is to get to know Arran and work out where the coin is. Not to tell you your business, but I'd suggest splitting your little soldiers out on an information and gathering mission, meet back, collate notes, then go get the coin."

"I want more than the coin," Victor said. "I want to kill that pathetic DOA!"

"That pathetic DOA will probably kick your behind once he realises his full potential in this place, every nasty element you see devouring you like antibodies with a purpose, but if you do find the coin before him, he'll be stranded here and left to die, job done. All that my boss is interested in is his sister Molly… Can I suggest we get moving?"

Victor nodded and turned to face the crowd.

"Right, you lot. Joss and Stammers are going to go with me; everyone else split up and find that coin. Everyone you meet will give you a bit more information about Arran, and hopefully a better understanding of him will lead us to where he would hide his coin in this place. If pounding on their faces doesn't work, you could try talking, I suppose."

They all stood silent, perhaps waiting for further instructions. Victor wasn't that intelligent; repeating Tribble's instructions was just about all he was capable of when it came to actual leadership.

"Come on then, split up before I pound each of *your* faces."

The children quickly dispersed in all directions, some mingling with the crowd, others thinking a simple, systematic search under rocks and amongst the grass to be a better way forward, the difference being that they were all being more proactive and working together for the first time since the death mask issued its demands.

Victor turned to say good-bye to Tribble, but he was gone.

Typical, he thought. *As soon as I have Arran I'm coming after you.*

"Come on then, you lot, we'll try in this tent here."

Joss and Stammers followed him inside.

Chapter Ninety-Five

The Last Drone Attack

Screams from outside her room woke the Professor from her slumber. She was not quite 100 percent but certainly feeling much better than she had when Mike laid her to rest. She inched her way to the door, opened it slightly, and peered through the crack. Two Spletka soldiers had a frightened doctor pinned up against the wall.

"What shall we do with this one?"

"No, please, we mean you no harm. I have a wife and two children," the doctor begged.

"And where are they now? Where is the Orb room? How about the Professor's beautiful daughter, where is she? Tell me something."

"Oh, stop crying, will you?"

"What do you think? Shall we just kill him?"

"Yeah, why not? Stupid idiots here would rather protect the Citadel and her secrets than save their own lives."

The Professor swung her door open and the two guards immediately turned to face her, dropping the defenceless doctor to the ground. He scurried away like a frightened rodent as the guards advanced on her.

"Stop!" she shouted, and to her surprise they did. At once they were frozen like breathing statues.

Well, that was easy, she thought.

"That wasn't you, my dear."

Richard Tempus's voice rang out in her ears.

"Jhonas Spletka wants control of the power you have been gifted. To do this he cannot use the abilities he has stolen from others. Here they must rest until the matter is settled. Under my influence, good and evil co-exist; people have the freedom of choice and there is a natural balance. If Jhonas were to control the power, then I shudder to think what this planet might become."

He appeared before her as an ethereal spirit.

"My child, this power cannot be taken by force; it must be given of your own free will. From here you must go to the Orb room and prepare for his arrival."

Chapter Ninety-Six

The Hack

Sophia tapped on the keys at a speed both Arran and Molly found hard to comprehend. Rudolph just looked on, pretending not to be impressed.

Reams of code flew across the screen. Reading it was impossible; no sooner had a key stroke been transferred to the screen than several pages passed. It gave Arran a headache to try.

"That's the speed, I think," Sophia answered, knowing what Arran was thinking. "Try not to look at it." Arran nodded and looked away. "There are a few bugs in the Tempus Network," she continued, not looking up.

"Well, thank you, Captain Obvious," Rudolph said. "The very fact that Spletka are running around killing people and none of us can leave—oh, and we're all on the most wanted list—would seem to support your statement."

"The bugs I'm talking about are literally bugs, Rudolph. One powerful spider to be precise, a hacking spider. It would explain the death mask we saw earlier. I'm guessing it comes from an animal surrounded by a hard light image, and the spider is using that as a gateway for Spletka to enter, and to stop us from getting out. As long as that spider is in contact, everybody here is trapped, including us, unless we find that coin."

She clicked a button on the keyboard, and back in the Citadel, Grombit, who had been lying unconscious on the recovery room bed, twitched as though he was receiving a tiny electric shock.

"Yes!" exclaimed Sophia.

"Looks happy," said Rudolph. "Bet she hadn't looked that pleased since she discovered that her massive ego actually fits inside that comparatively tiny head."

"That's a big word, Rudolph. Where did you learn it?" Molly joked.

"Oh, you now? Well, it was just a matter of time!"

"Relax, it was just a joke. Go on, you can say something about me. If I find it funny, I won't death stare you."

Arran, who seemed to have risen above the petty arguments and was becoming more comfortable with taking leadership of the group, re-established focus.

"What have you found, Sophia?"

"We've made contact. But…" She studied the code on the screen "…more than that. I think I've found the doorway, the one Spletka used to get into the network in the first place. Could be our way out of here. We might not need your coin. Speaking of which…"

Rudolph, Arran, and Molly shared a feeling of hopeful anticipation.

"So what are you going to do?" asked Arran.

"Well, first send a message for anyone out there to come help, and after that work on getting us through that doorway; if that doesn't work see if I can find your coin with this."

"Well, less talk, more type," said Molly, eager for the nightmare to be over.

Sophia didn't need this instruction and had already begun to type.

S.O.S.

Sophia Tel-Grasto with three friends: Arran, Molly, and Rudolph. We are trapped in the Tempus Network alongside everybody who made it into the Tempus Games. There are Spletka agents in here too. They have already killed some of the students and formed a militia with the rest to act as a manhunt to capture and/or kill Arran and Molly.

Professor Tempus, the daughter of the great Richard Tempus, is trapped in here too.

Please help. Time is running short. I will try to use this exit for us to escape. If that is unsuccessful we will have no choice but to find Arran's coin. According to my program his is now the only coin left in this place. Spletka must have destroyed the rest.

Sophia pressed a few buttons and the message was delivered.

Chapter Ninety-Seven

The Fake Professor Makes Contact

Less than a mile away Tribble's senses tingled. Sophia's message flashed in his mind as it was delivered. Slight change of plans, he now knew where they were and that too-clever-for-her-own-good brat Sophia Tal-Grasto must be stopped before it was too late. If she continued with her tampering, he might be trapped here too.

Sophia typed diligently. As before, multiple lines of code shot across the screen at lightning speed. The Spletka Spider Hacker was aware of her presence, and tried to block her access. It had never come across another living human with the intellectual capacity to take it on.

"Hack the hacker," she said quietly to herself, a phrase she repeated every time the spider anticipated and blocked her approach.

The spider couldn't simply break contact with Grombit (which would be the easiest way of blocking Sophia) because that would stop all movement in and out of the Tempus Network, including the Spletka. Its life expectancy would not be favourable should it do that.

This was every bit a battle of will as it was intelligence. Certain key strokes elicited a low grunt from Sophia with the accompanying words, "Hack the hacker." When her efforts resulted in progress, a tiny micro expression of a smile appeared on her face, which was just as quickly displaced with a stern look of concentration as she moved onto the next obstacle.

Whilst the battle between the spider hacker and Sophia ensued, Grombit's body tossed and turned with increasing intensity, as though he was strapped to an electric chair.

"I think we're doing it, shouldn't be long."

"By 'we,' she means her," said Rudolph.

"I know," said Arran. "Whatever she's doing I can feel it. Can't you?"

The other two shrugged but the statement prompted Sophia to stop working, look at Arran, and smile in recognition.

"Interesting." She turned to continue with her work.

Tribble was barely 100 yards away now. He sent a telepathic message to Victor and the child army outlining their whereabouts, then made his way to the tool shed. He still looked like an exact replica of their old friend Rebecca Tempus, but decided a little convincing would be needed to gain the trust of Arran and Molly. He lay on the ground and rolled around in the leaves and dirt. He ruffled his hair, then tore the pocket on the tweed jacket. He then slapped himself in the face a few times till a red mark emerged like a big glowing warning sign.

Perfect, he thought, then stumbled into the tool shed pretending to be dazed, tired, and upset, a performance that could have quite easily won an Academy Award. He fell forward, pushing the laptop to the ground with such force that it shattered into pieces. The link between the children and the outside world was now severed.

Sophia didn't believe in accidents or coincidence so instantly distrusted the Professor.

All but Molly took a step backward, giving the Professor ample space to fall, crashing hopelessly to the ground. Molly immediately knelt down and placed the Professor's head on her knee.

"Professor, are you all right?"

So this is the famous Molly in whom the general is so interested? Tribble thought. *This is going to be easier than I thought. I'll just keep these idiot children with me till the general contacts me, and then I'll... Uh oh.*

Sophia was trying to probe around Tribble's mind. She just needed a scrap of evidence to confirm her suspicion that the Professor was not what Molly thought she was. Had Tribble's realisation that Sophia was searching his mind been any slower, then the game would have been up and his plan and true identity would have been public knowledge.

As it happened all Sophia was able to get was a mental image of two dead mice: a mother and a child. As quick as it had arrived the image faded into non-existence. The Professor's brain, as far as Sophia could make out, was a barren landscape, devoid of thought, feeling, memory, or expression.

This in itself was not normal. All Sophia knew for sure was that the Professor was hiding something, not an ideal basis for trust. She glanced across at Arran, hoping he had managed to pick up something that she could not. If he did then he hid it pretty well. *It's the truth of human existence,* Sophia thought. *People see what they want to see and tend to ignore the rest.*

Arran slowly knelt down beside his sister, saying nothing for a while. He seemed a little more measured. He indicated that he should help the Professor to her feet, with his sister's help. Maybe it was the pressure and exhaustion of all that they had been through, but for some reason he was quite obviously not as elated to see his old friend Professor Tempus as one might expect.

Molly seemed puzzled by Arran's apparent lack of empathy, but chose to ignore it. Once the Professor was on her feet she flung her arms around her.

"Oh, thank goodness you're here, Professor." Her embrace was reciprocated in kind.

"There's space here for one more," the Professor said to Arran.

Arran shook his head and offered an apologetic smile.

"You know me, Professor; I don't go in for all that hugs stuff."

Molly glanced quizzically at him. Arran was generally very affectionate and the real Professor knew it, but the imposter simply let it pass as though she knew Arran was very passive when it came to public shows of affection.

Chapter Ninety-Eight

The Flies Converge

Victor Graston, Joss, Stammers, and most of the child army stood outside the tool shed, waiting for them to come out.

"I know you're in there, DOA!"

Tribble stumbled to his feet. "They must have followed me! That boy, he did this to me. I just managed to escape."

Rudolph felt his legs turn to jelly. He knew he wasn't the main target but that wouldn't stop Victor pounding him as an appetizer before he got to Arran and Molly. Sophia stepped outside closely followed by the others.

Tribble wanted to transport Molly out of there and to the General. As long as he had physical contact with her, it should have been a formality, but whatever Sophia had done must have severed the connection temporarily. He knew that once her laptop was broken, the spider hacker would have ample time to re-establish the link and they could leave. Till then the charade must go on and Tribble would have to act and behave as the good Professor.

No one dared to move forward, including Victor. Molly's death stare was still a real threat and they were all facing her. Stammers removed his gloves.

"Any ideas?" Arran asked Molly, who shrugged.

Sophia was almost snarling at her brother. Rudolph looked behind the shed. The door with "Do Not Enter" etched across the front was the only possible escape, and for the first time, it looked infinitely inviting. He nudged Arran and pointed it out. Sophia glanced behind to see what they were looking at.

Victor sniggered. "I reckon with one touch of Stammers here, your death stare would be rendered obsolete."

He was talking to Molly but his eyes were firmly fixed on Arran, who was trying to decide if the unknown terror that lay behind that door was preferable to the child army he had to face down. It didn't take much for him to make up his mind. Stammers took a step forward, Victor smiled triumphantly, and Arran turned and grabbed his sister.

"Run!" he shouted as they pelted toward the door, followed by Sophia, Tribble, and Rudolph.

Barely a second later Victor and the entire army gave chase.

Arran swung the door open in one swift movement and out stepped John Pentka, their father, looking more annoyed than ever. He glared at Arran and Molly.

"You two are coming with me!"

Tribble stepped back, both stunned and amazed, thinking this man to be Jhonas Spletka.

"Sir, it's you. But how…?"

Tribble telepathically ordered Victor and his army to stop, which they did without question. He didn't understand what Jhonas Spletka was doing here, but he wasn't about to do anything that might displease him.

"Er, hello, Father," said Molly and Arran simultaneously.

Father? thought Tribble. "I don't understand."

"What he's doing here?" interrupted Molly. "It's a long story."

John Pentka looked at Tribble but saw, as the rest of them did, Professor Rebecca Tempus.

"Oh, it's you. The children are going to stay with you for a while. I trust that's fine with you."

Tribble nodded. "Of course but…"

Sophia smiled. She knew that the man before them was nothing more than another phantom of Arran's mind.

John grabbed Arran and Molly by the hand and marched them over to the big circus tent, followed closely by Tribble, Sophia, and Rudolph. Victor and the others made to follow them, an action which was soon halted when Tribble, without turning around and using the power he had in the network, turned them all into still breathing statues.

Once the flap to the tent was pushed to one side, they walked inside and found themselves standing in the Professor's laboratory. In front of them stood the time machine and beneath that, a glowing coin.

Of course, thought Arran. *Where safer than the Professor's house?*

They all saw Arran's coin and breathed a collective sigh of relief. They all needed to have some form of physical contact with Arran to leave the network. Sophia and Molly held Rudolph's hand, and Molly held onto Tribble with her free hand, still believing him to be her Professor.

"Pick it up," said Sophia, reaching out her arm for Arran to hold.

He touched Sophia on the arm as he picked up the coin and held it between his thumb and forefinger. A blinding white light surrounded them, obscuring their surroundings from sight. When it settled they were out of the network and back in the Orb room in the heart of the Citadel. John Pentka, being but a phantom in the network, had disappeared.

The real Rebecca Tempus had arrived in the room moments earlier at her father's request and had been pacing, frantically waiting for Jhonas Spletka to arrive. When Arran and Molly materialised in front of her, there was a stunned silence, before tears of joy ran gleefully down her face.

"Is it really you?"

Rudolph could not help but to point out the obvious, as his glance shifted from Tribble, then back to the Professor. "Why are there two of you?"

Molly released her grasp of Tribble, who moved closer to the real Professor Tempus.

"Is this a trick?" Molly asked. "Are we still inside the network?"

Sophia was about to speak when Mike walked into the room, relieved to see the two children were safe.

"No, you're not still in the network. I received Sophia's message, then one from Richard Tempus telling me to come here."

He studied the two Rebecca Tempus's, who were now facing one another.

"One of these ladies is an imposter."

Chapter Ninety-Nine

Death to the Spider Hacker

The once paralysed spider had been searching for Grombit's room, looking for the Spletka spider that was restricting access out of the network.

Now at the foot of his bed, he silently crawled up the post. His life was soon to be extinguished, but he had one final task to perform before he could go.

He made his way silently across Grombit's sleeping body, then onto his head till he found the Spletka hacker. In one swift movement he sank his fangs into its body. There was no struggle; the Spletka hacker was no match for its opponent. It simply died.

Moments later, every living child previously trapped in the network woke in the real world, for the most part tired and exhausted, but alive.

Chapter One Hundred

The Final Battle

Tribble touched the Professor's hair.

"Fascinating," he lied. "She looks just like me."

The real Professor looked at Mike, who was crossing the room toward them.

"Don't be ridiculous," she said. "Anyone can see that..."

She motioned toward Arran and Molly, who both took a step back, unsure which Professor to trust.

"Oh, for Pete's sake, I can't believe that..."

"Rebecca Tempus. I can't begin to express how glad I am to see you here!"

Jhonas Spletka, the general, stood in the doorway, Bellonta by his side, playfully twirling a pointy dagger between her fingers.

"I'm assuming one of you is my loyal servant Tribble?"

Tribble stepped back quietly to stand by Bellonta's side. The two children then ran into the welcoming embrace of their own Professor Tempus.

Jhonas, Bellonta, and Tribble marched forward, past Mike, Rudolph, and Sophia till they were face-to-face with Rebecca Tempus, who instinctively ushered the children behind her for safety.

"You are the double of my father's old friend John Pentka from my time. So you are, what, relatives, a descendant?"

Jhonas shrugged. "From your time? I see your memory loss is still in full effect. You are of this time, Professor, as are your children."

The Professor's eyes widened. "My children? But I don't…"

Before she could finish the sentence, great segments of information hit her consciousness, and memories began to return like concrete slabs of previously missing jigsaw pieces as they fell into place.

Perhaps for the first time in thirteen years, everything was clear. She recalled her fight with Jhonas, she remembered the desperate struggle in the time machine when he kidnapped the children, and she understood in part why he had done that. The time machine needed someone inside with the same genetic code as Richard Tempus to make it work. Who would be more willing than two sleeping babies?

Her babies.

She turned, crouched down, pulled Arran and Molly close, and held them tight, an embrace they both welcomed and returned.

"Oh my children, you *are* my…" She stood up suddenly to face Jhonas. "And John Pentka?"

Jhonas smiled. "A fiction, the name at least. After we fought thirteen years ago. I trust you remember now?"

The Professor nodded and Jhonas continued.

"Part of me was taken and travelled back to wherever the time machine landed. What was left stayed in this time, scavenging, waiting for you to return. I suspect my other self has been waiting patiently for you to complete the machine too. Part of your memory was lost when I pulled you from the machine. But enough reminiscence, to business."

"What do you want?" Mike asked from behind Jhonas.

He had been quiet so far, carefully keeping Sophia and Rudolph from coming to harm.

"Keep out of this, Mike," Jhonas casually answered without feeling the need to look around. "Unless you'd like me to ask my dear wife to come dice you and your two little friends."

Bellonta playfully twiddled with her dagger and Mike pulled Sophia and Rudolph closer to him.

"As you know, the power that governs this planet is in you now. And since it can't be taken, I'm going to ask you to give up your power to me, Professor, and your daughter too. After which I'll take the time machine, join with my other self, and you all can go free. As a gesture of goodwill I'll even set the children currently trapped in the network free too."

Jhonas was unaware that the children in the network were already free and slowly recovering in the Tempus School for Special

Abilities. Unfortunately, everybody else in the Orb room was blissfully unaware of that fact too.

The Professor shook her head reverently. "That's never going to happen, Jhonas."

Jhonas smirked. "One thing at a time, eh? Tribble, go get Molly, will you?"

The Professor blocked Tribble's path and Jhonas sighed.

"Okay, let me put it this way; if Molly is not here with me in three seconds, I *will* kill every child still trapped in the network."

There was a pause.

"Oh, do I really have to do a countdown? We both know that the power you possess is only yours while you remain strong to your beliefs. I don't think allowing every child to die a terrible death is quite in keeping with that, do you?"

Bellonta laughed, knowing that the Professor had an impossible decision, and her husband had the upper hand.

The Professor shook her head and her father's voice rang out in her ears:

"Jhonas is right, my dear. To give up on your belief is to give up on the power you have been gifted. It would automatically pass to Jhonas and there is no measure to the damage he would do."

"It's not fair!" she screamed. "Molly is my daughter; you can't expect me to…"

Jhonas spoke slowly.

"Three, two…"

Molly looked toward Arran and smiled sympathetically; he released his grasp on her.

"I'm sorry, Arran."

She stepped forward very slowly, tears streaming down her face. She walked past the Professor and into Tribble's arms, who pulled her back and next to Bellonta, who began to use her dagger to start playing with Molly's hair.

Once Molly saw the dagger she had second thoughts and tried to run back to her mother, holding out her hands.

"Don't let them take me, Professor."

Arran stepped forward and tried to pull her free from Tribble's grasp. Jhonas's eyes turned jet black and Arran froze, transfixed in the gaze.

"Stop, Arran, your sister is coming with me."

Jhonas turned his attention to Molly.

"If you resist, your brother will become a Spletka. Would you like that?"

Molly reluctantly shook her head and stopped struggling. He used his mind control to force Arran back behind the Professor, then released him from the stare. He telepathically spoke to the Professor and Arran:

Try anything like that again and Molly will die.

"Excellent," said Jhonas. "Now stage two, you will gift the power of this planet to me or, instead of converting Molly to the Spletka, I shall drive my dear wife's dagger through her heart."

"Help me, Professor," Molly pleaded.

"Come, come, Professor, time is of the essence here. I will do it. It wouldn't be the first time."

Jhonas said this matter-of-factly whilst stealing a glance in Tribble's direction.

Mike, who had been silent and searching Jhonas's mind, suddenly spoke up.

"You killed Tribble's son?"

Jhonas spun around, and his eyes flashed jet black and stared at Mike, releasing just enough negative energy to make him fall to the ground, conscious but dazed.

"It's rude to read another man's thoughts, Mike," Jhonas bellowed. He then turned to face the Professor again.

Tribble began to shake, fear and anger rapidly combining forces and extracting all rational thought from his mind.

"You killed my son?! All this time you've had me do your

bidding and…"

He snatched the dagger from Bellonta's hand and pulled Molly away from them.

Arran and the Professor lunged forward to rescue her, but halted when the dagger touched her back, its shiny point threatening to break the skin.

"Stay exactly where you are," Tribble shouted. "I'm sorry, Professor. He killed my son, and that murdering maniac said he'd set him free." He used his shoulder to wipe the tears from his face. "Now I'm going to take his daughter!"

"No, Tribble, stop!" the Professor pleaded. "He is not their father; you'd be killing *my* child, not his!"

Molly screamed, "Professor, Mother, help me. I don't want to die!"

Tribble shook his head. "I heard them in the network, Professor. They both called him father, and since he's so desperate to have her back…"

Tribble, consumed with grief, plunged the dagger deep into Molly's body and she fell to the ground. He dropped the blade and stepped away.

The Professor and Arran ran to Molly and cradled her dying body in their arms. She gasped her final breaths as she spoke.

"It hurts so much. I can't feel my…"

She coughed and tiny droplets of blood dripped from her mouth. The Professor was crying as she mopped the blood with her sleeve.

"Sh, don't speak, baby, you'll be fine, you'll be fine."

Molly's last act was to reach out and hold her brother's finger. As her final breath left her body, her limp and lifeless hand relaxed and fell to the floor.

Arran, full of fury and remorse, reached for the dagger, stood up, and pushed Tribble to the wall, holding the point to his throat. Tribble, who was in a state of shock, offered no resistance. At that moment death held no intimidation.

"Kill 'im then!" Bellonta yelled, excited.

Arran looked back at her, then at the Professor, who was holding Molly close.

"You're not a murderer, Arran," said Rudolph. "You were right before. What separates us from him if you do that?"

He pointed at Jhonas, who simply watched in interest, unusually quiet.

Sophia, who was paying much more attention to the Professor, simply pointed and said: "Arran, look."

The Professor's colour had left her cheeks, and she began to rock back and forth, her breathing laboured, with Molly still cradled in her arms. A deep wound began to form on the Professor's body, blood seeping out and soaking her clothes. At the same time Molly's wound closed and there they stayed, locked in each other's embrace till the Professor fell back onto the floor, finally releasing the grasp on her daughter.

Molly fell to her side like a disused rag doll and within moments her chest began to move slowly up and down as her heart started again to beat. Her eyes snapped open, as did her mouth. She gasped for air.

Arran dropped the dagger, released Tribble from his grasp, and ran toward his sister, followed closely by Sophia and Rudolph.

"I'll be okay," whispered Molly, who was still too weak to stand. "Just a little dizzy. Where's the Professor?"

Mike rushed toward the Professor as soon as she had lost consciousness, her still body resting on his lap. He shook his head slowly, indicating that she was either dead, or quite close to death. Arran, Sophia, and Rudolph crowded around her, leaving for the moment Molly, who had fallen back on the floor conscious but exhausted.

Tribble inched his way toward the door, seemingly unnoticed by the rest of the room.

"I'm sorry, Professor," he whispered meekly, before taking a deep breath and transforming back into the shy, timid field mouse that he had been before he was forced into the Citadel. He scampered out of the room.

Jhonas was firmly focussed on the soon to be deceased Rebecca Tempus, her heart rate becoming more laboured with every breath.

"It won't be long now, Professor." He clenched both fists as he spoke. "I can feel the power start to make its way through my veins."

A darkened shadow seeped out of his body and crept across the room to where the Professor lay. Her already greying features intensified once contact was made.

"Stop him," she croaked, her eyes still closed. "Please…"

"Leave her alone!" yelled Arran. "You're killing her!"

Arran's protest was short-lived, as the deathly shadow reached him and his three friends. They tried to move, but could not. It took all of their concentration and effort to remain awake. Life seemed to be systematically extracted from each one of them.

Molly had been lying on the side-lines, simply observing and mustering enough energy to stand. She slowly walked in between Jhonas and her friends.

"Leave them alone."

Noticing that Molly was inexplicably unaffected by Jhonas's

shadow, Bellonta picked up the dagger from the floor, screamed, and charged at her. Molly's eyes, bright blue, burned into Bellonta's soul and she collapsed on the floor. She then turned her attention back to Jhonas and locked eyes with him. His own death stare was more powerful than ever, but Molly's counterattack was keeping him at bay.

Though her friends were too weak to stand, they could not help but be impressed by Molly's performance. She and Jhonas had reached a stalemate. The shadow which had been draining the life from Arran, Rudolph, Sophia, and the Professor disappeared, he needed all the strength he could muster simply to fight Molly.

"This can't be right," Jhonas thundered. "My power is fading."

So is mine, Molly thought as she stumbled toward him; her weak body clearly not ready for such an epic and monumental battle. At once Moly and Jhonas's eyes returned to normal, they sank to their knees, and simultaneously both Molly and Jhonas fell to the floor.

There was darkness; no one moved. The Orb room looked like a near abandoned battlefield, with no survivors; that was until, from the stillness Jhonas moved a finger, then an eyelid, precipitating a weak but definite return to consciousness.

He rose, stumbled past the unconscious and weak bodies, and dragged Molly's body past her ailing friends and into the time machine.

In a flash the machine was gone.

Chapter One Hundred and One

Epilogue

The Professor lay in the recovery room for three days following her near brush with death. When she woke, Arran and Mike were sitting by her bedside. Her eyes sprang open and she jolted upright.

"Molly," she gasped. "We need to rescue Molly!"

Mike nodded. "And it's a little more complicated than that now. I don't know what Jhonas did in the past, but the world is a different place to what it was three days ago."

Outside the Citadel, darkness prevailed. Rain and thunder filled the night sky, illuminating momentarily a single but magnificent stone statue of Molly as she glared menacingly at the helpless civilisation down below.

Printed in Great Britain
by Amazon

52067218R00326